BOOK ONE
OF THE ANTEDILUVIAN LEGACY

LEVIATHAN

‹ R. M. HUFFMAN ›

LAMPION
Press

Lampion Press, LLC
P. O. Box 932
Silverton, OR 97381

ISBN:

Paperback: 978-1-942614-00-5

Hardcover: 978-1-942614-01-2

Library of Congress Control Number: 2015949905

Formatting and cover design by Amy Cole, JPL Design Solutions

Printed in the United States of America

For Dad

‹ ACKNOWLEDGEMENTS ›

First and foremost, I thank the Creator God for the words He has given to us, and for the Word through which He fulfilled his promise to the serpent in the third chapter of Genesis. Thanks to my sweet wife Meredith for her perpetual support of a husband who must seem to have no end of time-consuming projects he takes on. An enormous thank you to my dad, Rick Huffman, who has read this at least twenty times; without his support, this book wouldn't exist to be read. Also, thanks to my brother John, who nurtured this idea with me until it was ready to become a story, then graciously let me run with it in my own direction. Thanks as well to Katherine and Dustin George, Kathy Decker, Tim Chaffey, Ben Wiggins, Brian Niro, Billy Herrington, and Rachael Wilson for their valuable time and invaluable feedback. The graphic elements of the book were, for me, some of the most fulfilling aspects of this project to work on; thanks to Igor Desic for his colors, Justin Tumey for the map, Ashley Legler for the genealogies, and especially Lucas Graciano for the fantastic cover art (and thanks to Sarah Carlson for taking the author photo, which requires far more skill than one might appreciate in this cameraphone age). Thanks to Wayne House and Tim Demy for taking such personal interests in helping this book achieve its full potential. Finally, thanks to everyone who reads this; no matter who or where you are, you and I share a common ancestor, which makes us family. This story is about that ancestor. I hope you like it.

‹ DRAMATIS PERSONAE ›

Elohim – the Lord God Creator, Who made the world

Bene Elohim – meaning "the sons of God," a general term for angelic beings, as opposed to humanity

Nephilim (singular Naphil) – the name given to the offspring of *bene Elohim* and human women, and their progeny; the males are notable for their giant stature

EDEN

Noah – a farmer from the land of Eden; descendant of Adam, the first man, through his son Seth in a line of firstborn sons; subject of a prophecy made by his father Lamech

Lamech – father of Noah; son of Methuselah

Methuselah – father of Lamech; grandfather of Noah; son of Enoch the Scribe, a prophet of Elohim who was translated to heaven at the age of 365

Jonan – brother of Noah, second son of Lamech

Hadishad – brother of Noah, third son of Lamech

Emzara – betrothed to Noah; daughter of Rakeel

Merim – cousin to Noah; firstborn son of Rakeel

Rakeel – second son of Methuselah; father of Merim and Emzara

Elebru – wealthy owner of the lands bordering those of Methuselah

Dashael – an animal wrangler employed by Elebru

Denter – chief of the men-at-arms employed by Elebru

Suat – the seneschal of Elebru, in charge of household affairs

Enosh – grandson of Adam; son of Seth; Greatfather of Eden, a title given to the eldest living firstborn son of Seth's line

Kenan – son of Enosh; unlike most of his family line, left Eden to wander the earth before returning centuries later

ENOCH

Tubal-Cain – skilled smith in the line of Cain

Naamah – sister of Tubal-Cain, wife of the *ben Elohim* Samyaza

Lilith – descendant of Cain; wife of the *ben Elohim* Azazyel

Agrat – descendant of Cain; wife of the *ben Elohim* Barkayal

Eisheth – descendant of Cain; wife of the *ben Elohim* Tamiel

Jet – descendant of Cain, wife of Gloryon the Naphil

Malidoch – lieutenant-captain of the guards of Enoch; brother of Lilith

Onim – leader of the Scribes and follower of the teachings of Enoch of Eden

Gregan – member of the Scribes

Thims – member of the Scribes

Raposh – wealthy member of the council of Enoch

GRIGORI

Samyaza – chief of the Grigori, a group of two hundred watcher angels who left their stations to take human wives for themselves; husband of Naamah

Azazyel – Grigori captain; husband of Lilith; teacher of smithing, warfare, and cosmetology

Barkayal – Grigori captain; husband of Agrat; teacher of astronomy

Tamiel – Grigori captain; husband of Eisheth; teacher of astronomy

Asaradel – Grigori captain; teacher of the movements of the moon

NEPHILIM

Gloryon – captain of the guard of Enoch; son of Azazyel and Lilith; husband of Jet; father of Gilyon

Gilyon – son of Gloryon; grandson of Azazyel and Lilith

Dyeus – son of Samyaza and Naamah; father of many children by different mistresses; a leading citizen of the city of Enoch

Pethun – son of Samyaza and Naamah; unmarried and childless

Dedroth – son of Samyaza and Naamah; a well-traveled naturalist

Mareth – a son of Dyeus; skilled in fighting
Hamerch – a son of Dyeus and friend of Gilyon
Deneresh – a son of Dyeus and friend of Gilyon
Hoduín – son of Barkayal and Agrat; magician and sorcerer
Tiras – son of Hoduín
Tevesh – son of Hoduín
Gofannon – a smith under Tubal-Cain
Voland – a smith under Tubal-Cain

Bene Sheol – meaning "sons of the grave," a secretive group of assassins trained by the Grigori Azazyel
Scribes – an organization of descendants of Cain who worship Elohim and oppose the presence of the *bene Elohim* on earth

‹ PROLOGUE ›

Nine hundred and thirty years
after the creation of the world

Lamech raced down the gritty road, his scarf pulled over his face to keep out the dust. His crested dragon's clawed feet tore up the ground in long, pounding strides. Millennia from now, the beast would be called a hadrosaurid; the rider called him Gryp, and he was the fastest in the herd.

Terraced groves of lemons and olive stumbled down the rocky hillside on either side of the small road, just wide enough for two carts to pass one another. The trees gave way to vineyards that covered the slopes, where wooden trellises supported broad-leafed green vines heavy with grapes. A dignified future awaited those grapes, destined to be pressed into the best wine in the region. Indeed, the wine's superiority was no longer considered to be a matter of taste, but a matter of fact, by the many who had enjoyed it. The master of viticulture responsible, after all, had been practicing his craft for more than two hundred years.

A cloud of dust trailed behind Lamech as he coaxed as much speed out of Gryp as he was able. The day's mists had long left the tops of the hills, parching the roads and leaving their last wisps curling about the vineyard valleys. Lamech scanned for signs of the winemaker. An oxcart on the road, half-full of baskets of harvested clusters of grapes, marked the slope where he might find the man. He reined his animal to a halt near the cart, jumped down, and followed one of the small paths that led down the hill through the vineyards.

"Methuselah!" he cried, "Methuselah! Where are you?"

1

"Lamech? Over here, son."

The rider followed the voice down a row of trellises and found its owner, carefully harvesting enormous dark clusters of the famous grapes. Another man was engaged in the same task beside him; both looked up from their work.

"Father, you need to come with me now," Lamech said, breathing hard, his anguish traced in tears down travel-dirty eyes. A man for whom everyday experiences produced great highs and crushing lows, he often needed his hands to help express passions too expansive for voice alone, and he waved them now as if to gather the older man to himself. "He's dying—Seth doesn't think he has much time left."

Methuselah's stone brow trembled slightly. He dropped a last cluster into the basket. "Then come I shall. Elebru, I'm sorry to leave you with work unfinished," he said to his companion.

"Then leave not!" said Elebru indignantly. "He has brought this curse upon himself, and all of us in time—you know this. Because of him, we toil out here now!"

"I am sorry, my friend," said Methuselah over his shoulder, following Lamech, who was already hurrying back down the path. "And I assure you, he is sorry too—more than he could ever say."

"Bah!" muttered Elebru, turning back to his work.

Rolling fields of grain replaced terraced hills as the dragon carried his passengers to their destination. As they ascended a rise in the road, an old village—the oldest in all of God's earth—spread out before their eyes. Ancient cottages and farmsteads in the center of the village had transitioned gradually to more modern buildings as the growing population had expanded; and as the older buildings became unfit for use, they had been torn down and replaced by builders using the newest methods at the time. As such, what was literally the architectural history of the land of Eden could be seen in the structures of the village, radiating outward like the growth rings of a fallen tree.

In the very center of the town, one ancient cottage remained. Several acres of undeveloped land lay around it and were home to a menagerie of creatures, each with scars from nature's red claw, that the cottage's resident had rescued over his many centuries. To this place rode Lamech and Methuselah.

Lamech tied Gryp to the trunk of the tall pine that served as a gate-post while his father waited. The two men hurried down paths that led through hedged lawns and over rocky ponds, past a tortoise with a partly-crushed shell and a slope-backed kerit that had been lamed by a wolfpack. The animals were loud today, as if they knew what was transpiring at the house ahead. A man stood at the door to meet them.

"Methuselah! At last. Thank you for coming so quickly, son."

"Lamech is a strong rider," said Methuselah. "Hello, Father."

"Enoch, who has come?" called a woman's voice from inside.

"Methuselah and Lamech, Grandmother," answered Methuselah's father Enoch. "All are here now."

Lamech bounded through the garden and the three men entered the home together. The room was one long, low-ceilinged hall, framed by timber beams above and walled by clay bricks. Two hearths divided the hall into three sections, with passages to private quarters on either side. The room was full of solemn people, engaged in whispered conversation. Methuselah recognized many; every one of his seven sires was present in the room, save Adam. He greeted them in turn: Seth and Enosh, Adam's son and grandson, both still living in the village; the son of Enosh, Kenan, a wanderer seldom seen in Eden anymore, dressed in rich robes from foreign lands; Mahalalel and Jared, father-and-son potters who lived with their families several hours away; and finally Enoch, Methuselah's father and the best man he knew. Myriad great-uncles, uncles, and cousins from Eden's small farming villages were clustered in tight groups; many other men were present as well, strangers in strange attire, at least to Methuselah.

"Who are those men? From where do they come?" he asked Enoch.

"Emissaries and elders, and it seems they have come from every-where. When he first fell ill, Adam requested them to be here, and mes-sengers were sent to retrieve them. Some travelled for weeks." Enoch smiled sadly. "They have as much a claim on Adam's kinship as you and I. It is right for them to be here, I think. People will want to know of his passing."

Methuselah dropped his head. "Will it be soon, then?"

"I fear so. He has grown weaker."

An older woman bustled out of the doorway that led to Adam's quarters. Seth hurried over to her and exchanged several brief, hushed words, then approached Methuselah. "My son, Azura says he is ready for you," he said. "We have all said our goodbyes already." Methuselah gave the old man a quick embrace, then went to Azura. The woman was the second daughter of Adam and Eve, as well as the wife of Seth, and engaged herself now in the role of loving nursemaid to her ill father. She retrieved a water-filled sheep-goat's bladder from a pot that was warming on the dog-irons in the hearth. She wrapped it in several folds of cloth to fashion a compress, then motioned for Methuselah to follow her.

Adam rested in bed, woolen blankets pulled to his chest, gaunt from illness. The orange glow from a sconced oil lamp threw bluish shadows around the room and accentuated his ancient features. He coughed wetly as Methuselah entered. Azura applied the compress to her father's forehead, then drew a thick curtain over the doorway and left the two men in privacy. Rheumy eyes fell on Methuselah, and a weak smile lit up Adam's face.

"Methuselah."

Methuselah kneeled at the bedside and clasped Adam's wrinkled hand. "I am here, Greatfather Adam."

"And I as well," the old man said, "but not for long, I think." He coughed again. "I need to say two things to you. First: I ask your forgiveness. No, do not argue. I know you are gracious towards me, and will tell me that all have sinned. But I was first, and I am sorry."

"Of course I forgive you," Methuselah said.

"Thank you. Second: always obey Elohim, our Lord God Creator—always! I know that you do now, but you have many years ahead of you before you share my fate. Many of my sons have strayed from the old ways." Adam stopped and stared at the lamp's flickering flame. "Old ways. They do not seem so to me, but old they are, and still true."

"I will, Greatfather."

"I believe you will, too," Adam said, looking back at Methuselah. "The line of Seth is blessed; how much is the grace of God, and how much is your fathers' obedience to His instructions, I cannot say, but you have been touched." His brow creased slightly. "Remind me of your prophecy. My mind grows dim."

"'When he dies, it shall be sent,'" Methuselah quoted quietly.

The old man sighed and closed his eyes. "'When he dies.' Even prophecy cannot escape the Curse."

"More than two hundred years have I carried that prophecy, and I still do not see its meaning," Methuselah said.

"Redemption? Judgment? It is hard to know." Adam gripped his hand tighter. "Trust the Lord." A paroxysm of coughing suddenly wracked the ancient man's body, alarming Methuselah almost enough to call for Azura. Adam waved his hand against it.

"Ah…I thought I had understood the full magnitude of the consequences of that original sin…my sin…when my son Abel died. Then, when Eve passed, I realized that I had not, and would not until death came for me. And now my own time comes, and I must face the enemy I have brought upon the world." Adam's voice faltered and his vision fell unfocused, filmy eyes drifting like mists over unfathomed waters. With an effort, he raised his head. "My last advice I give to you, Methuselah. Resist the Serpent, the tempter and corrupter. Walk in righteousness always. Obey Elohim, and teach your children and grandchildren to do the same."

He laid his ancient head back on the pillow. "The light fades," he rasped. "Would you please call my sons and daughters?" Methuselah nodded, then kissed the old man lightly on the forehead. "I will do all you ask," he promised Adam, then left slowly, pondering many things.

Adam's funeral was an event not rivaled in the history of the world, not even by Eve's. Tens of thousands passed through Eden, wishing to pay last respects to a man known to all, but whom most of them had never met. Even some of Cain's descendants attended, traveling from their homes in Nod, east of Eden. They carried news that on the day of Adam's passing, Cain was killed by stones fallen from the crumbling wall of his own house. "A fitting end," some said, but to Methuselah, it underscored Adam's last words to him.

"He gave me that advice as well," said Lamech, as he walked with his father down the main village street. "Do we not do those things already?"

"Aye, son, we do, for the greater part. Our family has been blessed with good training, and we are surrounded by those who believe as we do.

Never forget, though, that any man can fall. Adam knew that better than anyone else could."

Lamech nodded slowly, then kicked a fallen coconut husk down the road with a long scream. He sank to the ground as his lungs emptied at last.

"Our faith can be lost in one generation, after all," said Methuselah, sitting by his son. "One can never have too many reminders to be vigilant"

"True." Lamech ran his palms over his face and looked full into the elder man's eyes. "But I promise you this, Father: it will not be lost with me, and if ever the Creator gives me a son, we will teach him to hold strong his faith, too," he said hoarsely. "Even if the whole world should turn against him."

◄ ◄ ► ►

Sunrise was the best time for bathing, Naamah always thought. She and the other girls would wake early, as their mothers and the older women began the day's food preparation. The working men—five generations of them—were already in the shops and markets, dragging the boys with them. That meant no fear of being spied upon by hormonal cousins. She was in no rush to bear children; after all, they were only young once. Centuries of motherhood could wait its time, thank you, and besides, none of the young men particularly interested her.

Agrat called to her to hurry. Typical Naamah—always thinking, always dreaming and dawdling. The other girls were in the water already. The morning mists were rising from the ground, another guard against peeping boys. She entered the warm, clear springs, wading through the trumpet-shaped lily blossoms up to her chest. Smooth shelves of stone clung to the banks; Agrat and her sister Eisheth were sitting on their favorite one, splashing their feet and gossiping. Lilith was busy brushing her long, dark hair with the comb the craftsman's son had given her. Of course, the one boy in whom Naamah might possibly have considered taking interest would fall for Lilith. Well, he could have her—soon enough he would discover that the sweetness of her tongue was far exceeded by its sharpness.

Naamah dipped her head under the surface. She stayed submerged for just a second, enjoying the feeling of floating. Keeping her eyes closed, she tilted her head up and rose, her hair streaming wet and straight behind her. She opened her eyes and quickly started, her mouth parting slightly in confusion and surprise. A man's silhouette came towards her through the mists. She kicked backwards to the other girls, each turning to look at what had caused such a reaction. Lilith let out a stifled mix of gasp and scream.

The quickly advancing silhouette had been joined by three more. Naamah wasn't afraid, not really, not after her initial shock. The descendants of Cain had always benefited from his being marked for safety ages ago; the same fear of sevenfold vengeance against anyone who killed Cain had extended to his children, then grandchildren, and now generally lay as a covering from harm over all of the city of Enoch. Apprehension turned to curiosity as the figures came closer. Naamah heard Lilith gasp again, this time in awe, as the men parted the mists and came into view.

They were tall, well over six feet. Their lean and hard muscles seemed more like a master sculptor's example of the ideal human form rather than those built from years of work and toil. The tallest man, the one Naamah had first noticed through the mists, gazed directly at her. She met his eyes. Their crystal, unearthly beauty caused butterflies to flutter in her chest, but the intensity, almost intimacy, in the way he looked at her made them race down to her legs. Had she been standing on dry land, her trembling knees might have failed her.

Naamah's world contracted to the magnificent being stepping into the water towards her. She was entirely oblivious to her three friends, each equally enthralled by another of the men. He drew closer, almost near enough to touch.

He spoke. "I have been watching you."

Had a boy from the city said that to her, he would have been slapped and his father would have been told. Coming from this, a more beautiful specimen of a man than Naamah had supposed existed, it was beyond flattery. She could form no words; she could only stare. She waited for him to speak again.

His voice rang like music and laughter. "From all the daughters of men, I have chosen you. I wish to make you mine. I wish to marry you. I will honor your father and mother with our children, and to your brothers I will teach the secrets of the heavens. Only say you will be mine."

Naamah realized that he was waiting for her to speak. Of the countless words that had come unbidden to her mind in these last few impossible moments, she found the simplest and forced them out. "Who are you?"

The man smiled. "I am an *irin* of the *bene Elohim*, a son of God," he said. "I sang for joy as this world was created. My name is Samyaza."

"I am Grigori."

ᐧ CHAPTER 1 ᐧ

TWO HUNDRED AND SIX YEARS LATER

The warm spring washed away the scent of the hunter, his sound masked by its rush. He wove silently through tendrils of leaves and vines hanging low over the calf-high water's edge, navigating submerged roots and rocks by feel with bare feet. Water brought life with it, now and in ancient times: the four great rivers; the mists that rose from the ground; the land of the earth itself, raised out of endless water on creation's third day. This stream widened into a pool, where the drake he hunted, just visible through the vines, drank haltingly, warily, but, thanks to the secrecy afforded by the water, remained ignorant to the man's presence.

Water brought life, but for some creatures, water brought death.

A woolen hood shadowed the man's tanned features. He wore a dun vest and buckskin pants pulled up past his knees, a sheathed iron hunting knife strapped to his braided belt. A long leather bracer wrapped his left arm to his elbow, and an arrow-filled quiver carved from yew wood was at his back. He went barefoot, as was his habit when hunting. His name was Noah.

On most days he was a farmer and a husbandman; occasionally, as today, he was a protector of his family's herds from the many predators that found their ways across wild wooded hills to the grazing valleys. The hunting party had left yesterday, when the half-eaten carcass of an ewe was discovered at the edge of the forest. They had expertly followed the reptilian tracks, never giving up any sign of their presence to the beast, and were now closing in on their quarry.

Noah tensed the string of his flatbow, broad-headed arrow already nocked. He crept forward. The drake, a reptilian creature roughly the size of a grown man, strutted stealthily on two hind legs among the mossy rocks and short, scrubby bushes by the pool. Its mottled green skin would have made it almost invisible in the forest, but in the open it wasn't difficult to follow. A head that tapered slightly from skull to snout ended in a mouthful of sharp teeth, and Noah recognized the single oversized claw on either foot as the instrument that had rent the ewe so ruthlessly. In many ways, it was a testament to its Designer; Noah wondered if it was much changed from its ancestors that walked with Adam before the Fall, when every animal ate only plants, so the Generations told.

The drake paused, bobbing its head. Noah quietly ducked his own head to avoid being noticed. He wondered if the creature had seen or smelled one of the other hunters, although he doubted it. The others, experts in these woods, would remain undetected if they wanted. Regardless, the momentary stillness of the beast presented an opportunity that he was ready to take. He quickly drew his arrow back, rising in an instant from his crouch in the stream.

The arrow flew wide as a snarling white blur flashed from the rocks, shattering the hunter's concentration. A rolling mass of fur and claws entangled the reptilian, its shrieking cry short-lived as snapping teeth ripped stringy chunks of meat from its neck. The new attacker stood over its kill and took another vicious bite from the drake's carcass. The feline beast, longer than a man was tall, rippled with muscle. Brown stripes decorated its legs, fading to bronze at its flanks and disappearing into a solid white coat. A short mane bristled from the huge cat's neck. Lips curled in a predator's sneer, and nostrils snorted as it sniffed the air.

"You are a bit smarter, aren't you?" Noah whispered to himself. The big cat may have taken care of the hunters' quarry, but their job was not done. Noah immediately recognized the threat that this beast represented to the herds, and he knew the others in his party were thinking the same thing. Two days' work had been lost chasing the dead drake. How long to hunt this hungry monster after it slaughtered more livestock, as it undoubtedly would? Not willing to wait to find out, Noah drew another arrow and fired.

His arrow hit the white cat high on its shoulder; another arrow, fired from the undergrowth on the opposite side of the pool, caromed at a shallow angle off of the big beast's neck, leaving a red stretch of wound. Roaring in pain and appearing more angry than hurt, the cat bounded away from the water, towards the treeline from where the second arrow was fired and disappeared into a wall of fronds and foliage.

Noah splashed out of the water and sprinted to the trees. "Blood and death," he swore as human shouts and sharp bestial roars reached his ears. He crashed through the underbrush, following the cat's path.

A quick survey of the scene showed the big white cat on its hind legs, two hunting spears stuck fast in its chest and holding its clawing, writhing body up like tentpoles. One spear was held by Noah's father Lamech, the other by his younger brother Jonan, both doing their best to hold the beast at bay. His grandfather Methuselah was backed up to the broad, knobby trunk of a large conifer tree to avoid the long swiping reach of the cat's claws. Two ends of a broken bow he clutched, one in either hand. He blocked a paw with a piece of the ruined wood, then struck the animal hard in the mouth with the other, but the blow did nothing but increase the animal's ferocious ire.

A running leap carried Noah full onto the cat's back. He grasped a handful of mane with one hand and drew his knife with the other. With all his strength, he plunged the iron blade into the muscled white neck. Warm blood spurted around the wound; the animal thrashed violently, but Noah held on.

Slowly, steadily, the beast grew weaker, until Lamech and Jonan jerked their spears from its breast and it slumped lifelessly to the forest floor.

Noah rolled off of the dead cat, exhausted, and laid on his back on the leafy ground. Jonan stood over him, hands on knees. "I had him, you know," he said, turning up a corner of his mouth in a half-grin.

"Of course you did," answered Noah. "Sorry for butting in." Jonan offered a hand and pulled Noah to his feet.

Lamech handed the ruined halves of Methuselah's weapon to him. "My best bow," the elder man sighed. "Now what shall I do?"

"Cheer up, Father," said Lamech, "After all, for a moment there, I was afraid that we were about to find out what that prophecy of yours meant." Noah and Jonan looked at each other with a smirk.

"Hmph! It would take more than a mangy beast like that to introduce me to my Maker." Methuselah examined the dead cat. "A fine hide, though," he said; then, rising and looking at his son and grandsons, added with a wink, "that is, if you three had not poked holes in it. Now! Let us skin it, then to home! I'm hungry."

Noah laughed. The more heated the battle, it seemed, the more humorous everything after. Although the hunt had lasted more than a day, a straight path back to the farmlands should take but a few hours. They ought to return home before nightfall, Noah guessed, and a good thing, too. Harvest began tomorrow, and the entire household was having a feast, a last celebration before a season of hard labor. And with Methuselah and Lamech in such fine spirits, Noah anticipated a night to remember.

They arrived at the sprawling farmhouse as dusk was falling. Methuselah's home, whose first stone had been laid by his own father Enoch, fell in staggered levels from a rise in a hill. Verandas walked down the slope around the huge bole of an ancient cypress tree, several cellar-cave entrances below embraced and bordered by its roots. Below this were outbuildings, silos, and animal pens; fields of crops, planted in the lowlands to take the most advantage of watering mists, lay beyond these. This was Noah's home, and he was thankful to return to it.

Methuselah's and Lamech's wives, Edna and Betenos, met their husbands with warm embraces, naturally relieved at their safe return. Jonan entertained his younger brothers and cousins with a ballad detailing the hunters' adventures that, despite repeated good-natured punches to the ribs from his elder brother, he had insisted on composing on the long hike back from the forest. He, of course, had expanded his role in the hunt to epic proportions, and his exaggerated descriptions of their grandfather's plight brought forth many worried noises from their grandmother Edna, much to Methuselah's chagrin.

"Hello, Noah."

A young woman approached Noah, walking with a light bounce to her step. Her bright eyes and pretty smile complemented the lovely figure of a woman exiting gracefully from the last stages of girlhood. She was, Noah thought, the most beautiful creature he had ever seen.

12

"Zara!" he exclaimed, embracing her waist and spinning her once around. He held her tightly to his chest and inhaled deeply. "Mm, you smell wonderful!"

She pushed away playfully. "And you have smelled better," she said, "not that I mind. Come see what we've prepared!" Zara took Noah's hand.

"Should we tell them now?" asked Zara in a whisper, as she led Noah to the dining hall.

"After the feast, love." answered Noah, smiling. "I would rather enjoy my meal in peace than be interrupted by congratulations every minute." Zara rolled her eyes in mock annoyance. Noah laughed and whispered, "I love you, Zara."

Zara kissed him on the cheek. "And I love you, Noah," she said. "Now see what we have done while you were away!"

The long, wide dark wooden table stretched almost the entire length of the spacious main hall at the center of the farmhouse. The foods prepared for the feast completely covered the table, and a feast it was.

Towers of fresh fruits cut carefully into different designs rose at either end of the table. Broad platters of sliced apples and apricots shared space with bowls of mixed berries. Entire wheels of cheeses, made from sheep-goat's and cow's milks and crusted with herbs or crushed garlic, were placed at intervals, with plates of sliced cheese and grapes atop them. Dishes of nuts and dried fruits wrapped in grape leaves, savory cruciferates, fried plantains, and yam cakes rested in arm's reach of each place at the table. Breads of all kinds, some filled with dates, some with mixtures of pine nuts and spices, some plain, and all freshly baked, were abundant. Saucers of honeys smelling of orange and lemon accompanied grain puddings, and decanters of wine were placed regularly about the table, as were pitchers of cider and steaming pots of white and black teas.

Noah's eyes widened and he took a step forward. Zara stopped him with a tug of his vest. "Oh, no," she gently scolded. "Go wash up and change your clothes. Worry not, we shall not start without you." She pointed him in the direction of his quarters. "I will save you a seat. Now, hurry!"

Noah sent a silent prayer of thanks to Elohim as he jogged to his quarters. Life did not get better than this.

The feast filled the hall with the laughter and conversation of family and friends who truly enjoyed each other's company. Food and drink disappeared and were quickly replaced, most often by the young men who took the opportunity to first taste some new morsel on the way back from the kitchens. The fine women who had cooked and prepared the feast received much praise from the men, with one or two jesting comments of "you ought to do this more often." Eventually, appetites began to fill; the adults picked over the last few bites of their favorite dishes, and the children roasted sweet chestnuts and cocoa beans in the wide, crackling stone fireplace at the end of the room. As the empty trays were cleared and the oil lamps around the room were refilled, Methuselah rose. Silence fell as he began to speak. "As this season's harvest draws near, we thank Elohim for the bounty with which He has blessed us." A few murmured thanks to God were given in reply. "This year, as every year before, we honor Him with sacrifices, as well as our continued obedience."

He continued. "Let us speak now of wine. Who remembers the vintage from seventy years past?"

"Best you've ever made, and that's saying something!" called Noah's cousin Merim. The men in Methuselah's line typically knew their wine vintages as they knew their own families.

"I acquiesce to your excellent taste! There is one barrel still in the cellars," he said, pausing to scattered applause, "and the wine therein will be poured out as a drink offering in three days. For some of you, it will be a sacrifice indeed," he added to a few chuckles, and more than a few wistful looks from the younger generations. "As well it should—remember, we are simply stewards of what our good God has given to us for our short lifetimes. It is only right for Him to receive the first and best fruits of our labor." Heads nodded in agreement.

"Noah!" Methuselah addressed his grandson, "This farm has many herds, and you know them all. Which animal would you say is the best of them?"

Noah thought for only a moment before answering. "I should say that I have seen none finer than that young white bull from Ghestel's northern herd."

"Again, I agree. Ghestel," Methuselah directed to a quiet herdsman sitting with the younger men, "you have worked diligently for me for five years now and have multiplied our herds. Although you came to this place not of our family, I do regard you as such now, and I am proud to call you friend." Jonan clapped Ghestel on the back, and many of the other men made sounds of affirmation. Ghestel seemed a bit stunned. "I want to honor you and your labor. The best of our herds will be given as a burnt offering, and the culmination of our sacrifices will be your bull. I thank you for your work and stewardship, and I thank all of the esteemed cooks responsible for this excellent meal." Methuselah bowed to his wife. "Now everyone, finish up—preparations begin early tomorrow, and I wish you all well-fed before!"

"Pardon me, Grandfather," said Noah. He stood up, gesturing to Zara to do the same. "We have an announcement to make. All of you here know of my esteem for Emzara. By God's great grace, she feels the same for me. Her father," he said, inclining his head to his uncle Rakeel, Lamech's younger brother, "has given his blessing, and she has consented to be my wife. We are betrothed to be married!"

Cheers erupted from the younger crowd, and many of the older women looked at each other knowingly, as if they had expected the announcement. A wide smile spread on Methuselah's face. Lamech and Rakeel clasped hands. Rakeel approached the couple, embraced them both, and said to Noah, "What can I say? Welcome to the family!"—drawing general laughter from the table. Noah and Zara spent the next few minutes accepting congratulations from those gathered at the feast, receiving the many exclamations of *such a perfect couple* and *I'm so happy for you both* with genuine joy and thanks.

After the line of well-wishers for Noah and Zara had ended, Methuselah spoke once more. "Everyone who did not have a hand in the making of this meal, will have a hand in its cleaning up! That means you, Jonan—and yes, you may leave the wine on the table." A bustle of activity later, the table was cleared and dishes rinsed in the kitchen's large basins. The older generations and children retired to bed, but the younger adults remained in the hall, drinking wine and talking.

"Where will you live?" asked Merim.

"My father has given us a plot near the east vineyards," Noah said. "I have been storing wood and stone in the old barn for a year." He grinned at Zara. "Designing our home for longer. Now we have but to build it."

Merim tilted his cup to them. "Strong motivation to finish harvest quickly, I suppose."

The conversation naturally turned to the upcoming harvest. Noah's youngest brother, Hadishad, began arguing with Merim about the merits of hornfaces over aurochs as plow animals, with promises to compare the upcoming crop yields as proof. Several of the women, concern on their faces, were listening to Jonan's greatly-overstated descriptions of the difficulties and dangers he might face in the vast wheat fields at the foot of the vineyard hills.

Arm around his newly-betrothed, Noah's thoughts were on Zara and the life they would soon begin together. He absently listened to the various discussions around the table, not paying much attention to any of them, enjoying his own quiet reverie.

"This must be what life in the Garden was like," said Hadishad, tossing a last grape into his mouth and leaning back into Jonan as if his elder brother were a comfortable chair. Jonan shoved him away, laughing. "Does that make tomorrow the fall of Adam?" he asked. "Toil, plants of the field, sweat of our faces…we'll be well aware of the ground's curse for certain."

"You're quite right, dear brother," said Hadishad, adopting a false look of concern. "Noah! When are you going to fulfill that prophecy of yours, anyway? This harvest is going to wreak havoc on my lyre practice." Several cousins snorted.

"All in God's perfect timing," answered Noah. "Besides, little brother, you have far too many calluses from plucking strings, and not nearly enough from wielding a scythe."

A distant female cousin from the village who was spending some months at the farm leaned across the table and asked, "I know of Methuselah's, but what prophecy is this?"

Jonan stared at her, his expression feigning shock, and drew in a deep breath. "You mean you haven't *heard*?" He climbed on the bench, cleared his throat, and recited portentously: "This one will give us rest from our work and from the toil of our hands arising from the ground which the Lord has cursed!"

Joining in, Hadishad took out his lyre and began playing a tune. Jonan and Merim linked arms and started dancing around the table, singing the words of the prophecy to the melody. Ignoring their antics, but now engaged in the camaraderie around him, Noah noticed one other who seemed lost in thought. Ghestel sat quietly by himself, nursing his wine and staring blankly. "Ghestel," he hailed the farmhand, "I would thank you as well for your work. Methuselah thinks quite highly of you, you know. For him to choose a bull of your breeding for the sacrifice is a great honor."

"Indeed," said Ghestel. "Please excuse me. I think I shall go to bed."

"Sleep well, then," Noah said. The farmhand rose from the bench and left without another word, taking his cup of wine with him.

The sacrifice was more difficult for some than others, thought Noah. The farmhand was right about one thing, though—it had been a long night, and it was time to go to bed.

"I ought to retire too," he told the group around the table.

"So soon?" Jonan asked, taking a brief rest from the dancing that started. "You *are* getting old. In all honesty, though, congratulations to you both. And I do not mock the prophecy our father gave you. I only hope to be there when it is finally fulfilled. Until then, though," he said, rising again with a sigh, "our toil continues. Goodnight! And Zara, enjoy these last nights of sleeping alone—he snores!"

Noah stood and pulled Zara to her feet. "Goodnight, my love," he said, embracing her. She kissed him wordlessly. "Rest well, Noah," she said, smiling. "I will stay a while longer. There is much to tell the other girls!" Noah glanced at the table, where sisters and cousins were waiting for Zara eagerly.

True, long hours of hard work would begin soon. Still, Noah thought, he had more blessings than he could count. God was truly gracious, and he had been right; this had been the best night of his life.

As he fell to sleep, the evening's many pleasant conversations drifted through Noah's head. Of all the happy words he had heard, though, the last ones in his thoughts before he succumbed to slumber were his brother Jonan's.

"Tomorrow...the fall..."

‹ CHAPTER 2 ›

Nighttime bothered Ghestel none at all. He knew every path in these
farmlands and could walk them in the dark. What did bother him
were the outrageous plans for the upcoming sacrifice. He had spent
the last three years raising the magnificent bull to be a sire that would be
the envy of every farmer and herdsman for miles, all for Methuselah. How
many times had Master Elebru offered to buy Mut—as Ghestel had privately named the bull—every time increasing the price? And each time
Ghestel had refused him, out of loyalty to the family he had worked for—
slaved for, really—these five years. His hard work had paid off. This bull
was by far the strongest and healthiest the family had ever bred, and they
had Ghestel to thank. And now, just as he was reaching his prime, Mut was
to be burned on an altar! He would not even be sold for leather and horn
in the beastmarkets of Tanin, much less be allowed to breed. Ghestel would
not stand for it.

That is why he was leading the bull across the river, to Master Elebru.
The last offer was more than enough to buy a nice room in the city, and the
skills he had learned during his years here, on the most prosperous farm
around, would let him make a comfortable living. One bull would be easy
enough to conceal on a big farm like Elebru's—let Methuselah wonder
where his rival's exceptional calves were coming from. And Ghestel? He
could disappear into the masses who migrated to the market towns, maybe
keep traveling until he found another estate where his talents would be
appreciated rather than wasted needlessly.

Ghestel took the long way around from the stalls to the pastures,
past the mango groves, to avoid the ostrich pens. The big birds were almost
impossible to rouse at night, but if one of them started booming, it could
wake up the whole household. No point in risking it.

He had tried, truly tried, to see the matter from Methuselah's point
of view. He simply could not. Why would God want the squandering
of such a fine creature in His honor, anyway? Surely a good steward, as

Methuselah stressed to them all to be, would be the one who allowed Mut to live and thrive.

He led the bull down to the river, to the trampled, muddy banks where the herds often drank. The river ran deep in places, but Ghestel knew where he would be able to cross. The river would mask any scent trail that might be followed, and any hoofprints would be impossible to pick out from the hundreds there already. Once across, he would head straight to Master Elebru, take his offer for the bull, and be gone well before sunrise. He had little in the way of possessions, content to escape Methuselah's lands with only the rough clothes of a hardworking farmhand on his back. All he needed was a belt full of coin and he would be off. Master Elebru was clever enough to come up with a story to thwart the questions that were sure to come his way; he had coveted Mut long enough that Ghestel was quite sure he would not give the bull up once he had his hands on it.

The plan was simple, but it would work—was working, really. Ghestel smiled as he led the bull into the slow-flowing river. Tomorrow was the beginning of a new life—for him, and for Mut.

‹ CHAPTER 3 ›

Noah awoke from a restful sleep full of pleasant dreams. He ambled to the kitchen, where his father was eating his breakfast. Edna had laid out leftover datebread, along with cheese and fruit that had not been eaten during the feast, stored overnight in the cold cellars. Dawn had not yet broken, but most of the household was already awake and preparing for the workday.

"Morning, Noah," Lamech greeted his son. "Have a seat." He gestured at another wooden stool at the small round table in the kitchen alcove. "The women have already gone out, but Emzara brewed us some tea. She is a good woman, Noah, and you are a fine man. I am very happy for you—for you both." He took a last bite of breakfast. "And your mother wanted me to tell you to set a wedding date soon. She wants grandchildren." Noah chuckled.

Marking his arrival with a loud yawn, Jonan shuffled to the table. His half-shut eyes looked to be fighting a losing battle with the dark circles beneath them. "Tea. Hot. Good." He reached for the steaming pot on the table, pouring himself a cup and taking a sip. "Sorry I'm up late, Father," he said. "It would seem that I'm nursing a bit of a headache." Lamech muttered something about "too much wine and too little sleep."

After breakfast, the men gathered in the wooden barn that had been cleared out to store the sacrifices. The barn was the most recent addition to the complex that wrapped around the farmhouse. Many of the newer structures Noah had designed and built himself; of the many jobs at which he had become proficient during a lifetime on a farm, he enjoyed building most of all. Methuselah briefly reviewed the day's tasks. He, Lamech, and Rakeel would head to the altar, built upon a green hillock in the wide west field. The altar had been constructed centuries ago from uncut, unadorned stone. Although it was in reality merely a necessary prop for the sacrifices, the men would still ensure that it was clean and in good repair, free of creeping moss and accumulated grime.

Noah and his brothers, along with most of the younger men, were charged with gathering the sacrifices themselves. The best sheep-goats, cattle, and birds had already been chosen, needing but to be collected and brought to the barn for preparation. The grain and oil offerings, stored elsewhere, were a simple matter of transport. The very best and biggest fruits, waiting in the orchards and fields that were even now ripe for the harvest, would need to be carefully selected and picked. The men divided the work among themselves; it fell to Noah to procure the wine that his grandfather had marked for the sacrifice. "I just can't do it," lamented Jonan, with great sympathy from his cousin Merim.

The wine cellar was carved out of the bedrock below the farmhouse. As the stores of wine had increased over the decades, so had the size of the cellar, until it was a vast maze of casks and barrels. Noah lit the torch outside the old wooden door that guarded the stone stairway to the cellar, kept in darkness for proper aging of the wine; although he knew the cellar even in the dark, he would take no chances with picking the wrong barrel today. The gravel crunched underneath his feet as he made his way to his destination. He smelled the humid air; it called to him fond memories of childhood, of him and his brothers, barefoot, stomping on crushed grapes in his grandfather's fermentation tanks. He smiled. Soon enough, his own children would do the same for Methuselah, master vintner. Finally Noah found the marked oak barrel, and with a small sigh and the wine in tow, he started back towards the barn.

With efficiency and care, the work was almost completed by mid-morning. Fresh hay and feed for the sacrificial animals, all perfect specimens of their kinds, filled the barns. Sacks of grains and skins of oils were covered and placed against the wall. Produce of all sorts, gathered across the breadth of the farm, was stored in cold stone chests to keep fresh until the sacrifice; this would be the first to be given. There were two conspicuous absences, though: the centerpiece of the sacrifice, the white bull, had yet to be brought to the barn, a task which had fallen to Hadishad; and the farmhand Ghestel had not shown to breakfast, nor to Methuselah's briefing earlier in the day. A few of the other farmhands had made comments, but Noah and Jonan had not given the matter much concern. It was early yet, and their younger brother was easily distracted, though usually dependable.

A loud bray announced Hadishad's approach. He pulled hard on the reins strapped to the bright red crest of his scaly steed. It slid to a halt and dropped to all fours to let him dismount. He ran into the barn, clearly distraught.

"I've searched the north pastures high and low," he panted, "and the bull is nowhere to be found. Neither is Ghestel—I checked with Grandmother, and none of the women have seen him since last night. They're missing!"

The news spurred them into quick action. Each man was assigned a section of the estate to search and was on his way. Noah took it upon himself to inform Methuselah. He whistled as he sprinted to the corrals where the horses ran free during the day. Two shaggy wolfhounds burst from one of the farmhouse's back doors, barking loudly as they fell in line with their master. Noah had raised the hounds since they were pups. Strong, fast, and loyal to a fault, they served equally well as herders, trackers, and hunters, and Noah's instincts told him that he ought to keep their keen noses close at hand. "Ho there, Raph!" he hailed a roan stallion galloping along the tall fence. The horse stopped with a snort. Not slowing down, Noah took one step on the middle rail and hurdled over the fence onto the stallion's back. Right behind, the wolfhounds scooted under the lowest rail and followed Noah as he rode with all haste to the corral's far exit, toward the altar's field.

The meeting with the older men was short, but informative. "I wager Ghestel will not be found in our fields," said Rakeel darkly.

"Elebru?" asked Lamech.

"Aye," answered Methuselah. "His eye has been on that bull for a time, almost since the day it was born. I had suspected he had made offers before. Perhaps the sacrifice was the push Ghestel needed to succumb to the temptation." He shook his head sadly. "I had no choice, though. The bull was the finest in all my herds. I thought the boy understood."

"He was behaving strangely after the feast, to be sure," said Noah. "Still, I hesitate to accuse him with no proof. He has been a diligent worker and a good man, as far as I have known him."

"The most direct course of action is the best here, I think," said Methuselah. "Noah, ride to Elebru. Ask him if he has seen Ghestel or the bull. Tell him our suspicions that Ghestel has taken the bull illicitly. Who knows? If Ghestel has deceived us in this matter, he may have deceived Elebru as well."

"Be quick, son—and be careful!" called Lamech as Noah galloped away, towards the river and towards Elebru.

The road to Master Elebru was well-known but seldom-used by any member of either farm. Methuselah and Elebru knew each other of old and had worked together for a long while, but these days their relationship was rather cool, although not altogether unfriendly. Elebru had never married, so Noah and his generation, and even Lamech and his, had never had any of the man's children or grandchildren to befriend. Still, Noah felt sure he would easily gain an audience with the landowner, even if their fears of Ghestel's theft turned out to be well-founded, since turning Noah away outright would be an answer in itself.

The river between the two farmlands ran wide and deep in most places, with the occasional small islands consisting of mostly mud and reeds. Several shallows did exist, crossable if one knew where to look for them, and at one point the river became quite narrow. Here the farmers had built a small stone footbridge arching over the river, which cut miles from the roundabout path travelers between farms would otherwise have to take, all the way to the market village's wide woodbeamed bridge. Had he been herding livestock to trade or sell, Noah would have been obliged to take the long path; alone on horseback and needing haste, he took the shorter way now.

After crossing the stone bridge, Noah found himself on an ill-kept dirt path that soon met a larger road paved with stones. Soon enough he was riding down a broad, straight road lined with tall teak trees; lianas climbed up their trunks to form a thick canopy, creating a woody roof. At its end, the avenue split and wrapped around a three-tiered fountain surrounded by beds of ginger and bright orange blossoms, meeting again at the house's front entrance. Two long wings of Elebru's manor house stretched out to envelop the circle entrance-road. Noah raised an eyebrow in recognition of the manor's grandeur; Elebru had worked hard to build his farmstead up over a century, and he was obviously quite willing to demonstrate his wealth.

Noah's approach had been no secret, and a stable boy immediately met him in front of the house. Elebru's seneschal Suat greeted him from the open, ornately-carved front door. "Hail, Noah, son of Lamech, son of Methuselah. Do you have business with the master?"

"I do. I wish to see him now, if I may," Noah said.

"He is taking breakfast. I shall announce you. Please, follow me." Suat invited him in with an outstretched arm.

"Thank you, Suat. Stay outside, boys," he ordered his hounds, who took up casual positions flanking the door. Suat followed him in, pausing to regard each animal with a small frown before shutting the door.

The halls through which the seneschal led Noah were vaguely familiar from the few times he had occasion to visit over the years, either on an errand for the farm or with his grandfather. The high, arching ceilings and woven tapestries on the walls were a far cry from Methuselah's sprawling farmhouse, where comfort, function, and simplicity ruled. The central passage opened to a spacious room overlooking a wide green slope hedged on all sides with white rose, blackthorn, and beech. White peacocks strutted around the enclosed lawn. The room had no walls, letting the mild breeze circulate and fill the air with the scent of the roses. Thick-napped rugs covered the stone floor, and short couches piled with lush pillows were arranged to form several sitting areas. On the central couch sat the master of the farm, back turned towards Noah as Suat escorted him into the room. Elebru wore only a silk tunic open at the chest; work of any sort was clearly not on this morning's agenda.

Elebru turned as he heard the men approach. "Noah, Lamech's son, to see the master," announced Suat, who was then promptly dismissed with a wave.

"Noah! How very pleasant to see you," said Elebru. "What brings you to my home this morning? It must surely be important, if Methuselah is sparing you from labor today."

"Thank you for seeing me, sir," said Noah. "I know you are a man who appreciates forthright speech. A white bull from our northern herd was chosen for our upcoming sacrifices. It is now missing, along with the man whose charge it was. We wonder if he has sold it to you." Noah paused, observing the older man's reaction, but Elebru made no change of his expression. Noah continued, "If the man sold it to you, he did so under false pretenses, for it was not his to sell. We have no wish to assign blame in the matter. We wish only for our bull. If you do have it, we will gladly reimburse you whatever gold you paid, and I will take the bull and leave you in peace."

For a moment, Elebru appeared to be considering how to reply. Finally he spoke. "First, young Noah, your bluntness suits you. More, it suits me, so let me answer in kind. Your sacrifice is absurd. Of course I know of the bull you speak. It is perfect in every way, and for Methuselah to use it in this manner is madness! In truth, I have seen neither your man nor your bull, but I will tell you this: I wish I did have it hidden away, if only to save it from you. To waste such an animal in obeisance to God because you suspect it pleases Him—He has made life quite difficult enough for us without demanding the best we have!"

Noah began to make a reply, but Elebru stopped him. "No, you have your answer. I do not have the bull, I have not seen the man who took it, and I would not be inclined to assist you even if I had. Now, good day to you, young sir, and please give my regards to your grandfather and father, despite their foolishness in this matter." Elebru sat back down and resumed watching the birds on the lawn; like an apparition, Suat appeared beside Noah. "If you will kindly come this way," he said, gesturing back towards the entrance hall.

A bit dejected, Noah exited the manor. He mounted his stallion and rode back under the liana tunnel, wolfhounds following. He could not tell if Elebru had lied to him or not. Regardless, that avenue was obviously closed. He formulated a new plan of action.

Elebru's denial had not convinced him, that was certain. Mentally, he placed himself in Ghestel's position. If he were the farmhand, stealing away in the middle of the night, what would he have done? "That is easy enough," Noah thought, "I would make my way to the shallows where the herds grazed and cross the river there." Tracking would be futile from Methuselah's side of the river, since any tracks and scents would be mingled and masked, even with the hounds. "But Ghestel doesn't know Elebru's lands like he does our own," Noah considered. "If he did lead the bull to the shallows, he would likely take a predictable path once across." Struck with inspiration, Noah whistled to his mount and turned off the stone road.

If his theory held true, perhaps Noah and his hounds could pick up a trail on Elebru's side of the river. Ghestel would have headed to the manor house first, and he would have taken a straight line from the river crossing. Noah rode on a course that would intersect with that line, taking care to stay to uncultivated or fallow fields. He had not felt exactly unwelcome at the manor, but he thought he ought not flaunt his continued suspicions by searching openly.

He soon arrived at where he believed was a good place to start. "Look sharp, boys," he said to the hounds, slowing his horse to a walk. Noah examined the tall grass around him for any sign of passage of something as large as the bull, and the wolfhounds kept their noses to the ground as they ran back and forth, sniffing for a scent. Slowly and carefully, they made their way back to the banks of the river, with no sign of either Ghestel or the bull. Noah trusted the hounds' hunting instincts and his own tracking skills well enough that he felt confident that they hadn't missed anything; Ghestel had not come this way.

Noah sighed, in some part disappointed in the failure of their errand, but also relieved that their suspicions of thievery seemed to be unfounded. He would be able to keep his good opinion of the farmhand. Still, the mystery of the pair's disappearance had not been solved; Noah was back where he started. There was no place to go but back home to resume the search. Perhaps good news would even await him there.

As they were already at the banks near the shallow crossing, Noah saw no point in riding upriver to the bridge. He urged his horse into the water. The hounds, sensing their work was ended, bounded into the river, splashing and wagging their hairy tails. The silted riverbed underneath them broke the surface of the water midway across, forming a low muddy island enclosed by thick, tall reeds. The wolfhounds reached the island first, shaking their shaggy pelts free of water. Almost immediately, they froze. They began snarling, stalking forward in unison to a mass of reeds on the downstream end of the island, noses to the ground.

Curious, Noah dismounted. "Stand," he commanded his stallion; it snorted nervously, but held its place. He approached the hounds, both growling at something hidden in the reeds. At first, Noah's mind failed to grasp what the object was, but as gruesome realization set in, an unbidden wave of nausea swept over him.

Ghestel's empty eyes stared from a face smeared with mud and small bits of flotsam from the river. His tongue lolled out of his mouth, beginning to swell in the sun. His left arm floated back and forth in the water, the flow of the river not quite strong enough to draw what was left of him from the reeds. The rest of the body—right arm and shoulder, torso, legs—was gone. Ragged pieces of homespun tunic covered the bloody stump of his chest. Noah swallowed the bile rising in his throat. He needed to bring this… him…to Methuselah, for burial if nothing else. He stripped off his shirt in order to wrap the grisly remains.

Suddenly, both wolfhounds looked up, out towards the deep river. They bristled and backed up from the water slowly. Noah stepped back with them. The wolfhounds' instincts were keen, and their behavior now filled him with a growing sense of dread. "I think we ought to head home, boys," he said calmly. "We can return for the body later."

Without warning, a massive dark head exploded from the water, and the closest hound disappeared in a snap and a whimper. Noah jumped on his stallion, which leapt off the island as if stung. "Go, go, go!" shouted Noah; this situation was quickly going out of his control. The horse dashed madly to the opposite shore; Noah spared a glance behind him, breathing a quick sigh of relief to see the other hound running close to the horse's heels. He turned to look ahead. A splash and a loud yelp drew his attention again behind him. Where the hound had been was now a bloodstain on the water, spreading outward in the wake of a scaly green back diving below the surface. "Blood and death!" The small part of Noah's brain not engaged in panicked retreat considered that his mind must be playing tricks on him; it seemed that the creature's back had stretched four, perhaps five times the length of his horse, and had still been hidden by the misty river at either end.

"Lord God, let me reach the bank! Let me warn my family," Noah prayed breathlessly. Flecks of spittle from the speeding horse spattered Noah's face as he ducked his head to avoid a low branch hanging over the river. They were almost to the other side. Noah heard something gaining behind them, but he dared not look. An endless second passed, and splashes turned to dull wet hoofbeats as the horse finally reached the bank. The elation of a narrow escape soon shattered into icy shards of horror, though; the sounds of pursuit did not fade, but changed to the thud of heavy limbs on the ground, the wet grind of a broad belly plowing a muddy furrow through the damp earth. Noah steeled himself against despair. His horse was tired but swift yet, and he was in familiar territory. Cutting among low-growing bushes of brambles, Noah perceived the sounds of the beast's pursuit grow fainter. A leap over the hedge that enclosed the guanaco paddock, and they faded altogether. He did not slow—would not slow—until he had given the news to his father and grandfather. A distant low, throaty growl rumbled in Noah's ears, sending chills up his spine that did not fade until he had ridden far, far away.

‹ CHAPTER 4 ›

The news Noah brought caused even Methuselah to forget preparations for the sacrifice. Sadness for Ghestel's fate outweighed any negative feelings towards his assumed perfidy. Noah's sketchy descriptions of the beast started an intense discussion on its identity among his brothers and cousins. The general consensus was that some sea monster had swum upriver and was camped out in the deep waters. "Hungry, most likely," opined Rakeel. "The fishermen at the river mouth cast too many nets. We let fields lie fallow for a time—ought to do the same with the seas."

Merim carried a warning to Master Elebru, stopping in the village to inform the watch and to recommend avoiding the waterways, in case the monster decided to travel upstream. Advice from Methuselah's household was generally regarded as sound, and most of the trading barges and pleasure craft were unloaded and docked in short order. Merim retold Noah's harrowing experience to Elebru directly, then quickly excused himself to return to his own household. When the news reached Elebru, he wasted no time sending runners to call his tenant farmers to the manor. The messengers made no mention of specifics for fear of inciting panic; it was clear to the tenants, though, that the matter was urgent.

Everyone of Elebru's farms, including the wives and children of his workers, gathered at his manor in a state of nervous uncertainty. The tenants were ushered into the dining hall, the largest room in the house. Lit lamps cast eerie shadows on the dark stone walls as Elebru entered the hall, flanked by his man-at-arms, Denter, and Suat the seneschal. Denter was burly and silent, with the reputation for acting rather than speaking. He crossed his arms and looked sternly around the room. Suat appeared calm as always. Elebru's tenants knew the seneschal to be shrewd, cold, and calculating behind his carefully polished demeanor; the opinion of the farmers was that he would be perfectly willing to stab any of them in the back if it would profit his master, smiling politely as the knife slid between the ribs. Elebru addressed them without greeting. "My lands and herds are threatened. Some beast—I know not what kind—has taken up residence in the river. I intend to drive it out. If you wish to continue to live off my lands, you will aid in this."

Worried muttering fluttered around the room. One cottager, a stout, florid young man who had only been with Elebru for a few seasons, spoke up: "An' say we want no part? A living is one thing, but it sounds like you're asking us to risk death. An' if we leave, who will toil for you?" A few heads nodded in agreement.

Elebru practically pounced on the man. "I built this farm from *nothing!* Not a piece of it do I not know better than you know your own mother! I will still thrive without you, but you are *nothing* without me. Leave if you wish, but you will find that I will send your reputation as a sluggard, oaf, and coward far ahead of you. No one will dare employ you, and your chances of marrying, slim as they already are, will dwindle to *none*." Humiliated, the man hung his head, his cheeks now as red as the beets he farmed.

"I would hear from Dashael," said the farm's blacksmith. Dashael was Elebru's master of beasts, with a small amount of fame for his skill at handling larger animals. The soft-spoken man paused thoughtfully, then said, "I've handled mammoths, big cats, and bigger dragons, but I've not often come across a beast such as this was described. Clearly it's not confined to water, but just as clearly it prefers it. Likely as not, it has not been around man, besides the ones it has encountered alone, and so it has no respect for man's strength." He paused again. "It may be that if enough of us confront it, we can drive it back downriver." Dashael looked at Elebru and said, "I would have a care, though, Master Elebru. We will need to be well-armed, mounted as many as are able, and I would suggest carrying at least a few torches. I've said my piece now, but I make no promises. Herds are one thing, but these wild beasts are different, and this one sounds to be a crafty old monster."

"There now," Suat said smoothly to the tenants, "you have heard the expert. If it pleases you, master, let the men gather weapons—pitchforks, scythes, whatever they have that seems best to them—and return again here. We will go together to the river and drive this animal from our lands, and tomorrow we shall wake, safe and secure once more."

Elebru nodded and ordered, "All of you, go to your houses and arm yourselves, and make haste! We shall rid ourselves of this beast once and for all—tonight!"

Elebru's tenants-turned-hunters met again outside the manor, with the exceptions of three farmers who left with their families and meager possessions. They mainly carried the implements of their respective trades: pitchforks and mattocks, sickles and scythes, hatchets and broad-axes. The blacksmith held a long iron spear, with a heavy hammer strapped to his belt. Secretly, Dashael was the most worried; this was reflected in his preparation. Two heavy hunting knives were strapped to his belt, and a long bull-whip was coiled around his waist. A case of long wooden darts hung at his side, and he carried an atlatl carved from elk antler. "I can hit a bird at eighty paces with this," he said to the men next to him, "and I won't get closer than that if I can help it."

Elebru's watchmen, three large men led by Denter, arrived on heavy black draft horses. Each had a hunting bow strapped to his back along with a broad backsword, and they carried lances. Suat and the rest of the house-staff came on foot, armed with hunting spears and torches. The stable boys drove three milk cows, recently culled from the herds due to infertility, that had been marked for market. Master Elebru himself joined them at last, riding an enormous moa with bright green feathers that darkened and turned faintly iridescent near the tips. Long, gaudy show-feathers crowned its tall head. Elebru was less ostentatious; he was dressed in supple leather boots and gloves and an embroidered burgundy hunter's tunic, and he held a curved bow made of wood, sinew, and horn. "What are we waiting for?" he shouted. "To the river!"

The plan that had developed was this: the useless cows would be driven into the river as bait—"A sacrifice that actually means something," said Elebru—and when the beast surfaced to take them, the archers would attack with a barrage of arrows. If all went as planned, the animal would simply leave, seeking a less hostile dwelling place. Denter, who would take command of the operation, did not intend for the tenants to become involved; they would likely be useless, and if they panicked, they might be an actual threat to the whole business. "They add to the numbers, in any case," the big man-at-arms had said to his master, "and that may aid in frightening the creature."

The mists had rolled down from the upland fields and now lay heavy on the river. Dashael cracked his whip loudly, driving the cows into the shallows. The animals waded into the water a good ways from the bank. Elebru's men stood well away from the river's edge, tense, with weapons held ready. For several minutes, the only sounds were the occasional lowing of the cattle and the quiet splashing of the cows' fatty dewlaps as they brushed the surface of the water.

A sudden roar shattered the silence as the monster exploded from the water. Long, dark jaws clamped over the middle cow's neck; blood mixed with a great spray of water as knifelike teeth nearly severed the cow's head from its thick body, and the monster dragged the carcass underneath the surface. "Fire!" shouted Denter. Arrows peppered the water where the animals had disappeared.

The wide-eyed men held fast on the bank, but the two remaining cattle panicked. One lost its footing on the treacherous riverbed and slipped from the shallows into the deeper water. It floundered, then was violently jerked beneath the mist. The last cow ran frantically toward the opposite bank. The mists parted and the monster surfaced in pursuit. For the first time, the men glimpsed the creature almost in full; for those who would survive, the sight would haunt their nightmares.

Two rows of knobby spines ran the length of its broad, scaly body. The spines and scales continued down a thick tail that gyrated in the water, propelling it through the river. The head was too far away to make out details; it was roughly shaped in a long, tapered triangle with a bulge at its snout. Four crooked, clawed legs jutted horizontally from the body. What filled the farmers with terror, though, was the sheer size of the monster. From snout to rump was forty cubits at least, with girth to match, and most of its tail was still hidden; the head alone looked to be larger than a man. Its size belied its speed, even with the shallow river impeding its movement, and with little effort, it was upon the fleeing cow; two gargantuan bites later, and only the monster remained. "God save us," whispered Dashael. "I know what this is."

"Run. Now," Dashael urged the men around him. They needed no prodding; almost every farmer turned without a word, their trembling legs moving far faster than was their wont.

"How dare you!" screamed Elebru. "Come back, cowards!" he shouted futilely.

Through clenched teeth, the wrangler said, "Don't draw attention, master. We must leave now, all of us. I am no coward, but this beast is beyond us."

From his mount, Denter asked, "What sort of creature is this, Dashael?"

Even the most stouthearted of the remaining men felt the chill of fear when he answered. "Leviathan."

Elebru spurred his moa forward. "Leviathan or not, my task is not changed. We can still drive it away!" The big green bird bellowed, as if in agreement. Elebru drew an arrow. "Watchmen, on my mark!"

"And what if your arrows drive it into Methuselah's lands?" asked Dashael.

"Let them look after themselves. My concern is for my own. Now, fire!"

Five arrows flew true and hit their huge target, but the leviathan did not appear to notice. "Again!" cried Elebru, and again the arrows flew.

"The arrows are bouncing off those scales, master," said Denter. "The beast doesn't seem to even feel them."

"Then I'll use something larger," answered Elebru. "Suat! Spear!" The seneschal looked sharply at a sick-looking houseservant, who gulped and offered his spear to the master. Elebru wrenched it out of the man's hand, spurred his bird-mount forward almost to the river edge, and flung the spear across the river. It stuck for a moment in the beast's back, near the head, then fell to the mud. A growl drifted across the misty river, and the monster lumbered around to face the river. "There! It felt *that*, to be sure," yelled Elebru triumphantly. "A few more of those, and we'll surely be rid of it!"

The men of the household haltingly stepped to the water's edge, torches glowing brightly in the fading light. Shockingly quickly, the leviathan darted into the river and submerged. "Back! Back from the river!" Dashael shouted. Fear of the hidden monster overthrew fear of Master Elebru; the servants backed away, slowly at first, then a mad scramble up the muddy bank ensued. Four of the men slipped to the ground; Dashael and the blacksmith, who had stayed after the wrangler's first warning, leapt down the bank to aid them. The blacksmith planted his iron spear in the mud, grabbed a slight young man under the arms, and heaved him up the bank. Dashael helped another to his feet, who dropped his weapon and torch, now extinguished, and ran away without looking back. Without warning, the leviathan's head shot out of the water; its terrible jaws closed over a servant still struggling to rise, and he was gone. The remaining man screamed in terror and began crawling on all fours through the mud; the leviathan shook its head, flinging bits of chewed flesh all about, and started towards the man. With a cry, the blacksmith jumped over the downed man. He thrust his spear into the bulbous protrusion at the end of the beast's snout, and the tip stuck. The monster snapped once, then twice, but the spear held fast; beads of sweat tracked down the bulging veins on the big blacksmith's neck as he strained against the terrifying impasse. The leviathan suddenly jolted forward, knocking the spear from his hands and him to the ground. In an instant, grimy teeth were clamped on the blacksmith's legs. He screamed in terror, but kept the presence of mind to draw his hammer from his belt. Two swings, heavy enough to bend iron, landed upon the monster's snout, but to no avail. The leviathan swallowed, great gullet drawing the man deeper into the ghastly maw. The screams ended as the leviathan's jaws pierced flesh, broke ribs, savaged lungs. One more swallow, and the blacksmith too was gone.

For Denter, this had suddenly become his element. He relished a fight. He and his men were battle-hardened and fearless, qualities for which Elebru paid handsomely. Countless beasts from the forests, drawn perpetually by Elebru's fat and happy herds, had met bloody ends by the watchmen's violence. Their horses were used to hard, but relatively safe, work on a farm, but the animals were also well-trained for the hunt. Even so, they bucked and whinnied in instinctual fright of the deadly monster. In the few seconds it took for the watchmen to master their mounts, the leviathan struck. It shot up the bank among the stamping horses, using its rock-hard, bulbous snout as a bludgeon. Two horses crumpled with ruined knees, pinning their riders underneath them. Denter was almost as fast as the leviathan, though; the big man jabbed his lance at the beast's eyes and face, and the other mounted watchman soon joined him. They drove the leviathan backwards, the monster snapping and growling in frustration.

The men still there could now see the leviathan in terrifying detail. Grotesque jaws unevenly sprouted jagged teeth, stringy bits of flesh stuck between them. Dark reptilian eyes, huge but somehow still beady, were set atop the scaled head, depressed in knurled, rough protective pockets towards the back of the skull. The long snout narrowed to the width of a man, then broadened again to form the knobby, boulder-like bulla at the tip. Disturbingly, the shape of the creature's jaws gave the impression that it was smiling.

Denter was more awed than terrified. He had heard tell from sailors of the sea monsters hidden in the endless depths of the ocean, stories of sleek, grey, dead-eyed giants whose jaws could bite ships in half and many-tentacled monstrosities that surfaced from the dark depths to rip boats to pieces; this, he was sure, was a beast to match any of them. As if reading his thoughts and wanting to prove the truth of them, the leviathan halted its brief retreat. It lunged at the head of the other draft horse. The horse braced its muscular legs and gave a great pull to free itself, then another; it abruptly went limp, tumbling down the bank, its headless neck pulsing a red fountain of blood. The quick watchman jumped from his horse and slid down the muddy bank, drawing his wide single-edged backsword as he fought for purchase. He halted his slide right beside the corner of the leviathan's jaws, actually putting his hand on the beast's scaly shoulders for balance in reflex. The leviathan tossed its head back, gulping down its bite of horse flesh. One black, fathomless eye stared for a moment into the terror-stricken brown ones of the unfortunate watchmen, whose desperate swing of his sword was no match for the swipe of the jaws that chopped him in half.

The sword blow had gouged a shallow furrow in the scaled hide of the monster's snout and nicked its gums. The beast was not injured by any means; it was, however, livid, for the cut must have been painful. Roaring, it barreled up the bank towards Denter, who recognized himself as the object of the leviathan's wrath. He dropped his lance and drew his bow; three arrows bounced harmlessly off of thick scales. The leviathan drove its snout underneath Denter's horse and pitched it into the air with a mighty snap of its head. Denter flew through the air, the surreality of the sudden attack ending as quickly as it had begun when he landed in the champing maw; his last thought was on the foulness of the creature's breath, and he was devoured.

The animal's deadly offensive had taken only a few minutes. Elebru had watched in disbelief as his strongest men were slaughtered like suckling pigs. Suat had observed the carnage by his master's side, coldly analyzing the creature as it wreaked bloody havoc on men he had known for years. "Master," said the seneschal, "this battle cannot be won by brute strength."

"This battle cannot be won at *all*," said Dashael heatedly at Elebru's other side. The wrangler had pulled one of the fallen watchmen from underneath his horse, but had found the other with a pool of blood under his head, dead after striking a rock when he hit the ground. "Please, spare these men their lives. Order a retreat!"

Elebru ignored him. "You have a plan?" he asked Suat.

"Of course, master," Suat answered. "The beast lives in water. Dashael himself suggested torches, and your loyal servants all carry one. Fire will put fear into it."

"Insanity!" cried Dashael. "You mean to approach it? Look around you!"

"Quiet, coward," hissed Elebru. "A fine idea, Suat. You always look to my best interests." He spoke louder, addressing the servants behind his seneschal. "Go! Drive this beast away, and you will see how generous your master can be!"

"Come on then, lads!" Suat rallied his underlings, prodding a few forward with the butt of his spear. None of the servants of the household were fighters; most were employed in menial services, all revolving around Master Elebru's uninterrupted comfort. Their training, however, ingrained in them instant and unquestioned obedience to the master, and to Suat by extension. Trembling hands held flickering torches, and faltering feet shuffled forward through the mud. Wet scales glowed orange as the servants approached; the leviathan's eyes reflected the flames like polished obsidian.

The seneschal took the lead. Suat was confident; he had always looked on Denter, Dashael, the watchmen—all those who engaged in physical labor, really—as mindless sorts of brutes whose muscles prohibited the use of their brains. The leviathan was no different from them, he thought. When faced with a threat other than direct violence, it would flee.

Brandishing their torches before them, the servants approached, spread apart in an arc. Suat faced the leviathan directly; it was still chewing its last mouthful of Denter, but it watched them carefully, not moving. The seneschal swept his torch before the beast's snout, making harsh hissing noises as he did so. The servants followed their leader, closing to within ten paces of the monster. It took a step back, adding to Suat's confidence.

"See?" spat Elebru to Dashael. "It retreats! No thanks to you." Elebru spurred his moa down the bank, closer to the contracting circle of torches. "Consider yourself unemployed," he called over his shoulder.

Growing bold now, Suat stepped forward. "Back!" he shouted. The leviathan growled, a deep, throaty rumble that Suat took as fear. It snorted and stepped back once more. "We have it now, lads!" Suat exulted. The beast snorted again, louder than before.

With a rushing roar, a blinding spout of flame and smoke spewed from the leviathan's bulla. A sweep of its head bent the course of the flames along the line of servants, engulfing them in blankets of fire. Screams borne of indescribable pain curdled Dashael's blood; he could only watch as the human pyres fell burning to the ground, or stumbled blindly to fling themselves in the river. Suat had received the blast full-on, and all that now remained was a charred corpse, contracted and smoldering in the mud of the riverbank.

All who could flee had fled already, save Dashael and Elebru. The wrangler felt the weight of failure; despite his best efforts, many good men were now dead. He realized that his initial advice to Elebru had been far too optimistic, though he had tried to urge caution, and it had resulted in disaster.

Elebru was no fool, and his mount was a coward. When the leviathan had loosed its flames, the moa had bolted back up the bank, spurred on by its rider in earnest. The bird's bright green feathers and fearful, squawking bellows drew the leviathan's attention, and another stream of fire shot from its snout. The flames reached the back of Elebru and his retreating mount, setting both ablaze. Elebru screamed in pain, nostrils filled with the stink of burning feathers. Behind them, the leviathan propelled itself forward on powerful legs, jaws open wide.

A long dart whistled through the smoke, traveling almost too fast for the eye to follow, and pierced the beast's exposed palate. It stopped its advance, roaring in pain. Dashael rushed to Elebru's side and roughly pulled him from his flaming mount. He shoved the burning man to the ground, slapping at the flames and dousing them with mud.

The moa had taken the brunt of the fiery stream. It ran around madly, its powerful legs tearing up clumps of sod at the top of the bank. Quick as thought, Dashael drew his knives; on the burning moa's next pass near the men, the wrangler slashed at its legs. The bird fell. Dashael dropped to his back and kicked the moa's thrashing body with both feet, right into the path of the rampaging leviathan. Not waiting to witness the bird's demise, he scrambled up and hauled Elebru to his feet. A sideways glance at the man revealed a badly burned back and scalded, hairless scalp; the flames had spread even to Elebru's face. His legs had been spared, though, and with Dashael's aid, they sprinted to the protection of the thickets nearby. With a mouth full of moa, the leviathan did not bother to follow. Satisfied with its opponents killed or fled, it began the lazy task of dragging the corpses of men and beasts to the bottom of the river.

· CHAPTER 5 ·

The tenant farmers who first retreated did not wait to hear the battle's outcome. Each went straight to his cottage or hovel, packed what provisions and belongings he and his family, if he had one, was able, and left Elebru's farm. They carried news of the leviathan into the village, with varying levels of exaggeration. The young beet farmer's version of the report was the most widely-spread; with little to his name, he had been the fastest to pack up and leave and the first to reach the village. He had gone immediately to the tavern at one of the inns, where men were just starting to gather after the long workday, and had found many ears eager to listen to his tale.

"Big as a house, it was," he said, his shaking hand spilling wine from the flagon he held. "The way it ate them cattle…" Weatherbeaten dockworkers and well-groomed merchants alike crowded in to hear more, but the red-faced farmer looked emptily ahead, replaying the carnage in his mind's eye.

"What of the others?" asked a fruit vendor who did quite a bit of business with Master Elebru.

"If they stayed, they're done for," answered the farmer. "T'weren't no fighting with a beast as that. One snap of those jaws!"—here the young farmer clapped his hands, causing a few of those gathered to jump—"and three big cows, just gone!" He talked and drank until late, answering what questions he could but leaving his audience hungry for the rest of the story; finally, he retired to his quarters and, thanks to the wine, fell into a mercifully dreamless sleep.

As the other tenants trickled to the village's inns or passed through on their ways elsewhere, the beet farmer's story was more or less collaborated. That the beast was truly a leviathan was doubted only by a few; Dashael was known to many in the village as a trustworthy man, especially on the

39

subject of animalia. There was much speculation on his fate and that of the household of Master Elebru, not much of it optimistic. "It will sort out in the morning," assured one innkeeper. "Perhaps some of us can head to Elebru's in the morning and see for ourselves." No one volunteered.

In truth, Dashael and Elebru had made their way to the manor house. They met the other survivors—the last watchman, the servants that the beast-master and the blacksmith had rescued, and a few stable boys who had surreptitiously fled in the chaos—at the house. Those who were still able-bodied loaded two packhorses with food, clothes, and several trunks. Elebru filled a satchel with gold and a few cherished items, wrapped his face and head in a thick scarf, and gave his last command as master of the house. "Let us go to Methuselah," he said quietly, "and pray he shows mercy I would not."

When the small band arrived at Methuselah's farm, they were immediately taken in as if family. Emilbet, Rakeel's wife, who had some knowledge of herbs and medicine, slathered Elebru's burns with a salve made of aloe, olive oil, lavender, and beeswax, after which he immediately wrapped his face once more.

Dashael told the tale, with the others adding details when able. Only Elebru remained quiet, lost in thought and regret. The beast-master's narrative was interrupted constantly by questions, exclamations, and sorrowful pauses; by the time the story had been related in its entirety, the morning's first light was stealing through the windows.

Methuselah set his household to work in short order. Laborers, overseen by Jonan, left for the fields and pastures near the river. They spent the day digging ditches on the inner side of the border hedges and laying them with thick, roughly-hewn pikes facing both to and from the water; as important as restricting the leviathan's movement was keeping the herds from the river's edge, and Noah and Merim, with help from Dashael, moved them well away. Elebru used a bit of his gold to hire out stout men known to Dashael to guard every entrance into his estates and farms, much of it already protected by long, tall stone walls overgrown with thorny, blackberried brambles.

Hadishad and some of his younger cousins armed themselves and set up a watch in the woods overlooking the river. The opposite bank was now cleared of corpses, but the mud was still red from the spilled blood of the previous night. Hadishad took first watch overnight, and his report the next morning brought new concern.

"We found three men in our woods," he said. "We stopped them, and they told us they were scouting for a group of villagers set on avenging kinsmen killed in Elebru's attack. I let them know they were denied access to our land, for their own good and safety, and they left."

Methuselah frowned. "At least they sound reasonable."

"They, ah, obliged us to persuade them." Hadishad reached behind him to tap the quiver of arrows at his back.

"Look on the bright side, brother," said Jonan. "You have diluted their ill will toward the monster with ill will toward us." Nobody laughed.

After several days, all of Elebru's party took their leave of the hospitality of Methuselah's home, except Dashael and Elebru himself. Dashael had taken a personal interest in ensuring that the events that decimated his former master's household would not repeat themselves here. He spent long hours talking with Methuselah and his men, especially Noah, on possible strategies to drive the beast back downriver. Hadishad and the others who kept watch made occasional wide-eyed reports of the leviathan sunning on the bank or lying partially submerged in the shallows. "It's like a whole other island made from scales just grew in the middle of the river," Hadishad had reported. "It hasn't searched for food, either, as far as we can tell."

"The beast gorged itself that night—I watched it," Dashael said darkly, "and I'll wager it stored what it didn't eat in the depths of the river. It likely won't need to hunt again for a long while."

"At least that gives us some time," said Noah. Emzara sat beside him, holding his hand tightly. Her new habit of doing so whenever she was able was, to Noah, the single happy thing to come about since the leviathan made known its presence.

"But time to do what?" asked Jonan. "It *will* come to hunt, or worse, continue up the river to the village, or one of the hornface herds will break through the barriers to drink. The south springs will not last forever. We tax them badly now already."

"Let us send messages to my brothers," said Lamech. "Father, call your sons, and their sons. We will bring a hundred strong men against this creature."

"Just because the beast might not hunt does not mean it will not defend itself if attacked," cautioned Methuselah. "I will not risk losing a single one of my blood—not unless there were no remaining options. Let my flocks and herds be devoured before I see any of my family perish."

"The hornfaced dragons are sturdy and strong," said Hadishad. "Could they drive off the leviathan?"

"More likely they would flee in terror," said Jonan. "And wreck the barriers, and the crops besides. A rampaging hornface herd would be as much of a threat as anything."

Elebru would usually listen to the discussions, never adding anything, but now he spoke up in a dry rasp. "Sacrifice. We will sacrifice to the new river god of Eden and pray that he will be merciful."

"A *creature*, not a god!" Lamech's flying backhand caught Elebru high on the brow and knocked him off his chair. Methuselah interjected himself and grabbed Lamech's wrist; Emzara instinctively—motherly, Noah thought—dropped to the older man, and Noah helped her pull Elebru to his feet.

"Peace, Lamech," said Methuselah. "Let him be."

"You would let this man blaspheme in your house?" growled Lamech.

Methuselah kept his hand clenched on his son's wrist, veins bulging in both men's forearms. "He has taken a blow that would numb any man, any faith," he said gently.

"Not mine," said Lamech. "Nor that of my sons," but he dropped his hand.

From then on, Emzara adopted the role of nursemaid to the burned man, dressing his wounds daily and bringing him food when he declined to come to the table, which was often. "Every day," thought Noah, "I find another reason to love her. Medicine might heal Elebru's wounds, but Zara's kindness will heal his heart." Indeed, the girl's service, freely given and not bought, created a bond between Zara and the childless man. He still seldom spoke, but he began to regard her as a daughter or granddaughter of sorts, and his countenance slowly began to change for the better.

The harvest sacrifices were not held, on Methuselah's decision. Rather, he and his sons brought the gathered grains and produce to the village's altar house and offered prayers for deliverance. The chosen animals were let loose to their flocks and herds.

The problem of the leviathan existed still. After six days of fruitless brainstorming, Noah recognized that no workable ideas would be forthcoming. At another long after-dinner discussion involving Methuselah, most of his sons and grandsons, and Dashael, frustration was beginning to set in. Lamech pounded his fist on the table around which the men gathered. "The leviathan cannot be attacked, but we cannot let it stay. What shall we do? Up and move?"

"We have got to learn more about the beast," said Noah. "The first week of harvest has already been upset."

"The men cannot be blamed for looking over their shoulders," said Methuselah, shaking his head, "and the work that is being done is indeed going slowly."

"Although the harvest may be soon moot," said Jonan, "with all the trade-bereft village merchants you keep letting on our lands to take our crops." Methuselah raised an eyebrow toward his grandson.

"Not that I mind, Grandfather!" added Jonan quickly. "More charity from you means less work for me!" Noah jabbed his leg under the table.

"Dashael, when will the leviathan need to eat again?" asked Hadishad.

"From what I know of its smaller cousins? Several moons, perhaps. Perhaps tomorrow, but no matter what time we might have, I see no answer."

"I do," said Noah. The other men looked at him, curious. "All here are able men of action, used to solving their own problems. But here, the solution, if there is one, must lie outside our experiences and abilities. We need to look for advice outside of this farm. These monsters have lived and hunted elsewhere, just as this one does here—surely others have faced our predicament. Someone must know what we can do."

"Where do you propose to begin looking?" asked Rakeel.

"To the oldest man we know," Noah replied. "Greatfather Enosh."

Enosh lived in the village, in Adam's old home. He had just begun his tenth century of life, celebrating his nine-hundred and first birthday during the planting season. An old man by any reckoning, he was retired to puttering in his garden. He had always been a gardener; he had been content to remain where his grandfather Adam had first tilled the soil after the expulsion from Eden's original Garden, as had his father Seth before him. His descendants, of which he had many, had not all stayed in the region of Eden, but had spread over the continent, as had his cousins from his many other uncles, including Cain. In those first few nascent centuries, the spreading human population had established farms and settlements that had grown to cities, then nation-states. Enosh had lost track of many of his descendants now, but he was remembered by them. He often received gifts of plant cuttings, bulbs, or seeds from some exotic clime, sent by thoughtful relations four, five, or six generations removed. As such, his home's garden was something of a marvel. Not surprisingly, Adam had kept his own garden in fine condition, but Enosh had made it spectacular, declining to populate his acreage with invalid animals, as his grandfather did, and instead creating his own botanical paradise. Raised beds of mint, tea, and rosemary rose in union with stone steps leading to patios enclosed by colorful perennials. Trellises formed walls and arches of sweet peas and morning glories. After Seth's passing, Enosh had renovated much of the roof to sod, so even the house itself was covered with herbs, vegetables, and flowers.

Noah had visited this house many times. As a child, he learned at Enosh's feet of the Creator God and the histories of Adam and Eve, Cain and Abel, Seth and Enoch. From Enosh, Noah had learned to pray. "In my day," the old man had said, many times, "men began to call on the name of the Lord." Many of the villagers, in fact, had been a pupil of Enosh or one of his brothers, and for the most part lived their lives with a strong undercurrent of trust in the Creator.

Noah took in the bustle of the busy village as he rode through its dusty streets. Most of its population was descended from Seth, and virtually everyone probably knew someone in Noah's close circle of friends and family. "It is odd," thought Noah, "how quickly one loses track of relatives. Here I am surrounded by distant cousins, but they may as well be strangers."

He greeted a few he knew, though, and was met with many proclamations of sympathy for his farm's current plight.

Noah's conversation with Enosh was brief. He explained the dilemma, bits and pieces of which Enosh had already heard. "I am sorry I cannot help you more," the old man said. "I have a lived a tranquil life, and leviathans have not figured into it." He hobbled about as he spoke, disappearing behind a line of fig cuttings. "I am a man of dirt, soon to return to it!"

Disappointed, Noah turned to leave.

"Wait!" called Enosh, head peeking above the plants. "I do know of someone who might be able to help you." He reappeared, but something about a cluster of spiny succulents demanded his immediate attention.

The younger man waited for Enosh's mind to return from the plants to which it had wandered. After a proper period of patient deference had passed, he asked, "Who, Greatfather?"

Thus reminded, Enosh answered animatedly. "My son, Kenan—your great-great-great…"—he counted his fingers—"…great-grandfather!"

After taking tea with the old man, Noah returned to the farm to relay Enosh's advice to Methuselah and Lamech.

"What do you know of Kenan, Grandfather?" asked Noah. "I have never met him, and seldom have I heard him spoken of."

Methuselah looked unsure. "Not very much, I'm afraid," he said. "Kenan was a wanderer. He left Eden early in life. He did come back to marry, but his wife passed soon after bearing his children. His son, Mahalalel, my father's grandfather, settled in Eden after his mother died, and Kenan took to wandering again. Of Kenan himself I know little—the last time I saw him was when Adam was dying."

"He is a sort of hermit now," added Lamech. "Mahalalel and Jared visit him sometimes. He lives in a papyrus swamp, four days' travel south. I have been there once myself."

Noah was intrigued. Here was ancient family history coming unburied. "Enosh told me how to get there. I would leave now, if I may—if Kenan knows of a way to help us, I would see him as soon as I can."

"I agree," said Methuselah. "If anyone could help, it would be him." He stopped, then added, "Thank you, Noah, for taking this burden on yourself. Go with God's own speed."

"And take some wine!" said Lamech. "Gifts loosen tongues of relatives not often visited, and from what I remember, Kenan's diet is…rather limited. He will appreciate it."

Before the next dawn had broken, Noah traveled south, alone. Between the ongoing harvest, the rotating leviathan watch, and the bolstering of the riverside defenses, such as they were, no one else could be spared. For longer travels with reasonable cargo, the farmer preferred a camel; a single beast could carry a rider and a fair load without needing to stop often, and it would still keep a decent pace.

Perched between the shaggy animal's dual humps, Noah watched several small settlements pass by before he exited civilized country by the south road. On the last day of travel, farmland disappeared and wild, verdant forest took its place. Noah occupied his mind with the peculiar dichotomy of joy at his upcoming marriage to Zara, and worry that the leviathan problem remained unsolved.

The road became more of a trail, and soon Noah found himself winding through a long jungle canyon. Tangles of vines stretched far overhead, traversing the width of the canyon. Chittering monkeys with red faces and bottoms and long, grey fur swung on the vines and threw rotten purple fruit at one another. Noah watched them play above his head. "Enjoy your diversion, friends," he said to himself, amused. "It seldom lasts long." As if Noah had given a prophecy, a felldragon's scaly head pierced through the tangle of green, gnashing teeth snatching a monkey in mid-swing, and withdrew as quickly as it had appeared. The monkeys retreated far to the opposite side of the canyon, howling in anger. Noah rode on quickly, continuously watching the jungle ridge above him, but the beast did not show itself again.

The sun had passed its midday zenith and was well on its course toward the horizon when the path finally descended to the lowlands. Meandering creeks crept alongside Noah as he went, joining one another again and again as lowlands changed to wetlands. Soon he was in the midst of the swamp. Cypress trees rose all around, shooting angled roots into the water from far up their trunks. Lotus leaves floated close together on the surface, creating waterborne fields of pink and white blossoms. The path stopped at the edge of the greenish water. Solid ground ahead was limited to mossy islands punctuating the swamp. "Where now?" thought Noah. He scanned the lay of the swamp and spotted a small mud structure along the water's edge to his right. Noah steered the camel towards it. As they approached, he noticed a greying wooden sign on a pole sunk in the mud. "'All who come in peace, visit freely,'" he read aloud. "'Stable here at need.' That solves that problem, I suppose."

The mud hut was indeed a small stable, with a trough of dried, pulpy mash that Noah's hungry animal happily started munching. A coracle was stored inside the stable. The small boat was large enough for one passenger only, but Noah found that it could also accommodate his small cache of cargo. A stout pole was supplied, and the farmer, not a complete stranger to watercraft and seeing no other means of travel, pushed the coracle off the bank and through the shallow water.

Soon the water deepened until every push of the pole required Noah to submerge his grip on it. An uneasy anxiety passed over him each time his hands touched the water. Throughout his young lifetime, he had learned that water was life: the river he traveled on, the springs he bathed in, the mists that watered the crops. The leviathan—its rank, rending jaws just below the surface, its plated form too huge for even the thick mists of morning to fully hide—had unveiled how terrible water could be. He calmed his mind with prayer, shutting his eyes.

A rumbling roar overhead jolted him, almost upsetting the coracle. The trees above shook, their branches snapped, and a head rose. The creature's neck was as thick as the boles of the trees it was consuming; three more joined it while Noah craned his neck upward, transfixed by the sheer size of the animals, none of which paid him mind. He grinned. "Behemoths!"

The Lord God had seldom spoken aloud to humanity since Adam (great-grandfather Enoch being a conspicuous exception)—and Noah's lack of hubris kept him from imagining he himself might ever hear His voice—but even so, gazing up at the gargantuan beasts, in that moment he was struck by words that seemed to come from beyond himself: "If this is the creature, how much greater the Creator?" The thought did a great deal to calm Noah's worry. He sat there, alone on the water, and watched the gargantuan beasts until they lumbered away. He pushed onward.

After a while the trees grew thicker, but Noah's path was clear and never impeded. He poled through a natural waterway, bordered on either side by wide swaths of long, thin green taro stalks with broad, arrowhead-shaped leaves. "Those look to be cultivated. It cannot be too far," reasoned Noah, and it was not. After only a few minutes, an odd hut appeared around a bend of trees. White smoke spiraled from a crude chimney into the sky. Noah had reached his destination.

The hut was built on a low hammock island of cypress, surrounded by thick bunches of papyrus sedge that nearly encircled it. The builder had incorporated the cypresses themselves; mud walls stretched between trees to form a structure that seemed almost organic. The roof was a combination of papyrus thatching and the broad, multicolored polypore mushrooms that naturally grew on the trunks, circling upwards like staircases. Woody protrusions jutted out of the water for a distance around the island like tusks, the visible portions of the cypress trees' roots. Some of these had been cut away to form a narrow channel to the island. Noah poled the coracle down the concourse to the mossy shore and nimbly leapt onto land, pulling the boat behind him.

The hammock was small, but it had many inhabitants. Tiny frogs hopped along the ground or sat chirping on the mushroom roof, brightly colored in reds, greens, and blues. Shimmering dragonflies, as long as a man's forearm, zipped among the roots and perched on the cypress knees over the water.

A man's hand, silhouetted by firelight inside the hut, pulled back a woven screen covering the doorway. "Hello! If you are of peace, enter freely!" said a deep voice, cracking a bit from disuse.

"Grandfather Kenan? It is Noah, Lamech's son—your grandson through six generations. We have never m-"

"We have never met," Kenan interrupted, "but of course I know of you! Come in, come in—the sun is setting, and the night predators are stirring!" The silhouetted man beckoned Noah through the doorway, and he quickly complied.

Noah entered a wide, uneven room lit by the orange glow of a peat fire. For the first time, he looked upon his grandfather's grandfather's grandfather.

Kenan was a tall man, tanned darker than normally were the men in Noah's family. His hairline had completed its recession, leaving him entirely bald on top; his straight white hair, in a natural tonsure, was cut roughly past his still-broad shoulders to match his long, thin beard. He was simply dressed, wearing a robe tied with a rope. Noah recognized familial features: a strong jaw, deep brown eyes; but the face was marred by a marked asymmetry, the cheekbone on the left side as sunken as the right was sharp.

The room was as sparse as its occupant. The only furnishings were a wide, slate-topped desk with a hewn stump for a chair and a woven bedroll in the corner. One mud wall had molded cubicles, each filled with a scroll of some kind. Several high round windows were open near the gilled ceiling created by the mushrooms. Another door in back led to a covered deck of sorts, where Noah could see stacks of slate on sturdy frames, resting over a fire pit; he was at a loss to explain what they were for.

Kenan crossed his arms and stared at Noah with bright, smiling eyes. "Noah. Firstborn of a line of firstborns," he said, adding, "not counting Grandfather Seth, of course, the Lord rest his soul."

He pulled the stump out from underneath the desk, offering it to Noah, then scurried out the back door. "Have a seat, please!" he called from outside. "May I offer you a drink?" He re-entered with a pitcher of pungent thick, yellow liquid. It looked to Noah as if it was something that had been chewed and spat; fortunately, he remembered the gift he had brought.

"Actually, I was going to offer you the same," Noah said, unslinging his pack and withdrawing the large wineskin within.

Kenan froze at the sight of the skin, like a hunting dog pointing at game. "Is that from your grandfather, my son?" At the younger man's nod to the affirmative, he hurried back outside, taking his mysterious pitcher with him, and returned with two clean golden goblets. "Pour, pour!" he urged. Noah did so. Kenan paused and said a rapid prayer of thanks, then took a long swallow and sighed in satisfaction.

"I have tasted this twice before, young Noah," the older man said, "once at Adam's funeral and once when Lamech visited, both times far too long ago." He sipped again, smaller this time. "Far better than the fermented root pulp that is my usual custom." He grimaced dramatically. Noah decided that he liked the old man; he reminded Noah of Jonan, in looks and manner.

The finely-wrought golden goblets struck Noah as being grossly out of place in such a meager setting, but as he took in the room, other fine details stood out, like diamonds in clay. On the desk, a long writing quill resting on a stand of onyx was engraved in curling gold, with an inkwell to match. A sheathed long sword lay next to the bedroll; the scabbard itself was plain brown leather, but a silver swordhandle inset with deep blue lapis gleamed above the throat. Set into the mud wall above the desk was a series of polished granite slabs, extensively carved with lines of text that were too small for Noah to make out from where he sat. Noah was fascinated by the contrast.

"Please, tell me about yourself, sir," the younger man requested. "You are, to be honest, somewhat of a mystery to me, and this room does little to shed light upon it."

"Ah…that would indeed be much time in the telling," said Kenan. "But I will try. You must promise to stop me when I bore you."

Noah leaned forward to listen, casually resting his elbows on either knee, and Kenan began.

"I was wild of spirit from my youth. Father and Grandfather had been content to work the ground where Adam did, but by my time, men had spread far beyond the borders of Eden. We all still held to the common bonds of family, though, and all were welcome to go from place to place as they pleased, even to Cain's city of Enoch. I loved the stars—not for sorcerous divination or astrology, mind you—and I learned how to travel by them. I loved the rivers and roads and wanted to go where they led. So, at forty years of age, I left Eden. I followed the Pishon River to the lands of Havilah in the north.

"Ah, the wonders I saw, Noah, even then, when the world was still young! Gold and jewels were as common as honey and grapes, and my cousins who had settled there were hard-working and clever. Thirty years I stayed, and saw a nation born. Towers encased in gold, marble floors inlaid with ruby!

"I often sent messages back to my home, and received many messages in return. My younger sister Mualaleth, in particular, took an interest in my travels, and when I was sixty-seven years of age, I returned to Eden and married her. Mine was the last generation to marry siblings; our son Mahalalel wed my brother's daughter Dinah, and it became the custom from then on. I loved my wife very much, and we had fourteen children. We traveled together—all over Eden, to Havilah, to the sea. When she died in her hundred-and-thirtieth year, I was devastated. I was one hundred and seventy."

Kenan smiled weakly. "I am afraid that I became the same sort of sire to my sons and daughters as I am to you. My wanderlust made me a poor father, but thanks be to God that Seth and Enosh were there for guidance if needed, and my children did not stray. I left again."

"I wandered to the lands of Cush, then Assyria, learning what skills and trades I could and moving on. In Havilah, Noah, men still worshipped the Creator God, though some had fallen away, often in lust after the treasure of the earth. In Cush and Assyria, though, I found darkness—great darkness." His tone grew deeper as he thought on evil memories.

"There was no wealth in these places as there was in Havilah. Villages in these lands were often set upon by wild animals, as well as other men, who hoarded what little there was behind high stone walls. In my travels I had learned the art of the bow and the spear, and I often had need to practice both, for defense and for hunting. I protected these poor people from raiding bands and marauding beasts, and I reminded them of their history and their Creator. In only three or four generations, men had forgotten the Lord. He blessed me in my role as protector, though, and in these years, I developed a reputation as a mighty warrior from the eastern wilderness; but even more, my passion to remind men of their Creator was inflamed.

"My zeal for our God created many adversaries in these lands. I slew the high priests of the Om-Ctherra snake cult, along with its monstrous 'deity.' I fought a warlord-sorcerer, possessed by one of Satan's princes, with the nomads of Nod." Kenan lightly touched the indention on his face with two fingers. "This I received from the mountain monster in the cedar forests of Hambabeh. After that battle, I returned to Eden and built this dwelling. See here?" Kenan walked to the cubicled wall and withdrew a scroll. "I make these of the papyrus that grows in this swamp. I hammer the pulp and dry it in sheets," he explained, nodding at the slate and fire pit out back. "Read it."

Noah immediately recognized the scroll's contents. "The Generation of the Heavens and Earth—and the Generation of Adam as well! I memorized this very scroll when I was a lad! Or if not this, then its identical twin," he exclaimed. His gaze turned to the granite plates set in the wall over the desk. "Are these the originals?" he asked in awe. He stood up, traced the first lines with his finger.

"No, my son, merely facsimiles," the old man said. "I copied them from the tablets held still by my father. One day, though, they shall pass to me—as they shall to you as well." Kenan placed his bronzed arm on Noah's shoulder. "I am pleased to see that you regard the words of the Lord still." He replaced the scroll. "Many, so many, do not. Man's heart is fickle, with a short memory."

Kenan swept his arm around the room. "That is why I do what I do. When I returned to Eden, I was…different than my kinsmen. I knew myself—I knew my mind was filled with the evil things I have seen in my life." He sighed. "I have seen too often the sin, the wrongness, that can creep so quickly and so quietly into a man, especially a man with power. I did not—*still* do not—trust myself fully that I could not do the same. And I *am* a man with power, in my own way."

Fascinated, Noah asked, "But why the scrolls, sir?"

"Two reasons, young Noah. First, my work is painstaking and engages me fully in the very words of God. My mind has not the time to dwell on anything else. Second, there are many people spread throughout the earth who do remember and worship the Creator. Their knowledge of Him, though, has been passed down by word-of-mouth from generation to generation. It is imperfect, tainted—I have seen it so myself. These scrolls I send to the lands I have travelled, to people who know me and know our God, so their knowledge may be complete." Kenan laughed harshly. "You know—I have met some of those named in the Generation of Adam. The sons of Lamech—I refer to Cain's descendant, of course, not your father—I have known a long while. It was Tubal-Cain himself who forged my sword. Yet though they are named, they still regard the words as nothing." He shook his head. "Often have I wondered why Adam was inspired to include these names in his account. I suppose they have some part to play in the Lord's grand design, though I do not see it. Still—it is a fine sword, to be sure."

Kenan sipped from his neglected wine. "Enough of me," he said. "I think you did not come to hear an old man's monologue. Tell me of yourself, and what has brought you to me."

Noah told him, briefly—of his childhood, of learning of Elohim from Methuselah and Lamech, of his family, of Zara, of life on the farm. He told him of the leviathan and the impasse at which they now found themselves.

"So you see, sir, we do not know how to kill it, and we do not know how to drive it away," he finished. "Can you help us in any way?"

The old man's eyes narrowed in hard thought. "Yes...yes, I think I might." He paced around the room, organizing his ideas. "I have seen a leviathan once before, when I sailed the southern edge of the earth. We came upon what was once a fishing village, totally destroyed. The piers had been smashed, the buildings on land were burnt to the ground. The next two villages had met the same fate. We suspected the work of pirates or pillagers, so at the next village, we warned the headman, hid our boat and lay in wait.

"The leviathan came in the dead of night. I remember the sight well—the moon was full. It killed half of the villagers and three of our men before we all retreated. The beast did not find our boat, and after two days of hiding, we moved on."

Noah's hope faded as he listened to Kenan's story. "Your story sounds like Elebru's. So there is no way to defeat it? Must we too move on?"

"I did not say that," Kenan said. "I only tell you my story to assure you that I know what you face. I believe that of the animal kinds, the leviathan was the apex of the fifth day of creation, just as the behemoth was the apex of the sixth. The leviathan I may not have defeated, but the behemoth...I have.

"The monster that broke my face—you must have noticed!—was a wild behemoth, smaller than its cousins that live in marshes and swamps, but far fiercer. It had wandered into the forests that supplied the cedar to the great city of Uruk, on the Euphrates, and made a home there. Loggers began disappearing; bodies were found, crushed and mutilated beyond belief. I had befriended a young Naphil hero called Gilgamesh, now king of Uruk. He and I found the beast, and we killed it after a hard-fought battle. Almost knocked my head off, it did."

"Must I go to this Gilgamesh, then?" asked Noah.

"No, no. It would be a journey of months, with no assurance that he would help you. He is fine in his way, but prone to vanity and exaggeration. But you have hit close to my thoughts," said Kenan. "What do you know of the beings called the Nephilim?"

"I have heard many different things," answered Noah. "That they are half-breeds of human women and demons, great warriors, giants. I have not known any, and I can say no more."

Kenan raised a white eyebrow. "Warriors and giants they might be, but their breeding is not diabolical. I will tell you what I know of them, then I will give you my advice."

"The fathers of the Nephilim are not demons. They were indeed angels, but they did not rebel as Lucifer and his followers did. They are the Grigori, who were charged with watching over the human race, but fell in lust with them instead. These fallen angels took on human flesh and took women for themselves. Their offspring are the Nephilim, men and women of great stature and powers. Gilgamesh is one, but many others are spread over the earth. A fair number of Grigori, however, congregate in Cain's city, Enoch; several of their leaders took wives from that place, and many Nephilim are there as well.

"My advice to you is this: travel to Enoch. You need knowledge of the creature's weakness; the Grigori were present at its creation. You need strength of arm; the Nephilim are mighty warriors. Petition the Grigori for aid. They have stayed away from Eden—perhaps its Garden reminds them too much of their own temptation and fall. But I think they will not forget the people of Seth, who were close to Adam's heart and still worship the true God." The old man drained the last drop from his cup.

"I will do as you say," said Noah, happy to now possess a plan of action. "And I will trust that the Lord will work it for our good."

"Excellent!" Kenan said. "I, too, will pray that my advice might be found fruitful. Now—take my bedroll, please. You have traveled much already, and I fear that you have many more miles to go before you see this matter through."

Noah was far too exhausted to refuse. "To tomorrow, then," he said, raising his golden cup, almost empty. "And to the Grigori—may we find our solution at last."

‹ CHAPTER 6 ›

Samyaza took a deep breath. He must be the calm, firm island in the midst of this chaos, he told himself.

Naamah was pregnant with their seventh child. "A portentous number," he had said to his fellows. He was fond of his children, but not as human fathers were. To Samyaza, fatherhood was the often-pleasant, sometimes-tedious price to pay for the privilege of enacting the love he had for Naamah.

His bride of two-hundred-and-six years was laboring now. A normal human pregnancy lasted forty weeks or so; a Naphil normally gestated for thirty weeks only, and Naamah's labor had begun at thirty-two. Her belly was enormous, bursting with child. Samyaza could tell that Zillah, Naamah's mother and midwife, and Peleg, his Naphil grandson and now family physician, were becoming nervous. They had both hovered around Naamah's bed in the birthing chambers since contractions had begun, and so far their concern had not left their faces.

In truth, the act of childbirth repelled Samyaza. The smells were foul: the stink of sweat and musk from the laboring woman working for hours, the cloying aroma of incense and perfume that never completely masked the stench. The copious blood and amniotic fluid offended his ordered mind as messy and distasteful, but still not as hideous as the open secret that the woman's bowels were occasionally loosed while pushing. Once he had watched the birthing of the placenta, which had flopped open like a meaty flower. He found it disgusting.

The worst part of the process, though, was knowing the pain that his beloved experienced. She had described it to him once; she had felt as if she were being ripped open, the crowning of the baby's head like a searing ring of fire. What was more, Samyaza knew that the Lord had not

55

intended things to be this way, and the knowledge galled him. He cursed the weak woman Eve and her fool of a husband, as he did at every birth he had attended, for falling so easily to the temptations of the Serpent.

Zillah's obvious agitation was not helping Samyaza's state of mind. She had been bustling back and forth all morning. Several times, she had mentioned something about "mother's intuition," which Samyaza knew was absurd; humans had not been given such gifts. Peleg appeared calm, as always, but he had been far more actively involved in the labor than was usual.

The fallen angel's pupils blazed with a white light, and his perception shifted from the material to the spiritual. He looked for any sign of the supernatural, but no protective angel or tormenting devil was seen through angelic eyes. Naamah was alone, subject only to the natural laws of this fallen world.

Naamah screamed, and Samyaza knew it was not normal. Zillah dashed to her daughter's head with a cool damp sponge, bathing her head and whispering intently. Peleg hovered around her swollen belly, palpating, measuring, his lips pursed in a tight frown. The Grigori paced madly around the room, at a loss for how to help. He demonstrated complete mastery of emotion in almost every situation. When it came to his bride, though, he was extremely vulnerable, especially since their unborn child was involved. Naamah loved her children, more than enough to make up for Samyaza's coolness towards them. For himself, he feared for her; for her, he feared for their child.

Suddenly, Naamah's belly jumped, and she screamed in horrible pain. Dark blood gushed out from between her legs. Zillah and Peleg did not bother to mask it now; something was definitely wrong.

Another piercing scream stabbed through Samyaza like a blade, and he heard the muffled sound of tearing tissue. Zillah, too, gave a cry as her daughter grimaced, then lost consciousness. Naamah's face was white.

Peleg felt her pulse at the wrist, then the neck. The Naphil physician looked at Samyaza and Zillah with horror. "She is bleeding," he said through gritted teeth. "We need to cut."

The mother-midwife sobbed; panicked, Samyaza screamed, "No! She will die!"

Peleg did not meet his eyes, but replied, "My lord…I fear we cannot stop that. But if we do cut, the child might be saved." The Grigori looked at Zillah for confirmation; with tears streaming down her face, she nodded pained agreement. Samyaza's eyes darted from one face to another, unbelieving, then turned and walked away in shock.

Peleg accepted this as the only assent he would be given. His skilled hands took up a hooked scalpel. He made a wide, curving incision along the belly; the billow of blood that met him was proof of his worst suspicions. "Help me, woman!" he barked to Zillah, who was stroking her daughter's hair. "I am trying to save your grandchild!" The shaking woman grabbed a clean cloth and began wiping away blood and fluid. Peleg now carefully sliced through the uterine wall, already torn through. Like some bizarre bubble rising to the surface of a pool, the top of a baby's head popped through the incision, dark wet hair plastered to soft scalp. Peleg gently but firmly pulled the head out, then the rest of the quivering body. Strong, mewling cries echoed around the bare walls of the birthing room. "It is a boy," Peleg whispered to the child's grandmother.

Samyaza rushed back to Naamah and collapsed at her head. "Do not leave me," he begged her frantically. "You cannot leave me."

He spun, the paradoxical personification of impotent power. "*Do* something!" he shouted at Peleg.

"I am sorry, my lord," the Naphil said softly. "I cannot replace her blood."

The three of them could do nothing but watch as Naamah's life drained away. Still holding the baby, Peleg felt her fading pulse; finally, he shook his head: she was gone. Samyaza wailed in anguish. Zillah sucked in hitched breaths, then abandoned any pretense of control and draped herself over her daughter's corpse. The Grigori staggered to Peleg. Not knowing what to do, the Naphil offered the babe to Samyaza. "Your son, my lord."

With tears streaming down his face, Samyaza glanced at his newborn son, shuddered, then walked away silently. Peleg looked sadly at the baby and cut the umbilical cord without a word.

"Oh, child-uncle," he murmured, "you cannot know the hurt you have accomplished today."

⋅ CHAPTER 7 ⋅

Yet again, Noah packed for a journey. He had returned to the farmstead after an uneventful trip from Kenan's swamp dwelling, bearing several scrolls to keep at the farm and some rare wetland mosses for Enosh. The old man's advice was well-received, and several of the men immediately volunteered to be the ones to travel to the city of Enoch to petition the Grigori. Lamech, however, insisted that Noah again be the messenger, and Methuselah agreed. To the others, they argued that Noah was the only member of the family that had seen the leviathan in action, and his lengthy discussions with Dashael, and now Kenan, made him the default expert on the situation. Privately, though, they also worried that the lures of the city would provide unnecessary and unwanted distractions for most of the younger men. Noah, however, was betrothed already, and his integrity was implacable regardless; he would keep focused on the task at hand.

If Noah was disappointed at his having to leave again, Zara was even more so. After she helped him pack, they strolled alone in the apple orchard. The couple came there often. In the spring, pink blossoms covering the trees made the orchard one of the most beautiful places on the farm, and now at harvest-time the sweet scent of the apples saturated the air.

Noah held Zara as the orange sun dropped below the vineyard hills. Her back pressed against his chest, she leaned her head back to rest in the curve of his neck. Noah wrapped his arms tightly around her waist, desperate to capture every fleeting moment with his beloved before he left again into the unknown.

"Ah, Noah," Zara sighed, "When will this end? I feel as if I were living a beautiful dream, and just as I was to discover the happy ending, someone shoved me out of bed."

Noah smiled, face pressed to Zara's hair. "I'm glad our monster has not swallowed your sense of humor," he said. "I have prayed every day for our deliverance, and though it has not come yet, I have concluded this— that our God will work all this for our good, as long as we remain faithful to Him."

"You truly believe that," Zara whispered. "I do as well, but sometimes the hardness of it all causes me to doubt." She turned her body to face him, still pressed tightly to his chest, and gazed up into his eyes. "You have unshakeable faith, Noah, son of Lamech. It is just one more reason I need you."

He kissed her, deeply, and they watched as the first bright stars appeared in the new night sky.

"You have all the fun, you know," Jonan told Noah as they strode through the farmhouse hall with Merim and Hadishad to Noah's quarters.

"Do you mean the unrelenting soreness from two full days of riding, with many days more ahead, or being betrothed to be married to a beautiful woman? Because on the last count you would be right, but that only," answered Noah.

"I heard the Nephilim are three times as tall as a man, and that the Grigori shine and cannot be looked at directly for fear of blindness!" gushed Hadishad.

"From where did you hear that?" asked Merim, eyebrow raised.

"Someone in the village. I don't remember. Still! I do hope some of them will return with you. To fight alongside giant warriors!"

Sobered by the reminder of the importance of his mission, Noah answered, "If fighting must be done, it will not be by us—at least, not directly." He held the door to his quarters open for his brothers and cousin. "Which brings me to what I wish to show you before I leave."

Noah had lived in his room since childhood, and it had the sort of natural comfort acquired by such places over years of familiar use. As he had grown and needed more space, several of the walls had been torn down, and now his quarters spanned what was once four of the farmhouse's rooms. The odds and ends of a lifetime of boyish, then manly pursuits lay scattered about in a state bordering on disorder, but not quite reaching it.

Lofts stretched along the tops of the walls, piled with collections of claws, skins, and teeth from predators he had hunted. Implements of various hobbies and projects lay on broad wooden tables: a trumpet made of a ram's horn, ivory carving tools, thin sticks of charred wood for drawing, a collection of bone and bronze knives. The largest table held models of buildings, animals, and other nameless contraptions in various stages of completion; a portion of the surface had been cleared as a workspace. On this Noah unrolled one papyrus scroll, then another.

The other men leaned in together to look. "Are these construction plans, Noah?" Merim asked. "I do not follow them."

"Hold, hold," said Jonan. He narrowed his eyes and leaned forward. "You intend to build this in the valley?" Noah nodded. "You should start right away. We will sit on the hillside and laugh at you while you work on some unfathomable, ridiculous wooden contraption."

"You cannot read these, can you?" asked Hadishad.

"Of course not."

"Move aside, move aside," said Noah. "Kenan gave me these blank scrolls, and I planned out most of this in my head on my journey back from his swamp." He pointed at the first set of diagrams and drawings. "The truth is that, while I am hopeful my next journey will lead at last to the end of our problems, I want to be prepared to try and end it ourselves. See? The hinges are here."

"But what will move these?" Hadishad interrupted, having already grasped Noah's plans. "The beast itself?" Noah nodded in assertion.

"Ah! I see it now. It is bigger than I first understood." Merim exclaimed.

"I leave you three in charge of building it," Noah said. "Grandfather's caution may make him reluctant to order men that close to the river, even with defenses, but they will follow you. Use the wood I have gathered in the old barn."

"Noah, that is for your home with my sister," protested Merim.

"I can cut more."

"Dashael will help, too," said Jonan. Despite his jesting, Noah knew he was already performing the necessary work in his mind. "This could actually work, I think."

"That is why I drew it up," Noah said with a grin. "Feel free to modify it as you must, but I think it will not need much." He clapped his brothers on the back while Merim peered over the plans. "Where brawn might fail, the mind may triumph. And do not forget…keep praying."

A longer journey demanded more provisions packed, but it was finished before sunrise. Noah's stallion and a camel would both be joining him; he would ride the horse himself, with the other serving as a pack animal. A hide tent, treated with oils to keep out the morning mists, would be Noah's home for the next fortnight. A few extra tunics and trousers were wrapped in a roll of woolen blankets, and four large skins of water and four of wine were secured in pack-netting draped across the camel's back. Grazing for the animals would probably be plentiful, but a sack of feed would be taken anyway. Noah's provisions were carried in two satchels: date cakes, seed-rolls, dried plantains and dried tomatoes in oil, hard cheeses, and roasted nuts were packed with care. The stallion's cargo consisted of Noah himself, a light leather saddle, two saddlebags holding a small amount of food and another skin of water, and an ivory-tipped hunting spear. Noah's bow and quiver were slung on his back, and his hunting knives were on his belt; in the wilderness between Eden and Enoch, he would not be found unprepared. Goodbyes were said, some tearful and all hopeful, and Noah began down the path that Cain had fled more than a millennium ago.

There was no formal boundary or border between the lands of Eden and Nod, but at some point on the fifth day of Noah's travels, he left his homeland for the first time. He journeyed through the vast heathlands that stretched from Eden's cultivated farmlands to the jungles of Nod. The travel was not unpleasant; the yellows of the gorse and the purples of the heathers were quite pretty, and the berries from bushes that grew thick along the path were a fine supplement to the food Noah had packed.

The fauna of the heathlands was far different than those of the farms and wooded hills. Wild deer with long, curling antlers bounded along grassy ridges, but never came too near. Large, lumbering, armored reptiles with mace-like tails would glance up at their passing, then resume chewing the leaves from the tough shrubs. Once, Noah saw splayed, three-toed tracks as long as his arm that crisscrossed their path for half a mile; after that, he rode with his bow at the ready, but they were never accosted.

Noah rested on the seventh day, just as the Creator God did after He made the world.

On the ninth day, Noah passed through a large herd of bearded caprids with curving horns and shaggy fur. Soon after, a line of bold crimson, citrine, and indigo tents came into his view. Two figures on dark moas rode to meet him. Noah hailed them and was hailed in return. He was now among the nomads of Nod.

The nomads were not unknown to the people of Eden, although the same would be true for the people of many lands; the wandering tribes were true to their name, having ranged over virtually the entire continent in the last few centuries. They followed the wild herds wherever they went, hunting them sparingly when wanting for meat or skins. They also foraged and gathered from the local vegetation for food and any number of other ingenious uses. Medicines, dyes, and spices from the nomads were highly valued in the many towns and cities in which they visited, and they would trade these for tools, leathers, weapons, and anything else they could not easily pluck from the ground. Over the years, Noah had met several nomads who traded in the villages of Eden. He had purchased his knives from one of them, weapons originally forged in Enoch itself.

The nomadic riders pulled up, and the tallest one waved a friendly greeting. Both riders, a man and a woman, were dressed in garb that matched the colors of their surroundings: tunics and trousers were natural greens and greys, but they also wore colorful scarves around their necks and waists, and bright-jeweled earrings and necklaces sparkled in the sun. They were unarmed. The man addressed Noah. "Our scouts told us of your coming, traveler from Eden," he said. "I am Ber-Cush, and this is my wife Evannah. Will you come dine with us before you continue on your way? We would hear news of your lands; the herds wander that way, and we have not been in Eden in some time."

"I will be glad to," Noah said. "My name is Noah, son of Lamech from the line of Seth. Human company will be a welcome change from my days of late."

"Come, then!" The nomads turned their avian steeds towards the tents. Noah followed. Mammoths with braided fur and painted tusks stood among the portable dwellings. Moas strutted about the camp freely, tame and content to be so. Several fires were lit. Nomads clustered around the flames, chatting; many looked up at the newcomer, waving in greeting.

Noah rode between tents woven in coarse hairs, colored with the deep hues of the natural world. The bold tents and bright scarves differed greatly from the creams and browns of the homespun fabric worn by the farmers and villagers of Eden. Curious, Noah asked, "Do you dye these?"

"We do," Ber-Cush answered. "And we do a good deal of trade with both the fabrics and the dyes themselves."

"How do you make them?"

The nomad smiled slyly. "Many wish to know."

His wife said, "We make them from many things—plants, earth, even beetles."

"Beetles," Noah repeated.

"Yes, beetles. The Creator has hidden many secret things in this world," said Ber-Cush. "And He has given us the years and wisdom to discover them."

"You know the Creator," Noah said. "I am glad to hear of it."

"Aye. The knowledge was mostly lost with Cain's sons, but it was brought to us once more by the Prince of An-Kadu and Chimuriah, Kenan. He lives now in Eden. Do you know him?"

Noah gave a nod. "He is my sire, actually. We just met."

Ber-Cush laughed as they stopped at the central tent. "Excellent! Well, this is certainly a happy meeting! Come and enter, and you shall tell us of yourself while we eat."

The interior of the tent was the picture of comfort. Deep carpets covered the floor; the room's only appointments were long pillows with intricate designs. Following his hosts' lead, he pulled off his boots at the entrance flap. "Please sit," said Ber-Cush to Noah. "Pillows are our sole furnishings, as you can see. Anything else is simply too much to take with us." He reclined along a round silver plate as big as a table top, covered with simple dishes of berries and grains. The nomad popped a blackberry into his mouth. "So, tell us, Noah—from where do you come, and to where do you go?"

Noah told the truth. "I come from the farm of my grandfather and father, where our peace has been upset. A leviathan has invaded a river bordering our lands." At this, the nomads' interest rose. "I go now, on the advice of Kenan himself, to the city of Enoch, home of the Grigori, to ask for their help and the help of the Nephilim."

Evannah looked at her husband with concern in her eyes; he cleared his throat. "I would offer advice, if I may."

"Of course," said Noah.

The nomad chewed another blackberry slowly, then swallowed. "I suppose I should first tell you about the lands to which you travel. As you no doubt know, the city of Enoch was named by Cain for his son, after he was exiled from Eden. The city began simply, just a stone hut and some outbuildings. Out of fear, Cain surrounded his small settlement with a piked fence. The settlement spread, though, as he and his sister Awán had other sons and daughters. The city grew, and with it grew Cain's paranoia; with every generation he built another larger, more sophisticated wall around the existing city.

"To some of his progeny, the walls felt like a cage. These left the confines of the city and became nomads, our ancestors. My grandfather was one of the first to leave. He and his kin tried their hand at farming, but they found that while Cain still lived, his descendants lived under his curse."

Noah knew Cain's curse from the writings of Adam. "'When you work the ground, it will no longer yield its crops for you. You will be a restless wanderer on the earth,'" he quoted.

"Aye, and so we were. But we were also free to go where we would, with no fear of harm from our cousins, who were fast spreading over the earth. The nations of the earth number seventy now, and I have traveled in most of them. We nomads of Nod followed the herds where they went, and we saw no reason to change when Cain died and his curse was lifted. But enough about us! You need to know of Cain's city as it is now.

"Enoch is vast, Noah, not like your villages in Eden. Half a million people at least live within its walls. Farms are few, so traders and merchants from all around are constantly coming and going, buying and selling in the markets. Nine walls spreading outward separate Enoch into districts, and a wide moat surrounds it, connected to the river." Ber-Cush shook his head. "'Moat'—it is a small word for such a grand thing; you must see it for yourself, Noah. A great waterway carved into the earth, bridges sculpted from the rocks themselves, with arches wide and high enough for the largest barge and tallest carrack to pass under. The stone that was quarried to make the moat was used to build the ninth wall around the city. Again, 'wall' hardly describes it. It is high and thick, with towers and battlements, and broad enough for twenty men to walk side-by-side on the top of it. The ninth wall of Enoch is the culmination of Cain's paranoia. A shame he did not live to see it built. It would have pleased him greatly."

"Who built it, if not at Cain's direction?" asked Noah.

"The Grigori did, when they settled there. Ask me not why. Perhaps to show men what wonders can be done with earth and stone. Which brings me to my advice, Noah: be careful when approaching the Grigori."

"The *bene Elohim* were tasked with watching over humanity," injected Evannah hotly. "They have a council of petitions to let them play that they still do so, but it is a façade. Angels they are no longer; they are selfish and fickle. Trust them little."

Taken aback by this outburst, Noah was speechless. Ber-Cush patted his wife's arm and said to Noah, "Evannah has strong feelings towards the Grigori, none of them benevolent. One chose her sister for himself when she was a girl. We do not speak of it now, but I do echo her advice. If you must petition the Watchers, so be it; but be wary."

Noah nodded thoughtfully. "The same God created me and them as well, and He is Lord of us both," he said. "I will trust Him, and I thank you for your excellent advice."

"Well said!" clapped his host. "And now to bed! You may share a tent with my sons, friend Noah, if it pleases you. We will keep you in our prayers."

That night, Noah slept deeply among the friendly sons of Ber-Cush. His sleep was troubled, though, by dreams of countless fiery eyes, watching him.

‹ CHAPTER 8 ›

Before the sun rose, Noah took his leave of the nomads. Evannah graciously gave him a gift before his leaving: a perfumed scarf, dyed deep vermillion. "Remember us kindly, and may our paths cross again soon," Ber-Cush told him smiling, and Noah said that he wished the same.

After another lonely day of riding, he left the heathlands as well. Lush trees began to spring up on either side of the path, which soon widened and joined others to form a well-traveled road. He passed several trading caravans, big bison and lumbering hornfaces laden with chests and sacks of goods from far-off lands. He did not stop; he was close to his destination now, and his thoughts flew more and more to Zara and his family in Eden. Noah wanted simply to perform his task and go home, preferably with the aid he so hoped for.

The vine thicket of the jungle proper came into view, a bold green line in the distance. Eager to pass through as quickly as possible, Noah spurred his horse on, but slowed to a walk as a foul stench assaulted his nostrils.

"Something has died here," he said aloud, wrinkling his nose and looking for a sign of carrion birds, listening for the buzzing of flesh-flies. He wrapped the red scarf around his mouth and nose, thanking the Creator for His provision, and rode on.

Along the path was a high-sided wagon covered with weatherstained canvas. The harnesses attached to it lay empty, but two scytales sat still next to it, the large lizards' sail-shaped spines shimmering like jewels in the sunlight. A thin man perched on the step at the back of the wagon, smoking a long-stemmed pipe. He wore billowing black robes, and a thick yellow snake was draped around his neck. "Stinks, does it not?" the man said to Noah as he rode past.

"It does," answered Noah. "What is it?"

"Them be the big flowers near the edge of the woods there. Always I like to fill my nostrils with smoke before starting through." He laughed, a coarse, creaking sound.

At the point where the vines began to creep into the grasses at the border of the jungle, there were indeed two kinds of enormous flowers, larger far than the many already familiar to the farmer. Some grew close to the ground without stem or stalk, like wide, short pottery with thick, flopping petals, reddish-brown flecked with white. Others thrust high in the air, graceful curling petals colored green and purple, with a tall central protrusion sticking upright.

"Which ones cause the stench?" asked Noah.

"Both! But the growth of them stops just inside the trees, so worry not! Care to buy a bag, or boots, perhaps? Finest snake leather north of Assyria!"

Noah declined, and he and his beasts moved on into the jungle. After a mile or so, he pulled his scarf down; thankfully, the stench was gone. "What horrors has Adam's fall wrought on those poor plants?" Noah wondered to himself.

The jungle was dense on either side of the road, which was now wide and paved with stone. Way stations and wells were placed every few miles, so despite the tangle of green around him, Noah felt as if he were approaching more civilization than he had known in ten days of travel.

He rounded a bend. A banyan tree had thrown down its roots along the inner curve of the bend, and its thick branches splayed above the road. In a swooping crook of one of the larger branches, high above Noah's head, crouched a person. He appeared to be a young man, but was, to the farmer's wondering eyes, easily over eight feet tall. He wore an open white tunic and light brown trousers, with curly hair and a handsome face that was just beginning to show the chiseled features of a man. A leather strap crossed his chest, connected to a pack at his back.

"Ho there, traveler!" he said to Noah. "Going to our fair city?"

Noah gazed up. "I am," he said. "My name is Noah, of Eden." He stared at the giant. "You are a Naphil, yes?"

"I am indeed," the young Naphil replied with a wide, white smile. "My name is Obereth, and I am honored to meet a traveler from Eden."

He rose up in the branch's crook, balanced on one foot. With the other, he kicked in a sweeping arc over his head, the momentum carrying him forward off the branch and flipping him backwards. Despite the drop of some thirty feet, he landed on his feet like a cat. He stood up straight, then shot out his hand to Noah. "I offer my services as a guide and escort, sir, courtesy of the citizens of Enoch. This road is protected by the sons of the Grigori. Our city depends on robust trade, and we need our visitors to arrive safely!"

Noah paused, then took his hand. "Well met, Obereth. I will accept your offer, with my thanks."

Noah prodded his stallion to a walk; Obereth's long strides kept up easily. "What brings you to Nod, Noah of Eden?" asked the Naphil. "Pleasure? You haven't much to trade."

"Neither," said Noah. "I come to ask for aid."

"From whom?"

"From the Grigori."

"The Grigori! What are your ills, that you need their help?" His words were colored with genuine concern.

Noah told him. "A leviathan threatens my family's lands. It has killed several men already, and we do not know how to stop it."

Obereth threw his head back and laughed. Noah furrowed his brow. "Our problem is real," he began to object.

"No, no, you misunderstand me," said Obereth. "It is only that fortune has certainly guided you to the right place. Perhaps you have heard of the great channel surrounding our city. After we connected it to the sea, we had quite the leviathan problem ourselves. We killed them—all of them. It will be easy enough to help you destroy a single beast."

"Truly?" asked Noah. "God be praised! My journey was not in vain."

"Certainly not! Come, stay in our city for the night—you'll find it far different than your provincial lands. And in the morning, you will leave with all the warriors you need to make this pest a distant memory."

His heart leaping for joy, the farmer silently praised the Creator while he listened to Obereth's cheerful monologue about the city. They traveled for several hours together. Noah found the Naphil to be a good companion, jovial but not vulgar, with an intelligent mind and many stories of life in Enoch. The jungle became thinner as they went; the trees grew bigger, and the canopy high above blocked the sun. Obereth stopped at a waypoint with a wide stone basin connected to a nearby stream. Noah dismounted, letting his horse and camel drink.

"Do you know," said the Naphil, "we are quite near the graveyard of the leviathans." Seeing that this had piqued Noah's interest, he continued. "It's not a graveyard, really—more of a carcass pit. We could not let the rotting beasts sully our waters and perhaps attract other monsters from the sea. Would you like to see it? It will only take a few moments. Your animals will be safe here."

The stallion and the camel were drinking contentedly, and the journey on the road to Enoch had indeed been pristinely safe. "I suppose I would, if the place is close," said Noah.

"Then follow me, friend Noah, and come see the fate that awaits your foe!" The Naphil sprung down to a trail that crossed the spring and disappeared into a wall of fronds. The farmer followed, by sound more than sight. This Naphil drew from a seemingly endless store of energy. Not once in the hours they had been traveling had he dropped behind Noah or slowed his pace, despite his being on foot and the farmer mounted. Noah smiled to himself as he chased Obereth. If every Naphil were possessed of such strength and stamina, he supposed, then his family's deliverance was assured.

The trail underfoot became a natural stair of rough, dark stone. Noah pushed a curtain of flowering vines aside and saw Obereth standing on a branch to the side of the stone stair, beckoning. The jungle ended abruptly, and Noah beheld a magnificent view. A crescent of black rock, topped with a tall tangle of green, faded to blue in the distance. The rim of cliff stretched around and met back where they stood, on the edge of a massive cenote, a sinkhole, where pools of groundwaters had pulled down the earth itself. Thin waterfalls all along the cliffside cascaded into misty depths of the cenote; the stream flowing off the cliff's edge near the Naphil obviously formed one of them.

"A pit!" Noah exclaimed. "You have the gift of understatement, my friend."

Obereth grinned. "Come closer—you cannot see from there! Look, there are the bones below!" Noah hopped down to the stone ledge below Obereth and took a careful step to the edge. He peered over, trying to catch a glimpse through the mists.

Without warning, the rocky edge gave way under Noah's feet. He reflexively clutched at a handful of weak tendrils of vines in a futile attempt to arrest his fall. Time seemed to slow to a stop as Noah plummeted down the face of the cliff, and for a moment, all was surreal and beautiful. Noah took in every detail: a flock of sapphire and yellow parrots startled by the commotion, flapping overhead; the glistening black of the wet cliffs interrupted by pale, pulsing lines of the waterfalls; the billowing mists masking the cool green of the water beneath.

The water was warmer than Noah expected, and he plunged deeply beneath it. Shards of stone that shared the fall pierced through the water around his submerged form; none hit him, but he heard the muffled splashes too near his head. He stroked up to the surface, farther than he expected. The mists lying over the water were thick, but not so much that he was unable to orient himself. He swam to the rocks near the roiling bottom of the waterfall and clambered onto a shallow ledge, soaking wet and breathing heavily. Noah examined the cliff face; it was rough and certainly climbable, but high. A brief glance at the expansive pool showed him what he already knew; no leviathan bones were to be found here. An ember of anger began to burn, but Noah quickly quenched it. He sent a quick prayer of thankfulness that he was alive and unharmed, and he began to climb.

A long time later, Noah pulled himself up over the edge of the cliff. The rocks had been slippery, but with care and patience they had been conquered. He trekked back up the stone stair, exhausted. As he had suspected, his stallion, camel, and all his supplies were gone, including the bow and quiver he had left with the horse; only his clothes and the knives still strapped to his belt remained to him. "A common thief," Noah thought, then amended, "Quite uncommon, really. Are elaborate lies and thievery a game to these beings? Is friendship so easily assumed, only to be traded for a few beasts and the meager possessions of a lone traveler?" He vowed to be more careful, but his quest stood unchanged. He drank from the stream, rested for a moment, then started walking.

· CHAPTER 9 ·

Like so many nights before in a bucolic youth on his grandfather's farm, Noah slept outdoors. He climbed the bulbous trunk of a baobab tree and made his bed in a broad bough, his pillow a clump of soft moss peeled from the bank of a stream. In one way, at least, the treacherous Naphil had spoken true: the road through the jungle of Nod was safe. Only once was Noah's sleep disturbed, by a giant anteater shuffling along below the tree, searching for a nighttime snack. The baobab provided breakfast for the farmer as well; the leaves and the pulp from the sour gourds growing on the tree could both be eaten raw, and Noah had his fill. Before the sun shone through the canopy, he was on his way.

The march was not so long. A furrier from Pey-en-Pishon on his way to Enoch's market offered Noah a ride on the back of his cart. The farmer gladly accepted, taking a comfortable seat on top of a stack of sleek marten pelts.

The furrier's name was Tophor, and his opinion of Cain's city was less enthusiastic than Obereth's, though he admitted his dependence on its economy. "Been trading in Enoch for nigh two centuries," he told Noah. "Believe me, you're not the only one been stolen from on this road. If the city's the heart, these trade roads are the veins—and you can bet that scoundrels and brigands are drawn to them like leeches to blood."

"The Naphil who robbed me showed no semblance of dishonesty," Noah said, feeling more and more like a simple country hayseed as he dwelled on how he had been tricked.

"No surprise there, and no shame in being fooled by it neither," Tophor averred. "The children of the Watchers have put their minds to do many things, all of them well. Why would thievery be any different for them?"

Before the morning ended, the fur cart passed among the sparse, struggling farmlands outside the city. Fields of sickly stalks of corn, with corpse-like scarecrows dressed in black tatters jutting above the ears, were at once familiar and disturbing to Noah. He and Tophor shared a simple lunch with a Cainite farmer the furrier knew, a frail-looking man with skin like rawhide. The conversation naturally turned to agronomy, and Noah soon gained an appreciation for the vast difference between the farming trades of Eden and Enoch.

"In Eden," he had said, "the land seems to be a willing partner in our work."

"Here, it is our enemy," the frail farmer replied. "We drag our crops from the ground with much sweat. Still, we make an honest living." He looked at his small sod homestead in the distance. "A word of advice from one man of the soil to another: many of those in the city are not like we are. They look for an easy coin, never mind an honest one. Be on your guard." The furrier nodded in agreement.

"I will take your advice to heart, and trust that our Lord God will watch over me," said Noah appreciatively. The furrier and the old farmer did not scoff at Noah's hope, but neither did they share it.

Past the farms, Noah and Tophor joined a trickle of travelers and traders that soon became a rushing river of carts, wagons, and beasts of burden, all bound for the markets of Enoch. "So many on the road!" exclaimed Noah.

"A far piece from the dusty trails of Eden, eh?" chuckled the furrier. "Remember that this is the oldest true city in the world. Cain's people have relied on trade for more than a thousand years, and generations of merchants have relied on them as well. Not all can be as self-sufficient as you in Eden."

"The Creator God has blessed us indeed," said Noah. "It is He who is sufficient, not us."

A faint frown played on Tophor's face. "You speak freely of your God, and that is well for you," he said coolly. "Be not surprised if not all here share your view of the world. Many in Enoch put their faith only in what they can see with their eyes and touch with their own two hands."

"But angels themselves make their home here!" said Noah, surprised at the hint of unfriendliness in Tophor's voice. "The heavenly live among these people, and they do not recognize the Creator of all? Whatever faults they might have, surely the Grigori speak of their Lord!"

The furrier's voice ran openly with scorn. " The Grigori! They take what they want and who they want, from what I have heard of them—and if they speak of a Lord, they do so amongst themselves only. If ambassadors for your God they be, they are poor ones. You wish to meet them yourself. You will soon see."

"And what of you, friend Tophor?" said Noah gently. "You seem to me to be a good man, kind and generous. Do you also believe only in what your hands can touch?"

"Let us speak no more of this matter," the furrier said shortly, and an uncomfortable silence fell between them that drifted along with the cart for several miles.

The cool silence was soon burned off by the bright sun overhead and the signs of the city fast approaching. Inns and taverns seemed to grow from the road like fruit off a branch. "There's good trade to be had in the inns," Tophor said, back to his friendly self. "In fact, some of the smaller merchants never make it to the markets. Good for them, and good for the innkeepers as well—the strong tavern ales make sure that many of the coins changing hands eventually wind up safe in the tavern-keepers' pockets."

A short while after, Tophor stopped the cart. "Look there!" He pointed to an opening in the treeline, and Noah had his first glimpse of the city of Enoch. The city wall, matte grey and devoid of details in the misty distance, was still an impressive sight. Soon, every slight bend and crest in the road afforded the farmer a new view of Enoch, and Noah became more awed with each. The wall rose higher and higher on the horizon, yet still appeared faded and far away.

"I have built many things in my life," said the farmer to Tophor. "Barns, fences, silos, granaries, carts and wagons—I am no stranger to wood and stone. Still, I find it hard to believe that human hands can make such things!"

"Just wait until you finally see it up close!" Tophor said. "I tell you, there is nothing on earth to rival it. If Cain's mark still provides his people with a measure of safety, this wall makes it absolute."

Despite Noah's growing eagerness to arrive, the last mile of travel was slow due to the throngs of traders clogging the road. Merchants haggled from horseback and from the backs of wagons even while they traveled. The words of the offers and counteroffers shouted around him were almost all recognizable to Noah, but many were slightly twisted, with odd accents and unfamiliar phrasing. He turned his head constantly, eyes darting back and forth, fascinated by the variety of clothing, hairstyles, mounts, and draft animals around him. "I'm not in Eden anymore," he said under his breath.

The great stream of commerce flowed into a wide thoroughfare and straightened. Over the bobbing head of a caged giraffe, Noah finally saw Enoch's ninth wall looming overhead, with only the broad bridge left to pass. The black stone of the ashlar masonry was shot through with white-gold streaks of electrum, matching the rough cliffs upon which the wall was constructed. Tall towers marking it into sections, the wall stretched to either side until its curve around the city took it from view. The water in the moat beneath was like ink. The breadth of it easily surpassed even the widest point of the river bordering Methuselah's farm, and perhaps would rival even one of the four great rivers that flowed out of Eden's Garden. Flat barges and sailed sloops dotted the blackness, and other boats were docked at piers jutting from shantytowns at the level of the water. These clusters of shacks were built on narrow shores of stone, with small arched openings in the rocks providing what Noah guessed were passages to the city above.

The staccato of the cart wheels on the stone of the road disappeared as they met the smooth grade of the bridge to the city. A similar bridge could be seen to the left, at the far bend of the wall. "Six bridges in all," the furrier offered, unprompted. "That's the Fowl Bridge there," he said, pointed to the left, "Then the North Bridge, and the Sea Bridge to the port. After that it's the Black Bridge, then the Bull Bridge—that one be sculpted in the form of a great bull, thus the name. This is Wide Bridge. Most of the trade uses this one, so they made it to accommodate." The farmer nodded in appreciation of the explanation. There were no joinings on the bridge, only smooth lines and contours. Just as Ber-Cush had said, the bridge was clearly sculpted from the rock, not built, an engineering feat impressive enough; but what arrested Noah was the artistry adorning it. Sculpted along with the structure itself were statues carved from the abutments and murals in low relief running down the balustrades on either side, depicting creatures and figures with familiar features, but in unnatural combinations. Noah turned from his gawking and hailed Tophor. "What are these beasts sculpted on the bridge? I see an eagle with the hindquarters of a lion, a man with the head and feet of a bull. What meaning do they have?"

"The Grigori made them, out of simple fancy, I think," answered the furrier. "They have a predilection for a few creatures before all others: the bull, the eagle, the lion, and, of course, humans. Much of the decor in their palaces and the courtyards within the ninth wall are of these, or strange combinations of them."

"I should have guessed as much," Noah said. "Seraphim have the faces of those four creatures. I suppose they must have some importance in the heavenly realm."

"Don't know about such as that, but the Watchers surely hold them in high esteem."

While Noah was expecting the same sort of chaos on the bridge as on the road, he found the crossing to be instead quite well-ordered. The shouting died down and the traders filed along efficiently. The source of the sudden calm was soon found: to either side of the bridge gate was an embattled tower, each with a sentry post at its base. A staircase spiraled from the post to a wooden door set into the stone of the tower between two burning torches, with a strange emblem on a bronze plaque above it. A pair of stern human guardsmen stood at their stations. Visored helms with protruding horns hid their faces, and the long bronze pauldrons and tan fur that adorned the tops of their calf-length crimson capes made their broad shoulders seem even more imposing. Their leather half-breast corslets bore the same insignia as above the tower door. Leather bracers and greaves completed their armor, and leather straps ran across their hips and chest. At each of their sides were a long sheathed knife at their left and a horn at their right. Visible above the furred capes, fletchings of eagle feathers denoted full quivers of arrows, and a longbow as well; more feathers were tied below the striking iron heads of the polearms held by the guards. The heads had a larger blade pointed up, a smaller, slightly curved blade to the front, and a fanning blade behind. Noah squinted at the curious design, then realized it was a stylized depiction of an eagle in flight, wings extended to the sky. The entire effect of the armed guardsmen on the passing merchants was one of unquestioned authority. Noah feared no man, but he had no desire to cross these.

They passed through the gate. Tophor tipped his wide-brimmed hat politely at the nearest guard and received a small nod in return. "Those men do a fine job at keeping the peace," he said to Noah in the cavernous stone tunnel traversing the width of the wall. "In Enoch, thieves are caught and quarrels seldom turn violent. Between the deference to the Grigori and respect for the guard and Cain's mark, a more peaceable place you'd have a hard time finding."

The tunnel ended at the raised inner gate, opening into a bright public square. Very little of the black stone had been used inside the walls; instead, white marble formed most of the surrounding buildings, as well as the ornate statue in the center of the square. The statue was of a woman, barely clothed, with arms raised to the heavens, and was four or five times larger than life-sized. While unaccustomed to such displays of art, Noah appreciated the skill the sculptor must have possessed, but his sense of modesty allowed only a brief glance; though it was subtle, the woman was posed too suggestively for his comfort.

The furrier, however, gazed up unashamedly. "She's called 'The Treasure of Earth,'" he told Noah, then blew the statue a kiss. "Well, sir, you've now arrived in the city of Enoch. The palaces of the Grigori are to the south of the city, rightwards from here and you'll come to it. I'm off to the textile district myself."

Noah hopped off the back of the cart. "You are not going to the market?"

"No indeed—I sell my furs to the clothing-makers in the third ring. You are welcome to come, of course, but it isn't much to see, and it smells right foul, on account of the tanneries."

Noah held up his open hand, and Tophor leaned down from his driver's perch and clasped it. "I am indebted to you, my friend," Noah said. "I will repay you for the kindness you have shown me, I promise."

"Never mind that," said the furrier. "Good luck to you, and may our paths cross again soon." He clicked his tongue and the cart started forward.

Noah waved once more, then took closer inventory of his new surroundings. The buildings around the square were multistoried, some built entirely from the ubiquitous white marble and some with timber framing atop marble ground floors. The smooth streets were well-kept, and white pillars at the corners of them supported burning basin-torches. Several domed towers ascended above the rooftops, rising from other unknown parts of the city. He followed the curve of the street that Tophor had identified. Street-level shops at both sides of the street exhibited their wares to passers-by with signage and displays. Many sold wares common to Eden's village bazaars: pottery, baked goods, clothing, wines and cheeses. Others offered stranger fare, at least to Noah. Women with outlandishly painted eyes and lips offered powders and perfumes for sale. Hazy-eyed men in shimmering robes tempted potential customers with colored crystals and decorated drums, calling in portentous tones. So close to his destination and in a hurry now, Noah ignored these; he considered stopping, though, when he spied a storefront selling weapons and armors. He paused only for a second, then remembered that the little gold he had brought had been in his saddlebags, current whereabouts unknown. He moved on.

The farmer's travel-worn clothes drew no stares from the city's residents, who were accustomed to anyone from ragged beggars to wealthy merchants to giant Nephilim. Noah, though, wondered at the masses of humanity, the diversity of the people walking the streets on a thousand different errands. He wondered, but he did not necessarily enjoy it: the revealing bodices worn by many of the women, open well past the navel, offended his decency, as did threads of coarse conversation spoken loudly and openly. A few Nephilim, literally standing out from the crowd at eight, nine, and even ten feet tall, walked past him, but Noah had been cured of his awe of the giants by his first experience with their kind.

Palatial structures marked the district where resided the Grigori. More statuary of eagles and bulls, of winged lions and men with hooves, decorated the architecture. Pennants emblazoned with the mark of Cain hung from high arches between towers. Men and women with fine attire and airs of self-importance hurried about their errands. Guardsmen stood posted at many of the doorways, and some patrolled about freely. After making inquiries to one of these, Noah was directed to a resplendent structure, wide and airy, with spiraling pillars and an expansive staircase that rose the entire width of the building's portico. Noah bounded up the steps.

He joined a slowly-moving, milling crowd of others desiring to see the Grigori. Some, he gathered from overheard remarks, were foreigners like himself, eager to see the *bene Elohim* in person. Others, most dressed in the styles of the city, would be petitioning the Grigori council as well. The group filed into a circular chamber with no ceiling, guided by armored Enoch guards. The curious observers were directed to the bench seating and balconies that encircled the chamber floor, where onlookers were already watching the proceedings of the day. The front rows were filled with men and Nephilim dressed in garb that Noah surmised identified them as city elders of sorts, confirmed by a guard's answer to another querent.

The petitioners were instructed to join a line of men and women already waiting for their turns in front of the council. Noah did so, then at last beheld the five Grigori who were the objects of his quest.

They were tall and beautiful, seated in finely-wrought, high-backed chairs. Simply dressed in undyed tunics, they emanated an air of unpretentious nobility. Their faces radiated grace and justice as they listened to the petitioners' request, although the central figure, who Noah quickly learned was named Samyaza, was quieter and sterner than the others, while the one to his right, named Azazyel, seemed bored at times. Most of the requests that Noah heard were simply for mediation in some minor quarrel among shopkeepers or neighbors. Verdicts were given quickly, but to Noah each seemed fair and reasonable. A strong hope rose in his chest; he had come far and his need was great, and these beings would not deny him. His turn came. He took a deep breath and a step forward.

Eloquently and succinctly, Noah explained his situation once more. The words flowed smoothly, having been rehearsed in his head for days. Murmurs flew around the chamber like sparrows as he described the leviathan, and from the furrowed brows and concerned mutters to one another, he sensed that his non-angelic audience was not unmoved. The farm's plight was a more serious matter than the relative trivia that had already been presented, but the countenances of the five Grigori did not change as they listened. Noah finished his plea. With the elders of Enoch and the rest of those observing, he waited for a response.

The Grigori on the far left, whose name was Barkayal, spoke first. "Noah of Eden, you have made an extraordinary request for a fascinating predicament. I must ask you—why have you come to us?"

"My sire of six generations, Kenan son of Enosh son of Seth, advised me to do so," Noah answered.

Barkayal's eyes narrowed. "Kenan, you say?"

"Tell us of your lineage, son of Eden," demanded Azazyel abruptly.

"Entirely?" Noah did not see where these questions were going, but he complied. "Very well. I am Noah, son of Lamech, son of Methuselah, son of Enoch, son of Jared -"

"Son of Mahalalel, son of Kenan, son of Enosh, son of Seth, son of Adam," the Grigori to the right of Barkayal, called Tamiel, finished. Noah looked confused; all five Grigori, however, scrutinized the farmer with renewed intensity.

"We know of Enoch," said the Grigori to the far right, who had remained quiet for most of the proceedings. "We called him the Scribe. I am Asaradel. I wonder if I might examine you. Please do not be alarmed." Without waiting for assent, Asaradel leaned forward. His pupils lit up with a blinding white flame, eliciting gasps from several of the foreign audience members. A moment later, he leaned back in his chair and turned to the others with a look of supreme interest. "This one has a prophecy about him."

The eyes of the four other Grigori blazed with the same white light. After it had faded from each, Barkayal and Tamiel showed the same interest in Noah as had Asaradel; Samyaza, though, had a faintly contemptuous look, and Azazyel still seemed bored.

Barkayal spoke again. "Fascinating. You are of Enoch's line, and you are here, and we are here, and he is gone ascended."

Noah failed to see the fascination, and he was becoming impatient with the Grigori's mysterious actions. "Honored Grigori, I did not know my great-grandfather and can speak little of him. Please, I entreat you with good will and sincerity. Will you give me the aid I have requested?" Tamiel and Barkayal ignored him, whispering between themselves, and Asaradel was lost in thought. Samyaza stood. The audience quieted, as did the other Grigori. He spoke.

"Listen well, son of man. We are *bene Elohim*. Before we were Watchers of your kind, before your kind even existed, we watched as the world was made, and every creature in it. Understand this: the leviathan is a masterpiece. I would as soon destroy this very hall with my own hands before I would aid you in destroying this beast."

A ripple of muttering arose from the onlookers, but Samyaza continued. "You say it has killed. Whose fault is that? Its kind was blameless when it was made, with no capacity for evil, created to eat the plants of the sea and the shore. Adam sinned, though, and because of that, the whole of creation is cursed. You were given paradise, son of man, and you could not keep it, and all suffer now. No, this problem is of man's making. Do not look to us to solve it for you." He sat again. Azazyel nodded his agreement; the others stayed silent.

Shocked, Noah opened his mouth to speak, but words would not form. His shoulders drooped. Someone behind him gently laid a hand on his shoulder, whether to comfort him or to draw him back he could not tell. Unbidden tears of frustration and disappointment threatened to well.

All eyes, Grigori's included, fixed on the Naphil who stood up in the front row. He was well over eight feet tall, with dark, braided hair, dressed in a long grey tunic. "That is Gloryon, son of Azazyel," a guardsman whispered behind Noah. The Naphil spoke without preamble, addressing the council of Grigori.

"Noble Fathers, esteemed Samyaza, you have spoken wisely concerning Adam. We do all indeed suffer from the curse of his fall. I humbly remind you, though, that Adam has not abjured you now. This man comes sincerely and in need, and you would deny him when you willingly insert yourself in much smaller matters? I must admit I do not understand. Why not help him? Surely not on account of cowardice, or laziness? I would not deign to think such things of you."

Samyaza's jaw clenched, and although Azazyel still maintained an air of boredom, the engorged veins standing out from his temple betrayed a building rage. The elders and the rest of those listening were clearly on Gloryon's side, though, and he continued.

"Once, you were Watchers, charged with protecting man. Will you not still aid in their distress while you are able?" The Naphil turned to Noah. "Noah of Eden, I can only speak for myself, but as such, I pledge the aid of Gloryon of Enoch."

This pronouncement was met with scattered applause and cheers. The guard behind Noah clapped him on the shoulder. "Some fortune, at least, smiles on you today. A finer warrior than Gloryon this city has never known. And his promise of aid will lead to more, I reckon."

Noah smiled at the man, then at Gloryon, who nodded back and took his seat. A young man ran up to Noah and identified himself as one of the Naphil's household. "The master would be honored if you would stay with him and his family tonight." With renewed hope, Noah accepted the invitation. As he left the council chambers, he paid no attention to the five Grigori, staring darkly after him.

‹ CHAPTER 10 ›

From the halls of the palace district, the main thoroughfare wound around the ninth circle of the city. As the road turned to the north, the great black wall blocked any view of the busy harbors, but the faint smell of salt on the breezes that flowed through Sea Gate gave away its proximity to the water. Past Sea Gate, the road canted up, and the cross-streets became long, lazy stairs sloping up to the eighth wall and down to the ninth. The staired streets, broad and low enough to still be traversed by horses and other beasts, wound among parks and gardens. These were immaculately kept and intriguingly designed, and in them grew many of the same trees and flowers common in the lands of Eden. Elegant stone and wroughtiron fences that occasionally ran on the sides of the street afforded glimpses of manors with oversized doors and balustraded balconies; towers too tall to remain hidden peeked above the verge alongside the fences.

Noah followed Gloryon's domestic through these streets, feeling at home among familiar greenery. Darkness was falling; the sky was a pale violet, with pinpoints of stars just beginning to brighten.

"These look like residences," he observed, confirmed by his young guide.

"Many of our elders and wealthier citizens live in this part of the city," the young man said. "Most of the Nephilim in the city live here too. The housing inside the eighth wall was simply not built to accommodate their size, so they build their homes here." He stopped at an open arch sculpted in the form of a falcon with downswept wings and said, "This way, sir, if you please." They entered an alley with vines of vanilla orchids covering the walls on either side. The way opened into the courtyard of a greathouse that was brightly lit, flames burning in myriad sconces affixed to the outer walls.

With a heave, the young man pulled the embossed entrance door open. He straightened and announced his guest: "My lady, Noah, Lamech's son, of Eden, to dine this night at the master's table." A bit embarrassed, Noah stepped inside, running his eyes up the door to the decorated lintel fifteen feet above him as he did so. While some of the larger estates in Eden's farmlands boasted grand entrances, he could not help but view this one differently, as its size was a function of need, and not decor.

The entrance foyer in which the farmer found himself was a spacious affair with a frescoed domed ceiling. Another man, dressed identically to the one now standing attentively by the front door, gracefully entered. "Lady Jet," he intoned formally. Noah raised his eyes, expecting some towering womanly figure to stride in; the lady who showed herself, however, was quite human, and a rather petite one at that. Her carriage added weight to her presence, though, and the ornate, curling hairstyle she wore added inches to her height. She smiled graciously at Noah, who was thankful that she was dressed a good deal more demurely than many of Enoch's women he had seen walking the streets. The fine folds of her dress fell to her knees from a thick silver collar necklace, with smaller drapes falling from the back of the necklace and rising again to silver bands around her arms.

"How do you do, madam?" Noah said, unsure of the particular courtesies of the city or these people, but certain that they must exist. "Your husband has graciously invited me to your home."

"Welcome, Noah of Eden. Please, do not stand on formality here," Jet said. Turning to Noah's young guide, she asked, "Is my husband soon to arrive?"

"Yes, Lady," he said politely. "He instructed me to bring our guest here while he finishes in council, and to expect him soon after."

"Father will be here soon? Excellent—that means dinner is not far off!"

Noah spun to the new voice, deep and with the clarity of youth. This time he did have to raise his eyes; the voice's owner possessed his mother's straight auburn hair, shaggily cut, but he had almost his Naphil father's height, standing over eight feet tall.

"Who are *you*?" the stripling asked Noah, not rudely. Noah suppressed a smirk. Abrupt, young, hungry—if this youth were not a veritable giant, he might pass for one of the farmer's brothers or cousins.

"My name is Noah. I -"

"He is our guest," Lady Jet said to the giant youth. "Let us treat him accordingly. Noah, this is our son, Gilyon."

"Meant no offense, of course," Gilyon said. "Father invited you? Hnh—you must be interesting!"

Cutting off her son with a scolding click of her tongue, Jet said, "Come into the dining hall, Noah. We may talk there while we wait for my husband, and perhaps you might care to tell us more about yourself."

"Only the *interesting* parts, of course" said Noah, raising an eyebrow as they followed the serving-men.

"Ha!" said Gilyon.

At the table, Noah recounted his story, from the discovery of Ghestel to his audience with the Grigori. Lady Jet listened attentively, while Gilyon wore the impassivity on his face so common at his age; however, he asked many questions as Noah went.

"Interesting, indeed," said Lady Jet, after the farmer had finished. "Small wonder my husband volunteered his aid."

"On the contrary," Noah said, "it was a grand wonder to me. Why did he?"

"Because he is a *hero*," said Gilyon, but Noah could not tell whether he made the statement in irony or sincerity.

"Boasting of my husband I will do gladly," Jet said. "A hero he is, in word and in deed. Before he was a city elder, he served as provost marshal of the Enoch guard for forty years."

Gilyon counted his fingers as he spoke. "He sunk the Pallai pirates off the coastal colonies, he destroyed the ravager gangs that lived in the sewer-caves under the city, he broke the back of the Great Sloth...you seriously have not heard of these things?" Noah shook his head no.

"Be happy," said Jet, "that there are other places in this world where peace is the rule and not the exception, my son."

"Sounds dull to me," yawned Gilyon, "Besides the whole leviathan business, of course."

The announcement of Gloryon's arrival interrupted the conversation. "Finally!" Gilyon said. "Time to eat!"

Dinner began with cheese, dates, and nuts, followed by breads and mushrooms. Noah bowed his head to pray before he ate, prompting Gilyon to ask what he was doing.

"Giving thanks to God," answered Noah.

"Oh? Which one?" the young Naphil said between bites.

"The only one. The Lord Creator." Noah put down his knife. "Do you mean to tell me that even the very children of the *bene Elohim* do not know of the Lord?"

"I suppose not," said Gilyon with a shrug. "They do not speak much of a God, anyway."

Gloryon looked sympathetically at his guest. "Noah, you must understand that Enoch is not Eden. I have heard of the God that is worshipped in your lands, but this city is full of people from many places, and they worship many things. It is hard to know what is right, and so many matters seem more urgent."

"But Cain's mark is respected still. Who do his descendants believe gave it to him?"

"As one of them myself," said Jet, "all that I will say is, if your God there be, He has withdrawn His hand from our people. Do not blame them if they do not worship Him."

"Perhaps you might let me tell you about Him some time," said Noah gently. "It saddens me that you feel this way; you might not if you knew more about Him."

Obviously wishing to steer the conversation in a different direction, Gloryon said, "We have a long journey ahead of us, you and I. I will gladly hear of your Creator as we travel, but right now, let us speak of things less weighty than gods. Bring out the next course!"

The savory smells of the main dishes preceded their quick arrivals. Six serving-men carried in platters of whole roast boar, stuffed geese, and piles of small, tentacled creatures, unfamiliar to Noah, which looked as if they were raw and unprepared, possibly still alive; upon further inspection, the creatures were indeed writhing weakly. Noah felt ill. The boar and the geese were disturbingly recognizable, and the tentacled things he could not reconcile as possibly edible. He had been taught as a child that while, since the Fall and the Curse, many animals became carnivorous that were not created so, God had intended a vegetarian diet. At Methuselah's farm, they did not partake of meat whatsoever. Even beyond the Creator's intention, for Noah, eating flesh was too uncomfortably close to acquiescing that something else's death could be a proper and good part of his own life.

He felt a pang of regret at the thought of denying the hospitality of the Naphil who had dared defy even angels themselves to offer him aid, a foreigner and stranger with no claim to it. He also feared that such a denial might end that offer. "Please, God, give me guidance in this, though it may be a small thing," he prayed silently.

The platter of tentacles was placed in front of Noah. He clenched his jaw, nose wrinkled slightly despite his best efforts to mask his distaste. The foulness of the idea of chewing and swallowing such things strengthened his resolve. He raised his head and looked toward Gloryon.

Before Noah could speak, the head serving-man stepped into the dining hall and announced in formal tones, "Master Dedroth, son of Samyaza." The Naphil who entered wore a weathered watchcoat and boots with leather half-chaps, all with a light coat of dust, as if he had spent all day out of doors or riding. He carried a rucksack made of hemp canvas, also covered in dust, its hidden contents causing it to hang heavily from his shoulders.

"My apologies for interrupting your dinner, Gloryon." Dedroth's soft voice contrasted with his rather rugged appearance. "I heard you had a guest tonight. It was him I was hoping to speak with. Noah, correct?"

Gloryon nodded at Noah, who excused himself from the table, relieved at the unexpected respite. "Use the salon," said Gloryon. "I will order the servants not to disturb you."

"Please, do not wait for me," said Noah to the others at the table. Gilyon saluted his assent with a drumstick and promptly tore off a huge bite.

The salon was furnished with numerous seats and settees, some sized for humans and others designed for Nephilim. Noah and Dedroth chose chairs near the fire that was burning low in a stone hearth.

"Forgive my appearance," said the lanky Naphil. "I have been outside the walls all day, and I have only just heard of your audience with

Father—that is, Samyaza Grigori. When I heard why you came, I had to talk to you myself, to see if it was true."

"To see if what was true?" asked Noah, perplexed by the burning excitement in Dedroth's eyes that had nothing to do with the hearthfire reflected in them.

"I heard that you have a leviathan," he said.

"A leviathan has killed our neighbors and threatens my home, if that is what you mean," Noah said. "I would not say I have one."

"Of course. I mean no offense. Please, allow me to explain," said Dedroth more soberly. "I wish to offer my help to you. I am no warrior, mind you—my interest lies in natural history, mostly the zoological branches. I am known as somewhat of an expert in the subjects, especially of anatomy and physiology." A twinge of shame turned his eyes away from Noah toward the glowing coals in the hearth. "Perhaps I might be able to find a weakness in the beast. And for what it is worth, I am sorry Samyaza denied your request for help. Grief has been gnawing away at him since my mother died, like a jackal at a bone."

"I am very sorry," said Noah. "Death of a loved one is no easy thing. His behavior and words make more sense to me now."

"Still," said the Naphil, "they were, to many who witnessed them, poorly made. Might I help you rectify them? Let me travel with you."

Noah discerned Dedroth's request to be sincere, and he readily assented. "I will, and I thank you. Although, I fear that even if you were able to find a weakness, and Gloryon fought as valiantly as his repute, we would still lack strength of arms."

"Oh, that! I almost forgot. I bring offers of help from my family, as well. My younger brothers Pethun and Dyeus and my nephew Mareth are mighty warriors in their own rights. They wish to join you as well."

A piercing ray of hope began penetrating the dark fog of uncertainty that had encompassed Noah for so many days, as if it shone from God's own heavens. "We shall be happy to have them!" exclaimed Noah, who remembered a question he had been meaning to ask. "This may be another falsehood given to me by one I know to be a liar, but out of curiosity, were there leviathans that infested the city moats when they were built?"

"Assuredly a falsehood."

"Then I suppose it is pointless to hope for help from one who has killed a leviathan before. It was not a hard lie to accept—you Nephilim are rather imposing, you know."

"Huh!" Dedroth laughed as one unaccustomed to doing much of it. He leaned in. "Noah, in my life I have explored much of the world, seen many strange places, talked to many great huntsmen, trappers, and other naturalists like myself. I may tell you this with no doubt in my mind: nobody has killed a leviathan before."

They talked for some time longer of many things: of all Noah knew of the leviathan, of farming and life in Eden, of his family and Dedroth's as well, of Samyaza and the recent death of Naamah, of Dedroth himself. Eventually the coals' glow faded to a dull yellow, and Dedroth stood. "I must take my leave now, though it has been a true pleasure. There is much to do! I will arrange for us to meet you early tomorrow. Tell Gloryon to expect a runner near dawn." He shouldered his pack and strode from the salon, beckoning a waiting servant to escort him out. Dusty footprints dulled the sheen of the polished stone floors behind him as he left. Noah left, too, to return to his host's table, but was intercepted by the young domestic who had first served as his guide through the city. "Master Gloryon wishes me to inform you that they have moved into the solarium. If you will follow me."

They passed through the dining hall, where servants were clearing the table. The appetites of the Nephilim had proven to befit their statures; only bones were left of both the boar and the goose, and the silver platters were empty of the tentacled creatures. Noah's young guide served just as well inside Gloryon's greathouse as he had out in the streets of Enoch. As they walked through the house, he told Noah of the family and explained many of the curious objects that served as decoration. Crossed weapons, mounted animal heads, and tiled murals depicting battles unknown adorned the passage to the solarium. Noah put little stock in signs, but the marks of a warrior so evident in Gloryon's home signaled renewed hope to the farmer, a hope that he did not have a day before. He imagined he heard his father's voice, saying, "God's provision takes many forms, my son, and these forms happen to be ten feet tall and well-armed. Be thankful!"

The solarium was a circular room, open to a sky that was right now filled with coruscating points of light. Gloryon and Jet reclined on a low couch, while Gilyon leaned on a pillar sipping from a drinking bowl filled with a golden liquid. Jet was dwarfed by her husband, like a shining star next to the moon. "Noah!" said Gloryon. "I trust your conversation was fruitful?"

"The chef kept a plate of meat for you, if you want it," said Gilyon. "If not…" He left the sentence unfinished and gestured to himself with a smile.

"Thank you, but I fear I am in no mood to eat. Dedroth will come with us, and he promised the help of his brothers and nephew," Noah said to Gloryon.

Gloryon clapped. "I thought they might join us! You wanted strength of arms, and now you have them, believe me."

"More would be better," Gilyon said. "This beast sounds…"—his lips pouted in an "o"—"quite scary. Only one option will avail you, Father." He drained the last draught from his bowl and wiped his lips. "I must go with you."

"Certainly not!" exclaimed Jet. "You have not fifteen years yet!"

Before the predictable defiance of youth found its voice to argue further, a commotion turned the attentions of all to the hallway. The slap of sandals echoed down the passage, followed by objecting shouts. A Naphil youth burst into the room. His thin, ice-blond hair was shorn close to his scalp. He wore a fitted long-sleeved tunic and loose, short trousers held with a woven belt. He uttered a monotone staccato of rushed politeness— "Master-Gloryon-Lady-Jet-good-evening-I-apologize-for-the-interruption"—and spun his hand in a familiar wave toward Gilyon. The flustered head servant ran into the room, stopped, composed himself, and announced, "Master Deneresh and Master Hamerch, sons of Dyeus."

"Welcome, Deneresh," said Lady Jet, as if he been making an afternoon social call.

Deneresh fixed eager eyes on Noah. "You!" the towering young Naphil cried, and held out an object that trembled slightly in his hand. "Is this yours?"

With surprise, Noah recognized one of the wineskins he had lost when he had been robbed on the jungle road. When last he saw it, it was secured inside the pack-netting of his camel, which had disappeared with the Naphil scoundrel Obereth.

"Yes, that is mine, but it was stolen from me. How did you come to have it?"

Deneresh ignored the question and fell to his knees before Noah, still a head taller than the standing human. He cradled the wineskin in smooth, giant hands like it were something very precious to him. "My good sir, I pledge myself to your cause, whatever it may be. I will follow where you lead, to the ends of the earth and the depths of the sea. Only tell me, I beg of you, that you know where I may get more of this *fabulous* wine!"

Gloryon rose, snatched the wineskin, and handed it to Noah. "Where *did* you find this, Deneresh?" he asked the young Naphil sternly.

"He got it from me, sir." Another Naphil stepped into the solarium from the shadowed hall.

"Obereth!" Fists clenched and knotted forearms twitching, Noah quelled the impulse to assault the thieving Naphil, aided by the hard fact that any blow thrown might reach only his chest at best. "False friend! Giant, son of angels, or not, I will know what you mean by coming here after what you did."

"What *did* you do, Hamerch? And who is Obereth? You? Come, speak," Gloryon said sternly.

"I called myself 'Obereth' when I met this man on the road to the city. I lied to him and robbed him. I must apologize, Noah, though it is hardly enough."

A righteous anger coursed through Noah's veins, barely cooled by an apology that felt far too small for the wrong done. "That fall could have killed a man," Noah snarled. "Would you commit murder so casually, too? What sort of person are you?"

"A question I will ask of his father Dyeus tomorrow," Gloryon said severely. "The guard will know of this, Hamerch. You are not above the laws."

"I mean to make recompense!" Hamerch said. "Your animals are outside right now, along with everything I took! Please, just hear us out, Noah!"

"'Us?'" asked Gloryon.

"Master Gloryon, I convinced my half-brother to come tonight," spoke Deneresh. "I appealed to his nobility, his sense of decency and hospitality, and his genuine desire for restitution of the good will of this good man here." A sweeping bow towards Noah brought the young Naphil's head near to the floor. "Also, I blackmailed him."

"Noah, I am sincere in asking your forgiveness. There is no excuse for my behavior." Obereth's smoothness was gone, and in its place was Hamerch's shamed hesitance. "You know, the talk of the palaces is your audience with the Grigori, and I want to help. Deneresh does too. Will you have us?"

Torn between a natural inclination to give grace and a rational desire to avoid being fooled again, Noah said, "I cannot afford to trust you again, not in this."

Deneresh looked crestfallen. "But…the wine!"

Ignoring him, Gloryon crossed his arms and examined the three young Nephilim in the room in turn. Presently, he spoke. "Noah, my lady Jet, what think you of this proposal? We will be carrying much on our journey, and we will all need to preserve our fighting strength. It strikes me that we will need porters as well as fighters. It is my right as an elder of Enoch to judge and sentence, and forced labor seems an appropriate punishment for Hamerch's actions. Unless Noah objects, I hereby conscript you, Hamerch, to be under my direct supervision at all times and to perform what tasks are needed of you until the man you wronged considers your debt to him repaid. Gilyon and Deneresh, you are both too young still to fight, but strong backs will be useful on our journey. I see no reason you both might not accompany us to help where you may. That is, if my wife and our guest approve." The two younger Nephilim looked expectantly at Jet, then Noah.

"I trust you in this, as in all things, my husband," said Jet.

"Work this to your purpose, O Lord," prayed Noah. Aloud, he said, "On your word, Gloryon, I will accept this arrangement."

"Thank you, Noah," said the Naphil lord. "Now, you three! Gilyon, to bed with you; Hamerch, Deneresh, to home. I trust your father will have no objections over your joining us. Get some rest—you will work like men tomorrow."

The sleeping quarters shown to Noah was tall-ceilinged, except for an opening to the sky at one end. An elaborate lavatory with a columned basin of cool water and a seated commode allowed the farmer to refresh himself in more comfort than even at his home in Eden. Despite his fatigue, he spent several minutes examining the toilet, which he was intrigued to find emptied itself with only the pull of a drawing-rope.

He exited the lavatory, prospect of a full night's sleep in a twelve-foot-long bed pushing itself to the front of his mind. A sleeping tunic, fitted for a human, had been set out for his use. He put it on with gratitude. Other thoughts—Zara, the many events of the day, giants and angels, monsters with man-sized jaws—flitted in and out like moths, but the need to rest overwhelmed all.

Two flapping shadows swept over the opening in the ceiling, black on star-studded black. "Just birds," thought Noah, and they found no more purchase in his exhausted mind. He folded the bedclothes back, ready to fade into the grey of deep slumber.

His exhaustion dispersed in an instant at the surreal sight of the giant hooded figure standing silently in his room. Shrouded in eerie shadows, the Naphil's face was hidden but for two braided forks of a long beard, color impossible to tell in the dark. The birds cawed, one after another in quick succession, as the figure pulled his hood back.

Noah recoiled, ready for action.

"Do not be alarmed!" The mysterious giant held his hand out in an unnatural grasping gesture, as if he were willing Noah to stay in place. "I only wish to speak with you! What I say will, I hope, be to our mutual benefit."

One last unexpected meeting in a day full of them seemed like an oddly natural event, so Noah relaxed his shoulders. "Speak, then. Who are you?"

Moonlight pooled in the Naphil's pale blue eyes and reflected faintly from subtle silver symbols and markings decorating his robes. "My name is Hoduín, son of Barkayal. I saw your coming in the stars, Noah, son of Lamech, which your God created for signs. Does it not say so in your sacred writings?"

"It does," said Noah, surprised at the first familiarity with the Generations he had thus found. "And for seasons, and days, and years. Have I at last met a child of the angels who knows of the Creator?"

"You have been only with the sons of Samyaza and Azazyel, I can tell. They do not teach of what they knew before, to their sons' detriment. Others, though—Tamiel, Armers, Asaradel, my father Barkayal—have opened the secrets of the heavens to us, though they follow Samyaza. He and Azazyel have embraced more earthy things. You want the aid of those who know both, I think."

"Is it aid you offer me?" asked Noah. "You know why I came here, I suppose?"

"Oh, yes! My father told me, after the council. He would have helped you, but none go against Samyaza. I have come, though, to offer you a trade. I will go with you, I and my two sons, to lend our skills and strength to yours."

"And in return? My family will certainly repay you what we can. We do not have much gold, but we have many herds and crops," Noah offered.

Hoduín stopped him. "You misunderstand me! I am no mercenary." His eyes shone in the moonlight, then darkened back into shadow. "My father knew your great-grandfather, Enoch, who is said to have been taken to heaven, never dying. This is so?"

"Yes," Noah answered.

"And you yourself carry a prophecy?"

"Also true," said Noah, guessing the end to Hoduín's trail of questions. "My grandfather, Enoch's son Methuselah, carries one as well."

"Ah! Better than even I hoped! This is what I wish from you, Noah. Let me meet your family, speak with them, learn from them. The hidden wisdom we have here is all once-removed from its source, you see. The Grigori know much, but they speak to no gods, and their knowledge does not increase. Most of Cain's people do not think of higher things than trade and earthly pleasures, and of those that do, I am already their teacher. But to meet a line that has been touched, truly touched, by spirit and prophecy! This is worth more to me than gold. What say you, Noah? My sons, too, are mighty warriors, and I am wise. Shall you have us?"

Of the Nephilim he had met today, this one was perhaps the most interesting to the farmer. Hoduín spoke of things close to Noah's own heart; he easily agreed to the Naphil's bargain. "I will, Hoduín, and not only for your help fighting the leviathan. I look forward to speaking more with you as we travel."

Hoduín bowed, the folds of his robes rippling faint silver. "As do I with you. Until tomorrow, then." He drew his hood over his head and faded into the shadows.

"He is quite stealthy for one so large," thought Noah as he finally fell into bed. It was his last before he slipped blissfully into sleep.

‹ CHAPTER 11 ›

Noah awoke at dawn, its light inescapable in the room partially open to the sky. He found his clothes, washed and mended in places, and dressed hurriedly. Gloryon was waiting for him in the solarium, where they ate a light breakfast of cakes and honey. Gilyon was the last to arrive, having been roused from bed by Jet, who followed her son with reminders to be careful and on his best behavior.

"Mother, I'll be fine," Gilyon said, affecting annoyance while smothering Jet with a hug. She returned it, barely visible in the embrace of his massive arms, then released herself and turned to her husband.

"Be careful, my love," she said. Gloryon smiled, lifted her off the ground with one giant arm, and kissed her.

"Always," Gloryon said. "Wherever I may go, my love stays here with you."

"On your way, then, the sooner to return to me," said Jet in a whisper. The runner from Dedroth was announced, prompting Gilyon to place his wife gently on the floor.

"Thank you again for your hospitality," said Noah to his hostess. He and the two Nephilim followed Dedroth's runner out, leaving Jet standing with clasped hands behind them.

Outside, the household servants had loaded three carts with crates of supplies, each pulled by two long-horned wisents. Noah was delighted to find his stallion and his camel prepared for travel, too. The horse whinnied happily; the camel only spit.

Gloryon and Gilyon were dressed similarly, wearing knee-length riding tunics and high boots. "Our journey begins, Noah!" Gloryon said. "Come! We have one place to go, then we'll meet our caravan outside Sea

96

Bridge." The three travelers left the house grounds through the orchid gate through which Noah entered the night before, but the carts were driven by several domestics in another direction. Gilyon knew no more of where they were destined than Noah; they both followed Gloryon on the main road as it curved northwards. After a while, they cut through to the seventh ring of the city. Here, multistoried buildings were stacked high and built close together. Wooden signs marked places of business, mostly at street level, while lines of drying clothes and modest potted gardens suggested residences. The giant Nephilim drew more stares from passers-by here, but people quickly went back to their business. From what he had already observed, Noah guessed that the Nephilim seldom ventured any further into the city than inside the ninth wall. None of the structures in this part of Enoch would have been able to accommodate them, anyway; every doorway was the size of those in Eden, and Gloryon standing easily spanned the entire height of the first stories.

Eventually, they came to one larger stone structure that stood out from those around it, both in size and style. It was one story only, but with proportions fit more for the Nephilim. Smoke poured from several short chimneys on the slanted slate roof. A dry heat emanated from the open doorway; through this Gloryon led them into the dimly-lit interior. The only light from outside drifted in from small windows through smoky air, illuminating floating motes that spun lazily upwards. Racks of upright instruments hid in shadowy alcoves that lined the walls. In the center of the room, a man in a dark apron, face lit red by the coals from a forge fire, held a bar of metal in the firepot with tongs. Towering over him, a Naphil barked instructions and worked bellows.

"Too dark still, too dark!" he scolded, pumping the bellows and inflaming the coals with blasts of air. "It needs to be bright red. You're not making ladies' brooches here."

"Volund!" called Gloryon to the Naphil, who looked over at the new arrivals and told the man to continue.

"Ho there, Gloryon," returned Volund. "And you must be Gilyon—well met, young one, your father has told me much of you—and who might this…" He stared down at Noah, pausing as if in recognizance of something, but in the dark Noah couldn't follow his eyes to guess what it might be. "Hey-o! Tiny friend, I do not know your name, but I know you have good taste. May I?"

Without waiting for a reply, a long, hairy arm flecked with black soot snatched one of Noah's hunting knives from its sheath at his belt. The knife spun deftly in Volund's fingers, flashing orange and red in the glow of the furnace. He examined it with practiced eyes only for a second, then handed it back handle first. "Human, you may not know this, but those knives you wear were born right here in that fire. Forged them myself. I hope they've served you well. They looked cared-for!"

"Volund, this is Noah, from Eden," said Gloryon. "We begin our journey there today, so we are somewhat pressed for time. Is Tubal-Cain here?"

"In his workshop, as always," answered Volund. "He and Gof are experimenting with some new edging techniques." His voice dropped to a loud whisper. "I would be with them, but this silversmith here wants to learn a male's trade. I'm doing the best I can, but as they say, the blade is only as good as the metal from which it's forged..." He shrugged and went back to the bellows.

The master forge was further back, easily found by following the clangs of hammers on metal. A muscular, dark-haired man and a ruddy, wiry Naphil worked in tandem, hammering and blowing on a length of iron and ignoring the sparks that scattered brightly with every strike. The human noticed Noah and the giants. "Keep going, Gofannon. This will take but a moment," he told his Naphil colleague. He acknowledged Gloryon with an uplifted hand, then disappeared into a dark doorway.

"How goes it, Gofannon?" asked Gloryon.

"Oh, it goes," the Naphil answered. Sooty hair hung dankly over his eyes; black specks, whether burn marks from sparks or bits of ash it was hard to tell, speckled his bare shoulders and face. "We received your message. Perfect timing. Tubal-Cain finished only two days ago."

Noah knew that name. He had not asked Gloryon about Tubal-Cain, since his interest in Cain's descendant did not lie in metallurgy and the Naphil knew nothing of Adam's writings, the second Generation. Rather, he wondered, as he had even since childhood, why Adam had been inspired to mention Tubal-Cain's particular family in the histories that the patriarch had inscribed. Social advances in smithing, husbandry, and music hardly ought to rate inclusion in the very words of God, and yet there they were: Tubal-Cain, Jabal, Jubal, and recently-deceased Naamah. For that reason, that mysterious mention of a family far removed from Eden, Noah hoped that this opportunity to meet his quite-distant cousin would shed light he could carry back to his father and grandfather.

The object of his curiosity returned, bearing a long spear with an ornate head. "Come, come into the oreyard," Tubal-Cain said to the gathered group. "See it in the light of day."

"What is it, exactly?" asked Gilyon.

"It," replied his father, "is your birthday gift. I commissioned it three months ago. You will soon reach fifteen years, and you ought to have a real weapon. All things considered, I thought you should have it a bit early."

Not far from the forge was an open yard, dominated on one side by a charcoal kiln, conical in shape and spewing smoke from a hidden opening at the top. A dark, toothless old man reclined on a pile of wood nearby, watching the plumes. Sunken into the other side of the oreyard was an oblong, pitted stone the size of an outbuilding. Subtle orange hues dusted the edges of the pits and highlighted the corrugated surface. The men and Nephilim gathered between the kiln and the stone in a marked area with several wooden sparring manikins set around the perimeter. Tubal-Cain handed Gilyon the spear, explaining the details of the weapon.

"Hold it, feel the balance. Eight-foot shaft enough for you, mm? Yes, I think so. See these lugs?" The smith drew his finger along two protrusions to either side of the base of the triangular iron spearhead. "They will prevent an animal from working its way up the spear. The spike on the end here," he said as he took the spear from the Naphil, "is useful for melee combat in and of itself, but if you find a bear or some such stuck on the head, plant the rear point into the ground and brace it that way. Here now, everyone clear a space."

Gilyon took back the spear and swung it in a wide arc, then spun through several thrusting maneuvers in practiced motions.

"This is fine, Father! Thank you," Gilyon said, obviously pleased.

"Thank Tubal-Cain," said Gloryon. The smith inclined his head. "His work is the best. It will serve you well, son. Tubal-Cain, this is Noah, a farmer from Eden."

"Eden, eh?" said Tubal-Cain. "I have been there once. When Greatfather Adam passed." His brow darkened, thoughts straying down dark paths of family history, strewn with the dead bones of Abel, Cain, Adam, and now his sister Naamah.

"Is it rare to travel there among your kin, then?" asked Noah.

"What do you think? This city was born from Cain's exile from that place. The thought of there is bitterness. Still, I had to see the old man for myself. He was practically myth, a specter we only knew from old Cain's vicious ramblings. In the end, though, he was just a frail sack of flesh and bone, wasn't he?"

"Shall we hex our quest with talk of death?" asked Gloryon. "Tell me instead about weaponry. What wise words do you have for us leviathan-hunters?"

"You want my advice on how to kill a monster?" Tubal-Cain walked to the enormous pitted stone and patted it. "Take iron! Much iron! You cannot be well-armed enough."

"This is the source of your iron, then?" Gilyon asked, rapping the hard grey surface with his knuckles.

"Fallen from the clear blue sky, young warrior. Its impact destroyed the buildings that were here, and I built my forgeworks around it. Enough metal to supply ten armies with all the weapons they would ever need. Now, I assume your party is more than you three?"

"Your nephews and great-nephews are joining us, actually, along with Hoduín and his sons," Gloryon said.

"Well, *they* need no more weapons," the smith said, rubbing his chin. "They do need to vent their anger, though. Their mother's death has been difficult for us all. Perhaps a good, bloody fight will do them good."

"I meant to tell you—I am sorry for Naamah's passing, my friend," said Gloryon. "My mother grieves still." Tubal-Cain frowned, then turned to Noah.

"And what of you, farmer?" he asked. "We make more than arms here, though I doubt you have enough gold for much. Trowel, perhaps?"

Noah ignored the barb. "I have all I need. Shall we away now?"

Gilyon led the way out, brandishing his new weapon. "Be sure to let me know how that spear serves you," Tubal-Cain shouted behind them. Once they were out of earshot, he muttered again, "That is, if any of you return."

Lilith descended the winding stairs to the grotto in the heart of the Grigori palaces. In her girlhood she and the others had bathed there; so much had changed since then, and Naamah's death had been the most drastic change of all. She remembered when the palaces had been built, along with the ninth wall, so many years ago. She and Naamah had begged their divine husbands to incorporate the springs where they had first met, and they had done so without a question. Such devotion! Few women could boast that they could bid angels (and bed them as well), but the fact did not humble Lilith. Rather, she wore her arrogance openly, and why not? Azazyel was, for all intents and purposes, the lord of the whole earth and Enoch, its greatest city—especially now, with Samyaza wallowing in despair.

Her husband rested in the warm spring waters, back to her as she approached. She shrugged off her immodest gown, letting it fall to the tiled floor. Only the very edges of the stony banks of the spring remained, surrounded by a cavernous interior done in the refined style of the rest of the palaces. Azazyel barely acknowledged her as she slipped into the water behind him and pressed herself to his back.

"Darling, what troubles you?" Lilith asked, as she began massaging Azazyel's shoulders and brushed her lips to his neck.

The Grigori growled in pleasure before answering. "Eh, Samyaza broods still. He will not see anyone outside of court, he will not even look at his new child. Naamah's death has destroyed him."

"Why can he not go be with her, then? She is spirit now, as you all once were, yes? Can he not simply leave this earthly plane and go where she has gone?" Sitting straddled and pressed to his back, she ran her toes up the length of his legs, the movement creating gentle ripples on the water's surface.

"You do not understand, Lilith. Marriage is a state created for earth only; we angels cannot marry in heaven. In death, Naamah is lost to him forever," Azazyel explained. He closed his eyes, enjoying the attentions of his wife, who slowed her massage as she pondered this new information.

101

"Keep on," he commanded. She resumed kneading his muscles, and he continued. "We Grigori are torn, you see. Each of us left our stations out of love for our chosen woman, but it is difficult for us to suppress our scorn for the human race as a whole. We watched as Adam was made, and then we watched him ruin everything. And now, Samyaza is paying the price for Adam's loosing of death into the world. I do not blame him for his feelings. I would feel the same."

Lilith rested her chin on Azazyel's shoulder. "All the more reason to enjoy the time we have together now, love," she whispered, kissing his earlobe and wrapping her legs around his waist. He stood and turned within her embrace to face her, pulling her closer to himself with a lascivious grin.

"It is, indeed."

‹ CHAPTER 12 ›

Tiras gazed out at Sea Bridge from the top of the watch ruin, an unused relic of Cain's paranoid past. Gloryon had yet to show with the human who had caused the stir yesterday, and the sun was risen high enough now that dawn's painted hues had already long disappeared in the bright daylight of the morning. He fingered the braids of his red beard.

"Come down from there, brother," called a broad-shouldered giant below. "Mareth and I need you to judge our spar."

Tiras leapt from the ruin to a mossy boulder, then to the patchy ground. "You both need new hobbies, Tevesh."

Tevesh grinned. "We wish only to fight boredom. I would not have thought Gloryon to be such a slowcoach!"

The Nephilim brothers jogged to the ring of resting indriks that made up the caravan. The beasts towered over the giants, even while kneeling, but possessed a tameness that was borne from a complete lack of fear from any other living thing. The indriks were laden with everything the group could possibly need during this foray into foreign lands; as they were a band of Nephilim who were prepared for battle, often hungry, and used to the civilized accoutrements of urban luxury, the cargo was considerable.

Mareth was already stripped down to a belt and loincloth and was violently slicing the air with two bronze dirks. Dyeus and Pethun chatted with Hoduín and watched casually, while Dedroth took inventory one final time of an assortment of chests and boxes, Hamerch waiting close at hand to load this last luggage when his uncle finished. Deneresh sat in the shade of a smooth-hided indrik, popping figs into his mouth and absently yelling for Tevesh and Tiras to hurry up.

Tevesh traded his fringed shirt for a basket-hilted broadsword and faced his friendly opponent. The two Nephilim appeared well-matched; Mareth crouched like a tiger, muscles etched starkly in the sunlight, one blade held down and behind and the other in front. Tevesh was broader, with wooly hair covering his chest and shoulders, and just as muscled. He stood straight, broadsword held at ease, and tilted his bearded chin up in challenge. Mareth smiled a predator's smile, bounded forward, and the spar began.

The weapons were scaled to the giants' stature; Mareth's dirks would have been small swords in human hands, while Tevesh's sword would have been immovable to most men and impossibly unwieldy to the strongest. The Nephilim, however, sliced their blades through the air with easy speed and precision.

"Do you really plan on using those ratstickers on a leviathan?" taunted Tevesh, dodging an upward thrust of a dirk. "Too short to be of any good, if you ask me."

"Be sure that he has heard *that* particular complaint before," Deneresh guffawed.

"We shall soon hear what the ladies of Eden will be saying about the matter," laughed Mareth, skipping backward to avoid the slash of Tevesh's sword.

Tiras was not amused by coarse banter; he never was, although such was so common among strong young males. Though he was alone among his comrades in his distaste for this, he was confident that the Nephilim would comport themselves in Eden with the courtesy that befit their breeding, despite the vulgar talk amongst themselves.

He watched closely for a clean spar. Tevesh and Mareth, more than others of their kind, loved the martial arts: wrestling, hunting, boxing, swordplay. In Enoch, though, chances to put their skill on serious display were few. The last pirates had been routed by Gloryon ages ago, and carrying weapons to keep the peace held no interest for them. Tiras was glad this farmer Noah had come with his unique petition; few beasts could stand before a Naphil, but from the sound of it, this leviathan hunt would task all of their skill and strength. Until then, though, Tiras tasked himself only with preventing one of the Nephilim from maiming the other. The giants who now fought were good friends, to be sure, but all of them knew that a competitive spirit could overwhelm the best intentions.

Mareth spun inside the radius of the broadsword, forcing Tevesh to retreat a step. Parry followed thrust and parry, oiled blades flashing in the morning light. Tevesh's reach countered Mareth's speed, and they were equal in strength. The older Nephilim, even Dedroth, became fully engaged in the spar, shouting encouragement and advice. Tiras circled the combatants, watching closely for fatigue and frustration, but the fighters appeared to be enjoying the battle immensely.

"If you had but followed that stroke, you would have split my guts," said Mareth, awkwardly bending to dodge the broadsword's edge by a hair's breadth.

"And leave my flank wide open?" Tevesh shook his head, flingling droplets of sweat from his beard. He caught one of Mareth's stabbing blades on the forte of his sword. "If I didn't have this guard, I do believe I would have lost a hand by now. A few fingers, at the very least."

"But then, you'd be more useless than you are already, and your brother would need to do your work for you," said Mareth as he feinted, then darted inside Tevesh's swing. In an instant, one dirk's edge was pressed against Tevesh's throat, and the other's point against his ribs. Mareth grinned. "And I like Tiras far too much to burden him with that." He looked to the spar's arbiter, expecting Tiras's decision in his favor.

"Draw," said Tiras, without expression. Shock flickered across Mareth's face, followed by a shadow of fury. Tevesh clucked his tongue. Mareth looked down, then rolled his eyes; Tevesh's sword was held low and angled, deadly point almost touching Mareth's chest below the bottom edge of his ribcage. Tiras clapped each of them on the shoulder. "Better luck to you both next time."

His conscription ended, Tiras walked over to the elder Nephilim, where the conversation had turned to the human from Eden. Pethun spun his weapon of choice, an ornate three-pronged spear adapted from those used by the fishermen of Nod's coastline. "What sort of man is this Noah, anyway?" he asked. "Rather small and sniveling, to hear Father speak of him—although I can honestly never tell which humans are properly judged small or not."

"And yet you are so adept at sizing their bosoms, brother. What a strangeness," said Dyeus.

Tiras got along fine with the children of Samyaza, but he wondered if every conversation among them must involve sex. Both generations of males seemed obsessed with it. Then again, perhaps that was the natural legacy of Samyaza, whose lust and love for a woman was strong enough to draw him and his fellows from another plane of existence entirely.

Dedroth ignored the banter and answered the question. "Quite an earthy fellow, from what I have seen of him. His knowledge of flora and fauna is exceptional, even for a lifelong farmer."

"Interesting," said Hoduín. "My impression of Noah was much different. I would say that never a more spiritual man have I met. He seems in tune, somehow, with the vibrations of the cosmos. In fact, I hope to coax him to return to Enoch and study with me. I feel as if the floodgates of the heavens might open to us to reveal their secrets!"

Hoping to stave off one of Hoduín's long rants on the mystic powers of the stars, Dyeus interjected. "And what of you, my son?" he asked Hamerch. "Really, of us all, you have spent the most time with him. What is this Noah?"

Hamerch stood quiet a few moments, then replied. "He is something that I have seldom seen in Enoch," he said seriously.

"He is a good man."

‹ CHAPTER 13 ›

They followed the sun, traveling westward. The indriks were too large to take the jungle road, so the caravan followed the windblown coastline, then cut cross-country to the heathlands. Each Naphil rode on wide saddles with silk-draped awnings to ward off the sun. Noah's meager remaining supplies were easily added to those with which the giants' beasts were laden. He alternated riding between his horse and camel, hard-pressed to keep up with the long strides of the lumbering indriks. The pace was brisk and steady, and fellowship was spare, but it was more than Noah had enjoyed on his lonely journey to Enoch, so he did not mind. Besides, every mile, each disappearing with rapidity, brought him closer to his home and Zara.

Camp was made at dusk, with three or four Nephilim taking turns to hunt. Noah joined them once, only to watch them in action. Dyeus and Tiras led the hunt that night, with Gilyon in tow, eager to put his new spear to the test. Riding horseback, the farmer followed the three Nephilim south of the night's campsite. Birch trees sprouted sparsely from the heathlands, which sloped gradually to create a large basin in which was a wide, still pond. The terrain was cast in harsh orange and deep blues from the light of the fading sun, and a moment passed before Noah noticed the striking structure that formed part of the pond's edge. A dam, built haphazardly out of mud and branches, stretched from one wooded bank to another. To one side of the dam brimmed the lake to match its height; to the other lay a dank, muddy bottom of puddles and strands of green pondscum. In the middle of the pond was an island-like mound constructed in the same fashion as the wooden dam. No stranger to the remote lakes of Eden's hills and their occupants, Noah immediately recognized what the island was, and he knew what the Nephilim's prey was tonight.

Dyeus, Tiras, and Gilyon crept through the coppicing remnants of a section of birchwood; young shoots grew out of the stools, which appeared to have been gnawed rather than cut. The Nephilim hunters demonstrated surprising stealth for their size, but their sheer speed and giant strength rendered it largely irrelevant. Like Gilyon, Tiras carried a long thrusting spear, and a stout hatchet was at his belt. Dyeus held spears as well, but his were smaller, some carried in a sheath at his back and one clutched in either hand. Noah watched on horseback from a raised copse of trees near the bank. He followed the hunters' long shadows as they tracked around the lake, pausing occasionally to inspect the muddy ground. Not long passed before Tiras seemed to find something; at his signal, they slowed and spread out along the shoreline. A splash at the edge of the water initiated a blitz of commotion, the details of which Noah could not clearly make out but which lasted only briefly. Gilyon whistled, and Noah clicked his stallion into a trot towards the Nephilim, who were gathered around their defeated quarry.

The beaver lay dead, killed cleanly by a spear wound at the base of its skull. Bristled fur, still wet and sheening in what little light was left, sprouted in a tangled mane. Of course, Noah had seen many of the aquatic builders in his years, but seldom with the proportions of this one. From snout to the end of its paddle-tail, the animal's full length was eight or nine feet.

Tiras hefted the animal's limp mass onto his shoulders, clearly a feat of strength even for giants. "We had better be getting on," he said. "I can already hear the complaints of near-starvation from the others. Dyeus, shall we trade off carrying? It is too heavy, I think, for Noah's horse to carry both it and a rider."

Gilyon's intense concentration had been focused on the hunt. Naturally, he had wanted to impress the elder Nephilim, and he felt that he had accounted himself well. Now, though, he noticed a low, rough croaking that came from the soggy bottom below the dam. "I may have a better use for Noah and his horse, Tiras. Will you start without us? That is, if it pleases you, Noah."

Noah consented easily; he would not be dining on beaver, regardless. "Promise to be close behind us, young one," Dyeus said. "What your mother would do to me if something were to happen to you…"

"What are you going to do, Gilyon?" asked Tiras, shrugging the giant beaver higher.

"Find us some appetizers."

Noah left his stallion on the river bank and followed his giant young friend down the slippery slope. The air was humid and smelled muddy and rotten, and the coarse croaking was louder and came from all sides.

"Here, sharpen this stick, if you would," asked Gilyon, who tossed Noah a thin, pliable length of branch. Noah did so deftly with one of his sharp hunting knives. While he whittled, Gilyon trudged through the black mud. Every few steps, he struck at the ground with the butt of his spear, reached down, and threw a dark lump into an increasingly-large pile near the bank. Noah picked up one of the slimy lumps and examined it. Finished with his work, the Naphil bounded up the bank. "Where there are beavers, there are bulltoads." Indeed, the toad's features, just visible in the dusk, were reminiscent of a bull. Two horny protrusions above the eyes curved up and around the wart-like knobs at the top of its head. A floppy, deflated sac hung below its toothless jaw, and it shared most of the other features common to its batrachian kind. It was an impressively large specimen. Gilyon took it from Noah and speared its bulbous body with the sharpened branch, then skewered each of the other dozen or so bulltoads in turn.

"The legs are the prize," said Gilyon, holding his spear in one hand and the toad-skewer in the other. "Sometimes they taste a bit swampy, but usually they're very good."

"You Nephilim do eat the oddest things," said Noah, shaking his head.

"Our appetites are as large as we are," replied Gilyon. "And there are so many delicious things to eat in the world! You have not really lived, Noah, until you have tasted roast bulltoad."

Dedroth dressed the beaver and prepared the toad legs, using an extensive array of knives taken from a folded leather case. Whether his skill had its origin in dissection or proper butchery, Noah did not ask, but the farmer was impressed. He did question the Naphil as to the purpose of the few quick cuts near the tail of the big beaver. "Scent glands and testicles," answered Dedroth. "I shall dry them and keep them with my other medicines. Relieves pain and fever. I hope it will not be needed after we meet your monster—still, best to be ready, eh?"

The meat was prepared quickly and was soon on a spit over a fire, tended vigilantly by Deneresh, who was licking his lips and lauding loudly the smell of the roasting fat. Noah did not taste bulltoad that night, nor would he have likely had the chance had he been so inclined. The toad legs were quickly devoured, and the beaver meat soon followed. Pethun scraped the beaver's pelt clean and packed it away to sell to some furrier or feltmaker in the Edenic villages. Not that any of the Nephilim needed the coin; rather, the idea of wasting anything marketable was anathema to the mindset of virtually all of Enoch's citizens. Even the bones of the beaver's digits and tail were cleaned, in hopes that they might be sold in one of the sorcery shops, or to some aspiring cleromancer.

During dinner, Noah contented himself with a loaf of datebread and a flask of spring water. The indriks, still saddled, grazed in the fields around the campsite. Having no fear of nighttime predators and no need to shade themselves from the sun, the Nephilim slept in bedrolls under the open sky. Sleep came easily to all, for different reasons. The youngest giants, Gilyon and Deneresh, were simply exhausted; not the irritable fatigue from labor unwanted and unenjoyed, but rather the excited exhaustion of adventure and accomplishment. Hamerch was fatigued, but every day of toil brought him closer to restitution. The elder Nephilim slept deeply in the knowledge of the strength and skill of their party and in the satisfaction that follows all unselfish endeavors. And Noah, in stature like a child among the Nephilim, rested securely in his faith that he—and those with him, whether they acknowledged the fact or not—was held tightly in the strong arms of the Lord God Who causes all things to work for good.

They journeyed uneventfully, and though the days were long and the miles were many, Noah and the Nephilim arrived at the borders of Eden well-rested.

The stares that met the caravan as it began to come across the people of Eden, out and about on their daily errands, were not unanticipated by Noah. He rode in front of the train of indriks on his camel, sitting high on the hump and preemptively greeting those he saw. The farmhands and housewives of Eden, though, while used to animals as large as the indriks, were simply not accustomed to the giants riding them, and most they met hurried into whatever doors were closest. One skittish-looking rake of a man riding towards the group on a mottled, strutting cock-drake had only a glance at them and, despite Noah's shouts, frantically spurred his mount in the opposite direction, the frightened animal madly honking and chittering.

"That's a man to cause trouble if he is able, mark it," said Gloryon. "Eyes open, everyone. Noah, is there a village with a watch nearby?"

"There is," answered Noah, "and if that fellow does intend to tell the watchmen of us, it is only with the best intentions, I'm sure."

"We'll soon see, I suppose," said Pethun. "Not that we have aught to worry from some bunny-hunting provincial guard—no offense, Noah."

"Shall I cast a bone on it?" asked Hoduín.

"Ah, Father, come now." Tiras rolled his eyes. "Is even a frightened farmer foretold in your auguries?"

"Tut, son! We are now in the land of prophecies and prophets!" Hoduín winked at Noah from under his hood. "Here, we may discover the future to be more discernible than you think."

"At any rate, my family is known to most in these parts," said Noah. "A simple explanation will calm any fears. And even if an alarm misplaced causes armed men to gather, perhaps they might be persuaded to join us."

The village was nestled in the middle of rolling green hills. The thatched-roofed homes built on the hillsides were tucked away behind gardens and orchards. Grassy paths and stone stairways from the front doors of the houses sloped to join one another, all meeting in the small valley in the center of the hills, where tree-shaded streets and scattered shops clustered around a long lodge that was the meeting place for the villagers. Toward this Noah led the Nephilim. The younger giants took in the georgic scenery with the same fascination that Noah did the marbled palaces of Enoch.

From the emptiness of the streets, it appeared that a warning had indeed been given and heeded. "Quite the impressive watch," said Dyeus wryly, swaying a bit from the gait of his lumbering mount.

"This is a place of peace. Can you not see it?" said Gloryon. "What need of warriors have they?"

"Well, if something like a leviathan ever came along, they might come in handy," said Gilyon.

Gloryon frowned. "Sarcasm does not become a son of mine."

"Sorry, Father."

Dedroth arrested his mental cataloguing of the Edenic flora, his planning of future forays into the hills and gardens of this fertile land. "Why, I wonder, did our fathers not choose women from here? This, it strikes me, must be closer to paradise than Enoch's stone walls."

"The locals could be friendlier, though," said Tevesh.

The main thoroughfare of the village led past the lodge, and the only soul Noah saw as they passed was an old man lounging on the wooden deck of its second floor, feet kicked up on the railing and smoking a short, stubby pipe.

"Heyo!" He called down to Noah, still riding ahead of the indriks. "News of you, sir, has given the folks a scare. Need they be? Scared, that is?" He peered at the giants, his vantage point on the high deck bringing him almost to eye level with them. A long, thin stream of white smoke whistled from between his teeth.

"No, truly," answered Noah. "I am Noah, Lamech's son, and these are Nephilim from Enoch. We are bound for my grandfather's farm."

"Huh. Tall, aren't they?" The old man said nothing more, but went back to smoking his pipe.

Who the old man was, Noah did not know, but the homebound farmer suspected that he played a role in the friendlier tone they met in the succeeding hamlets and villages. In some, people lined the streets, obviously expecting them and curious, not frightened. Most of these were younger men and boys, and Pethun asked Noah, "Where are the women?"

Noah liked Pethun, who had been a source of much friendly conversation over the last few days, but the leering undertone irked him. "Likely engaged in useful pursuits, rather than gawking at us strangers." Noah weighed his words. "You might find the women of Eden less obliging to flattery and flirtation than those in Enoch," he said.

Tiras, riding behind them both, appreciated Noah's veiled caution to the older and far stronger Nephilim. "Like a shepherd," he thought to himself, "unwilling to let that wolf run freely among his flocks. Good for him."

"Point taken, Noah, point taken, but never let it be said that Pethun backed down from a challenge, of any kind!" He grinned, a lazy, handsome thing that had initiated more than one amorous episode with a young lady.

"Perhaps you ought to save your vigor for the battle ahead, Pethun," said Tiras. "That will be challenge enough for all of us, I think."

"Are we there yet?" moaned Deneresh. Vineyards spread up the terraced hills on either side of the road. They did not belong to Methuselah, but the subtle scent of the ripening grapes was achingly familiar and heightened Noah's desire to be home. The sights and smells also made Deneresh near-frantic to finally reach the object of his oenophilic lusts, and he freely expressed his anxiety every few minutes or so.

Thudding footsteps heralded a crested dragon coming down the road towards the caravan of indriks. At the sight of its riders, a heady brew of elation, relief, and familial love burst through Noah's spirits like floodwaters.

"Jonan! Hadishad!" Noah spurred his stallion to meet his brothers, who were mounted on the long double-saddle strapped to the big reptile. They waved in happy greeting.

"We came to meet you when we heard the news from the village," Jonan said. "Well done, Noah!"

Hadishad stared at the long line of mounted Nephilim. Tiras, riding the lead indrik, smiled and waved at the farmboy. "Well done, indeed," the young man said in an awed tone.

Addressing the Nephilim, Jonan shouted, "Greeting, honored guests, and many thanks from our family! You are an answer to many prayers. I am Jonan, son of Lamech, and this is our brother Hadishad." Hadishad gulped and waved, and the Nephilim answered with a chorus of greetings in return.

"Noah, Hadishad and I will guide them the rest of the way, if you wish to ride ahead," said Jonan. "Father and Grandfather are eager to see you—and they are not the most eager. We shall enjoy proper introductions later."

Gloryon rode to Tiras's side. "Allow me to accompany you, as an official and ambassador from Enoch," he said.

"Hut! Hoduín and I will come as well," yelled Dedroth from the back of the caravan. "Then each family here will be represented." The road was wide, but only barely enough to accommodate the two Nephilim bringing their mounts abreast of the leaders. "These vineyards—splendid! I would ask to travel slowly, Noah—so much to take in!—but I know you must be in haste now."

"I will go too!" Deneresh shouted. The mention of vineyards begot visions of rows upon rows of barrels waiting to be uncorked. "Father, may I?"

"Yes, yes, fine!" said Dyeus, tired of his son's complaining. "Obey your uncle! And don't be a nuisance!"

"Come ride with me, nephew," Dedroth offered. Deneresh dropped from his indrik, ran to the front, and clambered up the netting draped over the side of Dedroth's.

Noah reached up to his brothers, seated higher than he on the bigger animal, and clasped their hands in turn. "Thank you both."

"Thank you, Noah," replied Jonan. "It appears you have brought our salvation."

Noah smiled at his brothers. "You are welcome—but salvation belongs to our God alone. Remember to rely on Him in our fight—I believe that it will take more than strength of arms to fell this monster. We are all simply His tools."

Still mesmerized by the Nephilim, who were all every bit as impressive as he had imagined, Hadishad said, "It is a good thing, then, that you brought such large tools for Him to use."

Twenty-one days had passed since Noah had last seen his beloved, his betrothed. At the gate leading to the stables, far before they reached the farmhouse, she was waiting for him. The sight of her was like a breeze on the face after an endless day of work in the sun, like a cool drink after hard labor. Zara's smiling image, which he had kept centered in his mind's eye since he first left Eden for Enoch, was shattered by the beautiful reality of her running towards him, never even glancing at the four giants riding behind.

Noah jumped from his horse. He had to brace himself on the fence to keep from falling as Zara flung herself to him and wrapped her arms full around his neck.

"I missed you so much," she whispered.

"You will never have the need again," he whispered back, "for I will never again leave you."

The Nephilim dismounted. Mindful of the couple's need for a few moments of privacy, Gloryon stayed silent until they broke their embrace. "May we use this field for our camp, Noah?" he asked, indicating the flat, empty pastureland to their left. Zara instinctively opened her mouth to offer guest lodgings at the farmhouse, but on realization of just how large her beloved's companions were, she again closed it.

"Zara, allow me to introduce four of the Nephilim of the city of Enoch," said Noah. "Gloryon, this is Emzara, my betrothed."

"I gathered," Gloryon said, bowing and smiling broadly. "I recognize in you both the passion I share with my own wife. I am very pleased to meet you."

Noah introduced Dedroth, Hoduín, and Deneresh in turn. Dedroth awkwardly nodded his head in greeting, vulturelike, and Hoduín, though polite, unfortunately confused Zara with an obtuse statement about stars and their courses. Deneresh, however, was suavity personified, his simple, "I am honored, dear lady," punctuated with an angelic smile.

Zara was almost overwhelmed; large animals—mammoths, dragons, aurochs, even indriks—were a part of farm life in Eden, but half-angel giants! Her grandfather Methuselah often said that Elohim blesses unexpectedly at times, and these companions of her brave Noah had proven the truth of it. "Well met to each of you," she said. "I am sure that the leviathan cannot stand against you four!"

"That does remain to be seen, I suppose," said Dedroth, not rudely. "But there are seven more of us behind, you know."

"When I go about a task, I do it well, do I not?" Noah took his wide-eyed bride-to-be by the waist, and the six together walked down the winding path to the farmhouse.

The farmhouse was the scene of a flurry of embraces, introductions, and endless questioning from a dozen relations. Grandmother Edna, always the attentive hostess, noticed her giant guests continually stooping and ducking. "Everyone out, now!" she shouted over the conversations. "We shall dine outside!"

"Ah, you are a gem among women," said Deneresh, turning toward the door and narrowly avoiding banging his skull on a rafter.

"The peril of my ceiling is not the danger you came here to face, I think," Edna said. "But surely you are too young to fight, tall as you are! Remind me of your name again, if you please?"

"My name is Deneresh, good madam," he said to her with a bow and flourish, "and I am here for the wine."

Approaching unnoticed, Noah embraced his grandmother from behind and pecked her on the cheek. "Honesty is not lacking in this one, Grandmother. Do not worry, Deneresh. I myself will take you on a personal tour of the cellars when we are through."

"Your servant," Deneresh said, bowing again.

Noah walked outside with Zara and Merim, chatting animatedly and answering questions. He spotted Gloryon, Hoduín, and Dedroth sitting on the ground under the old spreading oak, speaking with Methuselah and Lamech.

"Be back soon, Zara," said Noah, excusing himself and Merim.

"If it were not so dark, I would show you now what we've built," said Merim as they walked toward the oak. "It's just as you planned."

"I only hope it works," said Noah.

"Do you even think we'll need it? These Nephilim—if their abilities even come close to matching their statures, the beast must surely fall."

Noah shrugged. "I hope so. You have heard Elebru and Dashael. I will not make the same mistake they did. I take nothing for granted."

"My son!" Lamech broke from the circle of conversation, ran to Noah, and embraced him warmly. "You have done a good thing. Praise to the Creator!"

"To Him be the glory," replied Noah. He mentally browsed through a catalogue of questions, unsure what to ask his father first. Has everyone remained safe? How goes the harvesting? What of the leviathan's movements? But before he chose one, he felt his grandfather's firm hand on his shoulder.

"Noah, I am happy to see you—it is an answer to my prayers!—but this need not include you. Go rest. Heaven knows you have earned it," said Methuselah.

"But…we have so much to talk about!"

"This is true. However, 'we' does not include 'you.'"

"Noah, you have been the principal actor in all these matters," Lamech echoed. "There is nothing we will talk of tonight that you have not planned, done, or known already."

Methuselah smiled, an expression full of fondness. "Take it from two old married men—there is another who requires your time more." He looked at Zara, who stood nearby listening to the excited conversation among several of the younger female cousins. The girls stole glances at the giant Nephilim, mostly Deneresh, but Zara gazed only at Noah. She smiled sweetly at him when he looked her way.

"Go on," said Lamech, and Noah needed no more encouragement. He took Zara's hand, and they found a bench on the outside wall of the farm-house, between a wash basin and one of the many hitching poles, where they could sit and watch the conversations and the play. They shared no words; Zara nestled her head in Noah's neck, and he wrapped both arms tightly around her shoulders.

"The calm before the chaos," he said softly, watching a few of his child cousins take turns having a laughing Deneresh lift them a dozen feet in the air, then swoop them down to the ground, squealing in delight.

Her finger traced along his shoulder sent intoxicating chills swirling on his skin. "I believe there is no chaos you could not travel safely through. Our God is with you, Noah. Everyone sees it." Zara sighed and pulled his arms more tightly to her.

"And you are with me too," whispered Noah. "What is a leviathan to that?"

‹ CHAPTER 14 ›

Noah carried Zara, who had fallen asleep in his arms, to her bed inside, laid her down with a kiss on the forehead, and retired himself before Hadishad and Jonan returned with the rest of the Nephilim. The next morning, he awoke early, clear-minded. The morning mists swirled heavily outside his window, erasing shadow and depth from the fences and fields of the farm. Rather grimly, he put on his vest and pulled up his hood, strapped a full quiver to his back and his knives to his belt, and laced up his leather boots.

No one stirred in the farmhouse, so Noah walked outside. Methuselah stood under the great oak in his simple tunic and robe, quietly sipping from a bowl of tea. Silently, Noah strode up beside him. Grandfather and grandson stared together into the grey mists, each offering their own prayers to their Maker.

One by one, a few more men joined them. Merim, Jonan, and Hadishad were dressed for the hunt and carried bow and spear, though none had any intention of fighting this day, or illusion that their help might make a difference. Still, Jonan carried a hatchet newly-sharpened, and Merim's sling hung at his belt. The wrangler Dashael, too, armed as before with whip and atlatl, joined them. He had remained at the farm, lending a strong hand where it was needed and taking a special interest in what Jonan and Merim had begun calling "the leviathan project."

The honks of two crested dragons led by Lamech broke the silence. Noah's horse followed behind, shaking its mane. The three animals were lightly saddled, the stallion for one and the larger reptiles for two.

"Well, boys, what are we waiting for?" asked Jonan. He and Hadishad climbed on one of the dragons, and Merim and Dashael took the other. "Shall we see what our large new friends make of things?" Noah clasped the forearm of his father and grandfather in turn. "Keep them safe," said Lamech.

"I will do all I can," Noah replied, and galloped off behind his brothers.

The tall tents of the Nephilim pierced the mists ahead. Faint figures waited for the five riders to approach, details seeming to materialize from the grey haze. Hadishad whistled.

Gone were the Nephilim of the night before, garbed in traveling clothes, jovial and conversant. In their place stood grim giants armed for battle, like silent towers, indomitable and strong. Gloryon wore the armor of a commander of the Enoch guard, horned helm tucked under his left arm. His right hand held a battle-axe, iron head shaped in the same stylized eagle's form as the polearms carried by the Enoch guardsmen. A cordlike vein ran up his biceps between the bronze bracer on his forearm and the fur crest of his cape, belying the weight of the axe. "Lead on," he said. "We are ready."

The two crested dragons thudded at a trot toward the river fields, and the Nephilim warriors followed in a loose file behind. Noah and Raph brought up the rear. The dawn of battle had wrought stern changes on his late traveling companions; only Hoduín in his robes and Dedroth in his watchcoat were immediately recognizable. The two sons of Hoduín wore fur-trimmed leather studded with bronze. Strings of teeth and bone ending in heavy bronze bracteates hung from their necks. Leather-and-tusken helmets covered their heads and hid their eyes; only Tiras's red beard marked a distinction between the brothers. Tevesh's broadsword was sheathed at his back. Tiras carried his spear, as well as a one-handed battle-axe, leather-wrapped handle strapped around the Naphil's wrist, its head etched with symbols similar to those on Hoduín's robes.

Dedroth's kin were just as fiercely armed and attired. Mareth's bronze cuirass covered his chest, and matching bracers, shinguards, and helmet finished his armor. The cuirass was adorned with a crude representation of a skull, painted in white, eyesockets finished with a darker red paint, or something fouler. His two dirks were stored sheathless in his belt; a narrow crimson cape wrapped around his neck and face, hiding his clenched jaw, and fell over one shoulder. No one could see it for the cape, but a small fountain of froth bubbled at one corner of his mouth. Anticipation of battle had birthed a rage only barely chained by the Naphil's discipline. His lust for blood surpassed all other thoughts and desires; for a second, he wondered if he was mad, then he decided he did not care.

In beaten copper armor over white leather and gold-trimmed robes, Dyeus' regal bearing and appearance radiated superiority over any foe. This affect was conscious on his part; it also reflected his true opinion of himself and his battle prowess, an opinion he had no doubt would be strengthened after today. He fingered one throwing spear, flexible and deadly, and pictured it piercing the beast through the eye, or perhaps through some soft underbelly absent of scales. He had no doubt that he would be able to make the scene come to pass.

Pethun wore scaled armor, intricate and supple, allowing for more agility, conducive to the dynamic spearfighting style he preferred. He shared his brother's arrogance, but tempered it with indifference. This jaunt into Eden had broken the boredom of Enoch, but Pethun would be happy to see its end. He considered himself a lover, not a fighter, although he boasted impressive conquests in both arenas, and he was eager to return to the women of his homeland, hopefully with a new tale of heroism to make them swoon.

Hamerch, Gilyon, and Deneresh were dressed no differently than before, but each of them carried a tall shield, and Gilyon had his new weapon in hand. Hamerch was the last in line; he nodded quietly at Noah trotting up behind them, and Gilyon gave the farmer a small salute with his spear. The three younger Nephilim were uncharacteristically silent, but none appeared afraid of what lay ahead. Noah feared for them, though. He feared for all of them; who else but himself would be to blame if tragedy struck? He could do one thing only now, and he did it without ceasing during the entire march to the river.

He prayed.

A stripe of a valley ran between the riverside pastures of Methuselah's farm and the first foothills of the Eden's mountain wilds. It was too narrow to be used as a pasture or a crop field, so the family had allowed the land's natural vegetation to grow unchecked. In no way did the decision prove to be unfruitful; melon vines covered the gentle slope bordering the pastures, sending scouting tendrils to explore the mossy woods across the valley. The woods walked up the uneven hills in starts and fits, jutting roots and jagged rocks masked by layers of the thick moss, impossible to tell apart. Noah and his brothers and cousins had spent many childhood days in the hills, searching for mushrooms in the folds of roots and the cool walls of hidden caves, and lately, Hadishad and his younger cousins had come and gone daily, keeping watch on the leviathan from the safety of the rocks overlooking the river.

In the middle of the valley, where the moss and melons met, mists ebbed and flowed as they rose and rained, but seldom retreated entirely. Here had been the site of much activity lately, as Merim and Jonan pulled Noah's blueprints from scroll to reality. Guarded from the river monster by a sequence of pikelines and hedges, the men had first dug a pit, deep and long enough, they hoped, to hold a leviathan. They drove thick posts into the ground on either side of the pit, then laid heavy beams by the post ends, perpendicular to the pit edge. The posts and beams were crudely, but solidly, connected by wood-and-iron hinges scavenged from old plows. A thick weave of netting was tied tightly to the lengths of the posts and stretched across the mouth of the pit, such that a mass weighty enough to pull the netting down would pull the beams over the opening, creating a heavy caged roof. Long boards formed a floor over the pit and netting; sturdy enough for a man to walk on, the planks were cut thin so that a larger animal would break them and fall through. None of this, the product of two weeks' labor, could be seen by the warband; after they had constructed the pit, the workers had carefully camouflaged the entire apparatus in the vines, moss, and brush of the valley.

"The problem is," explained Jonan to Noah and the Nephilim as they approached the valley, "we cannot test the plank strength, and *something* will need to be the bait that the leviathan chases to the trap. A man would not fall through, but it sounds as if the leviathan would catch him long before he made it here."

"This is true," said Noah and Dashael simultaneously.

"And a dragon might be fast enough to outrun the leviathan," said Merim, "but it would assuredly break the planks. Would a horse? We dared not test it. We just don't know."

Gloryon spoke in a commander's tone. "The pit is a resource, that is all. I think it is time to see the beast for ourselves."

The barriers guarding the riverbank needed removal in order to create a clear path to the pit from the river. In minutes, the Nephilim warriors had lifted entire lengths of piked fences and chopped through the thick hedges, piling the thorny branches to the side. With the way to the river clear, Noah dismounted; his horse Raph snorted nervously, but stood in place. Silently, he motioned the Nephilim to follow. Giants they were, but even armed and armored, they cut through the mists with hardly a sound, until a rise in the terrain afforded them a view across the river. They crouched in the grasses and finally looked upon their enemy.

The leviathan lay in the mud of the opposite bank, clouds of mist swirling among the shafts of morning sunlight hitting its back. Only a pile of gristly bones, partly submerged, denoted the animal's murderous history; otherwise, the scene was almost serene, but all the more terrifying for being so pregnant with disastrous potential.

"Wonderful! Simply wonderful!" whispered Dedroth. "Fifty or sixty cubits, I would say, and likely on the greater end of that!"

"Direct assault out, Gloryon?" Dyeus' pomp was subdued, but still present.

"Yes, I fear so. At the least, we must draw the beast from its element. We have no chance near the river."

"Should we try the horse?" Tevesh asked. "Noah, are you willing?"

Noah glanced back through the mists to where his loyal stallion bravely waited. He closed his eyes, steeled himself, and nodded yes. "This is my portion," he thought. "I will see it finished."

Unseen by the elder Nephilim and Noah, Hamerch had laid down the shield he carried and quietly walked up behind them. "Down! It will see you!" Pethun whispered harshly. Hamerch ignored him and strode past them. In his hand appeared one of Dyeus' throwing spears. "Hurry back to the pit," he said, to none of them in particular. "I have this. Hey! Beast!"

"Quick, back!" said Gloryon. Dyeus cursed, but followed. The Nephilim fighters loped back up the valley, Noah just able to keep pace in an all-out sprint by virtue of his knowing the land. He leapt on Raph, kicking him to a gallop. "What now, Gloryon?" he shouted, coming alongside the Naphil commander.

"We take our positions and wait," Gloryon said, breathing easily at a steady run. "The boy is committed now, for better or for worse. We must hope that 'better' comes to pass."

"But he is on foot!"

"Do not worry about Hamerch," said Dyeus, running on the other side of Noah. Fatherly pride gilded the sharp edge of anger at having a weapon stolen right from the sheath at his back. "The beast will never catch him. That son of mine has wings on his feet."

Hamerch's heart pounded in his ears, and he could feel the pulse of his thumb pressed tightly to the shaft of the spear he gripped, white-knuckled. He did not know what possessed him to give himself as what amounted to bait. A desire to impress the older warriors? The culmination of his guilt and the hope that one act of courage would free him from Gloryon's sentence? Every step through the mud pushed these muddled thoughts from his mind. Only he, his weapons, and the leviathan remained.

The monster's scaled lids were shut, perhaps in sleep. It had not heard the young Naphil's shouts, or had otherwise ignored them. Hamerch stamped almost to the water's edge and shouted again. "Hey! Wake up, worm!" The leviathan did not so much as blink.

"Fine," Hamerch muttered, as he stepped back from the water's edge. "We'll do this the hard way." Taking three long strides, he flung the spear across the river, hard and fast enough that the missile's path had almost no arc. The spearpoint hit the monster low in its side, near the belly, but did not pierce the armored scales. One black eye blinked, though, and the scaly sac under the leviathan's grinning jaw rippled with a sudden, slight head turn.

Hamerch unslung the thin pack at his back and withdrew the platter-shaped bronze disk within. Half of the disk's edge was sharpened; Hamerch gripped the other half overhand, with the top of the disk pressed against his veined forearm. He spun once, keeping his balance in the slippery mud, then released the disk in a sidearmed slinging motion, violent and smooth.

The disk whistled as it went, seeming to hover over the surface of the waters. Inexorably it sped toward its target. The impact of the disk on the leviathan's skull was audible, even across the river. As the disk caromed into the reeds, a faint white sliver marked the scaled head, then darkened with oozing black blood. The leviathan rumbled and stirred. "Not so invincible, are you?" shouted Hamerch with confidence he was not at all sure he felt. "Come now! Let me lead you to your death!"

No pretense of stealth marred the leviathan's furious dart into the river. The reflexive quickness with which the monster submerged and swam in a mist-roiling path to the opposite bank struck Hamerch awed, but only for a moment. Still, in that moment the beast was already halfway across, terrible undulations of the massive tail propelling it at a preternatural speed. The Naphil backed up to the brambles and grasses at the top of the muddy back and planted a foot. The explosion of the roaring, rancid jaws from the water was the signal that began the race for his life, up the misty valley and to the farmers' pit trap. Like a waking nightmare, the leviathan followed at his heels.

◂ CHAPTER 15 ▸

After hiding the dragons in the forest, Jonan, Merim, Hadishad, and Dashael had positioned themselves on the mossy hill overlooking the pit. In earshot of one another, with weapons at the ready, they waited and prayed. Padded footsteps drew their attention into the forest above them; Methuselah and Lamech, armed for a hunt, scrabbled down the greened roots and rocks.

"Couldn't stay away," Lamech said in response to Jonan's quizzical expression. "Rakeel and Elebru are hidden on the other hillside. What is happening?"

"Noah and his Nephilim are scouting the creature," Merim said. "They are going to try to draw it back here."

Methuselah craned his neck, peering into the mists downvalley. "Here they come! Stay ready, but keep hidden."

Noah had ridden ahead of the Nephilim, cutting up the farmside hill and dismounting while still at a trot. At his whistle, his stallion continued on to the safety of the fields. Noah slid down the hill to where Dashael crouched in a patch of melons. "The Nephilim are right behind!" Noah shouted to his kin across the valley, then drew his bow and said no more.

Mareth arrived first, concealing himself as best he could near the root-entwined boulder that marked the downvalley edge of the pit. Tevesh mirrored his position on the opposite side.

"You may have been right about my knives," Mareth said to his sparring partner. He reached behind him to a scabbard at his back, swathed in his thin cape, and withdrew a sword as long as Tevesh's, double-edged and wavy. Despite the mists, the polished blade caught and reflected the morning sun's light unpredictably, prompting Mareth to cover it with some of the vines and underbrush at his feet. He crouched, and Tevesh did the same.

Gloryon and Dyeus, then Tiras and Pethun, paired themselves near the head of the trap, obscured by the mists and weapons at the ready. Dedroth and Hoduín followed behind, striding quickly up the melon-covered hill to Noah.

"Shall we not move closer?" asked Dedroth. "The brume is so thick, I can barely see."

"Do as you may, but I'll stay right here," Dashael said calmly. His voice hid his nervousness, but the way he shifted his grip on his atlatl back and forth in one hand and the compulsive spinning of a dart around the thumb of his other belied his affected nonchalance.

"I will come, Dedroth," said Noah, and the two crept further down the hillside. As they waded through vine-covered brush, a harsh rhythm of ripping and crashing crescendoed toward them. Hamerch's ghostly form came into view, nearly flying up the misty valley. Behind him, in terrifying obscurity, the leviathan trampled the valley floor, leaving a wide trail of leafy green casualties in its wake. Coils of mist swirled around the monster; the sheer mass and speed of the raging beast tore the air apart.

Fast as the leviathan was, it could not match Hamerch. His stride was high; he knew if he tripped, even stumbled, on a vine or brambles, he was done for. His step proved sure, and the pound of his feet changed subtly as he ran across the boards over the trap. Noah sucked in a breath through his teeth when Hamerch passed Dyeus and the other Nephilim who waited near the pit's end. The leviathan suspected nothing as it followed him; its gnashing jaws were halfway across, and the boards still held firm. The crack of wood echoed, then another, prefacing a final great crash as wood surrendered to the weight of the leviathan. The monster's head rocked back as the boards under its lower jaw maintained their integrity just moments longer than those broken by its enormous body. The net underneath caught the beast and pulled the cords attached to the hinged beams taut. Two snapped, but the rest worked as planned; as the leviathan hit the floor of the pit, which had indeed been dug wide and deep enough, the beams arced on their hinges and fell heavily on the opposite sides.

A loud curse from Mareth mixed with the beast's roar of surprise. At the far end of the pit, ten or more cubits of the leviathan's massive plated tail swung back and forth, pinned by a beam but otherwise free of the trap. As one, Mareth and Tevesh lifted their swords and rushed the tail from either side.

Mareth reached the leviathan's writhing tail a split second before Tevesh. He swung the sword, putting every ounce of his mammoth strength into the overhead strike, but before the honed iron had a chance to be tested on the beast's scales, a jerking whip of the tail caught the Naphil full on the hip and side. The impact threw Mareth flailing to the pit's edge. He cursed again, scrambling for the swordhilt; as his agile fingers closed over the cross-guard, another sweep of the tail lifted him off the ground and sent him crashing into the first thick beam that lay across the pit. Whether the loud crack that followed was of splintered wood or broken back, no one who heard it could say. Mareth dropped into the pit's back corner. The scrabbling scrape of a huge clawed foot drowned out the muffled thud of a body being slammed into packed earth. Not so much as a groan drifted from the pit. The beast resumed its writhing.

Tevesh dodged the tail and hacked at the scales once, then twice. His efforts created nothing more than shallow rends. The tail whipped again and struck a glancing blow; the Naphil stumbled backwards, but did not fall.

Growling in frustration, Tevesh changed tactics. He planted the heel of his hand against the butt of his broadsword and stabbed straight forward, aiming at the joinings between the beast's natural platemail armor. The tip of the sword hit just far of true but still scraped along the plate until it stuck in a cleft. Tevesh angled the blade, following the curve of the scale as it tightly tunneled under its neighbor, and put every ounce of his weight and strength into piercing through to the meat of the tail. The leviathan felt it and tried to swat the pain away, but the Naphil braced himself firmly, muscles taut, heel on a strong, gnarled root curled around a jutting splinter of stone. Finally, the sword popped through scale, skin, and fascia. The mighty giant stabbed the beast several times through the sword's insertion point, angling, thrusting, and reangling, but never drawing the blade out fully. The monster roared in pain; a powerful upward jolt of the tail yanked the sword out of Tevesh's hands, breaking a finger, but damage had been done, and while the thrashing became wilder, it was clearly weaker as well.

The heat of battle burned away any perception of the pain in Tevesh's finger. While he scrambled to retrieve his weapon, Pethun and Tiras barreled out of the mists brandishing their spears. They thrust the weapons into the bloody wound Tevesh had made, worrying the beast's flesh and both gaining further purchase into the muscles of its tail.

"Lift that beam!" Tiras called to his brother, who had retrieved his sword. He ran to the end of the beam trapping the leviathan's tail and gripped it behind his back. He squatted and, with a grunt and a mighty push of his legs, lifted the heavy wooden pillar several feet, freeing the monster. At the same time, Tiras and Pethun heaved up against their spears planted into the meat of the leviathan and drove toward the pit. Slowly but steadily, their straining forced the bulk of the tail past the edge of the pit.

"This is as far as we go if we do not want to lose our weapons," said Pethun, his grip on only the end of his tri-pointed spear. "The brute cannot escape now."

"Tevesh, drop it!" said Tiras. The beam crashed back to earth. Only the last cubit of the leviathan's tail, adorned with spines formed from the armored scales that finally met as the tail tapered to its end, still poked through the opening between the beam and the pit's edge, long enough neither to be trapped nor to be of any threat.

The three Nephilim ran back to the head of the pit, where Gloryon and Dyeus watched the darkness between the beams cautiously, listening to the leviathan's sinister, guttural growls. Noah and Dedroth hurried up to the group.

"Excellent! An admirable job!" Dedroth shuffled to the edge of the pit and leaned over, trying to catch a glimpse of the beast through the mist that drifted and fell into the black. The growls grew sharper, and he stepped back with a grimace. "Now, how do we bind it? How will we transport it?"

"Don't be a fool," shot Pethun. "We have to kill it."

"And how do you suggest we do *that*, then?" asked Dedroth.

"Bury it," Dyeus said coldly. "Fill the pit with stone and earth. Bury it alive."

"Blood and death," swore Noah. "*Mareth.*"

Gloryon echoed the farmer. "Dyeus, we do not know that Mareth is dead."

"Will you venture into the pit to find out? He is lost regardless. I will not have his efforts, poor as they were, be wasted."

Gloryon looked at Dyeus and frowned. "He is your *son*, Dyeus."

"And likely a corpse now." Dyeus stepped closer to Gloryon. "Let us not make this complicated. I have two other sons here. I do not wish to risk their lives, no more than you do your own son. Let us bury the monster and be done with it." Gloryon shook his head, but did not argue.

"Poetic. The first death of its kind in trade for the first death of ours," Dedroth sighed. "Such a tragic waste."

"Do you refer to the animal, or your nephew?" snapped Pethun.

"Mareth, of course." The elder brother did his best to look offended.

Noah felt terribly. Of the Nephilim who had accompanied him from Enoch, Mareth had proved to be the least personable. He had seldom spoken to the farmer, and when he did, his contributions to the conversation had been minimal, consisting mostly of grunts. Somehow, this lack of friendliness made the Naphil's sacrifice weigh all the more heavily on Noah's shoulders. He began to apologize. "Dyeus, I am so sorry. I did not mean…"

Dyeus cut him off. "Do not apologize. We will mourn my son later. There is more immediate business at hand." He picked up a man-sized boulder, wrenching it from the clutches of earth and moss and sending several small snakes slithering. He wrapped his muscled arms around and took a heavy step towards the pit.

A gout of flame shot from the misty darkness of the trap, engulfing the middles of the first two beams and sending even the Nephilim warriors scurrying for cover.

"By the bloody head of Cain! What in black Sheol was that?" Deneresh shrieked.

"Have you not been listening to *anything*? The leviathan breathes fire!" said Jonan.

"Honestly, I assumed the whole thing would be over by now," muttered Deneresh. "By the way, my brother did just fall into that pit you dug. You might be a bit nicer."

"My apologies, truly."

Deneresh sniffed. "You may make it up to me with wine."

While the wood over the trap burned black, crackling and smoking and sending embers spiraling up on streams of smoke, sprays of dirt began to spew from the pit. Pethun, Dyeus, Gloryon, Tiras, and Tevesh spaced themselves in a semicircle, well back from the edge. None of them dared approach any further.

The middles of the beams finally burned through, ends tumbling into the pit and removing one more obstacle for the leviathan. The showers of dirt became heavier, and the snorting of the beast and the scraping of its claws became louder, portending its inevitable escape.

"Shields!" Gloryon shouted. The three young Nephilim shieldbearers quickly supplied Gloryon, Tiras, and Dyeus with their tall shields, then ran back to the relative safety of the hill where hid Noah's kin, all with bows drawn and arrows nocked. Tiras had exchanged his spear for his axe. Pethun stood erect, three-pronged spear held in one hand parallel to the ground, the butt behind his back; the pose looked nonchalant, hardly battle-ready, but the Naphil exuded such an aura of mastery over the weapon that he made the stance look deadly.

"It's vulnerable inside the mouth!" Dashael called out.

"First strike to me," growled Tevesh viciously. This piece of rubbish, this filthy sea worm had taken his friend and caused him personal injury. When it showed its ugly maw, Tevesh planned to strike once and once only.

The beast's bulla, like a scaly boulder, rammed through the lip of the pit. Slowly, menacingly, the leviathan stepped one clawed foot, then the other, out of the trap and blinked its beady eyes at its armed adversaries. It was angry. It was hungry.

And it was free.

· CHAPTER 16 ·

Tevesh stepped forward, bronze icon at his neck swinging. He faced an armored shoulder to the beast and brought his broadsword above his head, blooded blade pointed at the leviathan. The monster opened its cragged jaws in warning; when the Nephilim held his ground, it snapped forward in a feint. Still Tevesh waited. The maw opened again, an unseen wave of stench and swampy decay washing over the giant warrior. The beast shot forward again, no feint this time. It aimed to kill, to rip and tear and stab with a hundred foul daggers and fill its belly with its foe. With uncanny timing borne of both instinct and skill, Tevesh swept his sword in an upward stroke, aiming to pierce through the pale palate of the leviathan into its brain. Jaws clamped down, and blade struck home. Time seemed to pause. A wisp of mist turned the combatants into grey statues, solemn and unmoving, locked in some unending mythic struggle.

Noah held his breath, hypnotized by the eerie impasse and the import of its outcome, and wondered if this, finally, was the end. The mists passed, and a deep, rumbling growl from the leviathan broke the spell woven by them. Tevesh's eyes were wide, whites conspicuous even under his tusken helm, and his grimace spoke of the shock of a thing formerly unthinkable coming to pass.

"My *arm!*" Tevesh bellowed. A flash of sun through the fog hit upon the metal of the enormous broadsword. The weapon was stuck fast in the leviathans's teeth, bent like a green branch in its fearsome jaws. That the beast was unhurt was painfully evident to all, but none more so than Tevesh. The leviathan shook its head, and Tevesh was slammed to the ground, right arm free but casting about aimlessly, left arm trapped at the wrist. The monster swallowed; the Naphil warrior somehow found footing and strained against it, but despite all of Tevesh's massive strength, his arm was pulled in almost to the elbow. Knifelike teeth found new purchase in the flesh of Tevesh's forearm and bit down hard. The adrenaline that masked the giant's pain gave way to cold, terrible agony, and he screamed.

Like a bird of prey, Hoduín swooped down from the hill, robes billowing behind him, their silver sigils shining and dimming in the valley's diffuse light like the sheen on a feather of a raven in flight. Murmuring incantations, he reached deep within his cloak and flung a cloud of white powder at the eyes of his son's attacker. The scaly beast blinked, blinded momentarily. Harsh, high-pitched caws heralded the arrival of two enormous ravens that flew from some hidden perch in the wild forest. Pecking and clawing, they further harried the leviathan around its eyes, while Hoduín withdrew a short, silvery spear and stood by Dyeus, looking for openings for attack. The leviathan shook its head to and fro to try to rid itself of the pestering birds; the action threw Tevesh about like a rat in a hound's mouth.

"Cut me loose!" the trapped Naphil yelled. Seeing no other option, Tiras darted forward, gritting his teeth and swinging his axe. The blow cleanly severed his brother's arm distal to the elbow. Ashen-faced, Tevesh clutched the stump with his good hand, bright red blood spurting between his dirty fingers. Tiras dragged him away from the still-blinking monster, which only just realized its prey had been stolen. Hoduín aided Tiras in the retreat. Snorts preceded a blindly-aimed spurt of flame; the fire bathed a swath of ground, turning bush and grass to ash, but none of the fighters was harmed.

With his father's help, Tevesh stumbled up the hill to where Dedroth and Noah waited. Dedroth roughly pulled Tevesh's good hand away from his injury, drawing a hiss of pain. Spurting streams of blood pulsed from the two arteries in his forearm in time with his racing heartbeat, fanning outward as they met to make a single spray that painted a rhythmic red pattern on the ground.

"Bite this, Tevesh." Dedroth opened his pack, reached in, and slapped a leather cord into the maimed Naphil's good hand. Tevesh bit it, grimacing. "We must stop the bleeding."

Quickly, the Naphil naturalist tied another cord tightly around Tevesh's forearm and pressed a roll of linen cloth against the hemorrhaging stump. "Pressure, pressure. Noah! Heat your knives, if you please—red-hot if the fire burns strong enough." He inclined his head at the nearest patch of flames.

While Noah hurried to his task, Dedroth fished in his bag and pulled out a glass cylinder covered with a waxen seal, along with a small set of metal tools. From the tools he chose a small, hinged instrument with long, pointed graspers and proceeded to advance with it to Tevesh's wound.

"Gah! What devilry is that?" hissed the bleeding Naphil through gritted teeth and leather cord, sweat beading on his forehead from the pain and the close flames.

"If those two vessels are not tied off, you will bleed to death," answered Dedroth in a clinical tone. "It is the only way."

Tevesh turned away and gripped his father's hand. Hoduín closed his eyes and chanted as Dedroth pulled the severed end of one artery away from oozing tissue and clamped it closed. With one hand, he deftly broke the wax seal of the glass container and pulled a thin string from a dark violet liquid. "From the intestine of a bull," he explained. "It will hold secure for a time, until the wound is healed, then it shall be resorbed by your own tissues."

"Don't *tell* me about it, just *do* it!"

Dedroth tied the strand tightly around the artery's end, stopping the pulsing flow of blood, then repeated the process with the second vessel. Noah rushed up, carefully holding one of his knives, blade heated to a dark cherry red.

"The flames are very hot," he stated, displaying his bald hand and knuckles, hair singed off. "The handle is cool enough, though."

"Well done. Young Tevesh, this will hurt." Dedroth took Noah's knife and pressed the blade to the still-bleeding stump. Flesh smoked, and the cloying, disturbingly appetizing smell of burnt meat mingled with the metallic scent of blood. Tevesh squeezed his eyes shut, but bore the pain silently.

"Hmm. Most of the bleeding is staunched, but it oozes still," observed Dedroth after his torturous, but fruitful, administrations. "How exceedingly frustrating."

"I have the very thing!" Hoduín unfastened a satchel hidden in his robes. "If the flesh fails, the spirit may be of aid." He pulled a black stick out. "Behold, lunar caustic! The mystical healing power of the silver moon, pulled from the night sky itself!" With a spin of his wrist and a sibilant hiss, he pressed the stick to the bleeding areas and rolled it about, turning the tissue dark grey.

Dedroth pursed his lips in interest. "It worked."

"An alchemist from Mu sent them to me," said Hoduín, eyes twinkling. "There is more to the world than what eye can see, Dedroth."

Noah agreed with that statement with all his soul, but he felt uneasy in his accord, felt a gnawing suspicion that the roots of Hoduín's belief in the unseen grew in very different soil than his own. The battle in the valley raged on, though, drawing his attention, and he thought no more on it.

After depositing his brother on the relative safety of the hillside, Tiras leapt back into the fray. He, Dyeus, and Gloryon, each now carrying a shield, harried the beast, darting to and fro like dire wolves facing a cave bear, avoiding further injury but failing to wound the monster. Several times the leviathan's jaws came within inches of taking a Nephilim life, but the farmers on the hillsides used their arrows and darts well, firing into the maw when it opened. The insults were no more than an annoyance, but they were painful enough to cause the leviathan to shut its teeth before they could close on any of the giants.

While the three shielded Nephilim kept its attention, Pethun lithely harassed the monster, dodging and searching for a weakness in the scales of the beast's back with his spear. Stab after stab found none.

"Might as well be stone!" he shouted, frustrated, before the leviathan shifted its mass toward him and he was obliged to execute an impressive leaping somersault to avoid being crushed.

"Keep pressing!" said Gloryon, beating the beast's bulla off with his shield. "It must have a weak point *somewhere!*"

"It's only a matter of time before another casualty," whispered Dedroth to Noah, after one well-placed arrow helped Dyeus avoid being bitten in two. "They want a weak point. Let us find one, you and I." Closer they crept, down the hillside and past still-burning bushes. The scuffling and shouting of battle was louder, but underneath the growls and yells Noah noticed a subtle snuffing sound. His instincts blared, and he yelled. "Fire!"

Shields rose, and Nephilim ducked behind them. A third geyser of flames shot from the leviathan's snout; incredibly, no one appeared to be hurt after the fire died down, but all three Nephilim who bore the brunt of the blast flung away their burning shields.

"Did you see that?" asked Dedroth. "The flames formed from two streams, one from either side of the snout."

Noah narrowed his eyes as he watched the Nephilim warriors below regroup. "How can the beast keep the flame from burning inside its body?"

Dedroth answered excitedly, pieces of his theoretical puzzle falling into place. "Two different elements, like flint and iron! They combust when they meet, but alone are inert."

Rapidly Noah engaged the Naphil's line of thought. "If that is true, and we could cause a mixing of the elements before they are expelled…"

"Wherever they are made, the substances must course closest to one another somewhere in its snout," Dedroth reasoned. "But how to cause the mixing? Pethun said that the beast is like stone."

Noah raised his head and looked grimly at the Naphil naturalist. "Stone cracks."

Dedroth nodded. He stood from amidst the vines, muddy watchcoat heavy with moisture from the mists and hanging damply, and cupped his hands to his mouth. "Dyeus! You must crack its snout!"

"If it would—agh!—stay still!" Dyeus dodged the leviathan and countered with the thrust of a javelin, which was dodged in return. "This scabrous whoreson is deceptively quick!"

From higher on the hill, Hoduín shouted, "The eyes! Go for the eyes! Blind it if you can!"

Hoduín's cry was the catalyst that sped the men on the hillsides to action. Elebru, Rakeel, and Noah on one side loosed a barrage of arrows in rapid succession, while Methuselah and his kin on the forest hill did the same. Dashael added to the missiles with his atlatl, flinging darts with abandon. A few almost found their mark, digging into the rough, thick hide around the inky eyes. The leviathan stepped back and blinked, pausing for only a second, but Dyeus saw his chance. He reared back and launched a javelin. Its tip pierced through the lid into the vitreous and beyond, sticking firmly in the eye. Dyeus followed it with another that bounced off the top

135

of the beast's jaw; the third pierced the ruined eye even further. Of a sudden, the leviathan's behavior changed. The rumble from deep in its cavernous throat sounded almost confused, and its movements became spastic. It opened its jaw slowly, then closed it and shook its head side to side, paying no more attention to the Nephilim or the ravens that dove in to pick off bits of ocular substance dripping around the impaling javelins.

Tiras and Gloryon hefted their axes with renewed strength of purpose. Blow after blow they rained on the head, spinning away from reflexive swings of leviathan's great bludgeon of a snout, now crisscrossed with shallow, oozing furrows. One lucky spasm caught Tiras on the shoulder and chest; he rolled and coughed, gasping for breath.

Gloryon sensed the arrival of the battle's endgame, and he willed it to be finally finished. Too many of his kind had been hurt, and more severely than any Naphil ever had. He let his battle-rage boil over and cocked his bloody axe behind him, gauging the staggered, swaying leviathan for the perfect moment. It came.

"Be cursed and thrice cursed, you *insufferable* worm!"

The Naphil captain poured every ounce of strength, every iota of skill he possessed into the blow. A crack resounded as the weakened skull splintered below the axe's blade. Noah's and Dedroth's postulate proved true, but to what great extent none could have guessed. Fireballs exploded from beneath the leviathan's eyes, burning Dyeus' javelins to ash in an instant. The monster's lower jaw was blown into the dirt; meteoric pieces of skull, meat, and brain matter splattered tree, rock, and root alike, all burning and setting everything they touched aflame. Gloryon's body flew through the smoky air in a rain of fire and flesh, hitting hard, then lying still.

"*Father!*" Gilyon sprinted down the mossy hill, but Noah reached Gloryon first, ignoring the searing heat that singed hair from skin. As he sent up a wordless prayer, he cut the cord fastening the Naphil's burning cloak and gripped him securely under his arms. Noah bent his knees, leaned back, and strained to pull the heavy body free of the enclosing flames. The effort, combined with the breathless heat of the many fires burning around him, sucked the air from his lungs. A shadowed curtain flashed across his vision, and he almost passed out. He pled silently, desperately.

"Creator God, give me strength!"

Whether the answer to a prayer or a fresh burst of adrenaline, or perhaps both, Noah felt his strength renewed. Despite the added weight of the now-blackened armor, the farmer dragged Gloryon away from the fire with much effort. Gilyon bounded over a patch of flames; together, they carried the fallen Naphil to the safety of the hillside nearest the farm. Beads of sweat dripped down Gilyon's ash-covered face, creating pale trails through soot-black, and though the young Naphil tried to mask his filial concern with a face of stone, Noah marked white streaks that could only be from tears.

"Father, wake up," Gilyon said, voice cracking. "Please wake up."

"Let me see to him." Dedroth knelt by Gloryon's head, Noah moving closer to Gilyon and putting a comforting hand on the young giant's shoulder. With two fingers Dedroth pulled Gloryon's eyelids up, examined them closely, then put a finger on his neck, then his wrist. Suddenly, the Naphil naturalist slapped the supine warrior's face. Gloryon's eyes cracked open. Gilyon barked a laugh of relief, and Noah joined him. The laughter was contagious: it spread to Rakeel and Elebru watching nearby, then found booming voice in Pethun. Hoduín's laugh was clear and high, and even Tevesh chuckled weakly. Exhausted, Dyeus and Tiras supported each other as they trudged up the hill and could only manage tired smiles, but the whoops of excitement from Merim, Jonan, Hadishad, and Hamerch echoed down the valley, and Methuselah and Lamech shouted praises to Elohim just as loudly.

Even Dedroth grinned when he said, "Rest, Gloryon. You will be fine." Head cushioned by a tangle of melon vines, Gloryon looked at Noah, then at his son. The corner of his mouth twitched up faintly, and he closed his eyes and rested.

· CHAPTER 17 ·

Dyeus sat down, rubbing his temples. He paused, then looked towards the pit and cursed. "Mareth." The giant got to his feet slowly, exhaustedly, as if his last reserves of strength had just been drained. Pethun and Dedroth helped him down the slope. On the forest hillside, Hamerch had apparently had the same thought and was already quickly making his way down to the pit edge, humans and Deneresh following behind.

Noah glanced at Gloryon. "Go on," said Gilyon. "I'll stay with him." With a whispered prayer for comfort for Mareth's family on his tongue, Noah went to help retrieve a corpse.

Under the netting that covered the top of the trap, mists swirled in the dark bottom of the pit. Piles of dirt and stones filled the corners, torn and thrown from the rents in the floor made by the leviathan's scraping claws. One by one, the Nephilim and the humans made their ways to stand at the pit's edge, all peering down through the gloom for a glimpse of the body.

"There!" Hadishad pointed at a pile of rubble. Glints of dulled bronze peeked through the dirt. Nothing moved. Methuselah fell to his knees, lips moving silently in prayer.

Pethun put a hand on his brother's shoulder. "We shall take him back to Enoch to be buried, Dyeus."

"No," Dyeus said. "He will be buried here, with the beast's carcass. This pit will be a fitting grave for them both."

Noah bowed his head. The euphoria of victory was gone now; all that remained was the heaviness of another death. Suddenly, he dropped to one knee, tilting his ear closer to the darkness. "Did anyone else hear that?" A faint cough, then another, echoed up from the pit, followed by the sound of some slight movement that sent small rocks tumbling down from their places at the top of the pile. A hand, dark with blood and soil, broke from the dirt and rose with clutching fingers, then fell limply back down.

"Ropes, quickly!" Lamech commanded his sons, running to the closest beam. He reached down, pulled up a stretch of netting, and began sawing at it with a knife he pulled from his belt. His sons were joined by Rakeel, Merim, and Dashael. In the space of a few minutes, the section of netting was cut away and transformed into several stout lengths of rope. Gripping the beams still overlying the pit, Dyeus and Pethun quickly lowered themselves into it, dropping the short distance to the floor. A few sweeps of giant hands uncovered enough of Mareth to pull him up to a sitting position. Dyeus unstrapped his bronze armor, now dented and disformed, and threw the pieces of it to the ground. Dedroth and Hamerch lashed the ends of rope to their forearms and threw the other ends down to Pethun, who deftly tied a harness and secured Mareth, eyes closed and groaning, under the arms. With the two Nephilim above pulling and the two below lifting, the unconscious giant was hoisted out.

"Move aside now, move aside." Dedroth knelt beside Mareth and held a vial under his nose. Mareth started and coughed harder, then dropped his head again.

"Come now, nephew, time to awake!" Dedroth roughly kneaded a knuckle into the young giant's chest and held the vial to his nose once more. With this, Mareth's eyes popped open and he sat up violently, swinging wildly with massive fists. None found a target, and with a few calming words from Dedroth he settled down. His still-dazed eyes surveyed the scene. Black smoke from the fires and the white mists that were slowly rolling to reclaim the valley mingled and obscured the details of the battle's aftermath, but the victory against the leviathan was clear. More importantly to Mareth, though, was that he had had no part in it.

"Real thing a bit different from sparring, eh, brother?" Deneresh asked, then actually stepped back when Mareth glared at him with a hatred that chilled the blood.

"What would you know of either, boy?" spat Pethun. Hamerch shook his head in warning to his younger brother, then extended a hand to his elder.

Mareth did not respond to Deneresh's ill-thought comment with words. He slapped Hamerch' outstretched hand away and barked a curse that made the righteous farmers wince. He stood uneasily and checked that his two dirks were still attached to his belt. His weapons thus confirmed, he flung the end of his crimson cape behind his back. His steps tottered at first, but quickly became stronger, and silently he disappeared into the mists in the direction of the wooded wilds.

From his wounded brother's side, Tiras noticed what was happening and rose as if to follow Mareth. Dyeus motioned him down. "Let him be," he said, and Tiras returned to his place by Tevesh.

Under protest and with the insistence of their comrades, Gloryon and Tevesh agreed to ride the crested dragons back to the farmhouse. "You are injured," Hoduín said. "Your pride should not be." Methuselah and Lamech went with them. The rest of the farmers and the other Nephilim spent the remainder of the day cleaning up from the carnage. Noah wanted to ride to the village for nets and a boat in order to dredge the riverbottom for the remains of the victims, but Pethun saved him the trouble. Accompanied by a solemn Elebru looking on from the bank, he pulled half-eaten corpses from the water until all were accounted for, adding them to the pile of bones on the shore.

As the mists ascended and fell again in their afternoon showers, the fires died and the rest of the party set to work on the leviathan. Many of the scales of its neck had been partially blown away from the skin, although each was intact and seemingly none the worse from the flames. Their job thus begun for them, the humans used knives to pry the scales off one by one. It was slow, tiring work: the scales fit tightly and were firmly attached to the tough underlying tissue, and they were surprisingly heavy. Still, the value of the labor became more and more evident as they progressed. "Armor made from this would sell for a fortune," said Tiras, hefting a smaller plate half the size of his giant hand. "Fireproof, rustproof, virtually impervious to arrows and blades…ho there, young farmer, be careful! We must not lose a single scale!"

The leviathan's flesh was slowly laid bare, and the Nephilim began the task of butchering the beast. Dedroth appointed himself a supervisory role, with no opposition. He directed with authority, telling the others to cut here and slice along there, and soon it became impossible to deny the efficiency of his direction.

"What are we to do with all this meat?" asked Deneresh, who had started the day hungry and had grown only more so.

"Salt it and dry it," answered Dedroth. "We cannot cook it with what we have brought with us, and, please correct me if I err, our hosts are not in the habit of eating flesh."

"That is true…" said Noah.

"Splendid! More for me," interjected Deneresh.

"…but I can certainly find salt for you, and a way to transport the meat besides."

By the time Noah had returned from the village market, the leviathan had been stripped to bone and offal. The farmer led a brace of preening cock-drakes pulling a long cart, front half filled with bags of salt, and another crested dragon in front of a stout cargo wagon lined with meat cloth. He stopped at the top of the farmside slope. Dyeus and Dedroth ran up to meet him with the first load of stacked scales.

"What price do we owe you, Noah?" asked Dyeus,

"Nothing, to be sure. This is only one small way to repay what you have done for us."

Dyeus smiled. "And I will not refuse it."

"Come, come!" hurried Dedroth. "There is still much to do!"

Hamerch, still under Gloryon's sentence, was made by his father and uncle to dispose of the leviathan's enormous innards into the pit. The bones were left out in the sun, and Hoduín took it upon himself to scour them clean. "No sense in wasting good bones," he muttered between whispered incantations that he took pains for the farmers not to see. He did not know exactly why he hid them; he simply felt that, just perhaps, these men from Eden were not as spiritually open-minded as his pupils in Enoch.

While Hamerch filled the pit, the others chopped the beams with axes Merim had fetched from the closest toolhouse. The piles of wood grew until a single large layer had amassed on top of the entrails and organs. Atop the wood the farmers laid sod that they cut from the valley; they then piled topsoil over all, creating a sort of long, low hill. "We shall plant over this," said Merim. "Perhaps this beast will provide us in death what it threatened in life."

The group loaded the scales and meat into the carts. The animals were hard-pressed to pull their heavy loads through the fields to the farmhouse, in some muddier spots requiring the humans and Nephilim to help push. The giants were obliged to shoulder some of the sacks of salt, but soon the victorious group arrived at the farmhouse. They were greeted with cheers and many thanks to humans and Nephilim alike, and not only by Methuselah's household. Many villagers had descended upon the farmstead, eager to hear news of the battle and see for themselves the giant warriors— "fathered by God's angels themselves, if you can believe it!" Methuselah and Lamech had already sated their curiosity with a full account of the battle, but that did not prevent the flood of questions from a dozen eager listeners.

"Peace, all!" said Methuselah, raising his hands and signaling for quiet. "Our heroes are tired and they are hungry. Let them take some time to rest and wash, and if they please, return here after to tell their tales. In the meantime, consider yourselves my guests. My pantries are open to you all, and my cellars as well!"

The evening's plans were established. Noah and the other farmers retired to their quarters, eager to return to the gathering of their kinsmen and neighbors, and the Nephilim went to their tents, all but Deneresh. "Priorities!" he said, and took his place at the front of the line for the wine.

‹ CHAPTER 18 ›

The funeral for the leviathan's victims was held the next day on Elebru's land. Dashael spoke, as did Methuselah and many others. At its end, Enosh sang a prayer, beautiful despite a voice that wavered with age. Elebru did not say any words.

Later that week, he and two servants moved back into the east wing of his manor. He also sold all of his lands, minus the manor grounds, to Methuselah. Zara, and Noah with her when he was able, visited him regularly. He never said very much. Zara continued to visit him anyway.

Gloryon and Tevesh were taken to the village's house of healing, built high in the hills overlooking the river. Hot springs and green lawns surrounded the grounds, bordered by extensive herb gardens. The healers had to refigure several rooms to accommodate the giants' size, but the Nephilim did heal in comfort. Gloryon was burned over much of his arms and back, and the healers suspected that he had suffered moderate trauma to the head. They evaluated him daily for signs of sequelae—memory loss, changes in movement, speech difficulties—but as he exhibited none in the next four days, they then focused only on his burns. The healers' salves were effective and the wounds proved to be mostly superficial. Masses of blisters soon burst and scarred over, and by the end of the week Gloryon was well enough to spend his time strolling around the grounds, conversing with his son, who visited every day, or another of the Nephilim. Methuselah came to see him daily as well.

Tevesh's injury was more severe, and he was treated accordingly. His stump was bathed daily with a solution that bubbled and frothed when it touched his raw skin. It burned, but the healers assured him it would aid healing and keep the wound clean. Without telling the healers, Hoduín administered lunar caustic again; as it seemed to have good effect, they were actually quite interested in its making, but became much less so when Hoduín informed them of its arcane nature. Nevertheless, the Naphil did allow them to have a sample, and they accepted it with thanks and, unbeknownst to Hoduín, with many prayers of purification to the Creator God.

Gloryon was given leave to go after the first week, but he requested to stay so he might keep Tevesh company. The healers did not argue with him.

While their comrades were recovering, the other Nephilim were not idle. The harvest was far behind schedule, and Noah and his family had no time to rest after the funeral. The next morning the farmers took to the fields, eager to salvage as much as they could from more than a month of interruption. Noah rose early and hitched a supply wagon to an aurochs bull. One of the dragons would have been faster than the big bull, but the reptiles had a bad habit of eating the fruits that needed picking. He sighed. A lonely day awaited him. Zara would spend her day sorting produce, and with Elebru's fields now adding to the workload, everyone was assigned his own area of the farm to harvest the best they could alone. His course took him past the Nephilim campground. None of the giants had yet woken, except one.

"Where to, Noah?" called Dyeus from outside his tent, dressed in a simple tunic and sipping a bowl of some steaming liquid.

"I work the eastern orchards today," he replied. "I am afraid that I and my family will be poor company during the day's hours. There is yet much to do—too much, I fear. We shall see you all tonight, though. Let the women at the house know when you are hungry. Our stores and hospitality are yours."

"Hold, Noah! You really go to work? You are the architect of a great victory! Rest! Be with your woman!"

"If only I could, Dyeus. Grandfather needs every able body, though, and the work will not wait." He clicked the aurochs into a slow walk.

Dyeus crossed his arms. "Wait once more, Noah." He entered each tent in turn. Noah heard Dyeus conversing with sleepy, muffled voices, but he could not make out what was said. Dyeus emerged. "What do I need take with me?"

"I miss your meaning, my friend."

"I mean we will help with your harvest! We have naught else to do. I shall come with you today. And if someone will assign these slumbering oafs useful labor, they have agreed to help as well."

"God be praised! This is a welcome offer." Noah quickly took count. Absent Gloryon, Tevesh, and Mareth, there were still eight Nephilim well and strong. The task ahead suddenly seemed infinitely less daunting.

"So what shall I bring with me?" Dyeus asked again.

"Just yourself, I think. We have all else we need." Noah gestured to the supply wagon.

"Well, here I am." Dyeus grinned. "Let us be off!"

"Unbelievable!" Hadishad swept the sweat from his brow. "He is like four of us!"

"Who?" asked Merim. "Pethun?"

"No—Tiras. Like *five* of us. Plus a brace of oxen."

"You should have seen Hamerch. His feet are fast, but I think his hands may be quicker. I look away once, and he has already filled another basket."

The young farmers walked into the farmhouse together. They made their way to the dining hall, but were waved away by Edna to clean up before supper was served. Noah and Zara hailed them from an alcove.

"Finished and washed already, Noah?" asked Hadishad.

"With Dyeus' help," he answered. "What I had planned on doing in three days, we were able to accomplish in one."

"And I, for one, am very much indebted to him," Zara said, nuzzling her nose behind Noah's ear. He laughed, and his cheeks reddened.

Merim elbowed Hadishad. "Think you that Noah's prophecy has been fulfilled? No more toil for us, eh, now that he's brought these giants to Eden?"

"Yes, cousin," Noah said. "We shall enslave our new Nephilim friends, and you shall spend your centuries doing nothing but skipping rocks in the river, thus fulfilling the prophetic words of the Lord our God." He rolled his eyes. Zara giggled.

"I must warn you, we Nephilim do not take well to enslavement." Hoduín's stooped head appeared around the corner.

"Hoduín!" Noah bowed his head to the hooded Naphil, and Merim and Hadishad excused themselves to their quarters. "We were just discussing prophecy."

"Ah, excellent," said Hoduín. "The very topic I was hoping to broach with you and your father and grandfather. May we speak after dinner?"

"Of course," Noah asked. "After dinner."

The old oak tree unfurled its boughs high over the front yard and terraces, and its thick roots radiated out, serving as the terrace borders. A dirt path ran from the farmhouse's front door, flowing down the natural staircase created by the twisting root system and the soil packed in between. Pink and yellow catkins hung from every branch of the oak in the spring, and in the fall the clatter of acorns on the roof was perpetual. The ancient tree had put down its roots long before Methuselah had laid the home's foundation, and no one doubted it would outlast them all.

Above the terraces, two of the bottommost branches, heavy with age and size, curled almost to the ground and rose again as they tapered and branched. The roots near them were knobby and squat, and the thick foliage above provided ubiquitous shade from the sun. The spot had always been a perfect place to sit and talk in peace, quiet, and comfort.

After a simple meal of spiced squash soup, apple cake, and cheese was washed down with ample wine, four figures found seats around the oak's natural meet. Noah settled in the crook of one of the low branches, perfectly content to just listen to the conversation and follow it wherever it led. Lamech and Methuselah chose seats made of the tree's roots, and Hoduín sat crossed-legged on the ground.

Methuselah began. "Noah tells us you are a spiritual creature, Hoduín, and that you know of the account of creation."

The Naphil nodded. "I do, and I know many others besides."

"Others?" asked Lamech.

"Oh, yes. I myself have transcribed, from foreign seekers of knowledge, at least six different creation legends, and many more can be found in our libraries."

Lamech raised an eyebrow. "And which do you hold to be true?"

Hoduín shrugged. "Honestly, my interests do not lie there. I ask myself—does it matter? It is in the past, and cannot change. What interests me is the future."

Noah's father did not let the subject drop. "Of course it matters! The Creator God Himself deigned to record His works of creation!"

Condescension bled into the Naphil spiritist's tone. "Lamech, every account of mankind's origins I have ever read or heard tell of claims some divine source."

"Perhaps," said Methuselah, "but the Generation of the Heavens and the Earth was inscribed in stone by the Creator's own hand."

Hoduín raised his eyebrows and pursed his lips. "An account hand-scribed by God. That is a bold statement." He stroked the roots of his beard, obviously intrigued by the farmer's claim.

"It is a true one," said Methuselah matter-of-factly.

"You have proof?"

"What proof would be sufficient for you?" asked Lamech. "The Generation exists, and it is the Word of God. If you believe otherwise, seeing it will not alter that."

"Lamech, my friend," said Hoduín, "you seem quite protective of this thing."

"We are," said Methuselah. "The Generation has been handed down from father to firstborn son since our line's sire Seth received it from Adam, who wrote a Generation himself. The writings are precious to us."

"We ourselves are seldom allowed access to them," Lamech added. "Noah has never seen them."

"The words themselves we share freely, though, and all our kin commit them to memory." Methuselah reached to a pouch at his belt and removed a worn leatherbound codex, small and square. "Here, Hoduín, have mine."

The Naphil reached out his hand, paused halfway as if reconsidering, then took the codex. "Many thanks, Methuselah," he said sincerely. "I will keep it safe." He stashed it into his voluminous robes.

Noah almost objected, but held his tongue. The codex was perhaps Methuselah's most prized earthly possession. His giving it away, especially to one as Hoduín, struck Noah as an action that would be regretted later. Then again, it was his grandfather's to do with what he would, and he was

147

not a man for rash decisions. "The value lies in the words, not the book itself," Noah thought, "and those are already inscribed on Methuselah's heart. Perhaps they will make a change in Hoduín's, too, and who is to say how many others?"

Hoduín spoke again, carefully weighing his words. "I suppose there is one in your line who will not be the steward of your Generations."

"You speak of my father Enoch," said Methuselah, face unreadable. Lamech stiffened, only just perceptibly. Part of Noah's subconscious willed the conversation to go another direction. Enoch was a subject almost sacrosanct to the family, especially Methuselah: his life, his mysterious ascendance, his time spent away from Eden in the city that shared his name, and, most acutely to Noah's grandfather, the fact that he was here with them on the earth no longer. Noah could not guess how Methuselah would react to Hoduín's broaching the subject.

"Yes, I do," said the Naphil. "However, my own father, Barkayal, does not, nor do any other Grigori. Enoch opposed them, openly. He wished them gone. He told them that they had abandoned their proper abode to lust after things they ought not have." He leaned in conspiratorially. "Samyaza *hated* him. Which, I believe, is why he treated you like he did, Noah. Did you know that?"

"No," said Methuselah, leaning forward as well and betraying his growing interest.

"Then you do not know this, either: he wrote while in Enoch—volumes upon volumes."

"Your father called him the Scribe," interjected Noah.

"And so he was. He wrote much about the Grigori, but of many other things as well. The peoples of the earth, the movements of the heavens. His family." Hoduín returned Methuselah's unwavering gaze. "And I know the libraries of the city of Enoch as I know my own home. I know where to find it all." Hoduín sat back, satisfied he had piqued the farmers' interests. "Come to Enoch, Methuselah. We will learn from your father's writings together. Lamech and Noah, you as well. In return, I only wish to learn of your God, perhaps at some point even to see the words He has written. We Nephilim still have many days left in Eden. Only think on this while we remain, I ask you."

Hoduín rose smoothly, his long, billowing robes hiding his legs and giving the illusion of levitation. He bowed to Methuselah. "We have much to offer one another, you and I." With that, he strode from the oak meet, leaving Methuselah, Lamech, and Noah sitting, each lost in his own thoughts. Two ravens perched in the branches above, watching silently.

‹ CHAPTER 19 ›

At last the farmers offered the year's harvest sacrifice. The ceremonies were more solemn than usual, with many prayers of thanks from the members of Methuselah's family for their deliverance from the leviathan. The firstlings of their animals spilled their blood upon the farm's altar; the carcasses were burned with newly-gathered grains and fruit. A new bull was chosen. Of the Nephilim, all of whom were invited to participate, only Tiras, Hoduín, and Dedroth came.

"Why sacrifice?" asked Tiras, as they watched the pungent smoke ascend to the heavens. "Why not enjoy the fruit of your labor?"

"To thank Elohim, Who has given us all good things," said Methuselah. "When we sacrifice our first fruits and firstlings, we only give what is due Him."

"Your God gives your harvest, you say," said Dedroth, motes from the smoke speckling his shoulders. "Is it not more reasonable that this bounty is a function of Eden's rich soil and thick mists? Why attribute to the supernatural what might be explained by actions we observe?"

"Because, my friend, we have a Witness that tells us," said Noah.

"Curses and prophecies," murmured Hoduín.

All became silent while blackened bones and husks lifted their aromas to the evening sky.

"These are incredible!"

Gilyon hoisted the last white-and-yellow squash onto the wagon. The harvest was all but finished, earlier than it would have been if the leviathan had never come. Noah and Hadishad watched the young Naphil; more

150

than a fortnight of working alongside the giants had not dulled the awe the farmers had for their prodigious strength.

"It would have taken three of us to lift that," said Hadishad.

"Ah, it is nothing." Gilyon rubbed his hands together and wiped them on his tunic. "These gourds would be worth their weights in gold in Enoch's markets. The harvests' fruits from our dead lands are stunted and sickly." He shook his head. "I still cannot get over the sheer size of these!"

Noah and Hadishad looked at one another, then up at the enormous youth standing three heads above them. "I think we know the feeling," said Noah.

A braying honk in the distance drew their attention to a figure approaching. Tiras hailed them with a wave, mounted on a burgundy dragon with a high, wide crest. The crested dragons were some of the only beasts that could serve as steeds for both humans and Nephilim, not to mention the only ones that could travel at speed carrying a giant, and the Nephilim had taken to borrowing them whenever they could.

Tiras slowed the beast down and looked appreciatively at the loaded wagon. "All done here?" he asked.

"Only just," answered Noah.

"Good! I am asked to fetch you all back to the farmhouse—especially you, Gilyon. Your father and Tevesh are back."

"Tevesh is well? Finally. I am more than ready to leave this place."

Dyeus tossed a plump grape into his mouth. He and his brothers reclined in Pethun's spacious tent, sipping wine and enjoying several large clumps of Methuselah's grapes, along with the particularly pungent wheel of cheese they had purchased in the village.

"Why so eager to be gone, brother?" asked Dedroth. "From what I have seen, Eden is a fascinating land. Have we not been treated as honored guests?"

"We deserve no less," Pethun said. "We saved these people's lands, then we saved their harvest."

"Hear, brother." Dyeus raised his glass.

"Well, for myself, I have quite enjoyed these days. Meaningful labor, the sun on my shoulders, the satisfaction of a job well done—it is a welcome change from the cold, dead stone of Enoch."

Pethun made a snuffing sound. "I happen to like that cold, dead stone. Moreover, the people there are not so arrogant."

"They have struck you as such, too?" Dyeus sat up. "No deference to us, no deference at all—and one of us is equal to ten of them."

"Several times, I have caught some village girl or another staring at me," said Pethun, "but as soon as I catch their eye with mine, they turn away and hurry on."

"Ahhh." Dedroth wagged his finger at his brothers, then tapped his nose. "I know what irks you. You two want to be treated as gods and princes, as you are in the streets of Enoch. Here, girls are not falling to their knees in front of you, and the only one they fear and worship is this God of theirs."

"Religious intolerance," sniffed Pethun.

Dyeus glowered at his elder brother. "One with his nose so often in the dirt should not put so much stock in his perception."

Dedroth ignored the look and laughed. "Come, brothers! We will no doubt leave this place soon, but until then, let us greet our fellows and avail ourselves of more of Methuselah's wine."

Pethun shrugged and drained the last of his cup. "I suppose you are right. And besides, we cannot leave Mareth here."

Dyeus peered out of the tent, past the fields to the hills in the distance. "Where is that boy?"

Light and laughter emanated from the farmhouse. The congregation seemed to be gathered mainly in the dining hall, not surprisingly; the high wood-beamed ceilings made the room the obvious choice for entertaining those of the Nephilim's size. As Mareth approached, the smells of freshly baked breads and roasted garlic grew stronger. Famished and exhausted though he was, he held on to his still-wounded pride and did not speed his steps.

He plodded toward the glowing open doorway, hitching his burden higher on his shoulders. He passed the ostrich pen. The male birds began booming and stamping. Mareth kept walking. The wild cacophony struck him as a fitting herald to his return from the wilds.

Silhouettes darkened the doorway, and men began filtering outside. Giant figures stooped under the lintel and gathered with the farmers.

"Mareth?"

He recognized his father's voice, and it held neither reproach nor fatherly concern. He did not answer. A few lamps were lit now, casting oily light on recognizable faces. Mareth imagined himself as they would see him: a silent, towering shadow, the burden on his back adding height and breadth to his already-massive form. More than one of the human farmers furrowed his brow in worry and fear. That was well; only a fool would not fear him. He had proven that to himself these last days, and the proof would soon be laid out for all to see.

Mareth reached the stone courtyard, heaved his shoulders, and dropped his burden to the ground. It hit the stone with a muffled thud. He straightened. "I am returned."

"Mareth!" Dyeus stepped forward, and it was the signal for everyone else to swarm around him, eager to share the good cheer of the evening. Edna recruited a few of her younger grandchildren to fetch Mareth food and drink from the kitchens.

"Where have you been?" asked Pethun, but Mareth ignored him, looking for Noah. He spotted him, holding his woman's hand near the doorway. "Noah!" he called, voice coarse with two weeks' disuse. "These are for you."

Noah walked to the big bundle. "I am well glad to see you, my friend," he said, but again the Naphil did not answer. Instead, he bent down and pulled away the bedroll that he had secured around his burden. At least a dozen furs and skins unfurled onto the stone, scraped of gristle and clean of blood. A smaller, but still good-sized, parcel lay in the middle of the unwrapped stack of furs. Curious, Noah stepped forward to examine Mareth's gifts; the younger men and Nephilim followed him. Noah pulled the parcel to the side and began untying the knots, while the others knelt around the furs. One by one each was pulled from the pile: patterned creodont pelts, long-haired boar skins, striped and speckled cat furs, iridescent scaled hides of warrior drakes.

"Blood and… Merim, hold this end!" With his cousin's help, Jonan lifted the last and largest skin. After a moment of orienting it, Jonan whistled. "That's from a cave bear, that is!"

"So is this," said Noah. He held a thick, sharp curved tooth as long as his hand up to the light of the lamp. Tusks, teeth and claws, many longer and more wicked-looking than the bear tooth, filled the parcel. With Hadishad's help, Noah started removing the trophies and handing them around to the other men.

"You have a collection here to rival my own," he said to Mareth, "and mine I have amassed over decades!"

"Keep them," said Mareth. "Remember who brought death to their owners."

"You killed these," said Methuselah, not asking. "In a fortnight." He shook his head. "A hunting party would have taken days to kill just one."

Tevesh threw his good arm around his friend's shoulder. "So you have been hunting, while I have lain on my backside? Hardly fair." He laughed. "Trying to save face as a fighter in front of these farmers, eh? Killing predators for sport? I do not blame you, after your poor showing with the leviathan."

Mareth growled and shrugged Tevesh off with a curse. "Oh, come now, I was only jesting," Tevesh said. "Take me with you next time. I will fight them one-handed!"

Ignoring the joke, Mareth pointed his steps toward the Nephilim tents. "Your herds are safe for a while, humans," he said over his shoulder. "I have foregone sleep for many of these nights to make it so. And now, I am going to bed." He disappeared into the mists.

"How glad I am that I have no children," Pethun said under his breath to Dedroth.

"None that you know of, anyway," replied Dedroth.

"You ought to see them for yourself, Emzara."

Noah caught the end of Gilyon's conversation with Zara as he sat down with a fresh decanter of wine for the table. "What ought she see, Gilyon?"

"I was telling her of the jeweler's guilds in Enoch," replied Gilyon. "In the sixth ring. Orichalcum, silver, gold, electrum—the smiths work them all."

"And you have yet to give me my betrothal gift," Zara said with a wink.

"My apologies, darling." Noah gave her a peck on the cheek. "There you are."

"Really, though, Noah," said Gilyon. "You must bring her to the city one day soon. You are welcome to our home any time, of course. My mother would love you, Emzara."

"Why not come to our city?" Dedroth interjected. He sat on the floor, leaning his back on a thick wooden pillar. "Good trade to be had in the markets there. I would guarantee that few in Enoch have seen or tasted the quality of your fruits, or the excellence of your wine. Why, even one wagon-full of your harvest would fetch a price in the market to match whatever golden bauble you could want."

Gilyon looked above Noah's head, and the farmer sensed that another Naphil had come up behind him. He craned his neck to see who it was.

"Hamerch, you are a *giant*," laughed Zara. "You are supposed to *lumber*."

"Careful with talk of golden baubles, Master Dedroth," Gilyon said. "Else we might find Hamerch picking our pockets."

Hamerch dropped to a crouch and blew a curl of hair from his eyes. "Really, Gilyon. Shall I never hear the end of that sort of thing?"

"You shall hear the end from me." Noah straightened to his full height, even then barely taller than the crouching young giant. "Hamerch of Enoch, son of Dyeus, by the authority granted me by Gloryon of Enoch's guard, on account of what you have done for my family, I release you from my debt."

Zara and Gilyon cheered and clapped, and Hamerch broke into an embarrassed grin. Dedroth clasped his nephew's hand. "Congratulations, my boy," he said in all seriousness. "Do not take such things lightly."

"My pardon, all!" Gloryon stood tall with one raised hand, his giant form seeming too big for the dining hall. "I wish to speak to you all. We Nephilim depart in the morning. Never have I had such gracious hosts."

"And never has anyone deserved it more," said Methuselah. "Each of you has rendered my family and myself a service we can never repay."

"Yet I will ask you to repay us now." Confusion flashed across Methuselah's face, but Gloryon returned it with a smile. "As an elder of Enoch, I request that you, Methuselah, and what members of your house-hold you deem appropriate, would deign to serve as emissaries of Eden to the city of Enoch, and that formal and friendly relations commence heretofore between our lands."

Silence reigned in the room. From the looks that passed among the Nephilim, Noah ascertained that none of them had been informed of Gloryon's request, but the looks were not unpleasant. Dedroth, Hoduín, and the younger giants actually looked quite pleased, and the tilt of Pethun's head to Dyeus indicated nothing more than an apathetic "it is what it is."

Methuselah furrowed his brow. "I, ah…"

"I have spoken to Enosh already, and he has given me his blessing. I know your lands have no rulers, but he is eldest of eldest, and it seemed proper to me. Come, Methuselah. Neither of us has any part in the history of enmity between our ancestors. We have a chance now to start anew. What say you?"

Methuselah closed his eyes for a moment, the only sign of his silent prayer for guidance. He opened them again. "Very well, Gloryon. I accept your offer, and gladly." Scattered applause started with Hoduín and erupted into a dozen excited conversations.

"Well, Noah?" Gilyon grinned. "What excuse have you left? The harvest is finished. Your grandfather will not object. Let us go to Enoch together."

"Yes, Noah, let's," said Zara, hugging his arm.

"Fine, fine!" Noah held up his hands in mock surrender. "We will go to Enoch!"

The remainder of the evening was spent deciding who would go and what they would take with them. Methuselah chose Lamech to come, while Rakeel would take charge of the farm in their absence. Noah and Zara, Jonan, Merim, and Hadishad made up the remainder of the party. Edna would not leave charge of the household to anyone else and declined her invitation to be included, but Noah's mother Betenos agreed to accompany them. The next morning was spent in a flurry of activity: wagons were loaded, goods were fetched from the village for trade on behalf of various cheesemakers, weavers, bakers, and potters of Eden, and Methuselah personally escorted Deneresh on a tour of the cellars to choose barrels of wine to sell in Enoch's markets. By the time the morning mists had risen to become a light shower, a long caravan of indriks, camels, aurochs, and crested dragons was facing east and ready to depart. Noah and Zara sat side-by-side beneath the awning of a wine-laden wagon pulled by oxen. "When last I began this road," Noah said, "I was alone and burdened with many cares. Now, I go with you, and my soul is at ease. I am thankful."

Zara leaned her head on his shoulder. "Good will come of this journey," he whispered to her, stroking her rain-dampened hair. "Nothing but good."

Mareth slept until his father woke him by uprooting the center pole of his tent.

"Up and ready! We are leaving!"

Mareth sat up, blinking his eyes. "When?"

"Now," Dyeus replied. "Get dressed. Your indrik is saddled."

While the tent around him began to disappear, Mareth threw on a longer riding tunic, hooded and sleeveless. He checked to make sure the one hunting trophy he had kept was secure; it was, tied tightly to his thigh.

After the battle with the leviathan, Mareth had tried to drown his shame in the blood of the hunt. Days had passed, kills were made, and he had traveled on, with only his own morbid thoughts for company.

He had stumbled onto the hut far into the wilderness of the hills. The stone-and-wood structure had been empty, but the hairy goat-ante-lopes in back were evidence of residence, as was the thin stream of smoke that drifted out of the crude chimney. He had not been hungry; indeed, he had feasted each night, but only on unseasoned meat cooked over an open flame. An outbuilding stood near the hut, door ajar. He had ducked inside, looking for a food store he might borrow from.

A coarse melody sung in a deep, earthy bass interrupted his search. He saw the singer before he himself was seen: a burly man, tall for a human, with wild black hair and beard came up the path. The man carried an axe over one shoulder and held a mass of honeycomb. When the man saw Mareth, his eyes widened in surprise and fear. He dropped the honeycomb and clutched his axe.

"Away, demon!" The hill man's eyes stayed wide and white, but Mareth recognized fear giving way to rage. He had no time to speak; the man champed and barreled toward him growling, axe cocked to swing. The man's rage was contagious. Mareth caught it.

After it was finished, Mareth cleaned his knives in the trickling stream behind the hut. The goat-antelopes he ate that night, all three, roasted with spices and nuts. The jars of milk he drank, but he stored the mounds of soft cheese in a sack to take with him. He pulled out the man's teeth, slightly bothered at first by the fact that the wet sound of each pull did not disturb him in the slightest, but the feeling passed.

Mareth plucked out strands of the long black hair and wove them together. He strung the teeth on the cord of hair, then let it dangle in front of his face. For a while, he had just stared at it, replaying in his head the drawing of his knives, the agile dodge of a powerful swing, the easy burial of his blade into the man's back. The howling of dire wolves snapped him out of his macabre reverie. He kicked the corpse face-up. The blood on the ground would draw the wolves, not that Mareth had feared anyone would have discovered the body anyway. He considered waiting for the wolves, but decided that the presence of bait was not sporting, despite the likelihood of the greater numbers of a pack.

Mareth tied the string of teeth around his thigh. He scooped a handful of honey and wax from the comb still lying where the man had dropped it, and then he went on his way into the wild darkness.

‹ CHAPTER 20 ›

The highest spires of the Grigori palace shone and shimmered in the light of the morning. The reflected light was multihued, changing with the course of the sun. Dawn's faint, pearly glow had shifted to a bright, clean white. It would soon fade to golden in the afternoon, and in the evening, the spires would gleam orange, like a candle's flame. This was the home that Barkayal of the *bene Elohim* built for his wife Agrat.

Fluted flowers grew in bold, colorful masses in the spire gardens overlooking the sea. Hummingbirds hovered and flitted about the beds, throats and wings shining like ruby and topaz. Agrat reclined on a gilded bench set amongst the flowers. She wore gemstones in silver settings around her neck, waist, and wrists, matching the birds in jeweled splendor. She wore nothing else, and she was perfectly still.

Barkayal squinted in ardent concentration, looking at his beloved wife, then at the stretched canvas upon which he painted. At points his eyes would adopt a faint shine, supplementing an artist's vision with that of a watcher angel. Agrat's pose was innocent, yet seductive, a tantalizing juxtaposition that he intended to capture fully. He stared for a moment at his wife.

"Have I told you," asked Barkayal, focusing back on the canvas' image, "that your beauty surpasses even that of the starry night sky?" Agrat's mouth shaped a satisfied smile, but she did not otherwise move or speak. At this point in the painting process, the pose was preeminent.

For a while, the only movements were the hummingbirds darting to and fro and Barkayal's brushstrokes. The Grigori's frequent glances to his voluptuous model began to linger; the appraising eye of an artist became the smoldering gaze of a lover. He stepped from behind his canvas.

"This session is finished for now." Barkayal untied the embroidered sash that served as his tunic's belt as he strode towards his wife. Agrat laughed and shifted her hips to adopt a pose much less innocent than her previous.

"Agrat, darling!" A woman's voice carried up from the spiraling staircase that led to the garden's pavilions.

Agrat closed her eyes and sighed in frustration. "One moment, Lilith."

Lilith certainly heard, but she did not pause, entering the garden as Agrat was fastening the delicate golden neck-clasp of a thin silk robe. Azazyel followed Lilith, nodding at Barkayal, who had retreated to his painting.

"I apologize for the intrusion," Azazyel said to his fellow Grigori. "A fine morning as this is ought to be enjoyed with one's wife. Alone." He looked pointedly at Lilith, too obviously a husband denied, at least for the moment.

"This simply could not wait," said Lilith breathlessly, mostly to Agrat. "My root cuttings this morning spoke of something of supreme importance beginning today, and that it might be seen coming from the coastline. You have the best view, darling." She took Agrat's hand and pulled her over to the flowered balcony.

After appreciating the swaying hips of their women walking away from them, the Grigori followed. "Do you have the cutting still?" asked Barkayal.

"See for yourself." Lilith gave him the small root, dozens of slices and slivers peeled back but still tenuously attached to the main body.

Barkayal took it, turned it, then frowned. "Indeed, something approaches. The portent is clear. But there is an illness about it that I do not like, though I cannot say exactly what."

"Examine mine."

Samyaza stood behind them, one hand folded nonchalantly behind his back. He offered Barkayal another cut root. It shared a pattern with Lilith's, but the cuts were fuller, more detailed. To Barkayal's divining eye, it was like examining a living rose compared to a finely-crafted golden sculpture of one.

"Yes…it is subtle. Momentous events come swiftly, that is to be sure, but there is an underlying promise of tragedy."

"But for whom?" asked Samyaza. "I cannot tell."

Barkayal shook his head.

"My lords, do not find dark omens where there may be none," said Lilith. "A student I may be compared with your excellent skills, but for myself, I read none of that."

Azazyel cared none for the divinations of his fellows and his wife. His interests were in earthly things—the strength of man, the beauty of woman—and he had contributed to the lesser creations accordingly. It had been Azazyel, he who had captained against Lucifer's rebels under Michael the Archangel, who had first taught the sons of Cain the arts of war. It had been he who had shown Cain's daughters how to magnify their beauty with powders and pigments, had shown them how to wield their natural powers over men with more surety and skill than a lifelong warrior with a sword and spear. This being so, he had stopped listening to the conversation on roots as soon as it began. He now peered over the garden's balcony at the coastline, winding like a vein of silver to the horizon.

The vision of the human form Azazyel had adopted was excellent, but only as good as the keenest eyesight of a mortal man. That was enough for him to spy the dark specks on the coastal road several minutes before Lilith and Agrat shouted their own discovery. He spent those minutes not in a futile effort to ascertain details beyond the capability of the human eye; instead, the white blaze of his angelic spirit's vision searched for that which was veiled from mundane sight.

He recoiled as if he had been struck, and the reaction drew immediate attention from Samyaza and Barkayal. Their eyes blazed white.

"Our sons return," said Barkayal.

Agrat looked out again, shading her eyes with her hand. "All of them?" she asked excitedly.

Lilith narrowed her eyes. "And why would such news make you start so, dear husband?"

"They do not return alone," Azazyel replied. He tossed his hand in the general direction of the coastline, as if waving off a gnat. "They bring the spawn of the Scribe with them."

He turned to Samyaza. "We need to deal with this now. We spent far too long putting out the Scribe's flames last time."

Agrat moved toward the staircase. Barkayal stopped her with a gentle touch on the small of her back. "I go to meet my son and grandsons," she answered his unspoken question. "And I cannot very well meet them dressed in this." She kissed him quickly and hurried to her chambers, Lilith following closely after.

As Barkayal scrutinized and compared the two root cuttings, Azazyel gripped Samyaza's forearm. "Enoch almost ruined us. His progeny are not welcome here."

"Calm yourself," Samyaza said. "They do not know enough to be of any danger to us." He raised his chin and peered down his nose at Azazyel. "Perhaps you should concern yourself with your son. His defiance of us is what began all of this, if you recall."

Anger darkened the Grigori's countenance. "I recall."

"We must meet with the Edenites, regardless. Come, let us join our wives" Barkayal said. Then, realizing the impossibility of Samyaza's doing so, he bowed and said, "I apologize, my friend. I chose my words poorly."

For a moment, the Grigori leader's face twisted in still-raw pain and grief, but he composed himself. "We need not plan a course of action now. Barkayal is right. Come, Azazyel—and behave yourself."

Samyaza and Barkayal exited the gardens, leaving Azazyel alone. He ground his teeth—a habit of the flesh that he had found to be quite calming, in a violent sort of way—and clenched his fists once, then twice. Then, in a literal flash, his hand moved like a spark from a flint. His fingers curled in a gentle cage around a hummingbird with feathers the color of jade and a sapphire tuft at its throat. It cocked its head, as if in inquiry, then gave a futile flap of feathers. Azazyel looked at it, then squeezed, eliciting a terrified chirp. He opened his hand; the bird was alive, but it hopped pitifully on one leg, and its wings were broken. Azazyel tossed it over the edge of the balcony and left to join his fellows.

‹ CHAPTER 21 ›

The council of Enoch had little to do. Before his death, Cain had been the final authority in serious city matters. The council, originally brought together by Cain's grandson Irad, had merely served as advisors of sorts, privy to Cain's plans but only marginally involved in actual city planning and dispute resolution. When Cain passed, his son took his place as the leader of the city bearing his name, but when the Grigori had come, Enoch receded to a figurehead, happy to live out his days in comfort and wealth. Still, the council endured, and they even now considered themselves the ultimate authority in Enoch. Why bother with the burden, though, when angels were happy to shoulder it for you?

The group of men had greatly expanded over the centuries; even old Irad still attended, and with the exceptions of Cain and Enoch, who were never really members anyway, the council had been depleted by just two: Enoch's third son had disappeared with a mistress, and his notorious great-great-grandson Lamech had removed himself after his infamous incident. Every generation had added its own illustrious and noted individuals to the council, and it had swollen to a collection of several hundred of the most gifted and talented men in Enoch's thousand-year history.

Despite the apathetic approach to governance adopted by the council, the young and ambitious men of Enoch still strived for a seat. The daily gathering of Enoch's eldest, best, and brightest was where deals were made, trade alliances were formed, and favors were traded back and forth like trinkets in the market. Many on the council were rich and worked hard to become richer, and all enjoyed the prestige that came from holding a seat, but few were true leaders. This, thought many of the elder members, explained the meteoric rise of Gloryon, son of Lilith, in the esteem of the council and the citizenry at large.

He was the firstborn of the Nephilim, two months older than Dedroth, son of Naamah. At thirteen he towered over the members of the guard garrison he had joined, and at fourteen he led them. He married Jet, daughter of the house of Aleum, when he was twenty-four, instantly becoming the object of hatred of a dozen powerful suitors; most of those would now follow Gloryon into mortal peril. His exploits with the city guard made him famous, and his fairness and sense of justice as its leader made him loved.

The men of the council met in a hall adjacent to the Grigori's audience chambers. To this place Gloryon led Methuselah, Lamech, and Noah. It was built in the old style of the original council hall in the third circle of the city, now claimed by Irad for his familial dwelling. Connected to the hall by walkways and tunnels were offices, lounges, stables, and bathhouses. A staff of aides and servants was housed full-time in the basements, and many of the council members lived for weeks, even months at a time in the palace halls, never needing to set foot in Enoch's streets.

Inside the walls of Enoch, the caravan from Eden split up. Jonan, Merim, and Hadishad, along with Hoduín and his sons, went with the trade goods to the houses of Dyeus and his kin, to unload and store for an early trip to the markets tomorrow. At Gloryon's suggestion, Gilyon escorted Betenos and Emzara to meet Jet and refresh themselves from long days of journeying. Methuselah, Lamech, and Noah followed Gloryon to the council hall. Although Noah had seen the sights of the city already—the great black wall, the craftsmanship and splendor of the palaces—experiencing it with his father and grandfather, whose eyes widened at each new wonder, rekindled his original sense of awe. The pride Gloryon had for his city showed in his knowledge of its history and lore, and he talked while they walked.

"And that," said Gloryon, "is how a ratcatcher became regent of the Ingari district."

"Is that not something," Methuselah said, while Lamech nodded appreciatively.

"And here we are!" The giant turned past two silent city guards into a terraced courtyard decorated with statuary, the majority depicting upright men in noble poses. Past the courtyard was the face of a wide building, blocky and primitive compared to the fluted columns and flowing spirals of the Grigori architecture. While the farmers absorbed their surroundings, Gloryon strode to a man tending a serpentine garden running through the statues. The Naphil leaned down and spoke to the man, who bowed and hurried into the hall.

Gloryon called Noah, Lamech, and Methuselah over. "The council will be gathered shortly. Come, I shall show you where you may wash and refresh yourselves."

"We are to be presented?" Noah asked.

"Why wait?" replied Gloryon. "We are men of action. Before the hour is out, a new chapter shall begin in our histories, and Enoch and Eden shall be recognized, at long last, as friends."

A basin of warm water, a vial of sandalwood oil, and another of the clever flushing toilets waited for Noah inside the hall's labyrinthine bathhouse. After refreshing himself, he met his father and grandfather in an antechamber, the spacious meeting hall visible past an open doorway framed in thick polished granite. Men, few of whom appeared younger than several centuries, filed into the hall and found seats around the steeply-sloping crescent-shaped gallery. They were dressed in formal tunics of ivory-white, dark green, or greyed blues and purples, some accented with fur stoles or leather belts, capes of silk or flaxen robes. For the most part, the conservative sartorial sense of the body had evidently reached a critical mass generations ago, and the fashions on the streets of Enoch had not much affected it.

Gloryon entered the antechamber, dressed in clean tunic the color of cornflower, heavily embroidered in silver on the chest and shoulders, long front and back panels hanging to the floor beneath a woven silver belt. A thin young man in robes, with a hood fallen around his head, stood beside him. Gloryon gave the farmers a reassuring smile.

"When the chorister announces us, follow me and stand behind." He nodded at the robed man, who glided into the chamber. The man waited for the scattered conversations to cease. In a clear tenor, he chanted a few rising notes, then called in an echoing voice, "Gloryon of Enoch, son of Azazyel Grigori and Lilith of Enoch, to present Methuselah of Eden, his son Lamech of Eden, and his son's son Noah of Eden before the council. All attend!"

An unanticipated wave of visceral terror, greater than anything that had been inspired by the leviathan, swept over Noah and threatened to shake his quivering knees out from under him. He steeled himself and took one deep, shuddering breath. Then, with a prayer to the Creator God, and like a chick under a protective wing, he followed Gloryon into the meeting chamber of the council of Enoch.

Granite columns spaced the walls of the hall like ribs, with rows of seats filling the wide intervals between. The columns swept high toward the tall ceiling, meeting their opposite fellows in arches from which fell banners adorned with the mark of Cain. Noah found himself, with Gloryon and his father and grandfather, standing in a circular recess in the stone floor. Light shone from above, and Noah glanced up. The sunshine streaming through the hall's many windows illuminated the chambers, but the recess was lit brighter by means of the dome in the ceiling directly above them, made of crystals and mirrored glass that seemed to gather the light and reflect it invariably in the same direction, straight downwards. Noah felt bare and uncomfortable in the light; Gloryon, however, seemed to become greater, taller. The sharp shadows on his face, cast by the brightness from above, gave the Naphil an air, an aura, that he was a being above mere mortal man. Noah, like his father and grandfather before him, had never been a great respecter of persons, but in that moment, he knew that Gloryon would bend the council in whatever way the Naphil wanted. His unease evaporated. He straightened his back, tilted his chin up, and waited for the proceedings to unfold.

"Honored council, fellow citizens of Enoch, hear me." Gloryon spoke loudly, and his voice echoed around the chamber. "This day I present to you these men from the land of Eden, our close neighbors, whose people, like ours, are peace-loving and industrious. We have much to offer one another, in both culture and trade. The time is long past for the enmity of history between our peoples to dissolve. This being true, I do hereby propose to this body the formal and immediate establishment of relations between the noble city of Enoch and the free lands of Eden. I leave you now to consider this proposal in good faith and wisdom."

Gloryon bowed. He looked back at the men from Eden and gestured with one mammoth outstretched arm. Methuselah, Lamech, and Noah turned to look behind them. In the dim, flat light outside the radiance of the recess, a guard of Enoch stood and motioned them to follow him. They did so, while Gloryon walked to the side of the hall to take a seat on floor pillows, next to several other Nephilim who Noah did not recognize. He did notice Tubal-Cain sitting several rows above the floor, with men of similar features who Noah guessed were the smith's brothers. Whispered exclamations and conversations lit up the hall like a hundred candle flames, creating a low buzz that filled the chamber.

"This way," the guard whispered to the Edenites. They followed him to a raised section of seating behind the illuminated recess, bordered with columns decorated with stylized birds, bulls, and lions. From there the entire council could be seen; Noah also noticed for the first time several low balconies full of people obviously not of the council.

"Observation galleries, for the citizenry," whispered the guard, following Noah's gaze. "I am Malidoch, lieutenant-chief of the guard of Enoch. Gloryon is my nephew."

Lamech craned his neck to take a better look at the man. "From his mother's side, I assume," he said with a smile.

Malidoch smiled back, but only one side of his mouth pulled up; the left side drooped low, slightly parted, and his left eye remained hidden by an unmoving eyelid, with only a sliver of white sclera visible above a sagging lower lid. A jagged scar ran from his hairline past his ear to end at his jawline. He made no notice of the farmers' recognition of the defect, but only answered, "Indeed. His mother Lilith is my elder sister."

"Well met," Methuselah said quietly, and introduced them by name. "What happens now?"

"Now, the council talks." Malidoch remained standing, but leaned a shoulder against one of the pillars. "I advise you to get comfortable. This may take a while."

The chorister's voice pierced the low din, and all quieted. "Irad, son of Enoch, wishes to address this body." An elderly man, thin but not yet frail, with a flat mouth and a straight grey bristle of beard that sprouted down like a broom, stood and swept his gaze over the council. His eyes settled on Gloryon, and he spoke.

"You have accomplished much, Gloryon, and have served our people well. But you are young still." He addressed the entire assembly. "Do you all not recall the reason for this city's being? Our father Cain was banished, to wander as a wild beast! He found a home, though, and it has become our home as well, and it has become great, it is true! But this city of Enoch was borne of exile—exile from the very lands and people to whom we are now asked to extend a hand of friendship. To our father Cain this idea would have been anathema. Without opining on the merits of our guests from Eden, I ask you to remember our history." Irad sat. Lamech snorted, clenching his jaw to contain a retort. Noah knew what his father was thinking, for he was thinking the same. Cain cast as a victim? Revisionist history at its most obscene!

A Naphil stood from his seat on the floor by Gloryon, red hair falling around his shoulders in a nest of braids. His sage-green tunic was decorated with intricate patterns that wove in and out like impossible knots. A simple cudgel hung at his belt.

"That is Dagdha, son of Tamiel Grigori." Apparently Malidoch would keep up a much-needed commentary. Noah nodded his silent appreciation and listened.

"If I recall the old stories correctly, honored Irad, Cain's exile *was* his anathema—a divine punishment for killing his brother," the Naphil said. A few of the elder council members shook their hoary heads and murmured. Dagdha held up a massive hand. "I mean no disrespect to our father Cain, and I have no part in judging what he did. But it *is* history. We cannot change it, and neither can these men from Eden. We must look to the future. If Gloryon sees value in this alliance, I shall support its creation." Dagdha sat.

Before the Naphil's hindquarters touched the ground, a wild-eyed man in a hooded, unadorned tunic was already out of his seat.

"The people of your land are of pure human blood?" the man asked loudly. Several hisses slithered about the chamber. With surprise, Noah realized that the question had been addressed in their direction. He and Lamech looked to Methuselah, who haltingly stood.

"We have no children of the Grigori among us, if that is what you mean," Methuselah said. The man smiled smugly, but Methuselah continued. "In our lands, the character of a man is judged by his actions, not his ancestry, and I speak for my son and grandson in saying that seldom have we seen the high quality of character and selfless heroism shown by the sons of the Grigori." He sat. Lamech clapped him on the back.

The man's smug smile stayed in place. "But there are no stray *bene Elohim* or half-blooded Nephilim in Eden. That is all I need know." To the council, he shouted, "I and my fellows approve wholeheartedly this alliance." With that, he sat, oblivious to the unfriendly glowering aimed at him from other council members.

"Onim." Malidoch said the man's name like a curse. "Racist bastard. One day he will go too far. But you spoke well, Methuselah." Methuselah did not reply, but stared at Onim with a furrowed brow, lost in thought.

A heavy-framed man in silk robes stood next. Black fur lined his sleeves and collar, and a golden clasp in the shape of Cain's mark held an ornate cape that draped behind him. He had the look of a once-powerful man gone soft: an iron jaw become meaty jowels, a muscular chest and shoulders whose bulk had migrated to rest around a thick belly. An enormous-eyed tarsier with tiny jeweled rings on each of its long, tapered fingers and pierced through its ears clutched the man's still-broad shoulder.

"Raposh, head of Enoch's merchant guild," whispered Malidoch. "One guess as to his interest in this matter."

Raposh cleared his throat. "Our trusted colleague Gloryon has spoken of industry and trade. I would know more of these, if one of our visitors would be so accommodating."

A familiar, booming voice filled the hall. "Why not experience the offerings of Eden yourself, Raposh?"

Dyeus, with his brothers behind, took the illuminated recession in the hall floor as if he owned it. The light from above him flashed off the silver trim of his dress tunic; Pethun was dressed in deep blue, and even Dedroth hadtraded his dusty greatcoat for robes of dusky grey. "I hereby invite all council members gathered here to a feast at the estate of the sons of Samyaza, celebrating our great victory over the indomitable leviathan of Eden, and our newfound friendship with the proud men of that land. Rest assured, the trade to be had with Eden is excellent and bountiful, as you may all see for yourself tonight. Until then!" The three Nephilim made their way across the floor to a section where Noah noticed Hoduín, Tevesh, and Tiras had quietly taken up seats. Dyeus winked in the farmers' direction as he sat.

A small-but-weighty leather bag dropped in Noah's lap.

"A bit of spending money, brother?" Jonan took a seat behind Noah, having entered the seating area from a passage at its back.

"What was all that about, son?" Lamech asked in a low voice.

"When we arrived at Dyeus' storehouses, he purchased half the goods we brought with us," Jonan whispered excitedly. "Merim and Hadishad stayed with the rest, along with the chests of gold Dyeus paid. A generous price, too—although he no doubt plans to profit much."

"I trust you were fair about it," said Methuselah. "Come, let us listen."

"If there is no further discussion wanted, let this body come to a vote," intoned the chorister. "In favor of the proposal of alliance between Enoch and Eden made by Gloryon of Enoch, those will now stand."

Almost all stood. Onim sprang to his feet before even Gloryon, joined by Raposh, Dagdha, an expressionless Tubal-Cain, and several hundred others. Even Irad, among his grey-haired cohorts, slowly rose to his feet as he saw the inevitable, although he did not look pleased about it.

"Is this it?" Lamech whispered to Methuselah, an odd lilt to his voice that drew Noah's attention.

"What, father?" asked Noah. "You look as you did when Hadishad was born."

"I only wonder—this restoration of relations between the sons of Adam and of Cain, a new age of prosperity and trade, an avenue to bring the words of the Creator to this lost people—you brought it all about, son. Is this the fulfillment of your prophecy?" Lamech squeezed Noah's shoulder. "Well, if it is or not, I am proud of you."

"The Creator's will be done," added Methuselah.

The chorister motioned for the council to be seated, singing a low note that rose in pitch and volume until none were left standing. Any further vote was unnecessary; the young man spoke. "Be it then confirmed by this body that the city of Enoch-"

A door slammed, and a sibilant voice called, "One moment, please." It was not a request. A cacophony of mutterings gibbered through the hall as heads turned towards the interruption.

"Well, this just became more interesting," Malidoch intoned flatly, craning his head to see the new arrivals as they walked down an aisle hidden to the seated farmers.

"What is happening, Malidoch?" asked Methuselah.

The lieutenant-chief looked at him with his sole functioning eyebrow raised.

"The Grigori are here."

‹ CHAPTER 22 ›

The three *bene Elohim* glided onto the council hall floor. They did not stop at the illuminated recess. They had no need. All attention was already fixed on the Grigori, each glowing subtly as if every stray particle of the hall's diffuse light was a moth, and they the flames.

Azazyel spoke first, and his saccharine words were directed towards his son. "Gloryon," he said, "how good to see you safe in Enoch once more. But why came you to this place before seeing your own mother? She searched for you so."

Had Gloryon been a youth, this veiled mockery would have brought laughter from many of the men in the hall. His reputation had long ago passed into unquestioned respect, though, and the silence in the hall brought a scowl to Azazyel's face.

The Naphil regarded his father calmly. "I will visit her soon, certainly. As you can see, this council had pressing matters of state to attend to. We are concluded now."

"Are you?" Barkayal slid forward, holding Samyaza's cut root. "I would have you make a more informed decision. Let all you who divine examine this now, then say if you would still have these men from Eden as friends."

Several men and Nephilim stood, Hoduín first among them. The chorister brought a thin, carved wooden pedestal to the floor, upon which the root was placed. A slight, smooth-faced man, on whose cowl perched several bright passerines of varied hues, was the first to circle the root. He looked, but did not touch. One bird on his shoulder flapped as he stepped back.

"What do you see, Sheyzan?" asked a younger man.

"My powers lie with augury. I have no gift for cuttings." Sheyzan shook his head. "Hoduín?"

The bearded Naphil was already staring at the root. He picked it up in one giant hand, holding it with the tips of his fingers and turning it. After a quiet spell, he replaced it.

"Have you seen, my son?" Barkayal asked.

Hoduín leaned in and narrowed his eyes. "I see the sea, or the coast. I see a band of men, uncommon men. I see great change coming to Enoch." He stretched to his full height. "One might argue, my father, that the divination here has been fulfilled today."

"No. *No.* That is not all." Barkayal almost shouted. "Have all of you learned nothing? There is doom here—for those wise enough to see it." He glared at the gathered diviners, a derisive sneer gathering on his handsome features, and despite the presence of his son and a few other giants who towered over him, he managed to somehow give the distinct impression of looking down on them. He snatched the root and held it over his head.

"Listen to me!" he addressed the council, speaking as he slowly turned. "This cutting presages suffering, but it does not have to be. Send these men back from whence they came, in peace—but send them. Will you trust the wisdom of the Grigori in this, as you have in the past?"

Gloryon stood again. "Wise Barkayal, I do not doubt you, though I find myself loathe to doubt your son's wisdom either. But my question is this: how do you know that this suffering you see is brought by these humans? We Nephilim traveled with them from the coast. Can you be sure that it is they, and not we, of whom this divination speaks? Shall we, too, be sent away? All on account of a piece of root?"

Lamech muttered in Noah's ear. "What business do these *bene Elohim* have, dabbling in this sorcery? It is an affront to their Maker." He did not speak loudly, but the ears of the Grigori proved to be sharper than the farmer had known mortal man to have. Both Azazyel and Samyaza whipped their beautiful faces towards him.

"*What* did you say, man from Eden?" Azazyel spit out the words.

Malidoch whispered out of the functioning side of his mouth. "Careful, man."

Lamech was uncowed. "I asked, son of God, what business has your kind with this base sorcery? The Lord of true prophecies does not approbate such things. You, of all beings, ought to know better. And if know you do, you ought to have a care."

Hoduín leaned his head down to Sheyzan the augur. "See?" he whispered. "This is what these men can offer. Powers to best what even my father can teach us. The future will be ours to know, my friend." Sheyzan nodded, listening with rapt attention, along with the other diviners of Enoch.

Nostrils flaring, Azazyel's eyes blazed bright. He glared at Lamech as if he were willing the man to die where he stood. "How dare you speak to me so? I watched as your kind was fashioned from *dirt*! And as your idiot forebears were cast from the Garden, so we will cast you out."

"Men of Enoch!" the enraged Grigori continued. "You may choose! Shall we *bene Elohim* remain, to instruct you, aid you, make your city the greatest on the earth, as we have all these years? Or will you spurn us for these mud-rakers, these weed-growers? The choice is yours. Be wise about it."

Onim stood. "An easy choice, Watcher! We choose humanity! Humanity!" Amid shouts of concord and discord, Irad called for order and quiet. Gloryon rose, and the council calmed.

"My father. Why ask this council to make a choice that is unnecessary? Of course, the presence of the Grigori as Enoch's benefactors is desired and honored. But much benefit to this city might also be gained by friendship with Eden." He stepped onto the hall floor, a giant stride closer to Azazyel. "If you leave on account of the Edenites, the choice will be yours, not ours. Meanwhile, this council must do what is best for Enoch."

Azazyel smirked. "This council. What does this council know of what is best for anyone?"

Somehow, Gloryon seemed to grow even taller. "This council, of which I am a member by right through the blood of my mother Lilith, is the ruling body of Enoch. The Grigori have aided us in charting a course for our people. Now, if they wish to diverge from that course, they are welcome. This council will continue."

Dagdha's clap was slow and hollow. In his periphery, Noah saw nods of approval from dozens of heads, but he barely noticed. He was drawn fully into the family drama playing out on the council hall floor: Gloryon, giant, a leader of men five times his age, standing over his father Azazyel Grigori, a being not born of earth, furious eyes aflame. One thing and one thing only could have drawn his attention away, and at that moment she walked quietly, wide-eyed, into the audience balconies: Zara.

Entering arm-in-arm with Betenos, she wore a dress that was simple but stunning, cut off one shoulder in sophisticated asymmetry. Noah had never seen it before; he guessed that it was borrowed from Jet, who followed Zara into the balcony. Lilith walked in behind her daughter-in-law, satin-draped curves catching glances like honey catches flies. Gilyon escorted the four women, coming in last. When he recognized the ongoing confrontation on the floor, he motioned the women to sit.

Noah's eyes were not the only ones drawn to the newcomers. Azazyel's gaze latched onto Lilith's as she sat; naturally, Gloryon's followed, and Jet met him with a slightly worried look on her face, wondering what exactly was transpiring.

Samyaza noted Azazyel's distraction, and he looked up at the balconies to find the reason for it. A quiet heartbeat passed. In that pause, and with a quickened pulse, Samyaza spoke. "Please, noble councilmen, forgive our intrusion. Only consider our concerns, I ask, but we will not attempt to force our will on you any further." He bowed, flashed his eyes almost imperceptibly at Barkayal and a stunned Azazyel, and led them out of the hall. Gloryon let out his breath, and Noah noticed for the first time that he had been holding his own. Methuselah opened his eyes—"Praying, likely," thought Noah—while Lamech noticed Betenos for the first time and gave her a wan smile of feigned assurance.

"Harmph." Irad cleared his throat. "With that, I call this council's business concluded. On behalf of the city of Enoch, I formally recognize the reparation of relations with the land of Eden. This council is adjourned."

"Hnh," grunted Malidoch as the council members filed from the hall. "*That* was not ordinary."

Methuselah held his hand out to the disfigured man, a piece of gold palmed in it. "For your help and trouble."

"No trouble. Just duty." Malidoch waved his hand away. "And if you will excuse me, there are more that I must attend to."

"And we as well," Lamech said, smiling as he spotted Betenos and Emzara descending a wide, curving staircase from the observation balconies. Gilyon and Jet came after; Lilith was nowhere to be seen, presumably off searching for Azazyel. The two groups met at the foot of the stairs, Lamech taking Betenos' arm and Noah taking Zara's. Gloryon soon joined them, finding his towering son in the milling, but thinning, crowd with ease.

"Do not bring trouble to yourself for our sake," Methuselah said to the Naphil.

"I only do what I believe is best for my people," replied Gloryon. "My father will not try to thwart the council's will. Between Samyaza and my mother, his anger will subside."

Zara leaned in close to Noah as they exited the council hall. "Trouble?"

"Politics, more like. We have a great ally in Gloryon, though."

"Should I worry about you?"

Noah kissed her forehead. "Never. I lie safely in the hands of the Creator."

"Noah! Zara!" In the street, Hadishad was mounted on a crested dragon, waving his hand. A long, open carriage, six-wheeled, was harnessed to the dragon, and the now-expansive party was already climbing in. "How went the council meeting?"

"Long story, little brother," said Noah while he helped Zara up the steps.

"Tell me later, then," answered Hadishad. "Right now, we must make our way to Dyeus' estate." He patted his lean abdomen. "It's time to feast."

Samyaza, Azazyel, and Barkayal walked at a rapid pace through an unlit tunnel, one of many that formed a maze that ran underneath the palaces and halls of the ninth circle. A man would have stumbled about in the pitch blackness; to the Grigori's blazing-white vision they now employed, the path might as well have been bathed in midday sunlight.

Azazyel's fury blazed as well, a rabid, mad morass of anger towards the Edenites, his mutinous son, and the human dirt-creatures in general. He attempted to contain it, an exercise he practiced less and less these days, but one red-hot spurt escaped.

"And what was *that*, Samyaza?" he growled. "Are we now thralls for the humans to dismiss as they please? Has your sorrow weaken-"

The back of Samyaza's hand flashed up and returned to his side, the only evidence of its movement the red mark on Azazyel's face.

"Peace now," the Grigori leader said. "This situation has become far more complex. I would value your advice, my brother, but you must *be quiet*."

"What mean you, Samyaza?" asked Barkayal. "What did you see in that hall?"

An image flashed in the minds of Azazyel and Barkayal: the face of a young woman, not much more than a girl, eyes widened with wonder and worry and all the more beautiful for it. She was followed by several faces, some familiar—Lilith's painted face and sensual lips, young Gilyon, a strong-faced woman about Lilith's age, the petite and cultured lady Jet. The image sprang back to the first girl, though, details sharpening and brightening. Her dress, though attractive, was nothing. Far more fascinating was the lithe body, unpampered and accustomed to activity, the smooth, tanned skin of a woman who spent her youth in the sun, the golden-brown hair that begged for a lover's hands to run through it.

The image lasted less than a second, but the imprint of it was timeless. Azazyel and Barkayal understood its import instantly.

"So that is your game," said a softened Azazyel.

"No game, my friend," answered Samyaza. "You see why I need your help. Ask Lilith about her. Find out all you can."

Samyaza smiled in the darkness, as he had not since before Naamah's death.

"I would know more about the bride I have chosen."

‹ CHAPTER 23 ›

Lilith found her husband in the grotto below the palace, completely submerged in a pool at the foot of the hot springs. She watched him floating, naked, eyes closed, just below the surface. She leaned over the water and whispered.

"Azazyel, my love."

The Grigori's eyes snapped open. In one breath he was out of the water, standing in front of her. Lilith shuddered, still in awe of his perfect form after all these years. She tilted her head to meet his eyes.

"First I cannot find Gloryon," she said, "and then you disappear. What—"

He kissed her violently, leaving a spot of blood on her lip. She licked it off, shuddered again.

"Speak not our son's name to me," Azazyel rasped. "This day has been tense. I need release."

Lilith melted into him.

Afterwards, in their private chambers, Lilith lay in a stupor. She sprawled on a sea of pillows, slowly blowing thin lines of smoke that curled about the dimly-lit room and collected in the ceiling's coffers. The poppy tears made her feel as if she were liquid, or light—an unexplainable feeling, really—and they also dulled her pain. Azazyel was not gentle.

He watched her, unblinking, and she began to laugh uncontrollably. When her fit subsided, he was still staring.

"What?" She giggled.

"You fascinate me," he said.

Lilith laughed again and drew on the long ivory pipe. She extended her neck as she blew a ribbon of smoke from her nostrils. Azazyel traced a finger from her shoulder to the back of her ear.

"Who were those women with you in the council hall?" he asked.

Lilith sighed at his touch, then seemed to realize he had asked a question. "Why, my husband, do you ask about other women?" she asked back, with no hint of jealousy.

Azazyel's tone was nonchalant. "Only curious. Their dress was as the women of Enoch, but they seemed like in color and face to those men from Eden."

"For good reason," said Lilith. "The elder was the wife of one of them, and the younger is betrothed to her son."

"Noah?"

"That was his name, yes," Lilith said. "Jet said good things about him."

Azazyel ground his teeth. "Jet knows naught of him. And what is the younger one's name?"

She had to fight through the fog in her mind to find the answer. "Emzara. They call her Zara. Quite provincial. Very pretty, though, in her way." Lilith rolled over and set the pipe down on the marble top of a low table. She crawled on all fours over the pillows back to Azazyel, languorously, like thick honey dripping down a spoon. She stretched herself on him. "We are talking too much," she said, slurring slightly. Azazyel did not argue with her.

"Trouble will come of this, Samyaza," Azazyel stated matter-of-factly. He had left Lilith sleeping, or drugged, or fainted, or possibly some combination of the three, to make his report to Samyaza. He had searched for the Grigori leader in the heart of his empty palace, where he was wont to pine since his widowing. The ambling walk over had given Azazyel ample time to consider what he would say. Any attempt to change Samyaza's mind would be futile, he knew; nevertheless, he would present the difficulties as he saw them, and they were not insignificant. A plan had begun to form, though, in the dark, dank recesses of his once-glorious mind, like a web secretly woven by some bloated black spider.

Samyaza's inner sanctum was a treasure trove of art in a variety of media, all featuring one subject: Naamah. Samyaza spent most of his waking hours there, replaying memories both sensual and sweet in an effort to drive away the echoes of his dead wife's last screams. When Naamah was alive, the chamber had been dedicated to her beauty, and had collected almost two centuries' worth of masterpieces done by the world's most gifted sculptors, painters, and muralists. Now it functioned as a shrine of sorts. It was lit by an array of bowl-shaped candles, each placed under one of the works. Azazyel found Samyaza sitting there as if he were stone, the only movement in the room the flickering of the candle's flames on his sculpted face. He gave his report.

"So the girl is 'betrothed,'" said Samyaza, after his fellow Grigori had finished. "A meaningless human contrivance. I care nothing for it."

"But Gloryon will. He will use it as another wedge to drive between us and the council."

"The council will not stand against us over this."

Azazyel paced in front of his leader, never breaking eye contact. "Can you be sure? I think not. Your divinations do not suggest it, and neither does this day's events at the council hall. These damned Edenites…"

The spider in Azazyel's mind wove another thread, and he continued. "Do not forget, Samyaza, our children have spent time with these humans. They have fought and bled with them. Battles can form bonds, my brother. You know this to be true."

Samyaza flashed back to memories as bright and crisp as the present. Shouting for joy, Azazyel beside him, as they watched the first sunless dawn fall across the infant deep in the new world. His being selected to lead a watcher host, choosing his nineteen captains, issuing orders to their company, two hundred shining strong. Gathering intelligence with a hundred burning, unblinking eyes, reporting the rebellion's movements to Michael himself, skirmishing in the timeless realm of eternity with Lucifer's forces in the Seventh Day War. The war was won and the rebels cast out, but the bonds among those two hundred watcher angels, the Grigori, lasted still. Through the task assigned them on the fledgling earth, to watch over the human creations as they multiplied across the face of the land, to the imprecation that led them all to possess their current stations in the mortal realm, the links were inseparable. Because of this, Samyaza knew that Azazyel would stand by him in his choice. Still, his points were salient.

Samyaza rubbed his temples. "You must think for me in this, Azazyel. Zara... My head is full of her. Her face will not leave my vision, even in this place. To touch her, hold her... What must we do?"

"Only recognize the obstacles we face," answered Azazyel. "The council has never contested us like this. They ask themselves even now if the *bene Elohim* are growing weak. As well, the brood of that malcontent Enoch are poised to insert themselves and their zealotry into this city, and one of them is betrothed to your chosen bride." His voice dropped to a whisper. "We have suppressed his followers thus far. You know of what I speak. Let these men into the city, and they could be the flame that lights the conflagration that engulfs us."

Samyaza cursed softly, still massaging his head. Azazyel continued. "Our children, too, become adversarial."

"*Our* children?" Samyaza looked up. "Mine are concerned only with sex and drink. Your son is the one who defied us openly—in front of the entire council, I might add."

"He has power, it is true," Azazyel said, "and more slips to him every day. Gloryon is become the cynosure for the leaders of this city, its guiding light. How long until he desires our own light to die?"

Samyaza seemed to study a cubit-high woodcarving of a nude Naamah posing between two prowling lions, her fingers stroking their manes. He picked up the candle illuminating the carving and turned to Azazyel.

"So, on the one hand, we have Noah and his kin, who you call a 'flame,' with no love for us and who will no doubt fight for Emzara when I take her. On the other, there is Gloryon, the 'guiding light' that burns brighter and brighter against us. What would you do about them?"

Azazyel took the candle from Samyaza. He held it before him, staring at the flickering flame. Without a word, he blew it out.

Samyaza took the candle back, a thin thread of smoke still rising from the dead wick. "Well. You will certainly never be accused of nepotism," he said. "I do not want to know about it." Turning from Azazyel, the Grigori leader sat back down in the middle of the room and sank into his fantasies.

Azazyel grimaced as he left, a sadistic smile that sucked all beauty from his features. The web was complete, the last wet strands in place. None would escape from it, he was sure of that. None.

NOAH AND THE NEPHILIM

THE LANDS OF EDEN AND NOD

NOAH

EMZARA

NOAH AND EMZARA

SAMYAZA, CHIEF OF THE GRIGORI

TEVESH THE NAPHIL

BEN SHEOL

BULLDRAGON VS BENE SHEOL

LEVIATHAN VS TEVESH

CITY OF ENOCH

EYE OF THE LEVIATHAN

‹ CHAPTER 24 ›

"**H**a! I won!" Hadishad placed the jade figure on the highest square. He glanced at Tiras, cross-legged on the floor. "I did win, yes?" Tiras nodded. "Ha!" repeated Hadishad.

Noah sat across the table from his brother over the game they now played in the large, firelit room central to the emissary suites of the council hall. Hadishad had purchased the game that evening, after it had caught his eye in a jeweler's display. The board consisted of alternating dark and light wooden squares arranged in a stairstep pattern, lowest in the middle and rising to the edges, and placed at either side were small sets of fantastical figures, one of jade and one of carnelian. Noah frowned and ran his finger over the unwound scroll that came with the set, looking for the endgame rules.

"Give it up, Noah," Hadishad said. "My otter with the mud armor-"

"Ichneumon," said Tiras.

"—killed your winged dragon fairly. See? I won."

Noah rolled the scroll back up tightly. "May I blame it on my intolerable distraction?" He leaned over and wrapped an arm around Emzara, who had been standing to the side watching. She laughed and jumped into his lap.

"Do you mean me? I am sorry, my love." Zara kissed Noah on the top of his head. "Plan on losing many more games in the future." She picked up one of the red pieces and turned it in her finger. "Winged dragons. Thank the Creator He did not make those."

"There are such creatures as ichneumons," said Tiras. "Although their armor has no spikes or plates."

"Well, even if He gave wings to a dragon, cousin Zara," said Hadishad, "we would kill it as we did the leviathan! What ho, Tiras!" They struck fists.

183

"Who would kill what now?" Jonan strolled into the room, followed by Merim and Methuselah. "Where are mother and father?"

"They 'retired' for the night," Noah answered.

"I do *not* want to know about it," muttered Jonan. He and Merim sat down in the empty chairs by the fireplace. "We did not expect to see you here, Tiras. No mood for feasting?"

"Dyeus' banquets have a way of ending in drunken excess," replied Tiras. "I care not to make a fool of myself—or to see my friends and elders do so."

"Aye, we left when the wine began to flow too freely," said Merim. "And I do like my wine, so be assured it was in excess truly. And now—to bed! Which room is mine?"

"Over there, with me," said Hadishad, pointing. "You had better wash up!" he called, as Merim disappeared.

"So that means I am with you," said Jonan to Noah. "Excellent. Merim snores so."

"Ah, you say everyone snores," complained Merim.

"You would share a room with your brother, Jonan?" asked Tiras.

"Five rooms in the suite, eight of us," said Jonan. "Someone must share."

"I mean...would not Noah rather share a bed with Emzara?"

Zara blushed. "It is our custom to remain chaste until married," said Noah.

"But the answer to your question is 'yes,'" said Jonan in a mock-whisper.

Tiras held up a hand in apology. "I did not mean to embarrass. I only thought, since you were betrothed..."

"Alas, betrothed is not married," sighed Noah. He pulled Zara's face gently to his and kissed her. "First I must build us a home. A man cannot leave his father and mother for his bride if he has nowhere to go, after all. But the wait will be worth it."

Zara returned the kiss, then slipped out of his lap. "You still owe me a betrothal gift..." she lilted. She went to Methuselah and gave him an affectionate hug. "Good-night, Grandfather."

"Good-night, child. Off to bed with you."

"I shall take my leave as well," said Tiras, standing up and seeming to fill the room to the ceiling. "I suspect that more than one member of my house will need help stumbling home. And Noah…when the time comes, I will help you build your home." He bowed and left the room, to general wishes of good-night.

The fire was dying, and the lights of the city flickered like fireflies through the window. They drew Noah, mothlike. As his brother Jonan examined the game pieces on the table, he took his place next to his grand-father, who had been quietly looking out since they had returned. When Methuselah broke his silence, a dull sadness edged his voice.

"Look there, Noah." He pointed out the window to the street below. "That man by the bushes, there along the street. He is dressed as wealthy, well-groomed, yes? Utterly drunk. Twice now I have seen him vomit into the hedge. And there, past the line of lamps. That girl—the one wearing the jewels, and naught else to speak of—she was at the feast. She was talked about in my hearing. A known whore, plying her trade in the open, and the man with her is on the council. A leader of the people, Noah, consorting with a prostitute, and none says a word." He exhaled, an old-sounding sigh that settled poorly on Noah's ears. The weariness evident in his grandfa-ther's voice, in the slump of his shoulders and his filmy eyes, was more than that of long travels and the business of the day. It was the soul's weariness, and it troubled Noah.

"This city…in some ways, it dazzles the senses," continued Methuselah. "The towers, the statues and murals, that magnificent hall—they stretch my dreams, my assumptions of the limits of what a man could do, could build in his lifetime. Yet at the same time, I have already seen such debauchery here that it shames me for them." He backed from the window as the faint sounds of retching reached them. "I fear that this city is dead and dying, Noah, and that all the elegance, the pomp and pulchritude, is nothing more than a beautiful tomb."

Images of the Nephilim he had come to know appeared in Noah's mind's eye—Gloryon, Hamerch, Tiras, flesh peeling off bone under sunken, lifeless eyes. He shook his head to clear it.

"If dead and dying these people are, Grandfather," he said, "then we must show them how to live."

Ribbons of colored light danced across the new night sky. Gloryon watched them through the open dome ceiling of his bedroom, red and green curtains falling and curling on a deep violet backdrop of pinpoint stars. The lights were not often this active, but they matched his mood well, basking in the afterglow of a good wife's warm welcome home.

He and Jet had not stayed long at Dyeus' feast. Before the tables were cleared of a market's worth of dishes that made up the Nephilim banquet, the couple had discreetly made their leave. Jet now lay in bed, embraced and sleeping, but he was wide awake, staring up at the heavens.

In the peace of the night and in the comfort of his own bed, Gloryon pondered on the time passed since last he slept here. His life had not been a dull one thus far, by any stretch, but the events that had coalesced around the man Noah had succeeded in setting a new standard for excitement. Perhaps Hoduín was right about these Edenites; perhaps there was something extraordinary about them.

The thought of Hoduín brought Gloryon's mind back to the stars. Often had he gazed at them, but only as objects of beauty, or waypoints to be guided by in the wilds or on the open sea. He held no stock in divination by them, despite what the seers and the Grigori said. Never had he considered their origins, though. All his life, he had concerned himself with what exists in the *now*. At his core, he was a problem-solver, a reactor to things already instigated, events already set into motion. The past was lost to him, as it was to all creatures, upstream in the ever-flowing passage of time. But Noah and his kin—they seemed to regard the past as the foundation for understanding the future. They drew their very identities from it. Every night in Eden, and even on the road back to Enoch, Methuselah had gathered his sons and grandsons to read the Accounts that they held sacred. Without meaning to, Gloryon had imprinted the words in his head.

"In the beginning..." His lips moved without sound. Six days, their story said. Not enough time to ride even to Elash or the port at Lantagorah. What sort of being could make the world in such time? He, even Gloryon of Enoch, a giant among men, a son of the angels, could not hope to fathom that power. And why, if the *bene Elohim* knew of such a being, as the Edenites claimed, would they not speak of him?

"Why should I believe your tales?" he had asked Noah one evening, as they had made camp in the wilds of Nod. "What raises its truth above all the other accounts one might hear in any sorcerers' college? Why not the light of Larue, or the Infinite Turtle? Do not their adherents cling just as strongly to their beliefs?"

Noah had taken the question seriously. "I suppose," he had said, "it comes down to trust. We believe the Account of the Heavens and Earth because it was written by the very One who was there."

"And yet the Grigori do not relate this. Were they not there as well?"

"Kenan avows they were. Enoch too. They name themselves *bene Elohim*, sons of God. Why they secret the knowledge of Him to themselves, I cannot say." Noah shook his head. "Perhaps you ought to ask them."

Secrets and mysteries, thought Gloryon. He did not know what had stirred up these questions from the depths of his soul and kept him from sleep, but slumber at last began to clutch at the edges of his consciousness, and he surrendered to it. There would be plenty of time to consider the ways of the Edenites later, plenty of time to ask his questions.

Gloryon drifted off to sleep.

The high black walls of the city of Enoch could not keep out the mist. As the night grew cooler, it rolled out of the forests and in from the sea, filling the moat and surrounding the city, but never quite able to rise in a rainfall. It crept up the walls like ghostly ivy, curling over the battlements and masking the statues and carvings with its chill grey shroud. One by one the city's rings fell to its advance, but on most nights, the mist seldom met any of the citizenry walking about after dark. For the majority of Enoch's people, the day's hard work demanded restful sleep; the rich few who had risen above the need for daily toil would rather be curled around a warm fireplace, a pitcher of ale, or a woman or three, than be caught in the wet cold of the mists. The streets were not empty, though; far from it. Mischiefs of rats and swarms of rasp-roaches emptied their hidden homes for the crumb-filled market gutters. Sewer badgers, vicious if confronted, emerged from fetid burrows, and feral fisher-cats from the docks prowled the walls and rooftops. Unlike the myriad animals kept safe and indoors as pets and familiars, the city's nighttime denizens were not benign.

Far more dangerous things than those were out tonight.

Three shadowy figures glided over the wall surrounding Gloryon's estate, silent as the mists that hid their movements. They moved close to the ground, snaking through the front lawns and avoiding the pools of light cast eerily into the fog by garden lanterns. They fell upon the greathouse.

The old domestic at the door had served Jet's family for nigh on five centuries. He was a simple man—had known it even before his apprenticeship had fizzled into a serving position all those years ago—but he took his duties seriously, and he performed them well. Times had certainly changed in the last few generations; still, whether man or giant, folks always needed someone to see to the door and tend to supper. No doubt he was getting on in years, but his eyes and ears were keen as ever, and he would never be caught napping on the night shift, not like some of the younger set.

He never saw the darts that flew from the dark to blind him, but he did feel the iron hands that capped his mouth, muffled his cries, and snapped his neck at its base like dry bamboo.

Gloryon opened his eyes. He had been deep in dreams, but something had plucked at him like a loose thread, had pulled him from sleep. He felt Jet curled beside him, breathing softly and evenly on his bare chest. His own breath he held. Something…

A flicker of a shadow caught the corner of his vision, and his battle instincts took over. Gloryon threw one massive arm over his sleeping wife, catching two darts in the meat of his left forearm. Two more hit the wall as he let his momentum carry his body over Jet. He rolled, wrapping her in his arms as he did so and covering her with his body, and dropped off the side of the bed to the floor. He thrust her under the iron frame and bedclothes even before she fully awoke; a glimpse at her startled face, the thought of her having come so close to harm, enraged the Naphil as he had seldom known. Gloryon sprang up to face his attacker.

A grey-clad figure flew through the open bedroom window to deliver a vicious kick to the small of the giant's back. Gloryon roared and spun, just in time to dodge the curved metal claws aimed at his head. The missed killing blow was the only opening the grey assassin would have; with speed that seemed incongruous to his size, Gloryon grabbed the figure's arm and twisted it violently. The assassin jumped into a front flip, trying to avoid his shoulder's being ripped from its socket. As soon as his feet left the floor, Gloryon redirected the motion. With all his prodigious might, he spun towards the wall, smashing the grey figure face-first into the side of the granite windowframe. The assassin's head met the stone with a wet crack. The body slumped to the frame, leaving a dark stain that dripped black in the moonlight.

Gloryon released the assassin's body, continuing his spin to face the next attacker he knew would be there. There were two, in fact, almost invisible in the darkness of the moonlit room. One slightly-built shadow crouched at the top of a short flight of stairs. The other was tall and lean, swathed in dusky cloth but for a metallic belt that glinted faintly in the glow from the open windows. He stood at ease, hands behind his back. A dark mask covered both figures' mouths and noses and hung down past their necks, giving their silhouettes an inhuman aspect. The Naphil stepped forward, tensed for action, readying himself for the next attack.

It came from the tall assassin, whose hand snapped forward, pulling the metal belt from his waist. Gloryon had not been fooled by the relaxed facade; even so, he was taken aback by the sudden metallic hum of the long, flexible blade coming towards him with whip-like speed. He flowed with his reflexes, turning sideways and bending backwards. The strike that would have cut through his neck missed. The assassin snapped the blade back; its recoil drew it back across Gloryon's chest, leaving a red line of blood. His assailant readied for another strike. Weaponless, Gloryon gritted his teeth.

The head of a spear appeared from the assassin's chest. A muffled huff of breath escaped from a ruined lung; the spearhead disappeared, and the body dropped limply to the ground.

"*Father?*" Gilyon was poised to strike again. He was dressed in loose linen pants and held his spear with both hands—hands that, even in the darkness, were stained darker still with the assassin's blood.

"Watch out!" Gloryon's warning answer was slower than the last assassin, who sprung towards the newcomer with a sound like a bellows. Gilyon thrust with his spear, but the last grey figure had already danced back out of reach. The young Naphil coughed, then pitched forward as if he were going to be sick. Like a felled cedar he tilted, then dropped hard on his backside without a sound.

Gloryon rushed toward the assassin like a charging bull-dragon. The shadowy figure was quick and impressively agile, dodging the Naphil's onslaught with two steps up the wall and an aerial acrobatic that carried him over the giant. Gloryon threw his left hand behind him as he turned with the assassin's flip, using his long reach to his advantage. His hand gripped the cloth garment, but the assassin wrenched free with ease. The Naphil suddenly realized that his left arm, the one that had been struck by the darts, was surprisingly weak. His resolve had not changed, however; this person who had attacked him and his family in their own home would die in agony.

"You filth," he snarled, facing the last assassin. From behind the dark mask came a stuttering hiss, like a laugh from a nightmare. Gloryon pounced. The nimble grey figure was no doubt quick, but Gloryon had a giant's span and a speed borne of unbridled rage. His good hand caught the black-clad neck. The Naphil then lifted the grey figure off the floor, took three charging bounds forward, and rammed him into the wall. Gloryon held him there, crushing with all his strength, until the assassin's spine gave way with a distinct pop. He let the body drop.

"Gloryon!" Jet had crawled from the bed. Quickly, she lit a lamp. Gloryon turned to face her, relieved beyond description that she was safe. Her gasp drew his attention to his own chest. He looked down.

Plunged into the thick muscles of his chest and torso were a dozen darts, buried to the fletching. He pulled one out; the point was short, too short to cause any more damage beyond a prick, but Gloryon knew that was not its purpose. He sighed.

Jet ran to her husband, pulling him in the direction of the bed. He sat down. "See to our son, love. Does he live?"

Jet knelt by Gilyon's slumped form. His eyes were glazed, and he looked as if he were drunk to the point of insensibility, but his breaths came regularly in slow, noisy gulps.

"He lives, Gloryon." She ran back to him, almost tripping in her haste. She sat by him, tears in her eyes. "They hurt you. I do not understand." Her finger rose to touch one of the darts still stuck in her husband's flesh, but he gently pushed her hand away.

"Hush, love. Do not touch them. They are poisoned." Gloryon smiled down at her. His left arm hung uselessly, and already his breathing grew labored, but at least he was still able to smile, to speak, to look at the woman more beautiful to him than any other. "Jet…I love you, more than life itself. Kiss me—please, just kiss me."

Moved by an urgency and a terror that she did not understand, Jet rose to her knees on the bed and grasped Gloryon's face with both hands. In that kiss, Jet poured out every drop of love she felt for her husband, her protector, every treasured memory they shared, every hope for their future together, all together with every prayer to every god she had ever heard of. She pulled back. His tears matched hers. "I am sorry," he said. With a groan, he laid himself down on the bed.

"Gloryon! I will get help!" Jet started to rise, but Gloryon's hand clasped her leg.

"Stay," he whispered. He pulled her to lie down beside him. Already he felt the muscles that drew in air grow weak and fail. How strange, he thought, that such a natural, instinctual act as breathing should suddenly occupy every thought. His breaths grew shallow. He knew what words he wanted to be his last.

"My lady Jet." The words grew softer still as his exhalations grew faint. "I love you. I love you. I love you." His lips still moved, though no sound escaped them.

Gloryon took one last, minute breath. He locked his eyes on his beloved Jet's. She was sobbing now, but she returned his gaze with strength. Quickly, so quickly, the urge to breathe, the need for it, built up until it was overwhelming. He wanted to thrash his head about, to do anything that might force the smallest bit of air into his lungs, but instead he kept his focus on his wife's lovely, tear-stained face. *I love you*, he mouthed once more. Eventually, finally, a colorless haze edged his vision, growing until it blurred Jet's visage. Only then did Gloryon allow his eyes to close. All went black, and he knew no more.

◂ CHAPTER 25 ▸

Cold, sweaty hands clamped over the mouths of Noah and Jonan, awakening both of them with muffled screams.

"Shh! We must away—come now, quickly!" The harsh whisper might have been from any of the three hooded figures, details obliterated in the deep darkness of the unlit room. Noah clutched at his sleepy wits, trying his best to gather them. Bits of breathed conversation fought past his confusion, but the desperate edge to the voices woke him like ice water.

"How close are they?"

"A minute, at most."

"We have *no time*," the first voice interrupted. "Draw the guards. Do not be seen."

A robed shape opened the door from the dark bedchamber to the suites' central room. The figure stooped to the fireplace to gather some still-glowing embers in some hidden container. He ran to the stone-framed door that led to the palace halls, and in one flowing motion he flung the container's contents out. The ensuing explosion of light sounded like a rattlesnake's hiss magnified tenfold. For a moment the flash illuminated the figure; before the sudden brightness obliged him to shut his night-accustomed eyes, Noah glimpsed a face shadowed by a wide hood. A dozen leather pouches shared the cramped space along a thick, dual-strapped belt, its tightness the only indication that the man inside the loose-fitting robes was at least somewhat trim. The garment billowed at his legs as he ran back; suddenly, he was jerked off his feet by a force unseen and dropped hard to the stone floor. A shadow clung to the stones where the top of the fireplace met the ceiling. It leapt down, some sinister instrument glinting evilly in its fist. The fallen man in robes was quick, though; with panicked speed, he rose to his feet, flinging something from his belt at the ground as he did so. A billow of white smoke appeared as if conjured and enveloped him. The curtain of smoke parted as he rushed back into the bedchamber, robes flapping behind.

A grey blur burst from the smoke and hit the retreating man full in the back. They fell to the floor as one, no way to tell exactly what was happening in the darkness. A pained cry made clear that at least one of the grapplers had been wounded.

Another of the robed figures, taller and broader than the others, jumped over the combatants on the ground. He swung something—a weapon of some kind—and the blow rang true. A grey figure, so slender as to appear almost skeletal, rolled away from the first robed man, who now lay still. The ghastly shape made a huffing sound, like the *whuff* that came with stepping hard on a puffball mushroom. The tall man swept the arm of his robe to cover his face. The skeletal figure did not follow his attack; instead he ignored his adversary and leapt, to his surprise, at Noah. Noah had been frozen by the surreality of the scene to which he awoke, but this unexpected turn shocked him into action. He met his assailant with a straight-legged kick to the face. His foot was bare, but the impact on the cloth-clad face was solid; Noah felt the unmistakable crunch of nasal cartilage under his heel. The grey skeleton stumbled back, right into the powerful swing of the—was it a cudgel?—that rocked him stumbling right back into Noah, who caught the slumping figure under the arms.

"Hurry!" rasped the first voice. "Into the—"

A blade flew from the dissipating smoke, aimed straight at Noah's heart. He reflexively jerked up the thin body he held; the blade sunk deep into its neck. In the darkness, he found that senses other than sight waxed stronger. The gurgle from the cleft throat echoed like a waterfall in his ears; the hot, wet blood spurting from ruined vessels to soak through his tunic seemed to stream unending. Noah dropped the body. In what remained of the smokescreen, another grey figure crouched ominously.

Shouts came from the hall, followed by the thud of the heavy boots approaching the open doorway.

"Thanks to the Creator! The guards are here!" Jonan said.

"You think they are on your side?" The man to whom the first voice belonged pulled Jonan roughly to the chamber wall. He ran his hand over the stone, which disappeared to be replaced by the pitch black of a hidden passage. "Go! Thims, bring Gregan—hurry!"

The dim realization that he had heard this voice before was lost in the whirlwind of Noah's thoughts. Worried questions flew by, only to be immediately replaced by another: Is Zara safe? Who are these men? *Why is someone trying to kill me?* As a hand pulled firmly at his elbow, Noah glanced back into the smoky room. The grey figure had disappeared, but the ethereal shapes of the guards began to coalesce in the haze as they filtered into the room. He had to trust these men; moreover, he *did* trust in the Creator God. He could do nothing else. He gripped his faith tightly, ducked his head, and entered the passage.

· CHAPTER 26 ·

The space between the hidden passage's walls was narrow, but the big man, Thims, was able to push past Jonan to lead the way, even carrying the fallen Gregan on his back. The three of them were already hurrying as best they could into the blackness. Once inside the passageway, the man following Noah pushed again on the wall, and the stones slid back in place with barely a grind. He took a moment to pull out a small glass vial with a cork top. With a twist of the top and a quick shake, the vial began to glow with a moonlike light. The glow illuminated the man's face, and Noah had a name to match the voice.

"Onim!"

"You paid attention at the council meeting. No time now for proper introductions. Hurry on!" Onim pushed Noah down the passage. The smooth, cut stone underfoot held no risk for stumbling, and they soon caught the others.

"Questions." Onim spoke the word as an open invitation, and Jonan accepted readily.

"Yes!" Jonan's panic and confusion cracked his voice. "What in the black void was that about?"

Onim frowned. "That is simple enough. Those creatures tried to kill you. We saved you—at great risk to ourselves, might I add."

Noah put a reassuring hand on his brother's arm as they navigated the passage's turns. "Who tried to kill us, Onim? Why?"

"We do not know what they are called truly, but we call them the 'nameless.'"

"Ironically, providing them with a perfectly suitable name," muttered Jonan.

195

"They are men, trained in secrecy and stealth," continued Onim, "and to kill. But who is responsible, ultimately? Who gave them their black orders? Azazyel Grigori." A chill settled on Noah's skin and raised the hairs on his arms.

"We knew they served as Azazyel's hidden eyes and ears," Onim said. "Never before have they openly attempted murder, though. They have past preferred poisons and 'mysterious disappearances' and the like, not frank assassination. These are murky waters now. Elohim be with us."

Noah and Jonan shared a look of surprise. Noah spoke for them both. "How do you know of Elohim?"

For the first time, Onim smiled. "It is He who we worship. No, do not be surprised, men from Eden. Our legacy is yours. We are, all of us, the disciples of your forefather, Enoch. We call ourselves the Scribes."

Before either of the brothers could speak, Thims dropped to a knee in front of them. Both Noah and Jonan stepped forward to catch the man he carried; Gregan's face fell to Noah's shoulder, and the farmer was relieved to feel a brush of shallow breath on his skin. "He is alive," he said.

Onim pushed past him. "But I fear Thims will soon be otherwise. The mushroom dust is taking him." Leaning down, Onim waved a vial under the large man's nose. Whatever the contents, they had an effect. Thims shook himself like a hound just out of water, then pushed to his feet once more.

"The dust." Thims' voice was soft and tenor, incongruous with his physique. "It makes one to see things…bizarre… Onim, I had not thought I inhaled much. It is become more potent, I think."

Onim pulled the man's thick arm around his neck. "Come, just a bit further." He spoke without exaggeration, stopping not ten paces later to peruse the passage wall. His finger traced a vertical crevice to the height of his chin. He pressed, and a block of wall pulled back.

"A secret passage within a secret passage?" noted Jonan. "Cain was apparently not alone in his paranoia."

"But we, at least, have good reason to be," retorted Onim. "Quickly, down the stairs."

The mouldering stairs were a drastic and difficult change from the smooth stones of the palace passageways. The going was slower, but Onim was obviously much more at ease now, so they maintained a cautious pace. The stairs ended in a cavernous mélange of natural rock and manmade additions: complicated series of granite conduits crossed high overhead, rubble-and-mortar barriers circled grate-covered pits in the rough, uneven stone, and openings hewn by human hands were flung about the cavern at random.

Onim knew well enough of the water systems of Enoch that carried the clean waters of the Danbadan from the north, where they flowed among the foothills of Mount Armon, eventually to fill the basins and bathhouses of the city's richer residents. He knew the underclass, scraping out a living as fisherfolk or mushroom-gatherers or ratcatchers, struggling to sleep in the moat-level shantytowns while wrapped in cold, heavy mists. Above all these, though, he knew that Noah and Jonan, accustomed to Eden's fresh air, would notice only one thing.

"Rub this under your nose," Onim told them as they entered the cavern.

"Smells good," commented Jonan, smearing the ointment as directed and passing the small green bottle to Noah. "Like fawn's-mint."

"Very strong, though," added Noah.

Onim chuckled. "You shall soon be thankful for that when we pass under the tanneries. And beneath the animal markets. And by the sewage pools."

"Mm, I can smell it now," said Jonan. "Gah! I really *can* smell it now! Wonderful. Mint mixed with feces."

Onim allowed himself one more chortle at the farmers' expense. "Welcome to the underbelly of Cain's city."

The fetid maze wound deeper and deeper beneath the city. Thims' head seemed to clear as he breathed the sharply pungent air; with his added help carrying Gregan once again, the group picked up its pace. The bare feet of Noah and Jonan were soon black with grime, but the bedrock underfoot was worn smooth enough by the endlessly dripping water that the lack of boots or sandals did not impede their speed. After a while, the natural rock floor flowed into the unmistakable even plane of tool-worked stone, and they went faster still. "We are safe enough now," said Onim, "but Gregan needs tending-to at once. Come, come—quick, but careful!"

The domain of the Scribes was marked primarily by smell. No gate, no signpost gave overt signal, but the warm air of their catacombs and secret halls, bolstered by the sweet scents of pipe tobacco and olibanum candles, crashed against the rank humidity of the sewer passage like a wave. All breathed deeper, save Gregan. Thims hastened his pace as soon as he sensed the safety of home territory, carrying the badly injured man to the aid that could be found in this place.

Onim led Noah and Jonan in Thims' footsteps, but whatever allowed Thims and Gregan free passage into the realm of the Scribes did not automatically extend to the Edenites, despite Onim's presence. Where the walls shed their accumulation of grime and the floor became clean and dry, a robed man sidestepped from an unlit alcove and blocked their way. A viverrid crouched at his feet; it resembled a long-nosed cat with an even longer striped tail, with a black pattern overlying grey fur that caused it to virtually disappear into the rocky wall. Noah noted that the animal's coloring had been somewhat duplicated on Onim's striped robes, and the sentry's as well, and he wondered if the desired effect was the same sort of camouflage. He supposed it worked, more or less.

"Heel there, Jenet," the man said to the animal, then looked up. "The one with appearance like to Onim, I ask you: was the world once good?"

"It was very good," Onim answered.

"And what is it now?"

"It is cursed and fallen."

"Will you vouch for these two?"

Onim spread his hands. "They are men from Eden, descendants of Enoch the Scribe himself."

"Very well," the sentry said. Addressing Noah and Jonan, he said, "The two of you will have to wash your feet—over there." He gestured to a small, shallow manmade pool in another shadowy alcove across the hall. They did so, with thanks. When they returned, the man said, "Mark them, Jenet." The viverrid raised its banded tail and, before they could protest, released its musk at the farmers' feet.

Onim had stepped out of his mucky boots and placed them in a long recess that held a dozen or so pairs of footwear, mostly leather boots and sturdy brogans. He let the animal spray his feet as well.

"Our steps are marked now," he explained, leading them up a shadowy set of stairs, then down a candlelit corridor. "We may walk safely here."

A feral scream, pregnant with an agony that imparted an almost-physical discomfort to hear, caromed down the corridor. Noah and Jonan shared a stoic glance, then ran down the hall towards the awful sound. No more would they be passive participants in this night's bizarre theater. Fists balled and blood coursing, they would face any other horrors head-on.

The screaming stopped. Out of the wide doorway from which it had come stood a nightmarish figure, apron soaked a deep red hue, bloodstained hands wringing a rag. The torches that guarded the door flickered off the sinister metal instruments that hung from the apron's leather loops. A dour face turned to the slap of bare feet approaching.

The two brothers held up, searching for weapons of any kind. Finding none, they spread out to either side of the doorway. Grimness turned to confusion, but the man just kept wringing his bloody rag. The brothers readied their attack.

"Hold, hold!" Onim yelled. "Noah, stop!"

"Noah, eh?" The man pulled the rag through a loop and ran his eyes down the farmer's bloodsplattered face and tunic. "Your clothes look like mine. My name is Kiribaoth. Chirurgeon by profession. And your comrade here?"

"I am Jonan, his brother."

"Well met, both of you." Kiribaoth gave no impression of being surprised or perturbed about the Edenites' pugnacious posturing. "Onim, we were obliged to pipe Gregan's chest. We evacuated much blood, but he will live, the Creator willing."

"I am relieved to hear it, old friend. Now, to my new friends: to the libraries. If you are to navigate the lay of this violent terrain in which you now find yourselves, there are things you must know. But first, Noah—we must find you a change of clothing."

The contents of the cloak room of the Scribes was mainly comprised of the cinereous-and-chestnut striped robes worn by every member of the group Noah and Jonan had seen thus far, save the chirurgeon. Jonan's sleeping tunic had escaped unscathed; to this was added a robe and a belt.

"I am sorry, Noah," Onim said, appearing after a brief hunt for a suitable replacement for Noah's ruined tunic. "The bathbasins we keep full and warm, and you are welcome to wash yourself, but we keep few extra clothes here besides our robes. I asked the others, but I found nothing for you."

Jonan chuckled as he flipped his hood up over his head. "Alas, elder brother, your fate as a naked sewer-dwelling savage is assured, as I always expected." Quick as a mongoose, Noah pulled the wide hood all the way over Jonan's face, to a yelp of surprise.

"Hold, now," Onim said. A curious, almost wondering, lilt colored his tone. "Perhaps...wait here, please. I shall return in moments."

Noah took his time cleansing his face and neck of the assassin's blood, now dried in places and stuck to hairs. By the time he finished, Onim was back from his errand.

"Try this, Noah." He held up a sleeved cassock done in an old style, simple and serviceable. It looked to be a close fit, and Noah found that it was, almost as if it were tailor-made.

"What ancient person did that belong to?" asked Jonan. "Adam himself?"

With a twinkle in his eye, Onim answered, "Not Adam. Your great-grandfather, Enoch."

"Enoch!" exclaimed Noah. "And how is it so well-preserved?"

"This is the garment he wore when he was translated," Onim said. "Wherever he was taken, his clothing did not follow him. We have kept it under glass, a memento of our departed teacher, but now...with you here... yes, it is fitting that you wear it. Here, try a robe too."

"Tell me, Onim," Jonan said, while Noah searched for a robe that fit. "Why do the Grigori hate our forefather so much? So much that they would try to kill us?"

"Listen more, brother, and you will need ask fewer questions," said Noah. "They hate Enoch because he condemned them."

"Condemned them! Who told you that?" Onim's bother was plain on his face. "It is not true."

"But I thought... Then why?"

Onim leaned in, eager to impart knowledge that he considered of supreme importance. "Enoch never condemned the Watchers of his own accord, although that might be the story they have told, and told them-selves. On the contrary."

The old Scribe's bright eyes dimmed as he walked the path of memories now centuries old.

"Enoch tried to *save* them."

‹ CHAPTER 27 ›

Lady Jet's anguished wails woke the servants from their cottages, but by
then their master was long since dead. Gilyon was still lost in a stupor,
and Jet refused to leave her husband, so two footmen were sent running
for help. The city guards came quickly, answering the need of one of their
own, but none, no matter how familiar with battle and death, believed that
Gloryon had fallen. To their shock and dismay, the tragic truth of it was
soon confirmed. Gloryon was not the only one, either; the bodies of all six
of the servants who had drawn greathouse duty that night were found, each
fallen at their posts.

The assassins' corpses were noted and cordoned, but the guards
would not touch them on account of Gilyon's malady. "If that is what happens to one of angel's blood," said a grizzled guard veteran, examining the
young Naphil's empty-eyed stare, "then best we wait for the chief before we
set hands on these bodies."

"The chief is here," barked a hard, stern voice, "and I command *all* of
you to perform your duties *now.*"

"Lieutenant-chief Malidoch!" The guard stiffened and saluted.

"Get those bodies out of here. This is a home, not some tavern or
slumyard." Malidoch marched to where Jet lay prostrate over Gloryon, and
with a gentle hand he moved her away. His fingers on Gloryon's neck gave a
fleeting moment of hope to the servants and guards in the room, but it was
dashed when he took them away and closed his good eye sadly. This small
act carried a finality that sent Jet into renewed sobs. Malidoch pulled her to
him, pressing her wet cheek to his armor.

"He was my sister's son," he said. "He was the best of us. He will
be avenged."

At Malidoch's beckon, two guards came.

"Find an apothecary of good repute," he instructed the first. "Bring him here to address whatever ails Gilyon. You, escort Lady Jet to her family's estate. This is no place for her."

He turned to the rest of the guards. "The servants will stay here. I want *everyone* questioned, understand? Every movement they made, every alibi is to be checked and rechecked."

The grizzled guard nodded agreement. "And what will you do, sir?"

Like a mask, Malidoch's crooked face distorted beyond its normal wont into an expression more grim than any of the guards had seen him wear before.

"I go to tell Azazyel Grigori that his son is dead."

‹ CHAPTER 28 ›

Sergeant Havak scuffed the toe of his boot on a stain on the council hall's floor. The dark spot disappeared, rubbed off onto the leather; probably wine spilled by some inebriated councilman, tottering about with a mistress to the secrecy of the council hall's offices to do their adulterous business. The thought had crossed Havak's mind that he had become quite cynical for one so young, but was it cynicism if it were so often true? Most of the guards assigned to the palaces looked the other way when it happened, anxious to curry favor with Enoch's rich and powerful. Not Havak. He knew who firmly gripped the levers of power in this city, and it was most certainly not the council.

His position as sergeant, the highest rank in the lowest echelon of the guard corps of Enoch, belied his true level of power. The guardsmen under him were loyal, both to him and the Watchers. Their boots were planted firmly on the ground, which made him and his men perfect for jobs like tonight's. Havak did not ask for details, only orders. He fingered the hilt of his knife, shrugged his shoulders to feel the heft of the broadsword at his back—the palace guards eschewed the longbows and quivers carried by the gatekeeper guards. Nothing to do now but wait.

The rover guard passed Havak's position, giving him a curt, conspiratorial nod as he continued his circuit. Havak envied the man. The waiting was bad enough, but having to maintain his fixed position while he did so made the tension worse. His eyes wandered to the hallway where the Edenite suite was. Patience and discipline, he told himself. The signal would come soon.

Bright white light tore through the lamp-lit halls, blinding Havak momentarily and hissing like a mountain of coals dropped into water. The sergeant cursed. That was not the signal. Something had gone wrong. He could not very well ignore it, though. He made a decision and put his horn to his lips.

He met his guards as he ran, each drawn from his post by the peal of the horn. He gave instructions on the move. "Follow my lead. Keep the Edenites in their rooms. Stay sharp, swords out."

Led by Havak, six guards burst into the suite's central room. An acridity filled the hazy air, but visibility was not so impaired that a quick scan of the room told Havak where the action had been.

"Secure the bedchambers," Havak ordered, pointing out the four doors still closed. "Have a care with the primary objective." One doorway stood open. He grabbed a lamp from the wall and went to it.

Behind him, Havak heard a shout, the clash of wood on iron, then a brief scuffle and a *stay in your room, sir*. One of the Edenites roused from bed, striking before observing, but his men handled such things as professionals ought, as he knew they would. His interest lay before him, but he almost could not believe what he saw. At his call, his rover guard joined him.

"Cover the body," Havak instructed, ripping off the woolen sheets from the bed and tossing them towards the dark corpse of the assassin, a pool of blood still spreading on the stone under his head. With practiced eye, Sergeant Havak examined the windows and walls, but could find no likely egress for the target to have escaped. The fact remained, though, that egress there must be, since no other option for exit existed—not even the rats knew all the hidden ways that ran through the city's edifices and under its streets—but that mystery could be solved later. A believable story, a well-constructed lie in the service of angels, was needed now, and Havak thought it up quickly.

"Where is the primary?" he signed to his guards, each stationed before a shut door. He motioned to the guard who answered to stand with the rover by the body, now fully covered by a sheet that blossomed red over the neck wound, and took his place by the door. At his signal, each guard opened a door and burst in.

A girl huddled up at the head of her bed, legs pulled into her body in fright, sheets clutched. She was indeed beautiful, vulnerable, and Havak's hormones flared unbidden, but he was a professional with a job to do; besides, she was marked for someone far greater than he.

"Quickly, miss." He injected the appropriate amount of urgency and concern. "My name is Havak, of Enoch's guards. Come with me, please—for your safety."

Too young, too confused to ask questions, she threw a robe over her sleeping dress and followed. In the central room, the Edenite men were yelling for explanations.

Havak asserted his authority. "Everyone outside, now. We must escort you all to a safe place."

"Meaning this is not?" The sergeant recognized the angry speaker from the day's council as Lamech, the fool who spoke back to the Grigori. The elder one—Methushael or something similar, Havak could not recall—asked a more useful question, if vague. "Guard, what is happening here?"

"Assassination and abduction. Beyond that I know no more than you, but rest assured you are under the protection of the city of Enoch now."

"Assassination of *whom?*" demanded Lamech. Havak glanced towards the target's bedchambers, knowing every eye would follow. He was strangely satisfied when the sight of a bloody sheet, the profile of a human body unmistakable beneath, prompted such dramatic wailing from the Edenites. Lamech and a woman of similar age—his wife, no doubt—darted toward the room, but their way was blocked by armored guards, and they were manhandled out into the hall. The primary objective, the girl Emzara, only wilted in his arms. "Is it Noah?" she whispered.

"The younger man at the council today?" He injected the right hint of familiarity from a guard who had watched the proceedings. She nodded weakly. His face fell in a way he knew would confirm her worst fears. The girl did not burst into hysterics, as he had expected. Rather, she paled to dead white, and the life ran from her eyes. She looked so disturbingly corpselike that, despite himself, Havak felt a twinge of remorse. A fitting reaction, though, he thought, since compared to the new life for which she had been chosen, she may as well have been dead in her former. The sooner he brought her to their destination, the sooner her revival would occur.

"Where are you taking us?" asked the elder—Methaniel, maybe?—as he wrenched his arm away from the guard who led him.

"To the safest place in the city," answered Sergeant Havak. "To the palace of Samyaza."

‹ CHAPTER 29 ›

In the libraries of the Scribes, Noah pulled the tightly-bound scroll from the horn tube in which it was sequestered. It unwound of its own accord, as if it wanted to be read.

"Sit, sit," Onim said, ushering Noah to the table where Jonan was already engrossed in another parchment. "Read the truth for yourself."

Jonan looked up from his reading. "So our great-grandfather interceded for the angels."

"He did," Onim said. "And the Lord God replied through him that it was angels who ought to be interceding for mankind, not the other way around. What is more, by taking human form and laying with human women, the Grigori became one flesh with humanity, in all its sinful depravity. Heaven could not be open to such creatures."

Noah ran his fingers along the scripted lines of his document. "'But you were formerly spiritual,'" he read, "'living the eternal life, and immortal for all generations of the world. And therefore I have not appointed wives for you; for as for the spiritual ones of the heaven, in heaven is your dwelling.'"

"The Creator's words, according to your great-grandfather," said Onim.

"But the Grigori were sorry," Jonan argued. "Should they rightly be denied restoration?"

"Was Eve sorry?" Onim replied. "Actions have consequences, my young friends. Contrition does not always absolve us of them. If you heed only one thing I say to you in your lifetimes, heed this: obey the first time."

"Now I understand their hate," said Noah. "The Watchers were in constant fellowship with Elohim, but now have none."

"And no female companion could ever compare, no matter how lustily she might inflame a man or an angel," interjected Onim.

"And our sire Enoch did walk with Him, speak with Him," Noah continued. "So when their plea was rejected, the Grigori's only hope became their object of hatred."

"Exactly." Onim sat down next to Noah. "And with him translated, their hate finds its target in us, in you—how long until their bitterness extends to all of humankind? We do not wish to wait and see."

Jonan carefully rerolled his scroll and reached for a worn codex. "What of the Scribes? How have you survived against the Grigori all this time?"

"Hiding, mostly." Onim smiled grimly. "At times here underground, at times in plain sight. The disciples of Enoch the Scribe remained secret, for the most part, while he walked on this earth, and we have remained so since he was taken."

Paging through the leaves of the codex he had chosen, Jonan rubbed the back of his neck. "This does illuminate things."

At the mention of "underground" and "illuminate," Noah was struck by the absence of something expected. The library had no lamps on the tables or torches on the walls. Rather, glowing glass domes were set about the ceiling, casting pools of light onto the tables, and Noah wondered, "Onim, how do you keep this place lit? The same way you set that vial in the tunnels alight?"

Onim smiled. "No, the library lights are more marvelous than my simple formulas. Directly above us is Jewelers' Square—specifically, the emporium of Sefiron the Miner. He is old, one of the first settlers of Havilah, but he has called this city home for centuries now. An expert among experts in gems and glass, and a fixture in the noble houses and palaces."

Although they were alone in the library, with immeasurable tons of stone between them and anyone above who might hear, Onim leaned in and whispered. "It was he who discovered the plot against you. He feigns to be a pompous merchant of pretty baubles to the wealthy and powerful, but he is as sharp as a drake's tooth, and a brilliant man besides. When Sefiron built his showcase above, he piped glass strands down shafts we bored from here, from below. The lamps in Sefiron's shops never die—he takes customers at all hours—and though I cannot begin to tell you how, the glass carries the light from there to here, undimmed. This way, the scrolls and books here are in no danger of burning, and the purity of the air is not spoiled from flames.

And now that you have heard tell of these lights, allow me to give you the opportunity to use them. I will go find more scrolls for you."

The passage of time in the library, having no candles or windows, was impossible to tell, and Noah and Jonan had been feasting on the writings for hours. Their quiet study was abruptly interrupted when Onim ran into the room, animated as they had first seen him at the council.

"I have news, and it is not good. Gloryon, Azazyel's son, has been murdered!"

Jonan shot from his seat with a cry of disbelief, and Noah sunk his forehead to rest against his fist, in complete shock.

The old Scribe paced purposefully to them and pressed his palms to the worn wood of the table, supporting himself as he leaned towards them. "Before, our people would disappear, and we could prove nothing. Azazyel has pushed too far this time, though. In his arrogance, he believes he cannot be touched. I was waiting for the right time to broach this, and it would seem this is it." Onim stared at Noah, a look so intense that Noah could not match his gaze. "As a group, we Scribes hide in our burrows, but as individuals, we have resources. What we lack is a leader, someone who can take the mantle of the prophet Enoch and free this city, our people, from the grip of the angels. That leader must be you, Noah."

Hearing that Gloryon had been killed had already rocked Noah back on his heels, and this sudden pronouncement from a man, a leader of men, who he barely knew was too much. He looked at his brother imploringly. Jonan put up his hands, at as much of a loss as he. Onim pushed his case further.

"Noah, you are the heir of Enoch the Scribe. We will follow you. I can guarantee that much of the guard will rise against the killers of Gloryon, even if they be Grigori, although some are on the Watchers' side. You might even be able to bring the Nephilim to our cause—*your* cause, rather, since they would never join with me." The fire of righteous rebellion smoldered in Onim's eyes. "Now is the time to push back against the usurpers, Noah—to regain our rightful stewardship of this earth, instead of ceding its rule to angels who have no natural place in it. What say you?"

Onim's heated request was weighty, and Noah felt for a moment like grapes in a winepress. He only wanted to be back in Eden. He did not know how to answer, but he prayed that the one he would give, whatever it might be, would be the one that might lead him most quickly to Zara, his family, and the road home. His vacillation was interrupted by Jonan, who burst out, "What in all this cursed earth could *possibly* kill a being like Gloryon?"

"Blood and death," Noah muttered. "I cannot, Onim. This is not my place. I am sorry."

"Ah. I see." The Scribe's fervor froze. "So you have no problem begging for our help to deliver your lands, but you will not lift your hand to deliver ours. Fool and coward! Think you Eden is immune forever from Azazyel's shadow? He will cast it long, and you will rue this day that you spurned the chance to stop him!"

"Calm yourself, Onim!" From an alcove stepped Kiribaoth, the chirurgeon, dressed now in the robes of the Scribes. "Noah is neither fool nor coward." Kiribaoth circled the table as he spoke. "You are a righteous man, Noah. I see that. Not hard to be, when you live in security, where all men believe as you. I knew your ancestor Kenan. There were not as many of our kind in the inchoate days of the fourth generation of men, but we fell away from the Creator quickly all the same, and the darkness of humanity spread throughout the earth. Kenan did not hide in peace. He searched out evil and fought against it. Enoch did too." He laid a hand on Onim's shoulder. "Noah might have those men's blood in his veins, but their legacy is not his. He is a reactor, not an actor. He is content to remain in the safety of his homeland, living and worshiping in peace."

The chirurgeon's didactic tone was far more infuriating than Onim's passionate condemnation, but Noah was quite done with being lectured. He stood, and Jonan stood with him.

"I will tell you how I will react now," Noah said. "We will leave here, retrieve our kin, and return home. I am indebted to you for saving my life, but I cannot do what you ask me."

The light illuminating an adjacent table flickered oddly, interrupting the response upon Onim's lips. It dimmed, and a faint cacophony reverberated above their heads. From the worried glance that the two Scribes shared, Noah knew that this went beyond normalcy. Coupled with the night's previous events, the light's darkening caused his innards to twist in a spasm of trepidation. He and Jonan stepped away from the light, and Onim and Kiribaoth did the same.

With a crack, the dimmed dome dislodged from the ceiling and fell, splintering the table in two and shattering in a deafening explosion. Long strands of dark glass followed, falling from a height unknown, to send wave after wave of sharpened shards skidding and scattering about the library floor. The last thing to fall was a human head, which caromed off the mountainous pile of broken glass and rolled ramblingly to rest at the bare feet of Jonan. He stared in horror, making no move to pick it up. Kiribaoth crouched, carefully brushed the hair free of glass with his sleeve, and lifted it, adopting the detached eye of an anatomist.

"Sefiron."

In the decapitated head's mouth was stuffed a cylinder of gold, far too big to fit comfortably in the oral cavity. Several teeth were torn from the gums, and the asymmetry of the mandible denoted a jaw ripped from the tendons of its hinges. Somehow, Noah suspected that the cylinder was inserted while the man was still alive, and despite his attempts to calm his stomach with deep, flaring breaths through his nostrils, his gorge rose and he turned away. Kiribaoth pulled the golden container out, and several teeth dropped to the floor. After a cursory examination, he flipped the hinged end of the cylinder open, and dropped a rolled scrap of papyrus into Onim's clean hands. In a moment Onim had read the scrap, and its contents were obviously not good.

"It is unsigned," he said. "You…should read it for yourself." He handed it to Noah with a trembling hand, and Jonan read it over his shoulder.

> Your kin are with the Grigori. Send news of your survival, show
> your face in the city, or do anything other than depart silently for
> Eden now, and they will die, beginning with the girl Emzara.

"It is direr than you all realize," said Kiribaoth, finally showing some semblance of his disturbance. "They know where we are, and they may even know our identities. This place will not stay hidden for much longer. When the nameless ones find their way here, we cannot hope to stand against them." He began grabbing codices from the closest wooden shelves and stacking them in his arms. "Onim, we must leave, now."

Onim's eyes widened in panic, and he too began to gather the library's contents. Jonan spun on his heels and walked briskly back the way they had entered.

"Where are you going?" Onim shouted after him. "Help us!"

"You want an actor? You want initiative?" replied Jonan. "There is glass all over the floor, and you luminaries walk around in your bare feet. I, for one, am going to put on some boots."

‹ CHAPTER 30 ›

The scrolls and books were packed in chests, and the chests were wrapped in old sails. Noah counted fifteen Scribes scurrying about the tunnels preparing for departure, although Onim said there were many more; no one could be spared to send a message to the others, and time was of the essence.

Finally they finished. The robes of the Scribes were tucked away, replaced by tattered cloaks of fisher-folks and laborers. Another maze deposited them onto a well-worn, wide slope of a passage, used by the moat-dwellers to make their daily trudge to the city above. Three weather-beaten vessels waited for them at the shantytown docks. Once these were laden with their new cargo, the square rigs were set, moorings loosed, and the boats quietly sailed into the new dawn, unremarkable in the motley flotilla of subsistence fishermen doing the same.

By the time the sun was risen full over the horizon, the boats had exited the river and were in the open sea, hugging the coastline. The men breathed easier now that the immediate danger was behind them, and the fresh salt air cleansed their lungs of the underground's dankness.

Kiribaoth surfaced from below deck, where he had been keeping a watchful eye on wounded Gregan. He walked up to Noah, who knelt at the ship's bow. Legs unsteady, the chirurgeon stumbled loudly on his way, but Noah made no sign of noticing.

"I am not one for boats," Kiribaoth said, as he knelt besides the farmer.

"I find I do not mind them," replied Noah.

"You have no intent of returning to Eden, do you?"

"Not in the slightest."

"Do you have a plan?"

Noah sighed. "Not in the slightest. Actually, I amend myself—I do have the first stage worked out. It is being implemented even now."

"What is that?" Kiribaoth asked.

Despite himself, Noah smiled. "Call on the name of the Lord God Creator. Beyond that, I have nothing."

Kiribaoth matched his smile. "Beyond that, we *need* nothing."

The scandal and gossip that erupted that morning in the city of Enoch was unmatched since the days of the Song of Seventy-Seven. Morning criers spread the news they had received from the night guard, and the predictable channels of gossip and hearsay ensured its maximum saturation in the markets and shops. Murder of a descendant of both Cain and the Grigori? Attack on the Edenites, the night after relations were officially repaired? Outrageous! The people demanded answers, and by midday, the hall in which the Grigori held council was filled to overflowing.

Samyaza, Barkayal, Tamiel, and Asaradel took their seats on the floor, projecting a calm in the clamor that none of them truly felt. Azazyel was not present. The rumor that circulated most quickly was that he and Lilith were sequestered deep in the bowels of their palace, concocting a curse that would make Cain's seem like a slap of the belt. Most people settled on the simple and reasonable excuse that he and his wife were privately grieving, as any parents would.

Several unsuccessful attempts were made by the guards before some semblance of order was finally restored. Barkayal stood first, having only one thing to say, and he addressed it to the council members and Nephilim present.

"Perhaps next time, when one of the *bene Elohim* warns of suffering and doom, you will heed him." Angry voices arguing from the galleries shattered the fragile decorum only just attained, but they quieted when Samyaza addressed the crowd.

"We all have the same questions here today," he said. "Perhaps if the Edenites had left, none of this would have happened, but happened it has. The wise course is to first understand fully what occurred. Rumors and untruths will only darken matters. I call Lieutenant-chief Malidoch to attend and give testimony."

The disfigured guard marched onto the floor and approached the Grigori. He carried his helmet under one arm, and to those who knew him, his marred features looked far worse than usual, with eye bloodshot and beard unkempt.

"Malidoch, I know this matter is close to you," said Samyaza gently, "but I ask you to do this in your capacity as guard of Enoch. Please, for your city's sake, give us an account of last night's events."

The guard coughed into his hand to clear his throat and exhaled deeply, then complied. "I arrived at Gloryon's home…ah, the scene of the crime…after the guards first on the premises sent word. We found ten bodies in total—six servants, identities confirmed; Gloryon…" Malidoch's voice hitched, but he regained his composure. "Gloryon son of Azazyel I identified myself, and confirmed his…demise. Three other bodies were cordoned off and removed to the district guardhouse for safety, due to the multiple evidences of poison use. Our consensus was and remains that these three were the murderers."

"*Were?*" Asaradel snapped. His eyes narrowed, flashing bright through the slits. "What are you withholding?"

Malidoch cleared his throat again. "Noble Grigori, the bodies…ah… have disappeared."

Tamiel spoke clearly and loudly above the anger that muttered through the crowd, outrage enough in his voice for all gathered. "Explain yourself, lieutenant-chief, and explain how you have attempted to rectify it."

"While I informed Azazyel Grigori of his son's death, I ordered my men to remove the bodies. When I returned to our guardhouse, the men were unconscious, and the bodies were gone. I have personally interviewed the guards involved, all of them veterans with no stains on their record. None has any recollection of what happened."

"Bring them here," Barkayal said. Malidoch turned on his heel sharply and gestured. Three guards in full armor marched stiffly out of the crowd. They faced the Grigori, spines rigid, sweat and stress hidden behind decorum and discipline. The eyes of the *bene Elohim* burned white as they examined the guardsmen, but found nothing of interest. Samyaza dismissed them with a wave of his hand.

"You will devote your time and resources to finding the truth of this matter," he said to Malidoch. "Now, what do you have to say of the attack on the Edenites?"

"I received a report in full from the ranking guardsman on site, Sergeant Havak. One deceased; one missing, presumed deceased. No sign of the assassins was found. As you know, the survivors were brought to your palace, under the safety of the guard."

"And there they will remain," Samyaza said, in a tone that broached no argument. "As their safety cannot be assured in either the council hall or the houses of the guards."

"We thank you for your report, Malidoch," said Tamiel. "Go now. You have much work to do."

With the lieutenant-chief's dismissal, the short session was called closed. The grist for the rumor mills had been sparser than many in the crowd had hoped, but its quality was high, with plenty of room for embellishment and hearsay to add flavor as needed. In a busy city of Enoch's size, idleness was only for a privileged few, and Tamiel's last admonishment might as well have been addressed to all gathered. The audience dispersed.

Every ray of light was a lance of agony, and every sound assaulted him like a sworn enemy. Even so, Gilyon would not have missed this council. His first memory since he had gone to bed was the reedy apothecary, smearing an acrid paste on his face. Between was a morass of nightmarish visions that could not possibly be true, but clung behind his eyes, more vivid than waking life. The reality to which he finally awoke was no less a nightmare: his father dead, his mother broken. The Nephilim around him—everyone who had traveled to Eden, save Gloryon, with the addition of Dagdha—were the only rocks to which he was anchored right now. Now that the Grigori had departed, the Nephilim discussed the matters amongst themselves, and Gilyon tried to focus and listen.

"Liars spoke this day," Dyeus said. "I would wager my flesh on it. Someone knows more than they are telling. How much of that was facade, and on whose parts, I am unsure, but this much I guess: our father is complicit in some way."

"I wish not to speak ill of my own father, or yours, Dagdha," said Hoduín, "but even if the other Grigori knew of deception, they could never go against Samyaza."

"Even in murder?" asked Tiras.

"Aye," said Dagdha. "They know our people. Fidelity to ancient Cain and his curse surpasses that which they have to our fathers. If Samyaza fell, the rest would lose their place here."

"Our people, eh?" said Pethun thoughtfully. "If it came to it, whose side would you take? The humans, or the Grigori?"

When no elder Nephilim spoke, Tiras did. "The right side. The side of justice."

Dedroth and Tevesh nodded. Dyeus, though, inclined his head to Pethun, and with a hint of conspiracy said, "*Our* side." He straightened, pulling at Dagdha's and Hoduín's elbows in a friendly way. "Come, all. Let us discuss these matters over the leftovers of last night's feast."

Gilyon found himself at the back of the pack, with Hamerch and Deneresh. The two sons of Dyeus said nothing, which Gilyon appreciated; attempts at comfort would be useless platitudes, and besides, anything above a whisper was as if the crystal bells of Jig's temple were set ringing between his ears.

Their path took them off the main thoroughfare through Shepherd's Park, and the clipping of hooves and clatter of cartwheels finally ceased. Unsurprisingly, it was Deneresh who broke the silence.

"Do you think Father is right?" he asked Hamerch, well out of earshot of the group of giants ahead.

"He may be," answered Hamerch, "but will he pursue it? Probably not. Not until he knows it will benefit him beyond any doubt."

"Your father would have, Gilyon," said Deneresh, setting the bells ringing.

"Much good *that* does us," snapped Gilyon. He shut his eyes and rubbed his forehead roughly, willing tears not to well in front of his friends.

"Let me finish. If no one else will, then we must."

Hamerch looked askance at his younger brother. "You mean, investigate for ourselves? Search for the truth?"

"Find the killers," said Gilyon darkly.

"Who better?" A serious set to Deneresh's jaw was uncharacteristic, but fit his face well. "No one will see us coming."

"I would not have thought this in you, little brother," said Hamerch. "Count me in."

"Very well," said Gilyon. "How do we begin?"

Deneresh grinned. "With wine."

‹ CHAPTER 31 ›

From the few buildings in the palace district that Methuselah had seen thus far, gilded and polished had been the common theme of decor. This was not so in the palace of Samyaza. The side gate through which they were ushered led to a garden that Enosh would have admired. The front of the palace had no walls, instead opening to the mazes of ferns and flowers. A glimpse through the cedar pillars that supported the levels above showed a fountain flowing from the interior of the palace into the garden, the waterworks dressed only in nature's ornateness. Herded by their guards, the Edenites skirted the garden's edge, then descended a stair to a more private entrance. The path through the palace was all wooden floors and exposed beams, carved at corners and across lintels with every manner of birds and beasts. They followed a carven skulk of foxes up a staircase, finally coming to a set of thick oaken doors.

"Inside, please," said a guard, and no one was in a state to argue. In the room, twin eagles flew from either wall, wooden wings upswept, soaring forever over couches covered with furs; on the far wall was a wooden case of codices, interspersed with horn-and-linden figurines of animals, from wolves to wyverns. The guards shut the doors. Betenos collapsed on a couch, crying; Zara, pale white still, flopped onto the other. While Lamech tried to comfort his wife, Merim and Hadishad milled about the room in a daze, before finally settling silently on either side of Zara.

Methuselah looked at the broken remains of his family and dropped to his knees. "Elohim." The words were strained in his anguish. "Be faithful. Give us hope."

219

Two thoughts answered his hoarse prayer, circling like doves from above to rest upon his shoulders and whisper in his ear. He breathed a word of thanks, then stood to face the others.

"Do not grieve so yet," he said. "If Noah is…gone, then his prophecy must have been fulfilled. Might it be? I do not think so. Therefore, he must still live. Furthermore-" Methuselah checked himself, considering that his second thought might be too macabre for the raw feelings in the room.

"Right now, that seems a handhold less firm than most," said Lamech, although he sounded stronger, and Betenos stopped her sobbing. "What else were you going to say?"

Methuselah stroked his chin and turned away towards the doors.

"We have not actually seen his body."

Exhaustion and despondency dragged the women into fitful sleep. Merim slumped at the locked oaken doors, snoring, having given up his efforts to open them either by force or finesse. The other three men, needing something with which to occupy themselves, perused the shelves' contents, finding many exquisite folios filled with drawings and paintings of flora and fauna. The same strange sigil was branded into the leather of every cover, but the text that accompanied the pictures was of the common script. They soon came to the conclusion that the author was Samyaza, and the sign was his own.

Lamech shut a thin folio depicting the monstrous denizens of the ocean's deep waters. "If an angel did this, then it is the work of one estranged from his Master," he stated. "No mention of the Lord God."

"There is no hint of *anything* spiritual here," Methuselah said. "As if in his infatuation with knowing the created, he severed himself from all knowledge of the Creator."

"Rather sad," said Hadishad.

"Rather?" said Lamech. "Nothing could be more tragic."

A lock turning sounded at the door, prompting Merim to move out of the way before the portals were thrust open. A being in the form of man, but with an ageless beauty that defied a natural origin, strode into the room, pure white tunic in perfect contrast with golden skin. He was unmistakable, even if the men there hadn't seen him at a distance in the council hall.

Samyaza was home.

Two attendants followed him, both carrying a parchment on board and a stylus in hand.

"A thousand apologies, and a thousand condolences," the Grigori said. "Have you eaten or drunk? Refreshed yourselves?" He swept his eyes over everyone in the room, but directed the question at Hadishad. The young man stuttered a negative, and Samyaza waved an attendant away to the larders.

Lamech sent a stern glare and a cold growl at the Grigori. "Whatever you may be, know this: me and mine will not be held captive like this."

"No, you will not." Samyaza interrupted the planned diatribe with perfect timing. "Consider this place to be your own. Roam freely as you like, but please, do not leave the palace grounds. I ask you to do this only for your own safety." He reached a hand down to Merim and pulled him to his feet. "I am sorry. There has not been a killing in the city since my late wife's father, decades ago. Enoch's guard proved overeager this night, bringing you here in such rough manner. In my role these people have given me, I have come to know them—they are good men."

"There is no such thing," said Methuselah.

Samyaza laughed. "No, I suppose there is not." The fallen angel glided further into the room. "I will not pretend I do not know who you are, honored Methuselah, or you, Lamech, but to the rest of you, my name is Samyaza." He bowed to the others as they named themselves, keeping his distance.

"We are not making a social call-" said Lamech through gritted teeth.

"I only extend to you the same hospitality you showed my own family."

"Listen, angel, and stop interrupting! My sons are gone!"

"Not only yours," Samyaza said, all empathy to Lamech's sharpness. "My fellow Azazyel lost his also. Gloryon was killed last night."

Hadishad let slip an epithet, and the surprise in the room arrested any reprimand. The Grigori let the unwelcome news settle.

"I have much to do," he said. "Despite what you might think of me, I hope you will judge me by my actions now. Many wrongs were done last night, and I will do my best to right them, or to see justice done. Until then, you all have but to request it, and it shall be."

"I have a request now," Methuselah said.

"Please, tell," said Samyaza. The attendant raised his stylus.

Methuselah spared a brief glance of pity at Emzara.

"Let me see the body of my grandson."

If the palaces and halls were silver and gold, the district guardhouse was iron in the midst of them—forged and formed by a master smith, but unmistakable in its hardness. Although capital crimes were so rare as to be legendary, the alleys and sewers were infested with every manner of sneak-thief and cutpurse, and robbery was always rampant. This kept the dungeons full and the guards employed. For the violent and covetous, the rich markets would always be too tempting a target to resist, and no spell in the prison cell would be deterrent enough. Cain's curse kept executions from being a final solution for lawbreakers, since no guard wanted to be the first to volunteer to put a local criminal to death, only to risk being on the receiving end of sevenfold vengeance. The iron bars were strong, though, and the guards were vigilant.

Ordered by Samyaza, a stout sergeant took Methuselah and Lamech through the barracks that housed the guards on duty. They marched down a bare hall, past room after barred room full of tariff chests and weapons stores. The door at the end was unlocked; the sergeant pushed it open.

"Go on in," he said, with eyes downcast. "Myself, I wish to stay out here. Never seen a dead body before—poor omen."

Lamech snorted, then entered. Methuselah followed, praying as he went.

"You ought not to touch the body," said the guard after them. "The apothecary said poison was used."

The corpse laid on a wooden table, and the same bloody sheet covered it from head to toe. Lamech took a deep, shuddering breath and stepped forward. He stopped.

"I cannot do it, Father." His voice cracked. A fearful tear gathered at the corner of his eye as he looked at Methuselah, imploring him without words.

His hand stretched out, Methuselah approached. Gingerly, haltingly, he pinched a corner of the sheet with his thumb and forefinger.

He pulled the sheet away.

· CHAPTER 32 ·

Emzara and Betenos were sitting by the fountain when the two men trudged into view. Their faces said everything, and crushed whatever frail hopes had taken root.

The body was Noah's.

Gloryon's funeral was held in the barrows outside the city, where Enoch, son of Cain, was entombed, along with his brothers and sisters who had already passed. A pyre was built high, and Gloryon's body was placed upon it. Malidoch had the honor of lighting the fire that returned his nephew and captain to the dust of the earth.

Gilyon stayed through the night, until the last embers had died.

He watched as Elohim's finger spun the dust of the new earth. Each inert particle was carried on His divine wind, randomness becoming order and symmetry as they coalesced into bone, sinews, muscle. The vessel formed, lifeless, waiting for a first vital spark to set it into motion. With the supremest satisfaction, Elohim breathed into it, its nostrils flaring as it accepted the Creator's gift of life into its lungs. Creation culminated in that first inhalation. Man was made.

Azazyel watched it happen just as it had occurred, a piece of history perfectly captured in his mind. He floated, suspended in the spring's scalding deep water, where even Lilith could not find him. A few days' disappearance had been the suggestion of Samyaza, who had been most displeased with the course of events. The Grigori's displeasure had been mild, though, compared to Azazyel's own fury with his *bene Sheol*, and himself for underestimating his son and the Scribes—be they thrice damned and cast headlong into Satan's foul kingdom! Losing three of his secret assassin corps was a high price to pay, even for Gloryon's demise, and with the death of the fourth—how did *that* happen, pray tell?—he could not afford to take his anger out on the scarred flesh of the survivor. More brutality in training, that was the answer—and first kills would never again be against a Naphil. Perhaps the sewer folk, or prisoners, or perhaps (and this was an inspired thought) he ought to pit the *bene Sheol* against one another. Bah. Dwelling on past failures would bear only so much fruit, none of it tasteful. Better to think on present successes.

Havak's lies may have been necessary, but they had indeed presented new problems. Fortunately, the oaf who had managed to die in the emissary suite was the skeletal one, an ideal fleshy canvas for Azazyel's deception. No human could have done what was needed; Havak had been incredulous at the thought (perhaps *he* might be a good first kill). For Azazyel, though—for a Watcher who saw the Creator mold the clay that would become Adam—it was akin to a child scribbling with a lump of talc on the pavestones.

True, having seen Noah with the spirit's vision did help. A reasonable facsimile would have been accomplished regardless—it was not difficult to fool the humans' dirt-vision—but as it was, every pore, every hair, every flake of skin could be pictured in a moment's recall. Sculpting Noah's likeness onto the *ben Sheol's* corpse had then been a simple matter, done in a night. Waxes and oils, tinctures and saps and treemilks, and a bit of patient craftsmanship had been more than enough to fool even the young man's father, which was exactly what had happened. The city's sculptors had come a far way from their crude clay figurines, and its dancers and whores might have become quite facile in painting faces since he had introduced the concept of cosmetics all those years ago, but he, Azazyel, was most certainly still the master in both arts.

The thought of Enoch's women of pleasure woke up a longing for Lilith that he could not deny. He surfaced for air and climbed out of the springs. Poor Lilith. She did mourn for her son, but her attachment was irrevocably to Azazyel, and he knew exactly how to assuage her pain. He was glad to have his woman.

And soon, very soon, Samyaza would have his new woman, too.

· CHAPTER 33 ·

It started with toasts. After seven days of mourning passed, Hamerch, Deneresh, and Gilyon began making daily visits to Gloryon's old captains, bearing wine and requests for memories of the departed Naphil hero. The guardsmen were themselves grieving, and none begrudged a young giant recollections of a father he would never know further. For Gilyon, the sessions were cathartic. His mother was sequestered in her family's ancestral home in the sixth circle, and a skeleton staff of servants was maintaining their own manor; Gilyon wanted to be in neither place.

City guards rotated their watches throughout the day and night. Likewise, the three young Nephilim conducted their surreptitious investigation at any and all hours, something Hamerch and Deneresh minded not at all: the former eluded the boredom he so dreaded, and the latter was able to drink all day.

The visits kept them occupied, but in a score of days and fifty-odd conversations, they had uncovered no conspiracy. Gilyon found time to help Jet move back to the manor house, accompanied by various sisters and aunts. If he had spared a thought on the matter, he would have found it rather odd that he had not seen his grandfather and grandmother, nor heard of Azazyel or Lilith paying any sort of visit to his mother. They were always so distant and absorbed in one another anyway, and he did not find occasion to worry on such a thing.

On the last day of the third week, everything changed. Hamerch, Deneresh, and Gilyon, on the invitation of a few guards with whom they had lately spoken, attended the retirement of a guardsman named Mozh in the fourth circle. Deneresh, as usual, livened the event with songs and copious wine ("courtesy of my generous father Dyeus," who knew nothing of it).

Hamerch adopted his gregarious persona, and Gilyon accepted the sympathy offered him with a stoicism that earned the respect of the guards who did not yet know him. By the end of the night, Mozh was convinced that the three Nephilim were his new best friends, "and one the son of Gloryon himself!" The request for a private interview later was instantly agreed to; when the last tipsy sergeant tottered into the dirt street, the giants clustered around a wooden table too small for them, and Mozh lit a lamp.

"Tell me, most excellent Mozh," said Deneresh, refilling his wine-cup, "why would a man in the prime of life want to leave the service of Enoch's guards?"

"Oh, I served my fair share. Thought it was time to move on, find a wife, travel a bit—three-hundred-and-fourty-four years is a right respectable stretch of time at the post." He stretched and yawned. "When I started, you know, all we guards had were staves. Wooden staves, I tell you!" Mozh obviously considered such a thing hilarious, and the buzz of alcohol made joining in his laughter easier for the Nephilim. "And a bronze knife when you made the nightwatch." He glanced at his polished iron knife, newly mounted above the modest hearth, a retirement present from a well-wishing colleague. "The Grigori changed everything, though."

"Come now," said Hamerch. "Our great-uncle Tubal-Cain was making leaps in weapon-smithing decades before the Grigori appeared."

"Steps, perhaps," said Mozh. "Azazyel showed him how to leap. Would have taken him centuries more than it did without the help of Azazyel." He spoke as a man relating facts about the *bene Elohim*, not in praise of him. "It was he who taught the painting of faces, too. I do admit, the ladies at the Kitten's Inn would not be so pretty—not that you young gentlemen ought to know about such a place."

Mozh grinned and nodded, a moment too long for a man completely sober. "But the best thing he gave us—by far, young Gilyon—was your father."

"Would you tell me what you remember about him?" asked Gilyon. He took a sip of wine, but quietly spit it back before he placed the cup back on the table. "It does me good to hear about him, sir."

"I will, gladly. Your father was one of the great ones," Mozh said. "Beholden to the city, he was. A servant of the people. That is how we all used to be, until the angels came down."

"You say it as if it were a bad thing," said Hamerch.

"No, no," said Mozh quickly. "True, there were hard feelings at first among some, what with the finest young ladies being swept up in an afternoon." He meant to lean in, but what he managed was more of a slump. "Had quite the fancy for a girl named Eisheth, myself, but she goes and marries Tamiel Grigori with not so much as a fare-thee-well! Ah, well. What was I talking about?"

"The Grigori," reminded Hamerch.

"Oh, yes. Well, the ones that made their homes in Enoch had much to offer us, and it was only natural that there were men who exalted them a bit more than others. What *my* problem is," he said, becoming more animated, "is that such partiality bled into the guard corps. We are honor-bound to the *city*, not to the Grigori."

"And there are guards who are not, you think?" Gilyon asked. He sensed that Hamerch and Deneresh were letting him take the lead now, and he wanted to tread carefully on these grounds, to see how far Mozh was willing or able to lead them.

"I do not think, young Gilyon." Mozh tapped his forehead, an adequately large target for his wavering finger. "I *know*." He sloshed the dregs of his cup into his mouth, spilling half down his chin. "You want to know why I really retired? I cannot prove anything, but I have…suspicions."

"Do tell," said Deneresh.

"I will," answered Mozh. "But you cannot. Promise?" They assured him that their mouths were henceforth sealed.

"Very well. The guardsmen are a tight-woven group. We keep our business *among* ourselves, but among ourselves, we know each other's business. I know who loves the Grigori more than others, same as we all do… the ones who buck and moan for council hall duty, or the palace beats… but what of it? All one and the same, as the *bene Elohim* have always done right by our people." Mozh paused, tilting his empty cup back and almost falling from his chair. Deneresh pushed him back into place and poured more wine.

"This will steady you, my good man. Continue, please."

"Right you are. Now, we guards are orderly men, and the captains set our posts on a regular schedule, like we like it. On the night when...well, when Gloryon and those Edenites were attacked...my place ought to have been outside the emissary quarters. Goose me with a stick, then, when I was informed that the posts had changed! I like a night off as much as the next, but I thought it right odd, with all that day's commotion already. I asked around, and I found that all the guards at the council hall posts had been changed, and the guards who had filled them were the openest Grigori supporters in the whole garrison. Odd, I said. But then the murders happened, and then the killers' bodies disappeared, and I knew it was all connected somehow, so I said to myself, 'That's enough for you, old man,' and now here I am."

Mozh stared sleepily into his cup, once again empty, then shot awake in a panic. "You'll not say anything, will you?"

"Our word is as iron," said Deneresh. "And what was that guard's name again, Mozh? The one who replaced you at your post that night?"

"Oh, yes. Young sergeant named Havak," he said, and drifted into drunken slumber.

⟨ CHAPTER 34 ⟩

A cage stretched between two acacia trees in the heart of Samyaza's garden, built of iron wrought to resemble the natural flow of the trees' trunks. A lion was held within. In appearances, the beast lived in luxury; fed with dragon steaks and aurochs marrow, with no need to hunt, it slept most of the day and all night. When it did walk about, there was no power in its prowling. Muscles rippled beneath the sheen of its coat, to be sure, but its mien was of an animal that was trapped, knew it, and could do nothing about it.

Methuselah visited the lion every morning, always with uneaten meat from breakfast. Today it was cold venison. He threw the meat between the bars; as he did so, he spotted an armored guard through the cage, standing attentively before a verdant archway, polearm at the ready. A gate lay beyond, the farmer knew, but for all the good the knowledge did him, it may as well have been the gate to Eden's Garden.

Methuselah watched the animal devour the venison.

"I know just how you must feel," he said, and sighed.

Hadishad, Lamech, and Merim were present, as they have been every day for almost a fortnight, for the report given by the guard to Samyaza. And like every day past, the news was conjecture and theory.

Today's lieutenant was an unsmiling man, with hair close-cropped but somehow still unkempt, as if a sheep-goat had mistaken it for grass and chewed it to the scalp. He held his horned helmet under his arm, and his hurried statement to the Grigori spoke to his obvious eagerness to retreat back into its authoritative anonymity as soon as possible.

229

"We are looking at malcontents in the city's inner circle," he said, "men who might have picked up rabid anti-Eden tendencies, maybe from Cain himself."

"Any sign of the missing Edenite, Jonan?" asked Samyaza. "Any arrests, any hard evidence?"

"No, and no. I am sorry I have nothing more." The guard made a twitchy bow.

Samyaza frowned. "Your men must work harder, Lieutenant." His frustration was visible, and the guardsman took his opportunity to exit. Once more, the Edenites trudged away disappointed.

Behind a carinate vase filled with tall ferns, unnoticed by her kin, Emzara listened. Nothing that was said interested her. Nothing could, save news of a miracle she knew would never happen. She walked off into the garden, seeking solace in strange surroundings that did not evoke memories of a life with her Noah, of a life promised to her, then lost.

Samyaza watched her go.

Noah's body had been burned without a funeral. Of the guardsmen who had touched the corpse since its discovery, three had fallen moribund, fevering and delirious; none had yet made a full recovery. Methuselah and Lamech had been quarantined for several days, and the captains of the guards had made the collective decision to dispose of the corpse before anyone else became ill. When Emzara and the rest of the family heard, Betenos only said, "May it be an aroma pleasing to the Lord God," and they made no complaint.

It was just another thing that Zara tried not to think about; these days, there were many of those. She had not lately been praying. The Creator felt far away. She was not angry at Him, though. She was not *anything*, really— anything but empty, a husk with no maize inside, a cold sky absent of stars.

The gardens were usually quiet, but today the hush was broken by a woman's soft babbling and a baby's laughter. Zara smiled despite herself. She loved babies, and in a family like hers, where a woman could and did have twenty, thirty, even forty children in her first few hundred years, they were ubiquitous. Few sounds could have drawn her from where she hid among the thorns and roses, but this did.

Zara recognized the woman who held the child: Zillah, mother of Samyaza's late wife. She held the baby securely around the waist and seated on her hip. Her face was familiar from their shared residence in the palace, but Zara had never had reason to speak to the woman. Zillah smiled invitingly at her, and she approached them.

"Hello," Zara said. "A precious child. Six months?" She held her hand out to the baby.

Zillah smiled again, this time sadly. "Not even three. He is my daughter's child, and Samyaza's. The children of the Grigori are large even from birth—the males, anyway." The baby boy reached for Zara's finger and gripped it. "You may hold him if you like," said Zillah.

The child held both arms to her. She took him from his grandmother, surprised at how heavy he was already. "What is his name?"

"Eudeon," answered Zillah.

"Eudeon. A good name." The child cooed, and suddenly a great weight of despair pressed on Zara, threatening to drive her knees to the ground. In a year, perhaps two, this could have been her child—hers and Noah's. The baby blinked his wide grey eyes as tears welled in hers.

A motherly hand alighted on her own, and the kind gesture was too much. Zara began sobbing, as the grief that she had fought so hard to hold back overwhelmed her. Zillah held her as she held the baby, until the wave of emotion passed.

The empathy in Zillah's eyes was genuine, borne of experience shared.

"This place is strange to you, I know," the older woman said, "but there are few places in this city where you might find others who know how you feel. I do. Samyaza does, more than anyone. He alone of the Grigori, alone even of your own family, knows how it feels to mourn the death of your true love." She took baby Eudeon back. "Please, talk to me any time. The pain will not last forever."

They walked away, and Emzara sat again among the roses, watering them with tears that seemed to flow unending.

Five days passed, every one the same. As soon as the mists faded, Zara would sit in the garden for hours. Betenos would join her occasionally, and Merim and Hadishad did their best to brighten her spirits, but in truth she preferred to grieve alone.

Footfalls on the grass gently interrupted her solitude, the intrusion from a source unexpected. Samyaza Grigori stood before her; in his hands was a thin wooden panel, blank, but he held it as if something adorned the side hidden from her.

"I did not feel right keeping this," he said, piquing the faintest curiosity from her. He turned the panel around. On the other side was a painting that was unmistakably of her, sitting in the garden. The details of her surroundings—the petals of the flowers, the light on the leaves—were done with masterful realism, but she was the centerpiece. She, or rather the image of her, looked very pretty, but the pitiable sorrow on her face nearly drowned the beauty from her features and the flora that framed her.

Samyaza offered it to her. "Please, take it. Excuse me. I will not bother you further."

Zara almost let him leave, but the picture, uncanny in its accuracy of both form and feeling, made her comment. "This looks just how I feel. However did you capture it so well?"

The Grigori examined the ground for a moment before answering. "I have felt the same. I live with the same sorrow I see on your face."

"It is...very good. Noah..." She swallowed. It was the first time she had spoken his name aloud, since...

"Do not speak of him if you do not wish to."

"No. No, it will do me good," said Zara. "He liked to sketch, and carve, too. We would go into the forests and sit for hours in the moss, waiting for the creatures of the woods to appear, and if they did not, he would draw the woods themselves. I loved to watch him."

"My subjects are the same," said Samyaza. "Birds, beasts—I have done my best to capture them all, pale imitations of the Creator's handiwork though my efforts may be. Working on them has been a true comfort to me since my wife...passed. I wonder—would you care to see them?"

"No, thank you. Please leave now," thought Zara, but she did not voice it. Something about the Grigori leader, something unexpectedly vulnerable, stilled her refusal. With some surprise, Zara heard herself say, "Yes, of course."

She followed him to the same room to which her family had been taken on the night of the attack. The memory of it was dim, as if from a dream, and no pain came from being there. One by one he showed her the folios. A study of bull, buffalo, and antelope horns caught her eye; she paged through it once, then again. Noah had done many of the same studies, although the charcoal sketches that had impressed her so at the time were hardly as sophisticated as Samyaza's paintings. He had been fascinated at the sheer number of variations descended from just a single bovid pair, and he had buried himself in the project for several months. She told the Grigori as much, minus the comparison, and this time the ache induced by Noah's name was not as acute.

"Keep it," said Samyaza. "I hope you think of him without sorrow tonight." She thanked him and left the room.

Three days passed. Dedroth and Pethun came for a visit, pushing past guards who did not dare to raise weapons against Samyaza's sons. The news they brought was much appreciated by the farmers: the family's dragons, camels, and horses were well-fed and safe in Dyeus' stables, the goods and produce from Eden had sold in the market for better prices than any of them had expected, and a reciprocal trading caravan was already being organized by merchants optimistic that the current trouble would soon end. The two giants were glad company for the Edenite men, and they promised to send greetings to Hoduín and his sons.

Zara still spent most of her days in the garden. The place had become pleasant to her of its own merit, and not only as a respite from the ache brought about by familiar faces and voices. She felt less sad, but this was countered by a guilt that she ought to feel sadder. Noah had been the anchor to which her emotions had been tied, safe and stable; with him gone, they now whipped freely to and fro against her mind and soul, and she tired of the pain.

A voice hailed her gently as she sat in the sunlight, and she was surprised how welcome she found it.

"Would you care to stroll with me?" asked Samyaza. "There is much more to my garden than these roses."

Zara ignored a fleeting concern that her grandfather or uncle might see her with the Grigori and disapprove, but Samyaza's manner was so benign, so polite. Besides, he had been most hospitable, especially for a host whose guests had been thrust upon him at neither of their choosings. She agreed.

"Thank you for the picture-book," she said. They walked among agaves with iron-blue leaves as broad as a man, some with tall, torch-like flower-stalks growing from their centers.

"The folio? Think nothing of it," he said. His hand rose, guiding Zara away from the agave spike that almost caught on her dress. He did not quite touch her, but the closeness of him made her start, and she stepped away. She blushed. Samyaza continued walking as if he had not noticed.

"Has the pain faded at all?" he asked.

Zara was glad for the conversation. She wished they could speak on a different subject, but as he was an angel who lived in a city palace, and she a farmgirl from Eden, they had little else in common.

"Only a bit," she replied, and realized that she spoke the truth. It had faded. "But at times it still seems endless."

The Grigori nodded. "The greater the love that is ripped away, the bigger the hole for the pain to fill." For a moment, he seemed to retreat inside himself, and Zara fancied that perhaps he thought of a happier day long past, another walk in his garden, but with a different woman.

"You loved your wife very much," said Zara.

Samyaza looked at her, returned from his reverie. "Enough to leave the heavens for her."

Zara thought again of her grandfather, and his father Enoch, gone long before she was born.

"You have been kind to my family," she said, "and please pardon if I overstep my bounds, but I must ask. I did not know my great-grandfather, but I know he did not trust you. Why?"

Samyaza sighed. "I tried to change his mind. In a way, I understand why he felt the way he did. But look around you. Look what we Grigori have helped build, how many lives we have made safe, filled with self-worth and useful labor. Your great-grandfather Enoch lived here. He saw it. He could have helped us, but instead he spoke against us."

"Why did he dislike you so?"

The Grigori became thoughtful. "You know of the history of Abel and Cain. You have read it, but I saw it acted. Sometimes, when two people strive to please God in different ways, one becomes envious—piously so, but the piety becomes anger and leads to sin. And sometimes when that happens, the sinner is removed—expelled." He left unspoken Enoch's translation.

"You cast him in the role of Cain," she said.

"Enoch lived his own role," he replied.

"What about the idolatry, the sorcery, the fleshliness of this city? You could teach these people the truth of the Creator. Why do you not?"

"Man is created in the image of God," replied Samyaza, heat in his voice that matched the flicker of white flame in his eyes. "I know this, because I watched as it happened. That means free will, which, poorly exercised, led to man's knowledge of good and evil, and the practice of both. We *bene Elohim* have seen the Creator God—not God on earth, but God in the heavens, the God who would burn the earth to dust should He unleash His glory on it. We have shared in that nature. If we used our full capacities to lead people to the knowledge of Him, none could resist. This city would be one of puppets, and we would be guilty of far worse than your great-grandfather ever accused us of." He seemed taken aback at the strength of his outburst. "Please excuse me," he said, "but I have other business to which I must attend."

He left her alone in the garden once more, her mind full of many thoughts both new and strange.

Zara missed the evening meal, choosing instead to stay in the garden and dine on a few figs offered her by a friendly gardener. She did not care to see Samyaza after their awkward conversation, but as she wandered, her thoughts returned to him. During the first days of their stay in the palace, she had ignored everything and everyone. However, she was surprised to realize that if she allowed herself, she could indeed recall glimpses, nothing more, of the Grigori—short vignettes poorly remembered, but that together had formed an impression of him that had let him talk to her, be near her, when she had wanted to be alone. He treated his servants with respect and kindness, and they responded with near-reverence. The guards, too, deferred to him. Even the members of her own family, who were no natural friends of the *bene Elohim*, had been shown as much hospitality as they might have expected in Eden. True, they had been given no other option, but she trusted the sincerity of Samyaza and the guards in believing that it was for their own protection.

The stars came out, bright and close, as if the Creator had painted the night sky with solid strokes of pure white light. A rustle behind her turned her head. She was not afraid—not in this place.

Samyaza was there. He approached, and she did not move away. He touched her on the arm. The strangeness of his hand was completely different than the familiar touch of Noah, and it sent shocks through her body. She began to tremble uncontrollably.

Before, she had appreciated that Samyaza was handsome beyond human, but only as a fact that had no bearing on her or anything she cared for. Now, with his eyes locked onto hers, the Grigori's unearthly beauty impacted her viscerally, violently. He whispered.

"Zara."

He kissed her, and she was simply not ready for the intensity of the desire that flooded her when his lips touched hers. He pressed closer to her, kissing her again. His fingers buried themselves in her hair, pulling her more fully to him. Zara surrendered to the flood and was washed away.

· CHAPTER 35 ·

Abutting the eighth wall of Enoch, on the very inner edge of the final circle of the city, was a row of tall houses called Galil's Folly. Before the moat was excavated and the ninth wall had arisen, the occupants of the row were generally of an undesirable sort; either their possessions were too meager or few to benefit from the protection of the city, or they wished to have no gates obstructing their larcenous movements. Some might beg, and some might steal, but either way, the folk of the Folly were after honest men's gold.

Years had passed, and times had changed. With the Grigori and the ninth wall came the halls and palaces, and with those came all the children of Cain drawn to the new center of power: monied merchants, patricians, politicians, scholars. The Folly underwent renovation and renewal, and its tenants became of a decidedly better class as the dregs of Enoch's society scattered into the hostel-communes outside of the city or burrowed into the underground. The observatories of the College of Astrology were built on the hills around the row, and many of the Grigori with an interest in the movements of the heavens, chief among them Tamiel, Barkayal, and Asaradel, could often be spotted in the chartmakers' and lens-crafters' shops. Of any district or any dwelling in the whole of the great city, none had ascended so high from so ignoble a beginning. And surrounded by stargazers, perhaps it was fitting that the cost of a home on Galil's Folly was astronomical.

"How is a sergeant of the guard able to afford a place in *these* rarified environs?" Deneresh asked. The question was to himself, and it was asked mostly so he might hear himself speak. His companions had been quiet, painfully so. Hamerch was too serious for a young giant currently

237

carrying four precious new skins of wine from Eden, and Gilyon had been smoldering in silence since their visit with Mozh. Deneresh had taken it upon himself to send a runner to Havak, informing him of the call the Nephilim planned to make. He used the same pretense under which they had been operating, with the addition of a message of gratitude "for the brave guardsman who protected our friends from Eden, those who could be saved." Havak had sent the runner back with quick acceptance, and the Nephilim set out on foot with the wine.

The Nephilim must have been watched from the window, for at their approach—which was unmistakable, for the least of them was two heads taller than a human—Havak swung the door open and welcomed them in.

The sergeant lived alone, and the sparse furnishings in the house's den spoke to the fact. There were no pots of plants, no dyes or patterns on the rugs, none of the appurtenance of a home with a woman living in it. What details were there were martial: the armor of a guardsman dressed a wooden manikin, and a rack of weapons took up most of one wall. Metal-and-glass windows, relics of the Folly's beggared past, let in ample sunlight. After proper introductions, Hamerch offered the wineskins to the sergeant.

"What is this?" asked Havak.

"Wine from Eden, in honor of our friends from that land, and in thanks for your duty well-performed."

"Duty needs no thanks," answered Havak, "but I will not refuse. Come in! My home is yours. I will return in a moment—I shall bring cups for the wine, and alebread, and I have been roasting the finest sausages I could find. Please, sit." He ran off to the back of the house, leaving the three Nephilim alone in the den.

The giants were gratified to discover that the bowl-shaped chairs were oversized and comfortable.

"'Finest sausages,' he says." Deneresh turned up his nose in distaste. "And I am sure his latrines empty into the cleanest sewers."

"Ah, now we are all in the proper mood for this business," said Hamerch. "Men have died, brother—men we knew. Do not let the thought of wine make you forget why we are here. Besides, sausage is delicious."

"Gristle and filler," retorted Deneresh.

"Quiet. He returns," said Gilyon.

The smell of savory meats and warm bread followed Havak into the room. He set the wooden platter of food down on a low table and handed out cups. "The sons of the Grigori honor this house. Anything you need, please ask."

"Thank you," said Gilyon, pinching a sausage between a piece of bread. "You know why we are here?"

"You wish to hear of your father," said Havak. "Other guards have spoken of your visits. I did not know him—not personally. I know all the tales they tell in the barracks, though."

"All the tales?" Gilyon asked. "I would wager you have not heard of his run-in with the juggler bandits."

"Jugglers? No, I do not think so."

"Ah! Then listen. Wine, Deneresh?" The youngest Naphil poured with enthusiasm, and their host took a sip.

"This is excellent!" Havak took a longer draught and wiped his mouth.

"Believe me, we know," said Deneresh. "This is some of the last that is left to us. Most of it was served at the feast that my father held—but I forget! You were otherwise engaged." He sighed. "A pity. With all that has happened to them, I would not be surprised if the Edenites leave this place as soon as they are able, never to return."

The sergeant looked into his cup. "Pity indeed." He raised his eyes to the young giant's, smirking slightly. "But then again, *some* may stay."

"Hm? Have you heard word from our grandfather Samyaza's palace?"

Havak head snapped up, his face denoting surprise at his own words. "No, no. I was only…" He trailed off and took another drink. "Only talking."

Rapping his knuckles once on the table, Hamerch excused himself to the washroom. Havak pointed the way, then listened attentively to Gilyon's story. Here he was, already favored of Azazyel, and now befriended by Nephilim, who were surely still young enough to be impressed by a warrior, a leader, like himself. A wave of good fortune was washing over him; he needed only to relax and let it carry him.

With a stealthiness and speed that came from much practice, Hamerch opened and shut cabinets and ran his fingers over wooden walls. A liar, he thought, can always tell another liar, and Hamerch would have recognized

Havak even if they had not already suspected him of being involved in… well, *something*. With dozens of new acquaintances in the guard corps, it had been easy enough to ascertain a sergeant's salary, and it was not near so high as to be able to rent a regular room at the inns around Galil's Folly, much less have a home here. Havak did not come from a family of any means, or else the Nephilim, who did, would know of them. So where did he obtain enough gold to live here, like this? Hamerch could not yet say, but he bet himself that if he found that gold, an angelic sigil would be stamped on it.

Enough time had passed that he knew he ought to return. His search had been unfruitful, and he was disappointed…but suppose the evidence of Grigori patronage was not hidden at all? Perhaps… Hamerch hurried back to the den.

Since his father's death, Gilyon had spent most of his waking hours absorbing the memories of others. Sharing his own, and discovering that he could do so with his grief overwhelming him, was gratifying. Sergeant Havak was a rapt audience, and when Gilyon had finished his storytelling, he looked sad.

"A true shame, what happened," Havak said. "I know hardened guards, men I could swear were made of stone, who wept openly when they heard. I still cannot believe…" He stopped himself as Hamerch appeared.

"An excellent home you have," the Naphil said to the sergeant. He paused at the weapon rack. "May I?" Havak nodded, and Hamerch picked up a broadsword, Cain's mark prominent on the butt of the handle and the middle of the sheath. "This is standard issue?"

The sergeant nodded again. "The sword of the palace guard."

"Superb. Gilyon has a spear made by Tubal-Cain. Deneresh and I have nothing so fine—our elder brother Mareth is the fighter in our family."

Deneresh sniffed and sipped from his cup. "I wish my hands to be stained with wine, not blood."

His brother chuckled, examining each of the weapons in turn. Most were blades of a type, with several blunt instruments rounding out the collection. Hamerch had a good feeling now; a hilt caught his eye, and he knew he had found success.

"What think you of this, Gilyon? Something here to match even Tubal-Cain's workmanship." The sword was double-edged and long, half of a human's height. Where the blade met the hilt was shaped like a bull, with horns extending to either side to form the guard. The handle was leather-wrapped, and a sigil was etched into the forte. Gilyon took the sword in his hands and inhaled sharply as he recognized the sign.

Sergeant Havak was no heavy drinker, but this wine was going to his head far faster than it ought. The sunlight streaming through the windows was too hot, too bright—he felt himself flushed, and his eyes hurt. As the Naphil appraised his prize possession—he dared not tell them no—his heart began to race. Suddenly his mouth went dry, as if his tongue had turned to cotton. He took another drink, but it did not help.

Gripping the sword, Gilyon strode to Havak and knelt to face him. "Where did you get this?" the young giant asked. His tone was mild, but menace laced it. The sergeant swallowed.

"From…from Azazyel Grigori."

"For *what?*"

Havak could not stop himself, although he tried desperately. "I am sworn to him." The three Nephilim were clustered around him now. A terror, not entirely inexplicable, began to rise in his chest; at least their giant forms blocked the horrid light.

"What happened the night my father died?" Gilyon asked. The words ground together like dry bones. "What happened to Noah?"

Havak felt as if the morning mists had condensed in his head, all of his carefully constructed lies hidden from his thoughts. Only the truth remained, a last bright thread of sanity in his confusion, and he could not help but grasp it, then pour it out with barely a stammer. He told everything: his small cell of guards loyal to Azazyel, the assassination plan, the existence of the *bene Sheol*, the cover-up of the body's identity. Havak had not known of the attack on Gloryon, though. He finally finished, slumping in his chair.

Quivering, Gilyon turned his back on the sergeant. The blade of the sword he still held, the gift of Azazyel, sang as he pulled it from its scabbard. He spun back around, reared back, and snarled, rage in his eyes. "Noah was our friend, wastebag."

241

Before he could send the blade through Havak, strong arms pinned his. "He is not worth it," whispered Hamerch. "Keep him here. I will run to get my father and my uncles. The council will know of this. Your father will be avenged." He tucked the panels of his long tunic into his belt and ducked outside.

Deneresh fell into a chair and threw one leg over a side. "Nothing to do but wait, I suppose. Gilyon, have you control of the situation?"

The seated sergeant stared blindly at the floor, his pupils enormous black discs that obliterated whatever color his eyes had been. Unsheathed sword still in hand, Gilyon nodded.

"Then I shall pass the time in the best way I know." The giant youth unplugged an untouched wineskin and drank straight from it.

"The sergeant was drinking more than wine, wasn't he?" asked Gilyon.

Deneresh smacked his lips in satisfaction. "Indeed. Mixed with a truth-telling potion—a derivation of henbane, according to dear Uncle Dedroth. It worked like a charm, I must say."

Gilyon smiled grimly and flicked the tip of the sword in Havak's direction.

"Or in his case, a curse."

· CHAPTER 36 ·

The next day, the guards did not show to Samyaza's palace to give their daily report. In their place, however, came a collection of council members: Irad, three of his sons, and Dyeus, Pethun, and Dedroth. Enoch's guardsmen were represented, too, with several captains and lieutenants accompanying the council, including Malidoch, but they were brooding and silent and said nothing. Irad did the speaking. He informed Samyaza of all Havak had admitted to them, this time under an oath rather than a potion: Azazyel's plans for assassination of Gloryon and Noah, the existence of his secret cadre of guards and the *bene Sheol*. Samyaza listened, his expression so impassive that the old man may as well have been speaking to sculpted marble.

Methuselah and Lamech listened too. An ember of fury began to burn in them at the details of Azazyel's evil schemes, but it changed in an instant to a flame of hope when Irad mentioned, almost as an addendum, that Havak had lied about the corpse. Lamech whooped with joy and immediately ran off to tell the rest of the family the unbelievable news; Methuselah stayed to hear the rest, all the while weeping tears and whispering prayers of thanks.

Zara was the last to know. She had slept late, exhausted. The night before had drained her, both emotionally and physically, but her languor now was a reminder that what happened had not been a dream.

She almost jumped from bed when Betenos' scream cut through her torpor. Her aunt burst into her quarters a moment later, near-hysteria making her three words shrill, but they were unmistakable.

"Noah is alive!"

243

Azazyel lounged in his private sanctum in the heart of his palace, drinking. The crests of half-burnt candles thrust upwards from chaotic beds of spent wax, spilling light unevenly about the room. He had been here for days, happy to let Lilith play mistress of the house to callers paying respects and offering condolences. He did not keep up on news of the aftermath of what he had set in motion—when? It seemed so long ago now. Had the moon almost cycled again?

The *bene Elohim's* drink of choice was a kind of distilled mead, made with honey and spices. He drank from a golden flask, savoring each mouthful. The nectar was sublime, and mortal man did not possess the secret to its making.

A figure darkened the doorway, and as only one being would dare violate Azazyel's sanctum so freely, he knew at once who it was.

"Do come in, Samyaza. You have clearly already made yourself at home."

"You lied to me," said Samyaza. "Noah is not dead." The alcohol's power over even his angelic mind kept Azazyel from recognizing the dangerous coldness in the voice.

"Ah." Azazyel wondered how that particular piece of information had come to light. He considered an excuse, but gave it up as too strenuous a mental exercise. "Ah, what difference does it make? He is gone, is he not? You yourself said you did not want to know."

Samyaza shook his head and chuckled. He beckoned for the flask and picked up a candle.

"This…purging. You said it would be like blowing out a flame, yes?" Azazyel shrugged. Samyaza took a long drink and studied the flickering tongue of fire.

Suddenly, he turned towards Azazyel and spewed a mouthful of mead through the flame. The liquor ignited, creating a massive fireball that engulfed Azazyel. The Grigori screamed and pushed away with powerful legs, crashing himself into the ground and breaking his chair to kindling. He rolled around on the rug underneath him, its bold, colored patterns curling into smoking black char. Samyaza ran to him and began to barrage his body with the vicious kicks of a madman. Azazyel's screeching turned to muffled whimpers, then finally stopped. Between his frenzied, spastic rolling and Samyaza's assaults, the flames were beaten out. Once-flawless skin was now angry red tissue. Samyaza spat on Azazyel's body, and a small spurt of steam arose from where his saliva fell.

The flames had died, but the ruined red flesh blazed like it were lit from within; at the places where the burns were deepest, a white light shone through. Azazyel sat up. He threw his head back and roared as the inner glow intensified. When it dimmed, his flesh was pristine once more. Samyaza tapped his toe in impatience as Azazyel rose to his feet.

"That," Azazyel said, every word broken by a heaving breath, "was Lilith's favorite rug! It was from Havilah! Gates of Sheol, how will I explain this to her?"

"Think you more on how you will explain to the council," said Samyaza. "Beyond that…how far do you think you can fall before our Father intervenes in our affairs?"

"*Elohim* stopped intervening a long time ago," Azazyel scoffed. "Long ago did Adam pass from the childhood of his creation and the bosom of his Creator. He chose his own way, as do his descendants, as do we. Was this not the purpose of the gift of free will? Do you still coddle your own children as if they were still babes? I do not."

"No, you simply ignored them entirely until they ran off to foreign lands. Except Gloryon, of course…whom you had *killed*. Do not speak! Only consider carefully what you will say to the council."

He turned and left, leaving Azazyel fuming.

Dyeus was a wealthy man. His estate consisted of several palatial structures sprawled on a dozen high acres near the luxury merchants of North Bridge, a lazy lion prince overlooking his pride. He was also a family man. He shared his home with his two brothers, their three sisters, and most of his children and their mothers. In truth, he was wedded to his sister Eila, who, being a jealous woman, demanded that his mistresses live apart from the central manor. He was an animal not amenable to taming, though, and considered every woman fair prey.

The den of the manor was a male's territory. Trophies from the hunt adorned the walls, as well as a dozen or so tastefully-done paintings of nudes. A fire was always crackling, and food and drink were never in short supply.

Words spoken in this place had the least chance of falling on strange ears, which is why Dyeus, Pethun, Dedroth, and Mareth were gathered here.

"We must wait for our moment," said Dyeus. "Bide *our* time, for the time of our father is soon over. If Gloryon can fall… We cannot be forever safe with the Grigori around."

"But we need a human face," said Pethun. "If we Nephilim act alone, even with the rest of the children of the *bene Elohim*, can we be sure that the humans will follow us? We need someone who will not be seen to rise up only to take power for himself."

Dedroth folded his hands. "Noah might have been perfect."

"Perhaps, but we do not know where he is," said Pethun.

"What about his brother, Hadishad?" Mareth asked. "He would be easily manipulated. He is enamored of us."

"No, Dedroth is right," said Dyeus. "It needs to be Noah. Survivor of Azazyel's attack, the firstborn descendant of Enoch the Scribe, friend of the murdered Gloryon."

"He could unite the humans who hate the Grigori—who would never follow their sons alone," said Dedroth.

"And after, he would simply go away," continued Mareth. "He would have no desire to share rule here."

"A wonderful plan," said Pethun, leaning back and draping his long arms on the back of a fur-covered couch. "Now all we have to do is find the man."

A bell rang twice, letting the giants know they had a visitor; the estate's servants were strictly forbidden from entering the den unannounced.

"Who is it, man?" Mareth shouted.

An unseen doorman answered from the hallway. "Councilman Onim, to see Masters Dyeus, Pethun, and Dedroth."

Mareth growled. "Shall I toss him out now?"

"Calm, son," said Dyeus, rising with his brothers. "If that fanatic has brought himself to set foot here, his business must indeed be important."

Onim paced back and forth only a step from the front entry. He jumped when Dyeus hailed him, but his face was stern when he spoke.

"I have come to tell you that we have a mutual friend," he said. "And it seems that we now have in Azazyel Grigori a mutual enemy. We are all councilors of Enoch, and we must work together to keep our city safe. Azazyel's threats of his family's deaths kept him away, but no longer, thanks to you."

"Speak plainly, man," said Pethun. "Of whom do you speak?"

Dyeus was not partial to any god, but when Onim replied, he felt for a moment that some divine providence must occasionally shine upon mortals.

"Noah, of course—and I know where he is."

ᐧ CHAPTER 37 ᐧ

"Thank you for doing this for me," Onim said, raising his voice over the clipping of hooves on stone.

"I am not doing this for *you.*" Perched on his crested dragon borrowed from the Edenite farmers, Hamerch tugged on the reins as they entered the courtyard of Samyaza's palace. "Noah and Jonan are my friends. If you are the vehicle that unites them with the ones they love, so be it."

"Nevertheless, I could never gain entrance here by myself. I am no friend to the Grigori."

"Or their sons, for that matter." Hamerch leapt to the ground and handed a stableman the dragon's reins. "Perhaps you ought to cease your raging bigotry."

"Hamerch!" Hadishad called from across the courtyard, where a line of packhorses stood by open chests and bags. Several men looked up, and Hamerch recognized some of them from their dealings with his father.

"What is all this?" the Naphil asked.

"We leave tomorrow for Eden with these men and their trade caravan," answered Hadishad. "Just my mother and I, though. Father and Grandfather will stay in the city until Noah and Jonan are found. Not surprisingly, Emzara refused to leave, and Merim would not depart without his sister. Which reminds me—I need my dragon back."

The young giant laughed. "Indeed you do. I shall miss him."

Hadishad whistled for the stableman, who brought the crimson beast to him. The dragon seemed happy to see him, sending a loud honk echoing about the courtyard. "Do not be too disappointed," said the farmer. "He *is* a breeder, you know. I shall send a hatchling back for you."

"Young man," Onim said, "your family need not split up again."

"Oh, right," said Hamerch. "Hadishad, this is Onim. He has good news for you and your kin."

"News that you all ought to hear together," Onim said.

Hadishad nodded. "I shall fetch them now."

Compared to the revelation that Noah still lived, Onim's news was met with fewer tears and more shouts of praise. Hamerch promised to send over their animals that night.

"And please give the gold your father paid for our goods to the poor," said Methuselah. "We are all in accord. Consider it a gift to the city in the name of the Lord God Creator Elohim, for all that you and your family have done for us. For our part, we only want to leave this place."

"But do bring our neighbors' profits," added Lamech. "From what we have seen of what this caravan carries, the men of Eden will want full purses."

"When will you leave?" asked Onim.

"The merchants say they will be ready in two days," answered Lamech. "Does Noah know where we have been? That we are all safe and coming to him?"

"He will tonight," said Onim, "for I go to tell him now."

Zara caught up with Onim as he and Hamerch walked to the stables.

"I would go with you," she said. "I must see Noah now. I cannot wait two days."

Onim smiled. "I understand, young lady, but I must be quick, and my horse is unaccustomed to two riders."

"Hamerch and I will follow you on the dragon," she said, in a tone that brooked no argument.

The Naphil shrugged. "I have naught better to do. Truth be told, I would like to see Noah myself."

"Very well! This old man will not stand in the way of a young love." Onim swung up to the saddle. "Let us be off."

Noah and Jonan had not been idle for the last month. They, along with a group of Scribes whose full-time residence had been their now-abandoned underground halls, had been staying at an inn on the road to

Fowl Bridge. The brothers paid for their lodging by laboring on the construction of a new wing. Some days they felled timber; others they fashioned the joinery for beams and crosses; and lately, they had begun to build the skeleton of the structure.

The other Scribes joined them, doing whatever work they were best able during the day, then gathering for food, drink, and songs in the evening. Noah's thoughts were constantly on Emzara, but the fellowship helped him to miss her less keenly, and the labor let him sleep soundly at night.

"We cannot stay here forever," said Jonan. The sawblade he and Noah worked together provided a backdrop of noise that lent their conversation a modicum of privacy. "It has been almost a month. You need to choose. Leave for Eden, or return to Enoch?"

"Yet I cannot choose either," said Noah. "So my choice is to put my trust in the Creator God."

"All I ask is that you do not let your faith be an excuse for passivity," replied Jonan. "Sometimes I fear that when you say, 'Trust the Lord,' what you mean is 'Spare me the burden of action.'"

"You want action, little brother? More sawing, less talking."

The arrival of new travelers to the inn always arrested the construction work. Fowl Bridge was the entrance to the Enoch's animal markets, and the road that ended there was well-worn. From stallion breeders leading lines of horses, to traders in pets and familiars, and even the occasional dragon tamer, the flow of men with God's creatures in tow was varied and constant.

A bray drew the brothers' attention to the road. A horse and a dragon approached, but these animals were no strangers to Noah.

"Burning blood. Can it be?"

Noah dropped his end of the saw, hurdled over a short palisade, and sprinted down the road. The dragon's red crest was unmistakable, as were the riders, even in the fading daylight. While the horse trotted on, the big reptile slid to a stop and crouched. The giant on the beast kept his seat, but the girl in front of him jumped lithely down and ran to Noah, almost matching him for speed. They met in a collision of an embrace.

"Zara! Praise God, Zara!"

Zara clutched Noah so tightly as to hurt him. "I thought you were dead," she whispered.

"Dead?" Noah laughed. "Not I. *I* was afraid for *your* life. Are my mother and father coming?"

"Soon," she said. "I have so much to tell you. Where can we speak?"

"I can ask the innholder to use his quarters."

Zara nodded, and Noah took her arm and led her to the inn.

The innholder was a generous man called Uphansim, himself a worshipper of the Creator God and partial to the Scribes, and he acquiesced easily. He and Jonan hosted Onim and Hamerch in the common room with ale, pickled gherkin, and cold meat pies for the giant, and left the couple to their privacy. For the first time since Eden, Noah and Zara were together alone.

"Here, my love, let me take your cloak."

He touched her on the shoulders to pull her towards him, but his hands slipped roughly from them as she resisted. She looked pale, ill.

"Noah, I have to go back."

Zara might have well been speaking in some unknowable angelic tongue, for all the meaning she imparted to Noah. He heard the words, but from her mouth, in this time and place, he simply could not comprehend them. He blurted through his aphasia.

"Where?"

"To Enoch. To…to Samyaza."

"*Samyaza?*"

Not that Noah noticed, but the chattering from the common room stopped. Though her features were cast in a sickly sort of expression, color had returned to Zara's cheeks. It was as if the words she said had been vomitus: unpleasant coming out, but all felt better once disgorged.

"And why, pray tell," said Noah, "must you do that?"

"Because I fell in love with him," she said. "Because…I am one flesh with him." She dropped her eyes, reddened cheeks plain even in the faint firelight.

A sick vacuum in Noah's gut sucked any response from his tongue, and he stared dumbly at her. A door's crash split the silence, and Onim burst into the room.

"Young fool!" His spittle flew as he spoke, and Zara backed away, surprised and fearful. "You admit that you have given your heart and your body to this *irin*. Know you not that you risk your soul, as well? Whore!"

The fist lashed out in reflex, and before he realized what he had done, Noah was standing over a prostrate old man bleeding from a lip split like a roast apple. The brief violence served as a catalyst for a rambling apologetic from Zara, one which she had obviously spent much time rehearsing.

"Azazyel fooled Samyaza too, just as he did the rest of us," she said. "He is a good…well, person. I mourned you every day in his gardens, and he comforted me. He needs me, Noah. I do believe that this happened for a reason—I *must* believe it. In time, you will see." She pulled the hood of her cloak over her head. "Meanwhile, please try to be happy for me." She paused at the threshold.

"I told you." She finally forced her eyes to meet his. "I thought you were dead."

Her soft steps out of the door were agony to Noah. "Hamerch, take me back," he heard her say. He stood there frozen, wracking his spinning mind for some plan, some word he could say to erase the ones already spoken. When he heard the creak of the common room doors and a girl's voice, at once so familiar and so foreign, call for a stableboy, he gave it up and rushed out.

The Naphil was already astride their dragon, and Zara was gathering her long cloak to mount in front of him.

"You cannot leave! Hamerch, do not let her leave!"

"Would you keep me here by force?" Emzara climbed the leather slings of the dragon's saddle. "Or have me walk the miles alone in the dark?"

Hamerch shook his head in mute apology and snapped the reigns, leaving Noah livid behind him.

"I forgave your betrayal once, Hamerch! Not this time! Do you hear?" He took up an axe that leaned against a stack of timber and hurled it as far as he could down the road, where a trunk-like tail was quickly disappearing into the dusk. "Not this time!" His head swam and he dropped to his knees.

"His gardens, eh?" Onim leaned against Uphansim, holding his tender jaw. An aghast Jonan stood beside them. "This is not the first time that a woman has fallen to temptation in one of those."

Onim and Jonan helped Noah to his feet. His rage—at Emzara, at Hamerch, at Samyaza—burned up his tears. Other Scribes were gathered around now, drawn to the drama, respecting his pain.

"The Grigori will never let her go," said Onim. "They take what is not theirs, and no one moves to stop them. I ask you again, Noah. Will you lead us against the Grigori?"

"They want the earth," Noah said. "We shall bring them blood and fire and death." With one last glance down the road towards Enoch, he pushed through the group of men and went inside the inn.

Jonan looked at Onim, then the rest of the Scribes.

"I think that means yes."

· CHAPTER 38 ·

In the deep of the night, Enoch was quiet. The towers of the Grigori palaces rose from the mists that blanketed the city, where Tamiel and Barakayal and Asaradel watched the stars, as they did every night while their wives slept. Azazyel brooded in the deeps beneath his dwelling, a hidden place where no light had ever shown, absorbed in his dark fantasies. Samyaza lay with Emzara in his bed, enthralled by the novelty of discovering everything about her.

Her family had not departed without vehement objection, and Merim and Lamech had threatened violence, but between Zara's insistence on staying and the prospect of soon seeing Noah and Jonan, they left with the caravan as scheduled. In some ways, Samyaza was thankful for the harsh words spoken, as separation from kin would be easier for an angry woman. Zara was still sad, but Samyaza had been agreeably successful at using his considerable talents to comfort her and put her mind on more pleasant things.

As far as they were both concerned, they were now husband and wife. Samyaza held no regard for human traditions; in his mind, the consummation of marriage was the only act needed to create it. He knew Zara wanted a wedding of some sort—it couldn't be what she had imagined for herself in Eden, but Samyaza desired so much more for her than some provincial ceremony.

He shut his eyes so the light that shone from them would not wake his new bride. One by one, the four other *irin* answered his call. They met in their minds.

"Found a few moments to spare, have you?" thought Azazyel.

"Quiet," thought Tamiel. "As if your free time has been better spent. Your troublemaking has cost us a century of goodwill with these people."

"What about Samyaza?" Azazyel snarled mentally. "Shall his lonely loins not share some of the blame?"

"Watch yourself," thought Samyaza. "If Emzara had her way, you would be rotting in the pit right now."

"She ought to tell Lilith that," returned Azazyel, "but then, you would need find another bride."

"I said there would be trouble," said Barkayal. "I warned everyone. And I do question the wisdom of keeping the Edenite girl here."

Samyaza sent a wordless mental rebuke to Barkayal. "She is my wife now. She belongs wherever I am."

Asaradel alone projected calm. "This all comes from having children, you know. I hope you are more careful in your relations with this girl, Samyaza."

"Keep your expelling poisons away from Zara. You know we suffer you to use them only with great misgiving."

Asaradel sniffed. "Your son Pethun makes common enough use of them."

"Please, enough bickering," thought Barkayal. "This is beneath us. Samyaza, why have you called us?"

"I believe I have the answer to our problems, whatever their cause," he thought. "And despite Asaradel's opinion on the value of progeny, I took the idea from my sons. We shall have a wedding, Emzara and I, held in Enoch, and it shall be unrivaled in the history of the earth. All of the Grigori shall come, bearing the finest food and drink of their lands. The city will feast beyond their dreams, and once more they shall remember the gifts we *bene Elohim* can bestow."

"That is actually not a bad idea," thought Tamiel.

"I agree," thought Asaradel. "After all these years, it would be nice to see our comrades and their wives in person."

"Then let us invite them now."

The furthest away that any of the *irin* had settled was several months' journey from Enoch by caravan, although since then mankind had spread beyond them, establishing colonies and continuing to tame the still-vast wilderness. Samyaza's white lances of thought, however, were unbound by time or distance, and each found its target: Kokabiel in his tall tower, watching over the lands of Mu; Amazarak, chief shaman of the Lephaur nations, in his forest dwelling with his witch-wife and his herbs; Armers, in the heart of Kalab, city of sorcerers. All in all, one hundred and ninety-five *irin*—councilors to kings, patrons of scholars, artists and healers, sires of renowned heroes and lovers of beautiful women—received word. None of them denied the call. A flurry of thoughts of a logistical nature flew back and forth in a matter of seconds.

In moments, the time was agreed upon.

"I will spread the word throughout the city," thought Samyaza to the others. "In four moons, we will have our wedding, and Cain's people will be witness to an event they will not believe."

In Irad's ancient keep in the third circle, an unlikely group of conspirators met in secret. Dyeus, Dagdha, and Hoduín stooped in an inner room too small for them, along with Tubal-Cain, Onim, Raposh, and old Irad.

"The merchants' guild will stand with us," Raposh said. "Days of city-wide feasting might be good for the masses, but I have convinced them that commerce will come to a standstill. Most are not so wealthy that they can afford it. Have we gained the support of the guardsmen yet?"

Dyeus shook his head no. "We still are not sure who we can trust. Our fathers are occupied now, but if word reaches them…"

"I told you," said Dagdha, "Malidoch is our man. He burns for revenge since his nephew's death."

"Yes—against Azazyel, the husband of his sister," said Dyeus. "He is too close to the matter. We need a cool head, a strategist."

"Besides, he is occupied with hunting the *bene Sheol*," added Hoduín. "My sons aid him on occasion. They say he is consumed by it—although he has found no sign of them."

Irad slapped a leathery fist on a table that was older than any of the other men there. "Azazyel must pay. My grandfather's curse must be honored, angel or no."

"It will, and more," said Tubal-Cain. "Relax, Greatfather."

"Someone must tell Noah of the wedding," asked Hoduin.

"Why do we even need that farmer?" asked Tubal-Cain.

"Because in the eyes of the people, you are one of us, turning against family," said Dyeus. "And Raposh cares only for his gold, and Onim hates the Grigori out of envy or bigotry. At least, that is what will be said. Noah gives us a figurehead who acts of pure motives, and he can unite us as no one else can."

Raposh glanced around the table and laughed, his jowls bouncing in time with his belly. "Look around you. It would seem he already has."

"And do not forget the power he might bring through his God," said Hoduin.

"Trust me," said Tubal-Cain, "I have all the power we need at my forge."

"I will send Hamerch to Noah," said Dyeus. "To tell him we are on his side. To tell him we will fight once more for his cause."

Dyeus gave Hamerch his new errand in the morning. "I am proud of you, son. You are more clever than I give you credit for."

"I still feel badly," said Hamerch. "I could have left her there at the inn."

"And then Noah would have had no need to join us," said Dyeus. "You did what you needed to do when the opportunity presented itself. Beg forgiveness if you must. He is a man who will grant it."

At Uphansim's inn, Noah and Jonan continued their labor, now aided by Lamech and Methuselah. Merim, Hadishad, and Betenos had continued on with the caravan and were now several days into their journey back to Eden. Other Scribes, including Kiribaoth, Thims, and a healed Gregan, were now congregated at the inn as well, and more arrived every day.

"How could she do it, Father?" Noah took a draught of cool wellwater and poured the rest over his head. "How could she give up all she has been taught—everything she believes?"

Lamech shouldered his own axe and held Noah's out to him. "In her way, perhaps she is not. If she and the *irin* are one flesh, she cannot undo it. Honor, rather than love, may be what ties her to Samyaza." He set a thick piece of firewood on a tree stump as Noah hoisted his axe.

"You did not hear her voice, Father." A remnant of bitter anger quickened Noah's heartbeat. "You did not see her *blush*. But whatever the ties…" His blow split the wood and blasted the halves off the stump. "…I will sever them."

When Hamerch arrived, again on Hadishad's dragon, Noah could not refuse him a hearing.

"I did not betray you purposefully," the Naphil said. "Please, forgive me. I knew not what to do."

As the young giant apologized, Noah was struck anew at how large Hamerch and his kin were. He felt a bit like the lion was begging pardon from the lamb.

"You need not be sorry. My anger bested me. No man ought to be able to wrong me so much that I cannot forgive him. Zara's choice was not your doing." Noah was rather surprised that his words truly reflected his soul. He had thought that seeing Hamerch would light his fury again, but that part of his heart where Emzara once reigned was scarred over. His fury, his anger, his bitterness, was drained to the dregs. He felt almost nothing.

"When I took her back, I hurt for you more every mile of the way." Hamerch stretched out his arm, a look of profound sorrow in his eyes; but there was something harder there, too. "I tell you this now instead of Onim so you will know that this is not zealotry speaking. Samyaza and Emzara are going to be wed in less than four months' time. They have invited the other *bene Elohim*—all of them." The Naphil took Noah's hand as the import of the news sunk in. "This is from my father. I shall see you again soon. Tell Hadishad that I thank him for the use of his dragon. You will need it now more than I." He set out down the road on foot at a pace that a horse would envy and was soon lost from sight.

Left in Noah's hand was a tightly-folded piece of parchment. Placing a hand on his son's shoulder, Lamech noticed the note almost before a stunned Noah. "Read it, son" he said, and in a daze, Noah did so.

"What does it say?" Jonan asked.

"The sons of the Grigori will take our side," answered Noah. He may have been numb inside, but Kiribaoth spoke with enough feeling for a dozen men.

"Then let the revolution begin."

‹ CHAPTER 39 ›

Eila, Temethe, and Asathea, the daughters of Samyaza, lounged in the cool of the morning on the shaded roof of their home. Eila's pet peacocks strutted about on thin silver chains, and fig trees were planted in pots at the corners of the roof. Besides these few strokes of nature, the decor was urban and refined. Silken canopies cast ample shade, and Pethun had created a waterworks that ran about the roof's perimeter and sent cascades of water falling into pools below.

Nephilim females were not giants, although if they had not been born of angels they would have been considered tall. Their beauty, though, was to human women what their brothers' stature was to human men, engendering envy and adoration in equal doses. None of the three shared in their male siblings' tendency for dalliances. Eila was a faithful wife to Dyeus, but jealous of his paramours, especially those who lived at the estate, and Temethe and Asathea were both virgins, though not for lack of suitors. All of them held their late mother in the highest regard, so it was not surprising that the topic of today's gossip was the news of Samyaza's upcoming nuptials.

"The least he could have done is told us in person," complained Eila.

"Yes, but have we ever known the men in our family to behave unselfishly in matters of sex?" asked Asathea.

Temethe sipped a crystal glass of cold rosehip tea. "At least he was faithful to Mother." Eila turned an uncomfortable shade of red. "I am sorry, sister," said Temethe quickly. "I did not mean to disparage Dyeus."

Eila aimed her venom at easier, absent prey. "Well, if Father wishes to sow his seed once more, I suppose some country-born coquette is a suitable field to plow. He shall do so without my blessing, though."

"Just so," nodded Asathea.

Temethe picked up a half-full decanter, a ray of sun turning its contents to ruby. "More tea, anyone?"

Three very different women skulked down a stairway, towards hidden chambers hewn in stone and far, far from any sunlight. Agrat and Eisheth came willingly at Lilith's insistence. Each of them carried a wriggling bag slung over their thin robes; hempen strings with pouches hanging served as belts to their scanty attire. Most else of what was needed was already at the firepit.

The pit was sunken into the floor, carved from onyx that was perpetually heated by the boiling springs that ran underground from the fiery core of Mount Armon, miles away. The rim formed a perfect circle, the inner surface scoured clean by the constant heat. Lilith, Agrat, and Eisheth took their places around the circle, equidistant from one another. They disrobed, casting their garments far away from the pit. As close as they were to it, the heat was enough to make the most meager covering feel oppressive; moreover, any clothing at all would disrupt the sorcery.

Agrat was the tear-bearer this night. She fetched a pitcher of scalding water from one of the pools around them, carrying it to the pit while softly singing a dirge in memory of the departed soul they desired. Tears trickled down her cheek as she went, and she was careful that they dripped into the pitcher. Agrat poured it into the firepit, the water hissing as it hit the hot stone, and took her place around the circle once more.

The women then took turns opening their pouches and throwing their contents into the now-boiling water. Their movements were methodical and ritual, their only sounds moans and guttural chokes that were not of human language. The steam from the firepit adopted new hues and odors at the addition of each new ingredient. Beads of resins filmed across the surface of the water as soon as they touched it; colored powders combusted and danced in green and purple and orange flames; spices and crushed herbs lent their scents to the steam arising from the concoction.

Beside each of the women was a piece of obsidian, easily overlooked among the chips and shards of shale that littered the ground. These were taken up by the three of them, then they turned to the bags that lay at their feet.

Eisheth went first. She pulled out a small bat by its hind parts, leaving it able to stretch its membranous wings to their full span, impressively incongruous with its tiny, hairless body. She gathered the wings in her fist, cracking thin bones; the animal let out a high-pitched squeak that was masked by Eisheth's incantation.

"Creature of the night, born in darkness, I send your breath and blood to find the hidden paths to Sheol, where dwells one whose words we wish to hear."

She drew the sharp edge of the obsidian across the spindly neck, almost severing the bat's head from its body. Folding the head back on its tenuous attachment, Eisheth swept the bleeding wound across her collarbone. Crimson drops slowly traced their routes down her bare chest; she squeezed the dead bat like an orange wedge, filling her cupped hand with blood and flinging the ruined animal into the firepit. She smeared her stained hands on her ears, arching her back and lifting her chin in a manner that might have been sensual in a setting less macabre. When she finished, she sat cross-legged on the ground.

The wolf pup whimpered when Agrat pulled him out by the scruff of his neck, his hind legs jerking futilely.

"Innocent hunter, twilight tracker," she intoned, "I send your breath and blood to find in death the one whose face we wish to see once more."

Downy grey fur marked the pup days old at most; his short life ended in the same manner as the bat. Agrat drew a line of blood across her chest in the same way her sister had, but she smeared her eyes instead. She joined Eisheth on the ground, eyes closed as they waited for Lilith to complete the ceremony.

From her bag, Lilith removed a white dove, gripping it roughly to thwart its flapping attempts at escape.

"Pure sacrifice, herald of the morning sun, I send your breath and blood to guide the one to whom we would speak, we who walk still in the daylight of the living."

Her slash decapitated the bird entirely. She painted a line same as the others, then put the stump of the neck to her mouth. She sucked at it, then spat the blood out and licked around her lips. The bird's body joined the bat and the wolf pup in the pit, and the three women waited, sitting in vigilant silence.

The air in the chamber was still, and the smoke from the burning animal corpses drifted up in an ethereal column. Gradually, the smoke began to shift and stir, though no breezes blew. Shadowy forms, only hints, brightened and dimmed like the appearance of shafts of sunlight through heavy mist. The faint echo of a bat's shriek was followed by a long howl that faded into nothing even as the women heard it. The shadows in the smoke gained definition, and the coo of a dove sounded, then cut short. When it did, the column of smoke burst and dissipated, then coalesced into a woman's form. The ghostly figure's eyes were downcast, and she wore a sorrow as she never had in life, but she was unmistakable to the three sorceresses.

"Naamah."

The apparition looked up. "Who is there?" she asked.

"It is Lilith, dear one."

"Lilith?" Naamah's spirit raised her spectral hands. The smoke she was made from bent and bowed as if it were trying to escape its source in the firepit, but to no avail. "Lilith...have you any water? It is...so very hot here..."

"It is hot here as well. I am sorry, Naamah, but we cannot reach you."

"Get...Samyaza. Show him...ahhh..." The spirit contorted in that forbearing sort of agony that only comes when pain is chronic.

"It is about Samyaza I wish to speak. We here wish to know your thoughts on his remarrying."

The spirit's blank eyes widened. It let forth a keening wail, and this time its agony was acute. Agrat clutched her ears and bent over double; Eisheth threw her blood-crusted hands over her face to hide her eyes.

"Naamah! *Naamah!*" Lilith's shouts were unheard or ignored, and Naamah kept screaming.

"Lilith, send her back!" Agrat cried. The bright red blood that seeped under her hands and trickled down her neck could have only been her own.

"No! Spirit of Naamah, tell us what you wish us to do!"

"Lilith!" Agrat sobbed. "*Please!*"

Lilith's words were lost in the ever-louder shrieks of the hysterical spirit, but they had their intended effect. The smoky form dissolved, its wails dying even as the echoes of them rang about the chamber. Eisheth broke the circle, helping her sister to her feet and gathering their clothing while Lilith kneeled, naked and dejected, at the edge of the circle, staring at the blackened, boiled carcasses of their sacrifices.

"Come," said Eisheth, holding out a robe. "We will be missed."

Ignoring her, Lilith pulled the obsidian across her palm and flung her hand over the firepit, spraying droplets of her own blood into their arcane brew.

"Hear me, Naamah, for I vow you this: Emzara of Eden will not live to see her wedding night."

· CHAPTER 40 ·

The moon waxed and waned as it had since the fourth day of creation, and one by one the Grigori arrived. Samyaza employed special sentries who kept watch at each gate for each new *irin*, greeting them with the sounding of great bronze lurs.

They came in every conceivable way. Some rode carriages, pulled by everything from drakes to deer, trailing long entourages behind. The ships of Ezequeel Mist-reader sailed into the port one early morning, bearing gifts and foodstuffs that took days to unload. Sariel and the nine *irin* under him came on foot, their wives and three generations of daughters dancing and playing instruments, giant sons laden with spices and delicacies on their backs and heads. Four *irin* under Barkayal brought with them live trees, heavy with fruits and nuts, planted in great carts and pulled by teams of bucktoothed bunyips. Storehouses in the ninth ring filled, and more were built.

The stream of Grigori families into the city meant commerce. Gold and silver flowed like the Pishon through Havilah as the Grigori guests filled the inns and shopped in the markets. When the inns were filled, citizens in the ninth circle gladly accepted the coin of the *bene Elohim* to vacate their manors and move in with their relations in the inner rings. For some, they hoped that hosting angels would bring good fortune to their houses; for others, the decision was mercenary, as the Grigori paid well. At the end of the four months, the interior of Enoch was packed full of Cain's children, while the outer ring housed a host of angelic visitors, with their attendant kin and companies.

Zara was overwhelmed. All this for her—it was too much! Each new and beautiful *irin* was so…well, heavenly, with their gorgeous wives and gilded words. Introductions at the palace were constant, and every time Samyaza spoke of her to his fellows, his ebullience lifted her spirits, and his praise for her embarrassed her less and less. Little by little, the humble farmgirl started a metamorphosis into a lady of the *bene Elohim*. She hung on the conversations of each Grigori wife she met; she emulated their poise, adopted their fashions, delighted in time spent with them and their daughters. As the days disappeared, Eden became less in her thoughts. Evenings became full of her beloved Samyaza instead of prayer; eventually, it did not strike her nearly so odd that none of the Grigori, not one, spoke of the Creator.

The Grigori's audience hall was prepared for the feast. According to Samyaza's plans, a fortnight of citywide feasting would begin with a banquet by invitation only. That being so, the guests would still be legion. All sitting counselors of Enoch were invited. Any son or daughter of the Grigori was welcome, although most of them, as children were wont to do, were scattered about the earth with their own lives and doings, and had not traveled to Enoch. Of course, every *irin* would be there—every one except Azazyel. Zara would not allow it, and Samyaza acceded to her wishes. Surprisingly to her, Zara found that her vehemence to Azazyel came not from what he had tried to do to Noah, but from the fact that thinking of Azazyel simply drew her thoughts to her jilted fiancé. When she pictured the hated Grigori, his countenance would often twist to Noah's as she had seen him last, at the inn, crushed and furious. Fortunately, the busy whirlwind of the last few days of preparation before the feast blew away all her thoughts on the subject.

Finally, the first feast was ready. On that day, Grigori vassals were sent throughout the city's circles with carts of small samples of the food from their various homelands, promoting the coming celebrations. The next two weeks would see Enoch's half-million citizens take turns by districts to partake in the feasts that would be held three times daily. In consideration of Emzara's tastes, the first feast would feature no animal flesh of any kind; not so with those planned for the population at large. Huge outdoor beds of coal were lit, underground ovens were dug, and any man or woman who had skill with a knife was hired to butcher animals and dress meat. The guards of Enoch maintained a thick presence about the palaces and halls, eager to show their mighty visitors that the protectors of the city were second to none.

At last the banquet was set, and the hall brimmed over with such a gathering as the earth had never seen. Every *irin* was physical perfection, every wife the pinnacle of human beauty, every daughter breathtaking beyond even their mothers, every son a towering colossus. What human children of Cain were there, no matter their station, were staggered to be among such beings.

If all went as some planned, many of those beings would not be on the earth much longer.

Dyeus, Pethun, and Dedroth had hosted dozens of Nephilim as they had arrived, speaking with them of their own lands and histories, but also attempting to ascertain who might be for and against them when the time came. Hoduín and a cadre of loyal diviners had spent their days reading signs and portents in every way they knew. Meanwhile, Tiras, Tevesh, and Mareth lent the strength of their arms to Tubal-Cain's forge. Under the guidance of Volund and Gofannon, and with Tubal-Cain overseeing all, they made weapons—many weapons. As each day passed and more were brought to their secret cause, the conspirators feared that word would fall on Grigori ears, but the feast preparations and the flow of angelic friends long missed proved to be ample cover.

The guardsmen had not been brought into the conspiracy—not formally. The primary conspirators, both Nephilim and human, decided that in light of the guards' sworn fealty to the city and the council, the purging of Azazyel's cadre identified by Sergeant Havak, and the lingering anger at Gloryon's murder, the guardsmen could be counted on when the time came.

"Guests of honor and friends of old, I and my bride welcome you!"

Samyaza raised a goblet of Charitian cordial, signaling a battalion of servers to deploy with apéritifs and appetizers.

"Irad, son of Enoch, son of Cain, has asked if he might say a few words on behalf of the council of Enoch," announced Samyaza as the servers milled about the crowd. "Please attend!"

The old man raised himself from his seat, brushing droplets of wine from his bristly beard. "Thank you, noble Samyaza. Watchers! Welcome to Enoch! You all know of this city's foundation. Our father Cain was exiled from Eden, but with hard work his sons and grandsons built this place, and our people grew. Samyaza and his fellows came to us, and they helped us make Enoch great. All the while, we stayed true sons and daughters of Cain, resting our safety on walls of stone and the curse of our bloodline. Now Samyaza marries a child of Eden—how the circle completes itself!"

The Grigori and their kin began to lose interest. Irad's address was veering off into the tangential ramblings of an old man.

"We now have the singular honor to host here each and every Grigori that has graced the earth with his wisdom and beneficence," Irad continued, "save one. Samyaza, where is Azazyel?"

Zara blanched, and Samyaza froze as if turned to stone. Several of the *irin* looked with interest or confusion, only just realizing that indeed, their number was one shy of two hundred. Whatever thoughts they shared with Samyaza in that moment did not increase their understanding; rather, some of them appeared more confused than before.

"Honored *bene Elohim*," said Irad, "did you know that our safety has been marred? Your comrade Azazyel has murdered without cause—his own son, no less!—by creatures of darkness of his own making. Samyaza!"

At this, most of the councilors of Enoch stood as one. Irad motioned the ones who had not known of these plans to stand in solidarity, and upon seeing the eldest and most prominent councilmen already doing so, every Nephilim among them, they also rose.

"This body, the council of Enoch, now calls upon the Grigori here to deliver Azazyel to be punished according to the curse of Cain, under which Gloryon, son of Azazyel, was protected through his mother Lilith."

If the Grigori had been humans, the commotion would have been great indeed. Instead, their white eyes flashed and flickered like a firefly swarm as questions blazed from mind to mind. Sensing momentum was against his father, Dyeus continued where Irad had stopped.

"I speak as son of Samyaza and councilor of Enoch. In bringing Azazyel to justice, our guards have had no success. His fellows, my father, have aided us none in finding him or his minions. We adjure you now—deliver justice for one of our own."

Samyaza had not foreseen this, and he was incredulous at the fact. He looked at his sons, Dyeus with his brothers beside him, and had a brief moment of empathy for what Azazyel must have felt towards Gloryon. He sensed the *bene Elohim* around him, and he was ashamed and angry that they should see their chief at such a loss. He glanced last at Emzara, scared and more precious for it, looking to him to set things aright.

He knew what he must do.

◂ CHAPTER 41 ▸

Emzara held her head down, picking at her plate. The tears that threatened to fall were stopped only by the comforting words of Eisheth and Agrat, sitting along with their angelic husbands at the table of honor.

The hall was quiet. The guests, both from Enoch and abroad, ate in silence, sensing the bride's mortification. For those present who had known nothing of the recent happenings until now, the feast had become theater, and now they waited for a confrontation that could not fail to entertain.

Samyaza had summoned Azazyel. The means by which he did was difficult for the humans and Nephilim to grasp, although Irad, Dyeus, and their fellows were confident that he had done so. The Grigori, however, knew that a simple thought of command sent by their chief would reach its recipient regardless of distance, and none dared disobey Samyaza's direct order. Azazyel would come; it was just a matter of how long it took him to arrive. Meanwhile, much food remained to be eaten, so the feasting continued, albeit subdued.

The first course was finished. The clink of crystal goblets being refilled with wine was the only sound in the hall. A full moon and a host of stars cast a glow through the open ceiling, matched by the white fire from the lit lamps on the walls and pillars. Shadows, some harsh, some soft, cast about the hall's periphery where the light fell on the statues and stairwells. Feasters' eyes darted about, everyone hoping for the first glance of the wayward Grigori's entrance.

He appeared, not in one of the many entries to the hall, but in a shadowy recess under a massive sculpted bull. Chatter rose as Azazyel stepped out from beneath the flaring nostrils and sweeping horns, then died as he sauntered through the tables. Zara stifled a sob; Eisheth and Agrat went to

269

her like mother hens, preening and petting while Samyaza stared, implacable, at the murderous *irin*.

"Well?" Azazyel asked, stretching his hands wide and facing the councilors' tables. "You wished for me? Here I am."

A nod from Dyeus steeled Irad's resolve, and the elder man stood. "Azazyel Grigori, your charge, by a witness whose word we trust, is murder, through agents under your command. Do you refute this?"

"I could," Azazyel sniffed. "After all, your 'witness'—where is he? And what evidence do you have of these 'agents' you suppose me to command?"

"You deny the truth of the charge, then?" Irad said. Pethun and Dagdha exchanged glances; Hoduín raised his eyes to the stars above, in case of some portent newly appeared.

"No," answered Azazyel. "It is surely true. Alas, not all died who I intended." The chattering swelled, and many eyes lit white. Zara turned away with a cry, instantly embraced by Agrat; Samyaza rose to his feet and shot a white-hot look of warning to Azazyel.

"My question to you is," continued Azazyel, ignoring his leader, "what exactly do you intend to do about it?"

Irad wavered in the face of this defiant Grigori, and Dyeus took the opportunity. "Your sentence will be thus, Azazyel. Eight men died on your account, by the hands of your assassins, which you freely admit in the presence of all here. All of them were sons of Cain, and his vengeance will be seen. Of your assassins, you will deliver seven times those killed; if they be not fifty and six in number, then you will deliver every one. These will be executed by the sword."

Among the feast-goers, hearts raced and skin flushed at the mention of so many deaths at once, and more than a few women grew faint. Some of the Grigori came from wild places, far from where the curse of Cain held sway, but even these, their wives, their Nephilim sons and daughters, had seldom heard of such loss of life at one time. To those there who had been raised in the city of Enoch in the land of Nod, even the deaths of Gloryon and his servants, plus the jeweler Sefiron, had been a number almost unfathomable. Dyeus let the import of his words saturate the room, then continued.

"You yourself, as the captain of this evil, will suffer seven deadly wounds, thus repaying your misdeeds with your life. Accept the judgment of this council now, and deliver yourself and your agents to this city's justice."

Azazyel's smirk grew wide, then burst into full-throated laughter. "Have you considered, child, that you possess no weapon capable of killing me?"

Surrounded by Enoch's sorcerors and stargazers, Hoduín spoke. "If such be the case—and I very much doubt that it will be—then we will prepare the spells to banish you to the place from whence you came."

"You have not such power," snarled Azazyel. More than one Grigori apparently did not share his assurance, and many burning pairs of angelic eyes pulled in Hoduín's direction.

"Perhaps *they* do not," said a voice. It came from the back of the hall. "Perhaps we do." A man stepped out from under an arch formed by carved eagles in flight, walking between stacks of wine barrels. He wore a simple hooded cassock and carried a wooden staff, and a beard of several months' growth clung to his face. He was not alone.

Behind him filed in three dark giants, their garb quite distinct from one another, but all very clearly meant to be worn to war. Two women walked in with them, severe, with beauty so striking that there could be no supposing their blood was purely human. Behind these came three older men: two were dressed in the dull, striped robes of the Scribes, but the third wore a rich tunic and leathers from far-off lands, and he had a scabbard strapped to his back. Two Nephilim youth completed the group. They were no strangers, but to those who knew them, it seemed that the last vestiges of their boyhood were gone, replaced by cares of men.

The group pierced through the sumptuous tables and the finely-attired guests like an iron blade through gilded silks. They arrayed themselves in front of Samyaza's table, curving around Azazyel. The *irin* furrowed his brow, inclined his head to the five dark Nephilim with an ironic smile.

"Hello, my children."

The tallest male, braided beard hanging to his belt, spat. The man in the cassock seemed to speak for them all. "Your wrong is more than mere murder, fallen angel," he said, "and it is shared by more than you." His piercing, zealous stare was locked onto Azazyel's sneer. He did not spare a glance even for the bride who the feast honored; being utterly ignored by him made Zara's heart wrench harder when she realized that the man was Noah.

He was changed in four months. He was lean, harder than before, and his archaic clothing lent him a weight that matched the aged presence of Onim, Kiribaoth, and Kenan behind him. The heat of anger was gone, replaced by a cold purpose that Zara could not guess, nor did she want to. She was afraid, though the exact source of it escaped her, and Samyaza sensed her trepidation.

"You dare?" he said. "You were not invited. Leave at once!"

"No!" Noah struck his staff on the gold-veined marble floor. "*You* were not invited! This earth is not yours, but you have taken from it as you please! I was not the first to damn you thusly, but I promise you, in Elohim's name, I will be the last."

"Councilors of Enoch!" Noah turned his back to Zara and Samyaza. "I tell you now, Azazyel's comrades will not allow him to be banished. I have read the scrolls of old, the writings of my sire who shares this city's name. These two hundred have bound themselves together here by mutual imprecations. Is it not so?"

A Grigori near Noah jumped up, livid, but the sinuous arm of a Naphil son thrust him back in his seat.

"Sit down, Father Danel," said the raven-haired giant. "Let us hear more of this, shall we?"

"Is this not so, Samyaza?" Noah faced the Grigori leader full now, and Zara reached her breaking point. With a sob, she ran from the table, Agrat and Eisheth close behind. Samyaza trembled in his fury, but before he could speak, Azazyel answered Noah.

"It is so, human."

"Then suffer you now the curse of Cain," pronounced Dyeus. "And if indeed you cannot be killed, we will bind you until we might banish you and your fellows with you."

Dozens of Grigori erupted from their places. "Samyaza, we did not come here for this," called one, but Samyaza raised his hand for calm. Something had changed in his countenance; the conspirators who noticed it hoped beyond hope that it was simple resignation. Regardless, their path was set. Irad gave the command.

"Guards," he ordered, pointing at Lieutenant-chief Malidoch and two others of equal rank. "Take this being to the street and execute him unto death."

Malidoch unsheathed his blade slowly, menacingly. He seemed to be savoring his approach to Azazyel, taking his time while the other two guards went ahead with drawn swords. His twisted features were unreadable beneath his helm. The other lieutenant-chiefs were only steps away from the condemned Grigori, whose feet were planted like roots in stone.

Like a striking snake, Malidoch darted forward. He drew the blade of his sword across the heels of the first guard, then drove its point through the second one's knee. He then walked between them to Azazyel, kicking them to either side even as they screamed in pain. Azazyel patted him on his pauldroned shoulder as the marred guardsman took up a fighting stance to the left of the *irin*.

"Noble councilmen," Malidoch slurred out of his mouth's working side, "I fear you assume much about our loyalty. To arms, brothers of the Grigori!"

More than half the guards in the hall hoisted their feathered pole-arms or drew their bows, all trained on a councilman or a fellow guard. Dyeus, Hoduín, Irad, Tubal-Cain, Onim—even the most astute, the most careful in the room had not accounted for this possibility. Kenan seemed unfazed, although as one not native to the city and its traditions, he could have no real appreciation of this unexpected turn. Noah simply closed his eyes and lifted one more prayer to the heavens.

"So many, many things about which you dirt men are mistaken," said Azazyel. For a moment, Noah thought some hasty guard or Naphil might start a brawl, and more than a few wanted to, despite the odds. Then, like the worst figments from a poisoned dream, the *bene Sheol* arrived. They dripped down on invisible lines from the ceilings, crawled out from hidden alcoves behind statues, the polished metal of countless deadly instruments gleaming like spiders' eyes in the torchlight. Hundreds of them, enough to erase even the most foolhardy hopes of a fight, clung to the pillars and crouched half-hidden in the shadows. One of Azazyel's sons growled a curse; behind Noah, Onim whispered, "I…I had no idea."

Samyaza stepped from behind his table. "Banishment?" He wore his scorn openly now. "I watched as Adam was banished from the garden. I watched as Cain was banished from Eden. Now I will watch as you all are banished from Enoch."

The *bene Sheol* closed in, forcing councilors to the exits, ignoring the Grigori and their wives. The turncoat guards did the same with their hapless former comrades, who laid down their arms without incident.

Irad exploded. "We will *not* leave our city!" Three *bene Sheol* crept forward, weapons raised, but Samyaza held them off with a lifted hand.

"This is no longer your city. It is ours. You shall leave, or you shall die." Several other councilors pulled the old man away, still sputtering, out of the hall. Samyaza regarded Noah, who had not moved or opened his eyes.

"I would kill you, Noah," said the Grigori, "but I consider that I have deprived you of enough, without adding your life to the list. Be gone."

As the children of Azazyel joined the Nephilim of Enoch, the last group to leave the hall, Noah finally met Samyaza's glare. "This is not over," he said.

Samyaza waved his hand. "Of course it is."

"I did not merely state my opinion."

Samyaza narrowed his eyes to lines of white fire. Nothing had changed about Noah himself. An aura of prophecy surrounded him as before. His staff, though, plain by human eyes, was wreathed in silver script.

"So you have carved the words of the Generations onto a stick. What is that to me?"

Noah tapped the end of the staff on the ground as he turned to leave with Kenan. "It is a token, that you might know Who you place yourself against."

When finally he left—the very last—the hall was still full. The *bene Sheol* retreated to their shadowy corners, the guards were again at their posts, and the Grigori and their wives remained at their tables, rather at a loss. Samyaza smiled, radiant in his beauty.

"I apologize for that unpleasantness. Now, if you will please excuse me, I have a bride to comfort." A few *irin* gave lascivious chuckles. "Meanwhile, we ought not waste this bounty. Feast! Feast! And let this be merely the pangs of childbirth that will lead to a new era—the era of the *bene Elohim!*"

Lilith watched from a darkened palace tower as the lamps carried by the exiled councilors marked their exits from the city. The lights disappeared as their bearers went under the ninth wall, then bobbed into view again when they had passed onto Wide Bridge. As they reached the end of the bridge, though, they multiplied. Like a spark on kindling, the points of fire seemed to ignite the far edge of the moat and beyond. And not Wide Bridge alone was strangely alight; to her left and right, Lilith saw the phenomenon repeated at Fowl Bridge and Bull Bridge. In a few minutes, all of Enoch was surrounded by a halo of flames, concentrated most highly at the bridges leading to the city.

The siege of Enoch had begun.

· CHAPTER 42 ·

Smoke from the sacrificed bull mixed with the morning's mist as the sun rose on Noah and the men of his family, on their knees in prayer. The altar they had built was set back from the road to Wide Bridge, in the midst of the small village of tents erected to house the leaders of the conspiracy against the Grigori, for however long the siege might last. Presently Noah took to his feet, standing in respectful silence as, one after another, Jonan, Kenan, Lamech, and Methuselah did the same.

The last spirals of smoke drifted over the treeline between the encampment and Enoch's walls; small specks, at first mistakable for motes from the altar's dwindling fire, flew higher and higher in the hazy distance over the city.

"The messengers return," noted Lamech, whose eyes were sharpest in the family. A handful of falconers from Eden were clustered around the embers of a dying fire, also watching the skies intently. Volunteers all and worshippers of the Creator God, they had heeded the call raised by Merim and Hadishad on their return, and they had traveled to Enoch behind the young cousins. Other Edenites had come, as well. Kenan had emerged from his hermitage, drawing to himself grandchildren and great-grandchildren who had grown up listening to his legendary exploits, and who now wished to join him in one last quest. Rakeel, naturally, was jealous for his daughter. Angel or not, the being who misused her and stole her innocence would face a father's wrath, fanned hotter by Merim's accounts of Azazyel's evil schemes. Elebru, too, was incensed by Zara's "imprisonment," as he called it. What forces he could raise from the countrysides, he did, and Dashael accompanied him.

Nine falcons in all soared over Enoch, on their ways back from their mission in the city. Parchments had been attached to their legs, detailing instructions to whoever received them to relate the goings-on inside the inner walls, then to reattach the response to the birds. The information might be sparse, they knew, but it was better than nothing.

"Why is he diving?" asked a falconer, as one of the birds suddenly dropped towards the earth.

Another chuckled. "Someone's skill in training is not so great as he thinks, if a rat or rabbit can distract his bird so badly."

"He is not diving," growled Lamech. "They are shooting arrows from the outer wall."

The falconers turned white, but could do naught but watch. One, two more birds faltered; the first recovered, losing altitude but flapping to stay aloft, but the second dropped as if it had been changed to stone.

The seven returning birds, one with a wounded wing, were met by their subdued handlers. The falconers untied the leather thongs that held the parchments and delivered them to Noah and Kenan, then left as a group to console their fellows whose falcons had been lost. Noah divided the parchments amongst his kin. The missives were of varying detail, quality, and legibility, but their story kept to the same path: the gates from the eighth circle to the ninth were shut, guarded by the *bene Sheol*, and food was already scarce.

"Well, I hope nobody was expecting some epic battle," said Jonan. "No food? Only a single night has passed!"

"Think to what you know of the city, Jonan," said Methuselah. "It relies solely on trade, and that is cut off. If the Grigori prepared for their week-long gluttony as thoroughly as Onim related, I am not surprised that the food stores in the inner circles are so quickly depleted."

"A fiendish strategy." The lines at Kenan's eyes tightened and darkened as he pulled his face into a mask of disgust. "Mark my words: they will starve their own people until desperation or death, then blame us for forcing them to do so. These angels have not fallen as far as the Serpent and his legions, but they come very near."

"By now they will know that our numbers are not as great as those first fires made us appear," said Lamech.

"Yes, but first impressions stay," Kenan said. "It may give us an edge, at least against their human lackeys."

Noah tapped his staff on the ground, coming to a decision. "Kenan, come with me to meet with the council. We shall be inside the city by nightfall."

"Is that a prophecy, then?" Jonan smiled wryly.

"No," said Noah, "but it will come true regardless."

The men from Eden were not warriors. They were shepherds and farmers, wearing wool and leather, armed with spear, sling, and arrow, riding horses and cock-drakes. Among them, the wrangler Dashael alone had come with a hornfaced dragon, a beast whose role in life thus far had mostly consisted of pulling rooted stumps and hauling stones from fields. The Nephilim, in whose camp the council of Enoch had gathered, were another force entirely. Azazyel's children had posted themselves as camp guards. Despite knowing they were allies and having his legendary sire Kenan at his side, Noah felt a fleeting terror as he walked past them. One son, the bearded giant, surveyed the camp astride a bull-dragon, and another, with heavy, muscled girth almost to match his great height, rode slowly in a chariot pulled by hideous pigs the size of bears. His two daughters, bodyguard-consorts for a faraway chieftain, looked every bit their role, wearing decorative armor that covered vital points and not much else. They moved together through practiced forms with thin-bladed swords, their motions as graceful and deadly as they were themselves. The last son was a dragon hunter of renown; clad in skins and scales, he sat on the ground, running a whetstone over a curved throwing dagger. Beside him, a black-haired Naphil, the one who spoke at the feast to his father Danel, sharpened the blade of a jeweled glaive. Beyond them, an expansive tent spread across a clearing, its two thick poles rising higher than the trees around. Armored city guards milled about, many still reeling from last night's events and coming to grips with their parts in the siege of their own city.

The canvas walls of the tent could not keep out the raised voices arguing inside. Noah and Kenan shared a glance, then walked in.

"…knew it might come to exile." Tubal-Cain was staring down a red-faced Raposh. "Or did you think that we had prepared this camp for nothing?"

"But we are cut off entirely!" Raposh's pet tarsier hopped from shoulder to shoulder. "I did not anticipate the sheer number of those...those creatures of Azazyel, and you cannot tell me that any of you did."

"The *bene Sheol* do not outnumber the children of Cain." Tubal-Cain patted a pouch at his belt. "I could arm the city if I could reach my forge."

"But what good is arming the city, even if we could?" said Onim. "The *bene Sheol* would cut through our people."

In a voice of command, Kenan spoke. "We will split their attention. Our forces will break through from the outside."

"Impossible," said Tubal-Cain. "The gates are too thick, and the walls are guarded too heavily."

"And who knows what nefarious methods the *bene Sheol* will use to guard the gate?" asked Onim. "Arrows will be poisoned, or aflame. What else might they have in store?"

"Have faith, Onim," said Noah softly. To the entire council, he said, "You have not been privy to all our doings in these few months. Let us rectify that now." He nodded at Dyeus, who had been silent thus far, and the Nephilim left the tent. Pethun and Hoduín both looked pleased, and Dedroth rubbed his hands together expectantly.

A grinding sound, iron on earth, drew the council members outside the tent. A massive construction wheeled between two towering oaks into the space before the tent, shuddering as it went. The construct was shaped as a long, tall wagon, covered on the top and sides by overlapping shields of fire-hardened wood. The interior was hidden, but from an opening in the front, a monstrous ironclad head protruded, capped by a thick mass of a metal snout.

"This is our leviathan," said Noah. "With it, we will open the gates of Enoch."

"Symbolism is powerful," added Kenan. "Even more so when backed by the strength of wood and iron."

Onim ran his hand across the darkened wood plates. "Whoever works this beast will put themselves in great danger. If you need volunteers, the Scribes are prepared."

"We have our volunteers already," said Noah, motioning to the wagon. "And they will be as protected as they can be."

Three warriors, faces masked by helms, came out from the back of the wagon. Several gasps escaped the group of awestruck councilors.

"Incredible," breathed Raposh, who then shook his head. "But even if we do breach the gate and gain the ninth ring, we must contend with the *irin* and the *bene Sheol* who now fill it. We still cannot get into the inner city."

Pethun stepped forward with a confident grin.

"I can."

The cenotes around Enoch were many and varied, and Pethun knew them all. His dual exploratory passions were water and women, preferably together; in pursuit of the former, he had come to know much that was hidden from the masses who were content to merely walk the streets of the city. He knew of the countless caves beneath the hills and forests surrounding Enoch, deep pools hidden in the depths, connected by tunnels and winding ways drowned completely. He knew which of them, every so often, opened to shafts stretching to the surface, letting the faintest air and sunlight down to give life to the blind creatures below. He knew that a swimmer, if he is strong, might be able to use the underwater streams to travel from a sinkhole to Enoch's moat, and he knew that in this, no one was stronger than he. The risk was great—many of the underwater paths were untested, and if he was wrong about any of them, he would most certainly drown where none but the eels could find him.

Once in the great moat, he would make his way inside the city through the underground paths that Onim explained. The Scribes also gave him several of their ingenious light-vials, which could burn even underwater, and his uncle Tubal-Cain had given him the iron key that would free the arms from the forge. It was, all agreed, the only chance they could see to save the city in time.

Now Pethun peered over the edge of a sinkhole cliff, a small one, less than a mile from the city. The twists and turns of the underwater passages would make overland distances irrelevant; even so, the closer his starting point, the more likely he would have success. He inhaled deeply, knowing full well that it might be his last breath.

He dove into the churning water and swam into the darkness.

· CHAPTER 43 ·

The creak and groan of the manmade monstrosity reached the guardsmen on the wall well before it parted the mists at the head of Wide Bridge. Its wheels crushed the dirt under them as it crept up to the bridge's smooth stone. Guards called their comrades over to watch the armored construct's advance, wary but largely unconcerned. The rough tone of the rolling wheels sharpened when they met the bridge. A guard drew an arrow, then another did the same.

Its speed increased. The pace picked up slowly at first, but it built upon itself, coming faster and faster. The iron beast-head at its front shook as it sped inexorably toward the gate, and to the guards' surprise and dismay, two spurts of flame roared to life at the tip of the effigy's snout. Arrows were loosed, clattering harmlessly off the wooden scales that covered the construct. Collision was eminent now; the men on the wall braced hands against black stone.

The crash was loud, like an angry wave against a cliff, but from what the guardsmen could tell, it may as well have been water hitting the bridge's impenetrable gate. At the second impact, another barrage of arrows rained down. Some stuck fast in the armor; most ricocheted onto the bridge or into the moat. An officer on the wall raised a fist, and the firing stopped.

"Do not fire! Those may be our brothers inside. Do you think Cain's curse is suspended just bec-"

As if birthed from the mists, three grey-swathed apparitions seemed to conjure themselves around the officer. His words died garbled in his throat, and whatever had been stabbed into his back burst into flames. Together, the *bene Sheol* hoisted his body over the wall, cape's fur catching

281

fire as it dropped. His corpse slammed into the construct, cracking several scales, but the flames did not die.

More *bene Sheol* appeared on the wall, armed with bows, and the guards did not have so little sense to display their objection or outrage. Most of them backed away to the closest stair leading down from the wall. If Azazyel's minions wanted this fight, they could have it, and may they rot in the pit whose name they bore.

The arrows fell again in earnest, this time lit with orange flames. From across the moat, hidden archers returned fire, but the distance was great and the targets were fleeting, and no arrow found its mark. Patches of fire decorated the field of scales now, yet the monstrous ram battered on, slamming the gate over and over. Its persistence was rewarded by a sharp crack, then another; the gate was falling.

The *bene Sheol* did not sit idle while it happened. On the parapets to either side above the gate, the masked figures lithely leapt to the stone eagles' heads that jutted over the bridge. They wrapped ropes around the sculptures' necks, then scuttled back to the wall. Fumes of smoke appeared further down the top of the wall, the only warning before two burning urn-like vessels, ropes attached to them, were flung over the wall's edge. The sculpted eagles acted as pivots, and the fiery vessels swung unerring to explode against the leviathan ram's protection, rending it from the right and left and sending fragments of fiery wooden scales to the waters below.

Still the warriors who worked the ram kept on, pounding the thick beams and iron bars of the gate with the same strength as their first strike. Metal bent and wood splintered, even as the wood burned around the warriors. They were visible now to those on the wall above, through the ram's ruined protection. If they could have spoken, the *bene Sheol* would have admitted their expectation of fifteen, perhaps twenty men inside. To their cold surprise, only three figures manned the ram, but they were enough to give Azazyel's assassins pause.

They were Nephilim, each encased in a suit of black-green armor that looked as if it had been grown, not forged. Fearsome masks hid their faces; weapons were slung at their backs and hips, the bands and belts covered in the same organic material. Though they were wreathed in fire, they seemed unperturbed by it and did not falter. Once they reared back, and the iron head stuck fast in the gate, ripping wood to broken bits as the three giants pulled it out. Twice, and the mangled bars failed to keep the gate shut. A third time the leviathan's head struck forward, and the wall was breached, its ruined doors charred by the flames that failed to protect them. The Nephilim triad hoisted the iron-banded cedar that served as the ram itself, running as a unit through the defeated gate and leaving the burning skeleton of scales behind them. Alarm bells sounded, echoing dully in the tunnel that went through the wall, but the three paid no heed. The inner gate, the last barrier between them and the ninth circle, was not meant to be impenetrable. This they proved, as it fell at their first pass. The ternion of giants let the ram drop, drawing their weapons and putting their backs to one another. A film of mist swirled at their feet. Down the walls, out of the gatehouses, from the shadows came the *bene Sheol*. Ten, twenty, forty of the silent assassins wove their webs around the giants.

"Fine work, brothers," came Tiras' voice, muffled by his leviathan-scale helm. "Shall we?"

Tevesh said nothing, simply whirling a short-chained mace where his left hand had been, a broad-bladed sword in the other.

"For Gloryon," said Mareth. "Let the streets run deep with blood this day."

"For Gloryon," echoed Tiras, hoisting his axe. The grey host fell upon them, and the battle for Enoch was joined.

"Come on, lads!" Kenan drew his silver-handled sword and ran to the bridge, the guardsmen of the city and the Scribes' fighters at his back. He dodged the flaming debris scattered about, remnants of the Nephilim sons' brave, and successful, charge. The whistle of an arrow and a cry behind him alerted him to the continued presence of a few *bene Sheol* on the walls. He ignored the sounds of skirmish as his forces fired their own missiles. Instead, he ran to the gate mechanism and opened the ruined doors fully. The iron bars caught, and the gate stuck. Kenan suppressed a curse; the rent in the gate would let three, perhaps four men through at a time, but that was all, and the burning wood would make the going slower.

"Move aside!" The call boomed out from behind and above them. A rhythmic, earth-shaking pounding prompted hasty obedience from the guards and Scribes, and down Wide Bridge charged a bull-dragon, with

Azazyel's son astride it. The beast plowed through the remains of the ram's covering, ignoring the flames and pushing the debris to either side of the bridge. While the dragon could not have broken the gate while intact, its sheer bulk now made kindling of it.

The pig-chariot of the dragon-rider's brother sped through behind it. Kenan called for the guards to regroup, but even he, the victor of a thousand battles over five hundred years, had to marvel at the Nephilim who walked past him to war. Dyeus and Dedroth led the giants, with Azazyel's other children close behind. Tubal-Cain, the only human in the group, was flanked by Hamerch and Gilyon, both looking grim. Dagdha and the other scions of Tamiel had painted themselves in harsh-angled patterns designed to intimidate enemies and allies both. After them, Hoduín led a group of Nephilim sorcerers, most from Enoch, but some from afar, their chants grating against Kenan's ears and leaving him chilled. The guards filed behind these, and Kenan let them. For him, the great-grandfather of Enoch the Scribe, this action against the Grigori was hardly mercenary, and neither was it for the humans whose home the city was. However strongly he might feel, though, for the Nephilim it was in every sense personal. The lead was theirs by right, and he let them have it.

Noah and the men from Eden brought up the rear of the invading force. Dashael's hornface finished the work started by the bull-dragon, while Methuselah, Jonan, and Lamech walked with arrows nocked, watching the wall for stray archers.

"If any of you doubt that this earth is cursed," said Methuselah, loudly enough that Elebru and his men could hear, "then consider that we are about to enter into the proof of it. Elohim be with you."

"And you as well," several replied in kind.

They passed into the tunnel, the din of battle audible ahead.

"I have a bad feeling about this," said Jonan.

"As well you should," said Noah. "We are about to stare the enemy full in the face, as you and I have not before."

"Aye, the *bene Sheol*."

"No," said Noah. "Death."

"Ah." Jonan furrowed his brow. "And what of us? Are we ready to spill men's blood this day?"

"Cain's curse is on this place. The *bene Sheol* have invoked it on themselves," said Lamech. "Let their lifeblood be on their own heads."

Carnage had come to Enoch. Bodies, swathed in grey cloth or armored in molded leather, lay half-hidden by the mists that filmed the streets. Noah could hear the crashing din of melees in alleyways and past the curves of the buildings, but what fighting had been done in the courts inside the gate was finished. The Edenites kept to the walls, scanning for signs of ambush. Noah alone walked through the open street, stopping at a long splatter of blood, not yet dried, that decorated the base of the great statue that stood there.

"Treasure of the earth indeed," intoned Noah.

A commotion drew his attention to a marble archway that marked the mouth of some stairway. A body, one of the *bene Sheol*, rolled with limbs limp to stop at the bottom of the stair, its chest crushed into a bloody crater. Another assassin flew from under the arch; Noah drew back his staff, but the sprinting figure ignored him. With a mad yell, a Naphil, one Noah recognized as a kinsman of Dagdha, leapt from the stairs. He spun his weapon, a leather-wrapped flail linked with twin chains held in his fist, so fast that it became hard to see. Azazyel's minion was far away, almost disappeared behind a corner, when the Naphil loosed the end of one chain. A bronze sphere the size of an orange hit the assassin in the back and carried him skidding over cobblestones for a dozen paces, and Noah realized that what he took for a flail was in fact a monstrous sling. With a nod, the Naphil acknowledged Noah as he loped past, scooping up the bronze shot with the leather cradle in one fluid motion, then ducking into an alleyway in pursuit of another target.

The Edenites went along the bending street, following the trail of bodies. Noah did not recognize anyone. The majority were *bene Sheol*, and of the few fallen guards, he could not tell on which side they had fought. The casualties thus far had included no Nephilim, as far as he could see.

The cries of battle grew louder ahead, and the Edenites pressed onward. Noah spotted two familiar giants standing on guard, and he ran to meet them.

"Hamerch! Gilyon! How goes it?"

Gilyon hoisted his spear, tip bloodied and glistening. "Their numbers are great. I know your thoughts must be on rescuing Emzara, but archers would be much appreciated."

"We are to guide you to where you are most needed," added Hamerch.

Noah nodded at his father and grandfather, who both nodded back. "Lead on, then."

"I never thought I would fight beside Baoth the Butcher," said Kenan, blocking a strike from a *bene Sheol* whip-sword.

"No one is beyond salvation," said Kiribaoth, and they both pressed further into the fray. The attack had been a resounding success that had turned into a rout of the enemy. As deadly as the *bene Sheol* were, they had not been able to match the prowess of Tiras, Tevesh, and Mareth, and the leviathan armor had withstood every attack. When the bull-dragon came, the guardsmen loyal to the Grigori had all but surrendered their weapons, fleeing for their lives. The *bene Sheol* who had paused to cut them down in their cowardice had been the first to be eaten, but they had not been the last. The Nephilim dealt death on a scale Kenan had seldom seen before. Gilgamesh had been as powerful, but the children of Azazyel, Samyaza, Barkayal, and Tamiel fought with a viciousness that left no room for quarter.

The *bene Sheol* had regrouped near Bull Bridge, swarming like rats from windows and gutters. Kenan and his allies—Enoch's guardsmen, the Scribes, the Nephilim giants—were pressed together now, surrounded on all sides. Only Azazyel's son on the bull-dragon ran free, but his was a fury that heeded no orders, and Kenan considered that it was best to keep the hungry dragon away from his allies.

"They are herding us," said Kenan, as the fighting brought him near Tubal-Cain, with his black hammer, and Dyeus and his javelins. "Trying to trap us."

Casualties began to accumulate. A guardsman, one of the council's, slapped a hand to his neck as he was hit by a dart, then another. A bestial roar and a chorus of triumphant hissing prefaced a great crash, and Kenan knew the bull-dragon was down, likely a victim of the mushroom gas he had been warned about. Bleeding cuts collected on exposed human and Nephilim skin. A Scribe who paused, briefly, to administer a quick salve to a wound at his thigh was rewarded for his troubles with another to his chest, and he fell.

The three Nephilim armored in leviathan scale fought on unharmed. If it were not for the ardor with which the *bene Sheol* focused on them, to no avail, Kenan knew the casualty count would be much higher.

"If you have any pull with Noah's God, Kenan, now would be the time," said Tubal-Cain.

Kenan looked past him, at the balconies that surrounded them and spanned over the heads of the *bene Sheol*, watching them fill with men in hoods of tan and brown, feathered fletchings visible at their backs.

"Oh, I think He might be far, far ahead of me."

Water could kill in so many ways, and each had its moment of terror before the end: with the slow, inexorable weakening of treading muscles in a cavern's darkness, caged by drowned stone slick with slime; in the desperation of panicked strokes in submerged passages, having made the agonizing choice to swim past the point where turning back was within the capacity of an ever-diminishing breath, not knowing that the next precious pocket of hoped-for air was altogether absent; at feeling the rush of water on skin in the instant before the bite of monstrous jaws.

Any of these would not have surprised Pethun. None of them occurred. His underground swim to Enoch's moat had been almost dull; he had even skipped several chances to draw breath in open caves, bypassing them to give himself more of a challenge.

He emerged near still boats. Peering above the water, Pethun scanned the docks to get his bearings. To his left, its topmost arch visible above weatherworn roofs, was the cavernous entrance to Enoch's underground, just as Onim had described. The docks themselves were normally empty, Pethun knew, their occupant vessels out harvesting sea-plants or casting the day's nets. Now, the piers were filled and the boats were still on the calm water, with no human activity apparent on either.

Pethun pulled himself from the water quietly, crouching on a pier. Pieces of discarded sailcloth and rough rope lay nearby; he wrapped up the still-glowing light-spheres of the Scribes and tied the bundle to his back. He crept forward.

Onim had explained in detail the fastest passage from the fishermen's docks to the inner city. Pethun was only familiar with the ornate, fountain-studded stairways from the Grigori palaces to the moat—rather, the pools overlooking the moat—but ingress into the ninth ring was not his endeavor this day. He went from shanty to shed, as quietly as he was able, and as he did, he heard raised voices in the distance.

The massive, soaring cavern was at the bottom of a sheer face of stone. A line of armored guards of Enoch stood outside of it with their backs to him. They faced a motley group of people inside the entrance, most yelling angrily.

"You cannot keep us from our homes and livelihoods!"

"We will starve!"

The turncoat guards were meant to prevent the people of Enoch from accessing their boats; of that, Pethun was certain, and he knew whose orders they followed. The men in the cordon were quiet, though, even in the face of entreaties and angry insults. His first desire was to attack, but the guards were too many, and he was weaponless. Retreat or defeat would end his task as surely as if he had drowned in the swim to the moat. He needed a plan. He turned away, back to the docks.

A quick and quiet swim took him to where foreign ships were docked. These were usually larger and of varied design, and for the last weeks, the grandest of them were the vessels of the many Grigori who had traveled to Enoch by sea. Unlike those used by Enoch's fishermen, the platforms jutting from the walls to the water were large and ornate, with neat stacks of nautical equipment placed every so often. More importantly to Pethun, these docks—at this moment, at least—were not desolate of people. Angry shouts carried over the water. He listened for a minute, then made his plans.

"And we are telling *you*," said the city guardsman, "that you may *not* debark." Like a dumb animal scraping its horns on the ground in front of a rival, he planted his polearm's butt on the wooden dock with a thud. Shipmaster Seselash rolled his eyes.

"Surely that weapon's shaft is bigger than he is able to handle," Uwyeh said to him, but loudly enough to carry to the dock. "For what smallness is he compensating, I wonder?" His first mate had ample spirit and a bawdy mind, both of which made her an enjoyable bunkmate on lengthy voyages. These accursed guardsmen of Enoch had confiscated all arms on board when Lord Ezequeel had gone up to the city with his wife, so words were the only weapons he and his crew still had.

"I promise you," said the other guard, "this command comes from the *irin* Ezequeel himself."

"Then let us go ashore and confirm it," said Seselash, "and afterwards we shall return immediately."

"We are not merchants to bargain with," said the first guard, puffing out his armored chest. Seselash gave up, touching Uwyeh on her sun-darkened shoulder. He would have gone below-deck to their quarters to wait for the next shift of guards, hopefully more persuadable than these mules, but just then, he beheld a most curious sight.

A small splash, no louder than a wave on a pier-post or a fish breaching the surface, reached his ears. From where it sounded, a bundle of rope arced high above the heads of the guards, blossoming into a wide net as it went. It fell upon the two guards, who both shouted in a way that promised swift retribution to whoever was responsible. They dropped their weapons to pull at the net; the more brutish of the pair drew a knife to slash at the ropes.

When something began to drag the net and its contents to the edge of the wooden platform, the shouts turned to cries of fear.

The brute guard was pulled over the side with a cry and a splash. The other was prostrate on the deck, trapped by the taut net. A deep voice, unseen, like some god of the seas, came from under the wooden planks.

"Guardsman. If you wish your fellow not to drown, slide every weapon you have under the net."

The guard did his best to obey. After a struggle-filled minute, two polearms, a quiver and bow, and a hatchet lay upon the otherwise-empty docks. Uwyeh looked at Seselash, and he knew she wanted to retrieve the weapons, but he considered that the owner of the commanding voice might take offense, so he shook his head against it.

He was glad he did. Over the side of the docks came a towering son of the *irin*. The sea-wet muscles of his bare chest shined in the sun as he stood erect; "sea god" was not far from the truth. Uwyeh gasped, and Seselash wondered what lustful thoughts had sprung to life in his first mate's mind.

The giant pulled the other guardsman from the water by a thick rope. The man screamed; it sounded odd, and terrified beyond what a little drenching would justify. He fell to the ground, flopping like a fish, and his hands went to his face. He tried to say something, but the words were garbled. He pushed himself up to sitting; as he did so, Seselash could see the large iron hook going full through his cheek.

"You there," said the giant to the trapped guardsman. "Free yourself, then help your comrade. After that, set a guardsmen's ship ready to sail. Can you sail?" The guard nodded yes, shaking the net atop him.

"Good," said the giant. "You will have a full crew of your fellows before long. I, Pethun, son of Samyaza, will make it so. Once you set sail, never come within sight of these city walls again, and consider me merciful."

The giant, Pethun, watched until the two men were gone. He took up the weapons abandoned by the guardsmen, then turned to Seselash and his first mate, standing rather dumbly.

"Who is captain of this ship?"

As shipmaster, Seselash supposed the answer ought to be given by him. "Lord Ezequeel is captain of all of his vessels, but I am master of this one."

"But this is not his flagship?"

"No. This is a cargo vessel. His flagship is there." Seselash pointed two ships over at a painted and gilded masterpiece of a boat a good deal larger. The shipmaster knew not if this Pethun cared one way or another, but he felt acutely compelled to oblige the giant in every way he could.

"If your crew is full and your stores are replete, I advise you to sail back to your homeland," said Pethun. "Do you have arms aboard?"

"Enoch's guards confiscated them," said Uwyeh, sounding more distraught and needful about it than Seselash knew her to be.

"Those traitors are not Enoch's guards," answered Pethun. "Here." He tossed a polearm over the ship's side, and Seselash caught it. "A memento from Cain's people. Now, away with you, and wait not for Ezequeel the Grigori." He smiled broadly at Uwyeh. "I hope we meet again in happier times. I would know your people better. Until another day, Captain."

Captain. Seselash liked that, and he appreciated that he, in great likelihood, would be the one to benefit from the fires of attraction that Pethun had kindled in his first mate's eyes.

"Come, Uwyeh," he said, after the giant turned away, loping silently like a lion. "Rouse the crew."

At first Pethun doubted that he was moving in the right direction. He should be hearing shouting from the fishermen in the cavern, but all was silent. Peering through cracks between the weathered wood of a fisherman's shed, he saw why. All of the guards lay dead, and in their places were three *bene Sheol*.

Pethun knew they were fast and deadly, but right now they stalked about with their backs to the Naphil, taunting Enoch's cowering fishermen, who shouted no longer, with guttural laughter. Pethun was arrogant and aware of it, and he recognized the same in these *bene Sheol*. This would be his best opportunity, and there was no point in waiting.

He loosed three fishing-spears as soon as he emerged from between shanties. As he anticipated, the surprise on the faces of the first fishermen who saw him spurred the *bene Sheol* to turn. For two of them, the reaction was too late; the spears hit their targets, and they fell. The last spear was dodged by the assassin for whom it was intended, but his leaping escape was met by a barb-edged net thrown by Pethun, and he fell entangled.

Pethun sprinted toward the downed figure, but the men of Enoch reached him first. A barrage of thrown stones, lumps of coral, and other dockside detritus preceded a small mob of furious fishermen lashing out with feet and fists. One bold man had taken up the errant fishing-spear and was beating the prone form of the netted ben Sheol.

"Enough!" said Pethun, and he held out his hand. Abashed, the man placed the spear in the giant's palm. Pethun thrust it through the chest of the ben Sheol.

The men of Enoch looked on in stunned silence. "So does Cain's curse fall upon all who would threaten his descendants," said Pethun. He handed off the spear. "Arm yourselves, men of Enoch." Some of the ragged bunch spread out among the fallen guards and assassins, while others ran to the docks, where harpoons, nets, and thin knives could be found in abundance. Pethun took up a dead guard's eagle-headed polearm. Made to be wielded by a human, it hardly matched his strength or reach.

"Would you prefer this?" asked a fisherman, his skin sun-darkened beyond the shade typical of Cain's people. With some effort of strength, he presented a harpoon, its butt resting on the ground and still taller than Pethun. "It is made for hunting whales, and it has blooded more than one monster of the sea."

"Yes, in fact," answered Pethun, handing him the guard's polearm. "Here, an even trade."

In minutes the makeshift warriors had regathered. They were not yet enough, but they would grow. The last few days had severed completely his emotional attachment to his father Samyaza, and all of the angelic kind; now, looking upon the humans who themselves looked to him, he felt strongly an unfamiliar kinship with the people of his mother.

"I am Pethun," he said loudly, "son of Naamah, a daughter of Cain's people. I come to free our city. Who here knows the fastest way to the surface?"

The man who had offered him the harpoon spoke first. "Follow me."

Slick with slime, the passages wound upward. Humble hovels lined their walls, many structures defying Pethun's comprehension of how such things could remain standing. Faces lit by greasy lamps peered out of doorways. At calls from the group, men poured from these rough dwellings and joined the procession, angels and assassins be damned. The source of their eagerness was obvious: these men, dependent on their daily work for their families' food, had been deprived of it. Pethun had never known starvation, but he imagined it could drive one to desperate things.

"You all live here?" Pethun asked his self-appointed guide. He knew the answer. "They do—like rats in warrens," he thought, though he would never voice it.

"Most of us," the man answered, looking straight ahead. "Like rats."

Pethun had no response to this, so they continued on in silence, but for the slap of feet on wet stone and constant dripping from the city above.

They exited into daylight inside the seventh ring. "My brothers," said Pethun, "some of you must go throughout the inner rings. Gather everyone able to bear arms. Use my name. The rest of you, follow me."

"To where?" asked a fisherman.

"We go to get arms for them to bear."

Now that Pethun was in the city—*his* city—he proceeded at a pace that left his human companions behind. Fortunately, there was none who did not know of his uncle Tubal-Cain's forge. The way there was quiet, devoid of the usual commotion of the shops and markets. As at the docks, he grew careful as he approached his destination, and again he found a group of Enoch's guardsmen surrounding it, their caped or quiver-adorned backs to him. He doubled back, finding his motley battalion hurrying along the empty streets. "Quiet," he said to them. "Stay back from the forge and spread out." He motioned the suntanned harpooner and a few other men to come with him. Keeping to the shadows of the walls, they drew as close to the forge as stealth allowed.

Among the gathered guardsmen, one being was head, shoulders, and chest above the others, and Pethun was disappointed to recognize him among the traitors to the city. "Come out, Volund!" the Naphil yelled. "All the metal in the world will not fill your belly!"

"Come closer, Gofannon," the giant smith Volund shouted through the iron-barred window. "There is metal here I'd like to fill *your* belly with."

Gofannon chuckled. He was shorter than Pethun, and right now he was an obstacle whose existence was an annoyance.

"Gofannon, you fool," said Pethun, striding into view. "You chose the wrong side."

The other giant rounded, startled, but the armed men all about him gave him quick confidence. "Pethun, son of Samyaza!" Gofannon said. "You interrupt our business, but it need not result in lasting harm to you. Surrender to Enoch's guards now, and be spared Enoch's demons." He held aloft a black tassel and waved it, grinning like a monkey safe in a tree. Pethun watched him silently for a few moments, until the utter lack of the action's effect caused him to slowly lower his arm.

"I suppose you call for Azazyel's creatures, do you? I assure you: they are men, not demons," said Pethun. "And I just killed three of them."

Gofannon looked surprised, but he buried it. "Three *bene Sheol*? I remain dubious."

"I often feel the same," said Pethun. "For example, I doubt that your arms, thick and powerful as they might be, are adept at anything beyond swinging a smith's hammer." He shifted his grip on the harpoon and raised it up, his elbow bent but not quite cocked. "I hunt sea monsters for sport, Gofannon. I fought a leviathan. What chance do you have against me, or your men against mine?" His voice grew louder as he spoke. While he did, the men of Enoch filled the spaces between the buildings surrounding the forge and spilled around the guards like water. Just then, as if timed by whatever god claimed Enoch as his own, distant clashes and yells drifted into hearing. Faint waves of smoke rose far away from somewhere outside the city in the same direction from where came the noises. Gofannon waved the black cloth again. The guards with him began looking around expectantly.

"A ship waits for you at the moat, Gofannon," said Pethun. "You and all these guards will unburden yourselves of any weapons, then you will all begin your new lives at sea, at least for a while. Go where you will, but you cannot return here."

"The curse of Cain," said Gofannon, who grinned no more. "Will you raise your hand against fellow children of Cain to force us to do this thing? I think not."

"The curse of Cain? Let me tell you about the curse of Pethun. It is when I bind you all, take you to the ship myself, cut off your hands and tie a stone to your feet, and throw you overboard into deep waters one by one, after which I try to divine what killed you each first: the drowning, the pressure of the deeps, or the monsters drawn to the blood that trails you as you descend into the blackness."

The disarming was brief, and the men who once were Enoch's guards filed out among the citizens. Gofannon went last of all, casting a rueful glance at Tubal-Cain's forge, but go he did.

The door to Tubal-Cain's forge opened and Volund stepped out with two swords in either hand. "Come on, then," said the giant smith. "Take these, plenty for all." Under Volund's gruff direction, men of all ages and stations formed a rough order and began passing out swords and spears, axes and hammers.

"I have something for you, too," Volund said to Pethun, when the forge's blades could no longer find free hands. "Better than that wooden relic, anyway." He disappeared, then returned holding the weapon, and with a leather-handled mace of his own.

Pethun hefted the gift. "A proper tool for the task, this," he said, then shouted, "Men of Enoch! Let us free our city!"

Volund's voice was nearly drowned by the cries from the raucous mob, but Pethun heard him.

"Lead the way, my lord."

The arrows of the Edenites took a morbid toll on the assassins, who were out of their element in the broad daylight, and soon keenly-aimed shafts protruded from shoulders, hands, thighs, and knees of myriad *bene Sheol*. Other creatures lent their aid: the sleek, spotted viverrids favored by the Scribes bit and clawed at the cloth-wrapped legs of Azazyel's forces; falcons and kestrels from Eden harried their heads; and Hoduín's two ravens did damage befitting raptors five times their size. What made the council's victory absolute was the arrival of Pethun, leading an angry mob from the inner circles. Tubal-Cain's workmanship was in the hands of a thousand men of Enoch, who crudely hacked, beat, and stabbed any grey-clothed figure they could find. Numbers overwhelmed the *bene Sheol*; when their cause was irretrievably lost, they scurried, roach-like, into whatever dark space was closest. When all was counted, more than three hundred of the grey assassins lay unmoving in the street. The council and their forces had lost a tenth that many, thanks in large part to the ministrations of the Scribes, whose apothecaries distributed antidotes and salves to counter the poisons and venoms flung about by the *bene Sheol*.

Noah found Dyeus, Dedroth, and Hoduín listening to Pethun give his account of his entrance into the city.

"...the worst part was not the swim, it was the passage under the city." Pethun wrinkled his nose. "Nothing should smell that foul."

"New weapon?" asked Dyeus. Pethun handed over the spear he had used in the battle. It was shaped as a boar-spear, but with the wings extending into blades that rose and curved to the length of the spear's tip.

"I quite like it," said Pethun. "After this, I think I shall ask our uncle to make one for me in gold."

"Congratulations, Noah," said Dedroth. "Our city is saved, thanks to you."

"And me," muttered Pethun.

"Our task is not finished," said Noah. "The Grigori are here still."

Dyeus wiped blood from a javelin and replaced it at his back. "We shall find our father, and Azazyel's children have asked for a…private encounter with theirs. They are not pleased, to put it mildly."

"The council has already posted guards at the gates," said Hoduín. "The Grigori shall not escape."

Pethun grabbed his spear back from his brother. "Then let the hunt begin."

"Noah!" Jonan ran up, the few arrows he had left rattling in the quiver at his back. "You ought to see this."

Amassed in the middle of the street running straight to the palace districts were Onim and several other councilmen, trying their best to calm a group of women. Pethun whistled, and Noah saw why. Every one was beautiful, and immaculately attired to accent the fact. Their demeanor did not match their dress: some were sobbing, others shrieking at one another. Noah chose one who seemed least hysterical and approached. She was pale, with temples and cheeks painted in a blue that faded to the pearl-white of her perfect features. She did not wait for him to address her.

"Samyaza," the woman said. "He is keeping our husbands together in that horrid chamber. He will not let them leave!"

"You are the wives of the *bene Elohim*," Noah realized aloud. "All of them are there?"

"I think not Azazyel. That one left for his own lair, wherever pit that may be. You must help them!"

"Was Samyaza's bride, the girl Emzara, with them?"

"She left with the wives of Tamiel and Barkayal when we were told to leave. I know not where they went."

Noah called Hamerch over. "Guide these women out of the city. Let them return to their own lands." Hamerch looked at Dyeus, who nodded his assent to his son. A unit of guardsmen was assigned to help, and the group of stunning women moved on.

"Save our husbands!" the blue-cheeked woman shouted as she was led away. "Please!"

Jonan clucked his tongue. "'Save our husbands,' eh? She was not paying attention at the feast last night, was she?"

"I pity her," said Noah.

"Not just because you wish to be able to pity Zara as well?"

"You question my motive."

Jonan sighed. "No. And even if Zara was your motive, I would still not question it. It is only...what will you do with her, Noah?"

Noah fingered the carved script that adorned his staff. "I must leave that up to our God. For now, we need to plan our next move. Help me gather the Nephilim." He cast his hood over his head.

"It is high time we banish some angels."

· CHAPTER 44 ·

Azazyel gazed out of his window and smiled as the first trail of smoke ascended from the inner rings. His defeated *bene Sheol* would not retreat without retribution. The cursed city of Enoch would burn this day.

In a way, he was glad it had come to this. After all, he had spent so much time forging his splendid suit of armor in the heart of Mount Armon, used every bit of his cleverness and skill to craft his weapon. What good were such things if one never had a chance to put them to their purposes?

Running footsteps signaled that the time was almost here. Lilith had been rather sad at the turn of events, but she was wrapped up in her own little schemes, and he knew she understood what had to be done. Azazyel shrugged, admiring again the perfect fit of his breastplate, pauldrons, vambraces, that allowed him maximum mobility with minimum discomfort.

The carved and gilded door burst open, kicked in without need, as Azazyel had not locked it. Five shadows, cast by the hallway lamps, stretched into the bare room, empty of the furnishings that the Grigori had removed in hope and preparation of this very confrontation. He spun on his heels and planted his weapon on the marbled floor.

"Ah, my children." Azazyel pulled his shining helm to his head. "Welcome home."

Warriors from Enoch and Eden, men and giants alike, gathered on the broad steps before the Grigori council building.

"Captain, post your men," ordered Dyeus. "Nobody leaves the chamber inside."

Onim tapped Thims and Gregan. "The Scribes will hold watch with you." They ran off, calling their fellows to them as they went. "Forgive me if I do not wholly trust the guard."

"Pray for us, brothers," said Lamech.

"We already have been," answered Kiribaoth, and he and Onim stopped at the immense stone lions that guarded the chamber's main entrance.

The party that entered the chamber was small. Hoduín, Dyeus, Pethun, and Dedroth represented both the sons of the Grigori and the council, while Noah, Lamech, and Methuselah went as scions of Enoch the Scribe. Gilyon came also; his uncles and aunts had not allowed him to come with them to Azazyel, but he would not be denied accompanying the group that would confront Samyaza. Truth be told, Noah had no desire to see the young Naphil, or his own father and grandfather, put themselves at risk more than they had done so far, but they had insisted, and part of him was glad.

They walked past sculptures fantastic in both subject and execution, spiraling pillars that rose to meet the audience balconies, high-arched windows that looked out over the walkways and streets that hosted continued scenes of battle and death, as Tiras, Tevesh, and Mareth led the hunt for the escaped *bene Sheol*. The portal to the chamber approached. Noah had every intention of walking straight into the Watchers' den, but Hoduín swept past him, his silver spear in hand.

"You have done much, my friend," he said softly as his sigiled robes brushed past Noah, "but now, allow me."

The sons of Samyaza wore expressions that told Noah that they knew no more of this than he, and they all hurried in. In a single high-backed chair set on a raised plinth at the end of the chamber, Samyaza sat alone. One-hundred-and-ninety-eight fuming Grigori were clustered in the middle of the marble floor.

"For once, Father is exercising his authority," said Dyeus.

Pethun's monosyllabic grunt was the only laugh he could muster. "I did not think he had it in him."

The collective attention of the *bene Elohim* turned to Hoduín, who raised his arms and spoke in a clarion voice.

"Grigori! Watchers! Beings from another plane! Since you have not left this place under your own power, you shall leave under ours instead!"

At that signal, robed figures filed into the audience balconies above. Some were Nephilim and some human, some with animal familiars and others with crystals at their necks or held aloft, and all began chanting.

Theirs was a dark, low song, conjuring images of decomposing detritus in a sunless wood, of rotten meat and children crying in cobwebbed corners. If Enoch's sorcerers were the chorus, Hoduín drove the melody. His monotonous mutterings provided the rhythm, and his grating groans reverberated deepest. The sound was oppressive; Noah shut his eyes, overcome by a sudden urge to pray for deliverance, and he heard his father gasp.

The chanting stopped, the sense of impending doom ceased, and Noah saw every pair of Grigori eyes burning bright white.

"A banishing spell?" Barkayal's tone was one of fatherly disappointment, almost disdain. "You and your friends dabble in powers you cannot possibly understand."

Hoduín doubled over, fingers threaded through thick hair, clutching his head as if it would burst. A scan of the balconies showed the same reaction in every one of the sorcerers; one vomited over the wall to the floor below, then dropped out of sight behind it. Even Samyaza's sons and Gilyon were rubbing their temples. Methuselah and Lamech appeared to be unaffected, though.

Pethun swore. "Enough of that, then. On me, brothers." He brought his bladed spear to bear. Dyeus drew a shining javelin, and Dedroth whipped a sword-sized handscythe from under his cloak. Their great running strides devoured the space between them and their father, and then they were upon him.

The five Nephilim spread out around Azazyel, their footsteps echoing around the empty stone space.

"You have much for which to answer, father." The speaker was his second-eldest son. *Eldest now*, Azazyel corrected himself. Gloryon would soon have familiar company in Sheol.

"Perhaps I do, but not to you, *child*." Azazyel put emphasis on the word, letting it diminish the halfbreed whelps surrounding their sire in hostility. Anger, frustrated rage at their rebellion, suddenly filled him, and he wondered if Elohim felt the same towards Lucifer and his angels. If so, Elohim proved more merciful than Azazyel; Lucifer's name had been taken, but he was given a new one and left free. Not his children. Their names mattered no more. Their fates were sealed. Each of them was dead already.

His daughters were human height, as were all female Nephilim, but his giant sons towered over him. Had he let himself, Azazyel could have felt as if he were back among his angelic brethren in his ordained station, taking orders from Michael's lieutenants, they warriors bright and tall and terrible, he a mere watcher, a scout.

He did not let himself. In this reality, *he* was the warrior beyond defeat. He gripped his crossblade lightly. "Who of you have killed a man, children? Any?" His daughters had stalked to either side of him, and his youngest son, the self-styled "slayer of dragons," had circled around to his back. None of them wasted words on a response. "I have never," said Azazyel, setting his weight to the balls of his feet, armor shifting around him like a second skin. "But I do enjoy new experiences."

"Speak no more," said his newly-eldest son. He swung a whip of three chains, metal spheres shaped like enormous spiked thistles at each end, and it was meant to be a killing blow. Azazyel melted away from it, laughing aloud at the surprise on the faces of his children. Each of them had been near babes when first he introduced them to arms, but he had never showed more than a hint of his dirt-body's abilities. He had never before had a need. Now, leaping and weaving in a symphony of motion, joy filled him as he explored fully the far limits of this form.

His full-bearded son brandished the chain-whip, working in tandem with his axe-wielding next-born, whose great girth belied his quickness. Azazyel backed away from simultaneous strikes meant as much to keep his attention as to be fatal. His sons were not dunces; after the first failed attack, strategy had replaced speed and strength in primacy. They were trying to drive him back toward their youngest brother. Azazyel allowed them their game, keeping his eyes fixed upon his direct adversaries. He gave the appearance of ignoring his giant son behind him, but in truth, no sound of mail or leather escaped his ears, no scent of sweat his nose. From the instant the third brother began his strike, Azazyel knew it.

The knife had been aimed at the base of Azazyel's helm. The Grigori watched it as it whistled past his backward-bending body. He sprung from his hands and delivered a metal-booted foot to the knife-thrower's groin, at the same time hearing a wet thud and dismayed gasps.

"You are slow, child—what comes from being as fat as the pigs you keep," Azazyel sneered, directing his words to his ax-carrying son, now sinking to the cold floor with a blade sunk to the hilt in his ample belly. "Did you not learn from Lucifer cast from heaven, from Adam cursed and banished? What of Cain, or your own brother Gloryon? When children rebel against their father, they do so to their hurt." He spun around his youngest, now on his knees in pain, which meant that his head was now at the level of Azazyel's, who ran his gloved fingers through his son's matted hair.

"Your mother only ever wanted three sons," whispered Azazyel. A massive elbow flailed; he caught it sharply on his gauntlet, satisfied with the crack of bone and cry of pain. His son tried to rise, but Azazyel spun his weapon, stabbed down, and put a blade through the dragon-slayer's boot.

High-pitched battle-cries signaled his twin daughters' attacks. He had a certain fatherly affection for his girls, so he let the first few slashes with their thin-bladed swords fall upon him. The resulting scratches would need polishing out, but the blades did no more real damage to his armor than poured wine did to a golden goblet.

His youngest stirred again, and another knife flew. Azazyel had witnessed the Creator write the very laws that governed the manner in which bodies moved in the heavens; the matter of deflecting the path of a bit of metal was simple. He raised his crossblade and did so, causing its course to intersect with his leaping daughter. It caught her bare side, and she fell hard, the impact driving the weapon deeper into her. The vanguard of a pool of blood advanced from her still body upon the smooth stone.

The remaining daughter paused, lips parted in disbelief. Rage malformed her face's beautiful features, and she attacked—not her father, but her brother who had thrown the knife. Once, twice, her sword cut thick arms raised in protection; out of desperation, her younger brother thrust out a fist. The backhand blow hit her full in the face, and Azazyel appreciated the sheer strength granted by the giant size of Nephilim males. His daughter crumpled, her head cracking hard upon the floor. Azazyel kicked her sword away, then pushed his bloodied son, who offered no resistance, to the ground.

"Mindless beasts," said Azazyel, walking slowly to his eldest son, who knelt beside his pale, diaphoretic brother with the knife-hilt protruding from his belly. "Humans, small and weak. Those have been your adversaries. Do you understand now how foolish you have been?"

"You butcher your own blood." His son's rage was contained by a dam of discipline, but barely, so Azazyel kicked it.

"I?" Azazyel poured condescension into each word. "Whose weapons caused these wounds? Not mine." He turned back to look at his youngest son, trying to rise on a ruined foot. "Except that one."

The dam broke. With a roar, the giant sprung up and swung his chains. Azazyel was already inside the arc of the spheres. He grabbed his son's long beard, wrapping the coarse hairs around one arm, the other gripping his crossblade, but not bringing it into use.

Azazyel tugged to one side, then the other, surprised at how amusing he found this. His enraged son was off-balance, caught like a lion by its tail, but still he flailed his whip. The Grigori dodged again, pulling hard on the beard; the metal spheres missed their marks, but found others in the flesh and bone of the neck and face of his belly-wounded son. The thick giant went down, and Azazyel sensed his spirit leave his body.

The Grigori released the beard. His eldest living son was aghast, jaw slack, unbelieving. "You…you are a *devil!*"

"Inaccurate," said Azazyel.

"With my brother's weapon shall you be repaid!" The giant took up his fallen kin's ax, but before he could bring it around, Azazyel had swept the crossblade's edge across his face, opening a cut over the length of the Naphil's brow.

"Devil!" The giant swung wildly.

"Again, no." Azazyel stabbed twice, the length of his weapon exceedingly sufficient. The two resulting gashes—one through the meat of his son's upper arm, one where his arm met his shoulder—impeded the giant's control of the weapon and diminished his strength, but not his mad resolve. Azazyel had intended such, and since he had places to be, the time for the end had come.

He grabbed his son's beard once more. Near-blind from his brow's blood, the Naphil stumbled as Azazyel led him. The clumsy swings of the ax continued. The first few Azazyel batted away with the crossblade. Now the ax was raised again; Azazyel pulled down hard on the tightly-held beard, at the same time catching the ax with the curve of his weapon as it came down, redirecting it. The ax-head would have shattered the stone floor, had a fallen female Naphil not come between them.

"Careless," said Azazyel over his son's bestial cries. "How am I to explain *that* to your mother?"

With rage-fueled abandon the giant swung. This time, Azazyel's crossblade met a leather-wrapped wrist instead of metal. Ax and hand spun away as one, the heavy metal head finding a resting place in the skull of the youngest brother still trying to stand.

"Nooo!"

"Alas, yes." Azazyel leapt and kicked his son full in the chest. His dirt-body did not have enough mass to knock the Naphil over outright, but as he landed, he lashed out the staff of his weapon behind his son's backpedal-ling feet. With a roar the giant tripped and fell, full upon the prone form of his other sister, crushing her like an iron boot on a serpent's head.

Azazyel stepped up his son's body as if he were cresting a hill. "And you call me a devil?" he asked, receiving a groan in response. "Because of me, only one of my children is dead. You have killed four of them." He aimed the tip of his crossblade at his son's throat. "Greet them for their mother and me when you see them again in Sheol."

He stabbed down hard.

Noah had seen his share of martial prowess of late, but he had not seen such a display as this. Dyeus's javelins sped fast as light and as sure as a falcon diving for a kill. Pethun wove his weapon, stabbing and slashing, in a net of pure fury, and Dedroth's flawless attacks were all the more imposing for their improbability coming from the more cerebral brother. For all this, though, nothing Noah had witnessed matched Samyaza.

He was unarmed, yet unafraid. His feints confounded in plain sight, his evasions and escapes seeming impossible but for some prophetic power.

He floated and spun as if weight meant nothing to him, defying earth's pull and blades' strikes alike, if but by hair's breadth.

Samyaza danced through the onslaught, and his sons' frustration began to show. Roaring, Dyeus let a javelin fly; Samyaza snatched it out of midair, with a flick of his wrist using it to beat down Pethun's spearthrust, then a sweeping strike from Dedroth's scythe. The Grigori paused, as if making a decision. Fixating on Dyeus, he reared back to throw.

He paused again, then staggered. The shaft of an arrow was embedded in his neck, transfixing his windpipe and exiting through the back, a bit to the left of the spine. Noah's hunter's perception took over, and he traced the trajectory of the wound to where the shot must have come from.

Lamech's eyes were locked on Samyaza, bow still held at the end of an outstretched arm. The farmer's drawing hand hovered over the quiver at his back, ready to fire again as needed.

"No one steals my son's bride."

Samyaza took another shaky step. He brushed his neck with two fingers, looking almost thoughtful. Then, to the utter amazement of the humans and Nephilim, the wounds began to glow like embers. The fletchings and arrowhead, charred black after its passage through the Watcher's corporeal form, fell to the ground. The wounds flared into flame, then disappeared. leaving behind not even a trace of a scar.

Samyaza chuckled. "Fool. Now you know the great secret of the *bene Elohim*. You cannot kill us."

"The same was said about the leviathan," said Noah. "And what difference is there between you and it? Vicious, unwanted, invincible." His family stood beside him and his Nephilim allies around him, all tall and unbowed, though not yet victorious. "But we defeated it nonetheless, Samyaza Leviathan, just as you will be defeated."

Samyaza scoffed and stepped nearer the Edenites. "Eden. Ever the land of trouble. So arrogant, so self-righteous. Do you know, it strikes me—I knew your father Enoch better than you did, Methuselah. I knew *Elohim* more fully than you ever could, Lamech. And I certainly know Emzara…in ways you have only dreamt of, poor Noah." The radiant smile was withering in its arrogance. "Perhaps I am destined to know everyone about whom you care better than you do yourself. Tell me, what now will you do at this impasse?"

"There is no impasse. Not when one of us is willing to do what you will not, Samyaza." Azazyel strode into the hall; from where he had entered the guarded building, Noah could not begin to guess.His armor was burnished to a shine like sunlight through diamond, golden sigils flowing along its surfaces. In his hands was a weapon taller than he was. A golden haft the height of a man ended in a long, straight blade, and where the blade's base met the haft in four jeweled langets, two more blades like those of an axe swept to either side. The glistening red that streaked each blade gave severe announcement that the weapon was no virgin to warfare. Noah spared a glance at Gilyon, and he suddenly knew he was looking at the last of a bloodline. Azazyel saw Gilyon too, and through the slit in his helm his eyes burned white.

Two steps to the side, and Noah interposed himself between Azazyel and Gilyon, brandishing his staff with both hands held in front of him.

"A staff?" Azazyel sneered. "You wish to be cut in half, dust-man? Very well."

Noah stood his ground. "You are able to cleave flesh. I carry the words of the Creator God, Who can cleave flesh, soul, and spirit. Azazyel, you are nothing. Come and meet your doom."

The Grigori drew back his weapon, growling, two glowing points still visible beneath his helm. Suddenly, his head snapped back as if it were tethered to a cord whose length had run out. He ripped off his helm, and his fiery eyes widened.

He stared straight up through the chamber's open ceiling at empty sky, then abruptly spun around and sprinted away from Noah. Leaping headlong, he disappeared in a flash of liquid flame, weapon and armor clattering to the ground.

Whatever had caused such a reaction in the fallen angel was noted by his comrades as well. Grigori everywhere stumbled about in confusion. Some, only a few, vanished in the manner of Azazyel, but most simply ran. Humans and Nephilim alike looked around, but they could see nothing but marble stone and clear sky.

Noah closed his eyes. "God of my fathers, give me eyes to see," he prayed. Hoduín, now recovered, glanced doubtfully at him, but when again Noah opened them, his pupils blazed with the same pure fire that burned in those of the Grigori.

From the open expanse above descended beings that defied description, at least in human language. They had color to them, Noah felt sure of it, more vivid and alive than the boldest bolt of dyed cloth, but every aspect of them shined so brightly that whatever hues they displayed were lost in brilliant white. Hundreds, thousands, of the beings circled above, wings like no creature found on earth streaming from them at their backs and ankles. Noah marveled at this magnificence for only a second before his eyes were drawn inexorably to what was in the midst of them.

Four more glorious beings faced outward from each other, bodies covered by a pair of the same spectacular wings that stretched back and upwards to touch those of their neighbors. Their forms were as flames meeting the lamp as it burns, like bronze glowing from the heat of the forge or a coal in the heart of a hot fire. The creatures' four faces were terrifying and noble, monstrously beautiful, of man, bull, lion, and eagle together, never turning, never blinking; their feet were hoofed like a calf's. A roiling, whirling fire was in the midst of them, and inside it spun wheels within wheels. Set into the rims of the wheels were rows of eyes, and Noah knew beyond all doubt that those eyes could see all.

The final figure he glimpsed in the flames, the one that made all else seem like a dull, grey memory, was the One on a magnificent crystal-blue throne. As He appeared, the roar of a burning fire became the rush of waters. His legs were like living fire, at his torso becoming more like heated bronze that had become crystal, transparent, and had trapped the fire within it. Around the Person's entire form pulsed light—not the bright, saturated whiteness of the first beings, or the pure, fiery light of the four around the throne. This light, this radiance was of many colors, each distinct, yet still a perfect complement to the whole. The radiance bent, and the Person on the throne seemed to hold it almost as bow, like Lamech still held his own. Noah was too awestruck to wonder what sort of missiles might be loosed from such a thing. Only afterward did he recall the flares of chains whipping down to ensnare the screaming spirits of the Grigori trapped in the chamber, or the twenty trails of cold light speeding away from the city walls toward Mount Armon.

He fell on his face, praising the Lord God Creator.

· CHAPTER 45 ·

For Noah, time seemed to pause while he lifted up his prayers of thanks. He had no words, only gratitude; he knew that it was enough. When he felt two strong hands on his shoulders, he regained his feet. No sign of the Grigori remained, no bodies, no piles of ash or blackened stains on the marble.

"Gone…they all just…gone!" Hoduín was trembling. "Noah, what did you see? Incredible!"

"Calm, Hoduín," said Dyeus, beaming. Whoops and cheering from outside began in earnest, as word of what had just transpired reached the guards and the Scribes. "Our humble farmer has things he must still do."

"Son, Rakeel and Hadishad have gone with Dagdha and his kin to his father Tamiel's palace," said Lamech, "and Hoduín will take Merim and Jonan to Barkayal's."

"Come with us, Noah," the Naphil sorcerer offered. "I would wager that we shall find your bride there."

"I…think I shall decline," said Noah.

Lamech wrinkled his tanned brow. "But son, you -"

"Please, Father. Emzara will find no comfort from me now, not when she has lost the one to whom she has given herself. Do not ask me to explain my feelings. I could not if I tried."

Two and three at a time, council members arrived at the scene of their final victory. Raposh supported old Irad, beside himself with a jealous joy that the city was theirs once more. Tubal-Cain, tunic soaked with the sweat and blood of battle, grinned as he came up to Samyaza's sons.

"You fought too hard," said Pethun, grinning back at his uncle.

"Nonsense. That was nothing compared to a day at my forge." His eyes twinkled. "The council has been petitioned by the people of Enoch, who you saved this day. We have much to discuss yet, but...well, some of them wish to make you head of a new council—a Nephilim council, to replace the Grigori. You, Dyeus, and Dedroth, and also Hoduín and Dagdha."

"A Nephilim council." Like a slow-breaking wave, a smile crested upon Pethun's face. "Yes, I suppose that makes sense."

"I thought you might like that." Tubal-Cain reached up and patted his giant nephew on the back. "Now, if you all will excuse me, I must go to find my mother, and your infant brother. She must be worried sick." At the edge of the growing assembly, the smith noticed Noah. "The architect of our victory seems rather morose," he noted to his nephews.

"Lovelorn," said Pethun.

"Ah. Noah!" Tubal-Cain ran over to where Noah stood, slowly turning his staff to read the words of the Generations that he knew so well. "Your mind needs clearing. Come with me, will you? I go to Samyaza's palace. I know you must hold no great fondness for anything that bears his touch, but I promise you, his gardens will make you feel as if you were in Eden once more."

Noah ran his eyes down the words on his staff, to the very end of Adam's Generation. "Strangely enough, Tubal-Cain, I was just reading about you. Yes, I shall come. Lead the way."

"You spoke the truth about this garden," said Noah, walking beneath the gold-hung branches of a pear tree heavy with fruit. Tubal-Cain picked two and tossed one to Noah.

They passed an empty wrought-iron cage, the only manmade structure they had seen since the garden gates. "I have been meaning to ask you," Noah said to the smith, who looked up while taking a voracious bite, "do you know why Greatfather Adam placed you and your family in the Generation he wrote? Could it really be only the metalwork?"

"Despite what you might think, I do know the words of which you speak," said Tubal-Cain. "My best guess is-"

A guard crashed out of the bushes like one of the Grigori man-bull statues come to life, driving through the blossoming hedge to their left with a toss of his horned helmet. The unmistakable ring made by iron leaving scabbard left little time for hesitation, and Noah instinctively pushed Tubal-Cain hard. The smith stumbled forward with an angry cry and hit the ground. The blow that was meant to cleave him from shoulder to navel missed, instead hitting him at the back of the ankle and burying deep. Tubal-Cain cried again, now from pain.

Noah positioned himself to make what defense he could. The truth was that he never intended to use the staff he now carried as a weapon. Despite all the fighting he had walked through thus far this day, he had not yet missed his bow or his knives, but he found himself wishing he had them now.

He stared into a mangled face that he could not help but recognize. "Malidoch!"

The lieutenant-chief, long disfigured and now disgraced, contorted his palsied face into an entirely new degree of sneer. "You. This is your fault, damn you!"

Malidoch cocked the sword, Azazyel's sigil catching the sun and blazing bright as if the departed Grigori were willing it to bring him vengeance. So focused was Malidoch on delivering the killing stroke that he did not notice the young giant behind him—not while rounding the towering rosebushes at a full run, not while screaming his name, and not while thrusting the point of Azazyel's golden weapon through his crimson cape and into his back, piercing flesh until it stuck fast to the inside of his leather corslet.

Gilyon tugged the long blade from Malidoch's back, letting his great-uncle crumple to the ground. His cheeks were wet with tears.

"My father was your sister's son," he said. "You could have saved him." He dropped to his knees, his shut eyes coming level with Noah's own, and he wept.

Malidoch gurgled on the ground, lips dripping bloody saliva. "Hurry on, Noah...yours will not be a happy ending." He sounded as if he were speaking underwater, but his words were intelligible. "My sister will see to that..."

Noah snapped to attention, every fiber in him suddenly burning for action, not caring if Malidoch's bubbling breath had been his final one. "Gilyon, see to Tubal-Cain." He sprinted past walls of greenery for Samyaza's palace.

The verdant borders opened into the yard before the vast open-walled structure. Noah burst into the space, then stopped short. There, above the wooden pillars of the first palace floor, at a balcony overlooking the gardens, was Zara. The woman behind her was wild-eyed and beautiful, and Noah instantly feared her as he had never feared anything in his life.

Zara was dressed in a gossamer gown that left little to the imagination, sending waves of jealousy crashing down on Noah that Samyaza had dared touch his beloved with such wicked hands. A green silk cord was at her throat, and her lids fluttered. She moaned.

The woman behind Zara jerked a hand, and Zara was pulled back harshly. Jealousy turned to horror as Noah saw that she gripped the same sort of green cord that was around Zara's neck.

"Greetings, Noah!" she called. "I am Lilith! So very sorry we have not been properly introduced." She cackled madly. "My husband, my love, is gone now, lost forever. Let me show you how such a thing feels."

Whatever the madwoman flung down at Noah, it burst as it hit the ground into a greyish cloud that seared his nostrils and throat. Lilith pushed Zara hard, propelling herself back inside the palace while Zara tumbled off the balcony like a girl's husk-doll kicked by a bullying brother.

Noah stumbled to where she hanged, stretching desperately, almost able to reach her feet. She swayed without noise, and Noah's vision swayed with her. Lights and shapes played at the corners of his eyes. The earth and sky turned upside down and inside-out, and he dropped onto his back. His senses were revolting: he fancied he could taste Lilith's fading laughter, hold the scent of the grass in his hands. He could see all of Zara now, the thin gown clinging to her figure, her pretty face turning purple shade by shade, or perhaps only seeming to.

Her lips moved. A choke escaped them. Through his mind's anarchy, Noah grasped the words he thought he heard.

"I am sorry."

The last thing he noticed before he succumbed totally was the green cord tight around her neck, but in that, too, his senses could not be trusted. In that final conscious moment, he could have sworn that it was not a cord at all.

He could have sworn it was a serpent.

‹ CHAPTER 46 ›

Barkayal, fleshless spirit for the first time in more than two centuries, screamed in frustration. "How? How could we have missed the signs?"

Twenty Watcher captains hovered over Mount Armon, the site of their original vows. Their human likenesses were gone, disintegrated, and now they were again as they were created. Six thin wings, three on a side, fell from their backs, drooping and curling around them to cover their loins. The spirits' most striking features, at least to beings of their nature, were the illuminate orbs that covered them, floating on the surface of their forms, even their wings.

"Only One can bend the heavens, hide the stars' courses," said Samyaza. "Be thankful we escaped His binding."

"Thankful to whom, exactly?" Azazyel's orbs rippled dark from head to wingtip and brightened again. "We escaped of our own power."

"We must remain free," Barkayal wailed. "Our vassals' sacrifices must not be wasted."

"We did not give them much choice in the matter, did we?" Azazyel snorted. "We needed their strength, so we took it."

"It is not something of which we ought to be proud," snapped Kokobiel.

"Why not?"

Twenty spirits turned a thousand eyes to the new presence. He stole among the Watchers, movements languid and dark as amber honey. His face and feet were as a bull, and his bearing would have marked him as a captain in that host but for the deep blackness that cloaked him, like a once-lit torch suddenly extinguished at the bottom of a well.

Ancient routine made Samyaza want to retreat and report, but he kept his place. "Belial."

"Samyaza. Captains." The demon's darkness trailed him like a sable cape. "I ask again, why not be proud? Would you rather be bound in Tartarus? For that is where your fellows are."

"If that is where they are, let us free them!" Asaradel's wings wavered and flitted as he searched for the idea's approval.

"From Tartarus?" Belial snorted. "Obviously you have never seen that pit, else you would not speak such folly from your ignorance. I assure you, they are lost…at least for now."

"It is not fair!" cried Barkayal. "He sent us to this cursed, fallen earth. It was only a matter of time before we succumbed to its fairest creations. He knew this would happen!"

"You remained under His authority and rule, blind fool," Belial hissed. "Look at us—we are not in chains. We do as we please. We have removed His yoke. We are free."

"What do you want, Belial?" asked Azazyel, curiosity infecting the question.

"Ironically, my dear Watchers, we have been watching *you*. The Lord of the Earth extends his condolences, and an invitation. Join us in rebellion against the Tyrant."

Samyaza sneered. "And we speak folly? He is infinite in power."

"A proper sentiment for an ant to feel for a basilisk, until the ants overwhelm with sheer numbers."

"We are not ants."

"Thank you for that wisdom, Samyaza. No wonder you are the leader here." Belial strode in a circle, leaving darkness behind him in a liquid mist. "Is 'omnipotence' not simply possessing more power than a weaker being can comprehend? Penemuel, would your weaponless scholars not feel likewise about Araqiel's stone-sorcerers, or Zaquiel's bronze-armored knights? We have not tested the limits of the Tyrant's strength, true. That does not mean He has no limits. We outnumber Him, and His favored creations are two things: ignorant, thus persuadable. We add to our numbers. We bide our time."

"Impossible," said Tamiel. "He made us, and He can unmake us."

"Then why hasn't He?" asked Belial. "You think we cannot win, because Elohim made us? Were your children not made by you, and have they not supplanted you? He is only invincible until He is defeated."

They had no choice, no other options left to them. The imprecation was made once more on the peak of Mount Armon. In an instant, with total understanding of all it implied, the deed was done. Belial melted into the earth, whispering behind him.

"Our Lord Satan is quite pleased to have you."

· CHAPTER 47 ·

Jet ran through the ninth circle, calling Gilyon's name. The moment word had reached her at her family's estate that Pethun and his mob had breached the eighth wall, she had left. She knew the streets were still perilous, but a frantic mother worried for her son gave no heed to danger.

The side street she ran down now emptied onto the main thoroughfare, meeting it as it made its way to the palace district. Jet followed it, keeping to the side of the street, where the stones were driest; the dung and dirt from heavy traffic mixed with the mists to make a trough of feculent mud where the sloping street met in the center.

She curved around a pillared building and saw, to her dismay, that she was not alone. A lion nosed at a wet, grimy lump that lay dead in the middle of the street. Its mane was lustrous gold, except in matted, muddy patches where it dragged on the ground. The beast sniffed, picking up her scent even as its nose was covered with filth. It began to prowl towards her, growling. Jet looked about for an open door or archway, but she saw nothing. She tripped on an edge of stone and sat down hard. The lion's pace picked up.

"Hey there, cat! Begone!" A long whip snapped at the lion's face, drawing a hiss and another growl. A man, hooded and dressed in the manner of Eden's farmers, cracked his whip again. The beast swiped at thin air, then ran off, obviously deciding that better meat and less trouble might be found somewhere else.

The Edenite man offered her a calloused hand, and she took it. He helped her up.

"My name is Dashael, of Eden," he said. "Are you hurt?"

Jet brushed herself off and looked at her rescuer. His eyes were the pale green of a field in sunlight.

316

"I am alright, I think." Jet looked at the man again, longer this time, and smiled as she had not since Gloryon was living. "Yes, I believe I am quite alright."

The *bene Sheol* had run through the city like foxes with their tails aflame. As demanded Cain's retributive curse, most of them had been chased down and killed, though how many survived none could be sure. They had set much of the inner circles on fire before the hunt, though. Of all the men who fought that day, it was Elebru who proved himself greatest in the battle's aftermath, at least in the eyes of those whose lives and homes he saved. He worked tirelessly, selflessly, fighting the flames with abandon, the scars he already bore removing his fears of adding to them. More than one child was rescued by his brave actions.

Back on Wide Bridge, Tiras ran a cloth over his axe's chipped edge. Considering the work it had done today, it offered no danger of cutting him. Scores of broken blades and severed limbs had dulled it to the point of uselessness, except perhaps as a giant hammer. The hunt for the fled *bene Sheol* had been good; if there were any verity to Cain's curse, it had been visited in full on Azazyel's murderous minions.

Mareth and Tevesh tossed the last of the assassins' corpses on the fire. Protected by the leviathan's scales, the three giant warriors had gathered up and consolidated the smoldering debris that littered the bridge, with the burning remnants of the great ram as the heart of the fire. Upon this they piled bodies and pieces of bodies; Tiras had been somewhat surprised at how poorly human flesh withstood sharp iron wielded by a Naphil.

Finished at last, the giants watched the smoke form a column that rose above the city walls and began to drift out towards the sea. Bits of gore and splashes of ichor were the only things that marred their remarkable organic armor. Despite the myriad sadistic weapons the *bene Sheol* had borne against them, the leviathan scales that covered each of them had proven as impenetrable as when worn by the monster from which they had been taken.

The ram's iron head, heated cherry-red, broke from its charred beam with a hiss and crack, sending embers flying.

"She was a grand leviathan," said Tevesh.

"The ram?" asked Mareth. "No."

"Mareth, you dog, do not disparage our poor battering ram," said Tevesh, a white grin in contrast with his sooted beard.

"The ram was not the leviathan," repeated Mareth, and he did not share the grin. "We," he said, placing a fist on the armored chest of Tiras, then Tevesh. "We Nephilim—we are the leviathan."

When Hamerch heard that while he had been escorting the Grigori wives, the Grigori themselves had been...well, whatever they had been... his thought went to his father's estate. His aunts and his father's mistresses, his mother included, were trapped there, along with Deneresh. Less than a day had passed, but Hamerch knew that plenty might happen in that time.

At a sprint, he drank in the distance like his younger brother drank fine wine. The broken main gate, the clear result of strong intent with no good purpose, spurred him to go even faster. He burst into the estate house.

At first, he thought his worst fears had been realized. The foyer and the front halls were wrecked, vases broken, marble facades shattered. Hamerch made his way further in, stepping over shards of glass and uprooted plants. Three still bodies of Enoch's guards blocked the arched portal to one of the sitting rooms. Their helms were askew, and their weapons were still clutched in gloved fists. Deneresh sat among them, chin at his chest, back against the white stone jamb. His bright tunic was stained dark, as dark as the red liquid that pooled on the floor and blended so subtly into the guards' crimson capes. Hamerch's heart fell, then leapt when he heard his brother's soft sob.

"Deneresh!" Hamerch stepped over the first prostrate guard. "You live!"

"Of *course* I live! But what is the purpose anymore?" Deneresh raised his head, followed by his hand, which clutched the broken neck of an amphora. The jagged edge of the white pottery dripped red.

"I am sorry, brother," Deneresh said, voice cracking. "I had to do it. I heard these...these *pigs* talking, planning to forcefully violate our dear, sweet aunts—and Aunt Eila, too! I stopped them, though, with the first thing I had at hand." He pushed himself to his feet, put his lips to the broken vessel he held, then flung it across the room with a cry. He stumbled to Hamerch, who accepted him with outstretched arms.

318

"The last of Methuselah's wine," Deneresh sobbed, "gone."

"Somehow, brother, we shall overcome," Hamerch said, and he knew then that everything would be just fine.

Noah convalesced under the care of the Scribes, where he recounted everything he remembered of what Lamech, Methuselah, and Onim were convinced was a genuine theophany. On a whim kindled by the farmer's hazy recollection of his white-eyed vision, Dyeus and Mareth went to Mount Armon to look for the Grigori. They found no one there, but what they did find, they kept close to them. Barrels of some kind of indescribable mead were piled in storeroom after storeroom. Opulent dwellings were built at the mountain's peak, with halls stretching further into the stone itself. A steep, winding stairway descended deep into the mountain, ending in a forge so grand that Dyeus suspected if Tubal-Cain saw it, he would never want to leave. Indeed, when Dyeus moved his sisters and household from his estate in the city to the mountain, a hobbled Tubal-Cain came with them, and from then on he seldom did.

"Will you be taking Father's palace for your own, Pethun?" asked Dedroth.

"That is *Lord Councilor* Pethun of Enoch now," said Pethun. "And to answer your question: no. I have given it to the Edenites to be their embassy. I shall take Azazyel's palace instead. Have you seen the hot springs and grottoes down there?" Pethun stroked his chin. "Speaking of 'down there.' Scrivener! Take a note."

An aide, female, newly-appointed and well-endowed, ran up with board and parchment.

"Draft an edict. The undergrounds are not habitable for any citizen of ours. The hovels and warrens therein shall be condemned, their inhabitants moved aboveground. The scions of Samyaza will raise the funds to build their housing if we must." She repeated it to his satisfaction, then she sauntered away, the back of her voluptuous figure also to his satisfaction.

"By the way, how were the autopsies of the *bene Sheol*?" Pethun asked, still staring after his aide. "Are they anything like us? Half goat, or half fish, perhaps?"

"Only human," Dedroth answered. "Mutilated, scarred, but no more than men. Whatever Azazyel did to them, it was brutal." He tapped his long fingers together. "My brother, I have a boon to ask of you."

"Anything, Dedroth."

"What are your plans for the underground?"

Noah lifted a heavy chest to the camel's back and tied it fast, exulting in his feeling healthy and strong once more. He had accompanied his father and grandfather to Upanshim's inn, the last waypoint before they would part.

"That is the last of it," said Noah. The sense of satisfaction that ought to have filled him was dulled by the ache in his soul he had felt since... No. He pushed the thought, that moment, away with all of his mental might.

"I wish you were coming back to the farm with us, my son," said Lamech. "But I understand why you do not."

"We received word," said Methuselah, just failing to meet his grandson's eyes. "Rakeel made it back to Eden safely. With Emzara."

The hurt in the older man's face reminded Noah that his loss was not his alone, and that understanding softened the pain of hearing her name. "He took her to...the grave orchard?"

Lamech nodded.

"Good," said Noah, willing himself to believe the word. "Good. It is where she belongs."

"Will you not come with us for *her* sake, Noah?" asked Lamech, as if one more swing of the axe would finally fall the tree.

"I have...said my goodbyes to Emzara already," answered Noah. "There is nothing else I can do. Nothing for me in Eden but reminders of what could have been, of what I have lost."

"Your family."

"Reminders of what I have lost. Besides, I feel the Creator's calling," said Noah, hoping to lift his father's spirit, and his own as well. "There is much to rebuild in Enoch, and much to teach, now that the words of Elohim might be spoken aloud."

Methuselah inclined his head, deftly darting into a different subject. "Quite generous of Pethun to give the Grigori's chamber to the Scribes as an altar house."

"Indeed it was." Noah showed the hint of a grin. "Besides, someone must keep Merim and Hadishad well-behaved."

"Co-ambassadors." Methuselah shook his head. "I still say they are young for it."

"It cannot be any harder than, oh, running your own farmstead and vineyard at their age," said Lamech, climbing the netting onto the camel's hump.

"What after Enoch, Noah?" asked Methuselah. "What will you do? Return to Eden?"

"I cannot say," Noah answered. "I simply have faith that Elohim will work my life to His purpose."

Methuselah mounted his own camel, and with two loud spits, the animals started down the road. Noah waved his goodbye.

"Mark my words, my son," Methuselah said to Lamech, as they began their long journey home. "The world will be changed because of that man."

"Of that, I have no doubt, my father," and he laughed. "Of that I have no doubt."

‹ EPILOGUE ›

EIGHTEEN YEARS LATER

Noah laid the last shaped stone on the watchtower and called for the scaffolding to be lowered. More than a year of constant construction, and thousands upon thousands of man-hours, had passed, but at last the citadel at the heart of the city was complete. There was a poetic aspect to it: the crumbling and fire-gutted crudity that had been there before, the ruins of Cain's original structure, was no more, and soon the name he had given his settlement would be gone as well.

Noah's friends and family, his closest circle, stood by while he descended.

"Well done, Noah," said Kenan. "I would wager this will last for a thousand years or more."

"You have foremen for this sort of thing, you know," said Jonan, and pride in his brother lurked behind his smirk.

Noah clapped powdery dust from his hands. "My prerogative. I am the architect, after all."

A Naphil with a boyish face imposed upon them. "Noah, Grandmother has given her blessing, along with my brother Pethun. I am to come with you!"

"Excellent, Eudeon!"

"Excellent for me, you mean." Gilyon clasped the other giant's hand. "Now I shall have someone along whose clothes I can borrow."

"Gilyon, have your brothers given up their plans to stowaway?" asked Noah.

The giant chuckled. "They have finally been dissuaded. Mother reminded them that they are but ten and eight years old, and Dashael promised to show them the unicorns just come from Cush."

"It is not hard to guess which parent won them over, I suppose," said Noah.

"Lady Jet, obviously," said Eudeon with a wink.

As they left the worksite, Jonan said, "Father and Grandfather sent one last wagon of provisions. I think we are ready."

"Everything comes to a head at once." Kenan raised his eyes to the heavens. "Almost as if Someone were directing our path."

"Then tomorrow we start," said Noah. "First to see our old friends Hoduín, Tiras, and Tevesh at the northern keeps, then on to follow the old journeys of the legendary Kenan, son of Enosh."

"Assuming you remember the way, old man," said Gilyon to Kenan.

"You mean, 'assuming you remember, old man, sir.'"

Noah laughed the easy laugh of a man with a task complete and much left to do. Looking at his kin and comrades, he thanked Elohim for like-minded men. Together, the five of them headed off to the ceremony that would name an heir, then a city.

"A new era begins today, brother." Pethun handed his infant son back to the wet nurse. "New era, new buildings, a new heir. A new city."

"Have you chosen a name yet?" Dedroth had ascended from his underground laboratories to attend the naming, that fact alone making the day one of rare occasions. With Dyeus now inhabiting Mount Armon full-time and Hoduín and Dagdha building colonies of their own, Pethun had become the sole remaining active member of the Nephilim council, and leader of the city by default.

"Indeed, I have." Pethun paused, as if confirming he still liked his choice. The answer apparently affirmative, he said, "His name shall be Atlan."

"The city—Atlan, then, as Cain did with his own son?"

"No, no, no. Certainly not. Far too confusing, people and places having exactly the same name." Pethun gazed outside, admiring his city's many new white spires tinted blue by the sea beyond.

"What, then?" asked Dedroth, covering his weak, dark-accustomed eyes from the glare.

The Naphil king smiled.

"Atlantis."

◄ ◄ ► ►

‹ GENEALOGY ›

GENEALOGY of ADAM

Adam ═ Eve

Cain   Abel   Seth ═ Azura   Awan   OSD

Enosh ═ Noam   OSD

Kenan ═ Mualaleth   OSD

Mahalalel ═ Dinah   OSD

OSD   Jared ═ Baraka

Edni ═ Enoch   OSD

OSD   Methuselah ═ Edna

Betenos ═ Lamech   Rakeel ═ Emilbet   OSD

OSD   Hadishad   Jonan   Noah ⋯⋯ Emzara   Merim   OSD

Notes

Plain Text = Humans
"OSD" = "Other Sons and Daughters"

GENEALOGY of CAIN

Adam ══ Eve

Abel   Cain ══ Awan   Seth   Azura   OSD

Enoch

Irad

Mehujael

Methushael

Notes

Plain Text = Humans
Script = Bene Elohim
"OSD" = "Other Sons and Daughters"

Adah ══ Lamech ══ Zillah

Jabal   Jubal   Tubal‑Cain   Naamah ══ *Samyaza*

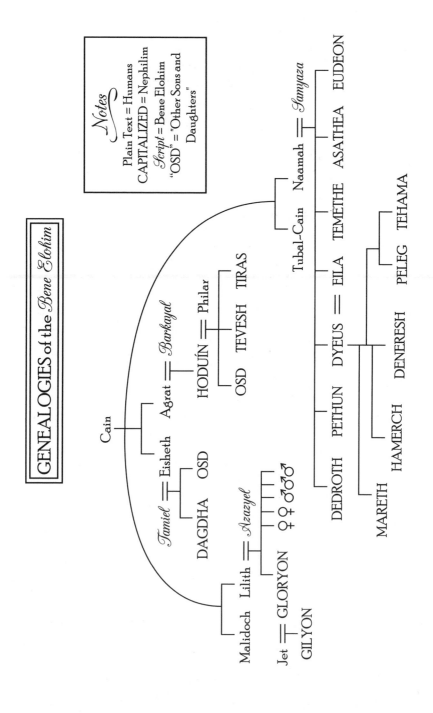

· BESTIARY ·

Author's note: I do not propose that these identifications are authoritative in whatever accuracy they may possess. Where a creature's name has its origin in mythology, I attempted to match it with an animal known from natural history with a credible etiology, whether in name or particular physical feature or description. All illustrations are my own.

AUROCH: one of the larger varieties of the cattle kind. These hooved quadrupeds are easily domesticated; provide leather, milk, and meat (post-Flood); and are suitable for sacrifice. Cattle, in many forms both wild and domesticated, are ubiquitous throughout history and widespread today.

BARAMIN: a grouping of animals according to their created kind. Although all individual creatures in a baramin share particular features, the baramin as a whole often possesses enormous capacity for variation within set genetic boundaries. In general, members may interbreed.

BEHEMOTH: the largest land animal ever to exist. The behemoth is cited by the Creator Himself as one of the grandest specimens of creation. This quadripedal giant has a tree-like neck and tail and a sheer

size that protects it from virtually any predators. While the animal is an herbivore, provoking one is fraught with as much, or more, danger than any predator. The modern name for the *baramin* is "sauropod." Notable examples include diplodocus and apatosaurus.

BULL DRAGON: a bipedal beast slightly smaller than a felldragon, but sharing many of the same features—strong legs, undersized forelimbs, fanged jaws—with the addition of two bony horns above the eyes. Its modern name is carnotaurus.

CAPRID: a member of the baramin that includes all variations of sheep, goats, and antelope. These creatures are ubiquitous both in captivity and in the wild. When husbanded, a caprid might provide a renewable source of clothing (wool or cashmere) as well as leather of various qualities. Exceptional members of this baramin are considered suitable for sacrifice.

COCK-DRAKE: a bipedal reptilian herbivore, but much slighter and more colorful than the vicious and predatory drake. A genial and docile nature makes this animal amenable to taming. The smallest variations are only suitable for pets, but larger specimens might serve as cart-teams and mounts. Examples, in modern terminology, include gallimimus and ornithomimus.

CREODONT: a group of carnivorous mammals that occupied a similar ecological niche (and ranged in similar size) as canines and felines. No known examples are living today.

DRAGON: a broadly used generic term. It encompasses the baramin of the largest bipedal reptiles including allosaurus, carnotaurus and tyrannosaurus; as well as other dinosaur kinds including tarasqs (ankylosaurs), horned dinosaurs (triceratops), and spined dinosaurs (stegosaurs).

DRAKE: a bipedal reptilian carnivore, in appearance much like a miniature felldragon. These hunters compete for the same prey as wolves, lions, and creodonts, and range in comparable size. Examples, in modern terminology, include velociraptor and deinonychus.

FELLDRAGON: a massive bipedal reptilian beast, and the apex terrestrial predator. The largest specimens can bring down all but the very biggest prey. Notable features include powerful clawed legs, stunted forelimbs, and jaws full of knifelike teeth. Notable examples, in modern terminology, include tyrannosaurus and allosaurus.

GOAT-ANTELOPE: see Caprid

HORNFACE DRAGON: a sturdy quadripedal reptilian creature. Most breeds are much larger than bulls, although the men of Eden use them both for the same purposes (with the exception of sacrifice). Its most prominent features, from which it derives its name, are the horns at its nose, brow, and edge of the bony frill that extends from and around its skull. These horns are greatly variable in placement, size, and number. Notable examples, in modern terminology, include triceratops and styracosaurus.

INDRIK: a massive member of the same baramin as the rhinoceros. This creature is the largest terrestrial mammal in history. Its size makes it an ideal mount for humans or Nephilim traveling en masse. Its modern name is indricotherium or paraceratherium.

331

KERIT: a lumbering, slope-backed herbivore with a horse-like face and stout hind legs. Its reliance on two long, clawed forelimbs preclude the kerit from being truly called bipedal. Its modern name is chalicothere.

LEVIATHAN: the crowning glory of animals created on the fifth day of Creation week. Although primarily aquatic, four splayed limbs allow it access to land if need be. Sheathed from jaws to tail with thick armored scales, it is nigh impervious to injury from other beasts or humans. Beyond sheer mass, the main feature that distinguishes it from the other crocodilians that comprise its baramin is the bulla at the end of its snout, from which it can spew a combustible discharge for attack or defense. Its growth is limited by environment, not age; older specimens with a large range can be truly monstrous in size. Its modern name is sarcosuchus.

MOA: a wingless (thus flightless) bird that grew to twelve feet tall with neck outstretched. Although herbivorous, its size and powerful three-toed feet were ample protection from all but the largest predators. In postdiluvian history, it dominated New Zealand's ecosystem until hunted to extinction by the Maori people, at which point its only local predator, the Haast's eagle, also became extinct.

PASSERINE: an enormous group of avian kinds, having in common the ability to perch. These birds can be drab, brightly colored, or anything between. Many are songbirds. Familiar examples include the sparrow, crow, thrush, and cardinal.

SCYTALE: a large lizard-like creature with sprawling limbs that carries it close to the ground. Its dominant and instantly recognizable feature is the iridescent, spine-supported sail down the length of its back. Its modern name is dimetrodon.

VIVERRID: a baramin of smaller mammals resembling felines with elongated snouts and short limbs. These animals are extant today and include the civet, genet, and binturong.

WOLFHOUND: one of the original members of the canid baramin. Others include wolves, foxes, coyotes, and jackals, which are globally ubiquitous. Today's domestic dog- every variation from dachshund to the Great Dane- is derived from the gray wolf. Wild wolfhounds can greatly vex farmers and shepherds, but once domesticated, they can and have proven to be "man's best friend."

PREVIEW FROM

FALLEN

BOOK TWO
IN THE ANTEDILUVIAN LEGACY TRILOGY

‹ CHAPTER 1 ›

The city of Phempoor sweltered and sweated in the morning sun. The morning mists crept through the alleys, prying into cracks in the crude wooden doors and empty windows with damp fingers. In other places in the world, the mists watered crops, orchards, gardens; here, they merely turned the filthy dirt streets into mud.

A man, neither very young nor very old, strode through the mud with a purpose, trying to avoid the patches of darker brown that marked where excreta had been tossed into the street. Working men and women were already about, trudging with dull, downcast eyes to toil in dry fields. The people of the city were impoverished, but they filled the warrens of their honeycombed dwellings with many children; after all, in a land such as this, what other entertainment was there to be had than procreation?

For eight years Noah had lived alongside the peasants. It was not the longest time he and his comrades had spent in one mission field, but it was longer than most, for the need was great. They had started in the small, dusty communities of the region, and for the last few years had worked in the slums of Phempoor itself. Much of his work had been of a practical nature. The application of sound farming principles, ingrained in him from his youth in the lands of Eden, to even this poor soil had led to markedly increased crop yields of the tubers and squashes that were staples of Phempoor's diet, aided by regular animal sacrifices in the altar houses they had planted about the city. The strong arms of the missioners had helped build many homes and dig many wells, and parts of the clay slums now had rudimentary waste channels running to the sulfurous bogs outside of the city. Phempoor's ubiquitous structures were the round-roofed clay hovels that clustered closely together and pressed almost to the high-walled palaces of the ruling class, like prostrate beggars clutching at the hems of noble robes. The palaces lay in the middle of the city, but for the peasantry that surrounded them, they might as well have been a thousand leagues away. After much work and prayer, though, Noah's invitation had come. He was finally to meet the reclusive prince of Phempoor.

His destination loomed ahead, broad and dark against the bright blue sky. Messages of truth and hope, of the Creator God and His will for the world, bubbled easily to the surface of his thoughts. They were well-rehearsed, given freely many thousand times and honed by study, prayer, and discussion to pierce a man's soul. Well it was, too, for times such as these, when the chance might not come again to witness the truth to these rulers of men, but a good word well-planted in fertile soil might bear fruit for an entire nation-state.

Noah smiled as he walked, reminiscing on the successes the Lord God Creator had blessed them with, on the many of His children who now called on His name and made sacrifice to Him out of fealty and love. This was his true work. Many others had joined the work over the last four centuries. Paths crossed and branched and began and ended, all weaving a holy tapestry for the Creator God's glory, and ancient truths had reawakened in many places they had been lost. Phempoor was one such place. While its barren soil bore the curse of the land poorly, the souls of its people had been ready for harvest. Noah found that this was often the case; those without earthly needs seldom realized their spiritual needs, but poverty bred hearts hungry for hope and a willingness to listen.

At first, their message had fallen on deaf ears, but care and persistence had paid off. Now, Machmanis, one of the first of the peasants to take up the faith of old, had assumed full duties at one of the modest altar houses, and Felun's zeal was as great as Noah or any of the others. Young Gaen had expressed interest in continuing with them to their next mission field, whenever and wherever it might be, and some of the missions they had planted had even begun to plant missions of their own.

Still, this was the opportunity he had prayed for. For all of its change for the better, Phempoor was still dangerous and dirty. The populace was hard-pressed enough, but crime was rampant. Women and children disappeared regularly. Gangs of brigands fought bloody, secret battles for control of alleys and muddy pools, answering only to rival gangs, since the Phempoor guard remained within the confines of the palaces. There was much idolatry; clay was in abundance, and sculptors made a steady living crafting sun-dried figures, blind and deaf to their supplicants. These things did not have to be. Noah had seen it before: a righteous ruler, living as the Creator intended, could bless his own people, change how they lived their lives, in ways Noah could never do.

The palaces were enclosed by a tall guard wall built of red salt-glazed bricks that caught the sun like liquid. Iron lamps sat atop the angular buttresses that supported the wall every so often; whatever fuel filled the lamps burned bright blue. Dark doors set in the guard wall opened for Noah, seemingly of their own accord. He walked through them.

The courtyard was barren. No one greeted Noah as he crossed the dusty space to the wide steps leading to the main palace entrance. Two bare-armed, leather-clad palace guards stood at the door, both holding barbed spears in one hand and long leather leashes in the other. At the ends of the leashes, iron-grey wolfhounds strained against their masters and paced back and forth, roughly describing the arc that the leash length would allow. The courtyard stunk of dog feces; obviously no effort was made to clean up the wolfhound droppings that littered the ground.

Noah took the stairs two at a time, smiling at the hounds despite their menacing growls. The guards' countenances were imperceptible in the shadows cast by their low-browed helms and faceguards that swept past their cheeks and nearly met a hand's length past their noses. The most striking thing about them was the symbols scarred into their necks, clearly a result of branding. They did not acknowledge Noah, but neither did they move to stop him. He strode on, through the door that again opened for him with no sign of human action.

The palace interior was swathed in shadows, and a moment passed before Noah's eyes recovered from bright daylight. As the darkness gained shape and hue, he raised an eyebrow in mild surprise. While the courtyard he had seen was in accord with the dirty quality of the city, the inside of the palace was opulent. Indeed, Noah would have thought he had stepped into a hall in Enoch—rather, Atlantis, as it was now named—or Havilah, had the stench of the courtyard not faintly followed him through the door. Sculptures and frescoes decorated the walls and columns, dim and dream-like in the low light cast by more blue-flamed lanterns. Details of the art were difficult to make out, but each example was obviously done by a master in the form. Still, the more Noah looked around the room, the greater an uneasy sense of malevolence nagged at the edge of his consciousness. Whether the simple dichotomy of beauty in shadow, or some intentional twisting and warping of the figures by the artists, done too subtly to pinpoint, he was relieved when a man finally greeted him from a doorway across the entrance hall.

"Welcome, Noah of Eden. You are expected. Come, enter freely, of your own will." The man was thin and severe, dressed in a simple, straight black robe, and strikingly pale. He spoke with a heavy accent unfamiliar to Noah's well-travelled ears, but the invitation was an answer to many years of prayer, and Noah gladly followed him.

They walked quickly through a maze of hallways, and the missioner soon found himself completely disoriented. Rather suddenly, a turn took them through a high-arched stone hall, and Noah stepped blinking into a flame-lit room, complete with a coterie of courtiers who stopped and stared as one at the newcomer, and the prince of Phempoor himself gazing down from his ebony throne at the end of the room.

Like the rest of the palace so far, there was no source of outside light, but the lantern flames here were a comfortable, homey, normal orange. Many of the courtiers' faces lit up at the sight of Noah, jovial and friendly. Each man and woman was dressed in dark clothing of fine fabric and cut, fitting for an audience with royalty. Like the man who ushered him in, the people who smiled at Noah now were pale of skin, as if none of them saw the sun. Many of them were quite fleshy, obviously well-fed, a stark contrast to the gaunt, bony physiques common to Phempoor's peasants. Noah suppressed a frown. What secret store of food were these fat folk hiding in these palaces, and why had they not shared it with the starving populace?

A loud, light voice pulled his attention to the prince. "And you must be Noah!" he said. "Come closer! I am told that we have much to discuss, you and I. Come!" The prince stood. He was young, or appeared so, trim and starkly beautiful, and just as pale as everyone else Noah had yet seen in the palace. His slender, almost effeminate, hands had clearly not known labor of any sort, and with one of them he patted Noah on the shoulder.

"What luck! You have arrived in time for our banquet. I know that you wish to speak to me—an honor!—so shall we walk and talk?"

"My message is for the ears and hearts of your courtiers, too."

"Of course! All of you," the prince said, clapping his hands, "follow us, and listen closely to what this man says! Now, Noah, if you please. What message is this? A good one, I hope?"

"The best." Noah took a deep breath. This court was certainly the most informal he had ever experienced. A camaraderie seemed to exist among these denizens of the palace, and the prince was surprisingly friendly and open. Like the farmers from whose stock he came, Noah had planted the seeds with toil and sweat, and now he prepared for a harvest. "Prince, I will tell you an ancient truth. We are immortals under a curse."

"Intriguing! Do tell more."

"You and I, and all here, were made by the eternal Creator God in His very image. The first of us, the man Adam and the woman Eve, were placed in paradise and fellowshipped with the Creator Himself, wanting nothing. They were perfect of form, undying, happy and fulfilled, but they were not merely playthings for the Creator God, not puppets. They were free to choose to do what they would, to go where they wished."

"This sounds very nice indeed! What happened next?" The prince leaned closer as they walked.

Noah's tone took a grim timbre. "They were deceived into disobedience, prince. Satan, the Serpent, once the highest of the Creator God's servants but now set in rebellion against Him, tempted the woman Eve with the forbidden fruit of the knowledge of good and evil. The man Adam followed. They disobeyed the one command that their Lord had given them. Fellowship was broken. The man and woman were cast from paradise, never to return, and a curse was set over the world. Death and pain, struggle and toil, was now the lot of man."

Quiet murmurs of disappointment and concern floated from the following courtiers. The prince frowned. "This story has become rather depressing, Noah."

"And depressing it was, prince. No tragedy could have been greater. But with the curse came hope! To our great benefit, mankind was not to live eternal in this cursed flesh, sinking ever deeper into its sin, apart from the Creator. His justice demanded punishment for disobedience, but His love remained. He promised a Redeemer, who would free mankind, and indeed the whole of creation, from the curse. Even death itself, the last, final enemy, would be destroyed, and all would be renewed to be what it once was, to what it was intended to be."

Scattered clapping came from behind, as if the courtiers had witnessed a bard's bravura performance. The prince's interest could not be denied. "A very fine story. So, tell me—what are we to do now?"

"We obey the Creator God," answered Noah. "We hope for the coming of the promised Redeemer, and we walk in righteousness while we wait. We treat our fellow men as we ourselves wish to be treated."

The prince slowed his walk and pursed his lips. "And this is why you have toiled alongside the people of this city?"

Noah smiled. "Earthly work can open minds to spiritual truth. If even one soul attains to the hope of redemption, I consider it well worth the effort."

"Ah." The prince grew quiet. His mouth twitched at the corners, as if he were suppressing some joke of supreme hilarity. "You believe all of this to be true, do you?"

"I know it to be true, prince."

"Know it! Well, Noah, allow me to share with you what I believe." The prince glanced back at his fleshy followers with a conspiratorial grin. "I believe in what I see with my own eyes, and what I see is this. Each of us has a time, a thousand years at most, to suck as much pleasure from this life as we have power. I will waste no time thinking on a god I cannot see, nor the origins of the world around. It is what it is. That is enough. Might there be things that lie outside my perception? Perhaps, but why should I concern myself with them?"

Noah had a dozen ready responses that leapt to his lips. He was not surprised at the opposition that he now encountered, that he had encountered countless times before. Before he could speak, the prince abruptly exlaimed, "At last, we come to the banquet hall! I must say, I am famished."

The smell of meat and spices was heavy in the air, mingled with a faintly sweet, metallic scent. At first Noah couldn't identify the curiously familiar smell, although he knew that somehow he was no stranger to it. As he struggled to place it, the group rounded another corner and arrived in a wide hall. Long tables were spaced around the brick-paved floor, with short staircases leading to shadowy alcoves in the hall's corners. Fireplaces lined either side of the hall, and servants with the same sort of scars on their necks as had the palace guards stood at attention around the room.

The prince gestured to Noah with a broad smile. "Please, sit at my table." Noah could not very well refuse, and he followed the prince to his seat. Each place was set with ornate silver settings, but the tables were bare of food. The smell of the feast was stronger now; Noah abstained from eating meat, though it did smell quite good, but the strange scent somehow decreased his appetite further.

Once the courtiers had been seated, the prince stood and clapped. "Bring food and drink! And be quick about it!" The servants disappeared into dark arched doorways.

All of a sudden, Noah recognized the smell. He feared nothing and no one but the Lord God, but a visceral terror now clutched his heart in an icy, shocking grip, and a chill swept over him. The color drained from his face, and he stared at the prince with unbelieving wide eyes.

The prince returned his stare with a cold smile. "Welcome to our feast."

◂ ◂ ▸ ▸

‹ ABOUT THE AUTHOR ›

R. M. Huffman, an avid reader from the time he was able, has had lifelong interests in biblical history, the origins of myth and legend, the power of epic storytelling, and the world-building fiction of masters like Lewis and Tolkien; in the first chapters of Genesis, he found the perfect setting in which to explore those interests. As a freelance artist, he has done work from gaming illustration to concept art, and those elements are finding their ways into this project as well. He has also authored the *Sweet Tooth* series of short stories collected in *Sweet Tooth* Omnibus.

He is a physician, author, illustrator, and lifelong Texan. He graduated from Texas A & M University and the University of Texas Medical Branch at Galveston, and practices as an anesthesiologist in north Texas. He lives with his wife, Meredith, their two baby daughters, and two young sons, and is a skiing enthusiast (water and snow) and tennis player.

◂ ◂ ▸ ▸

ALSO AVAILABLE FROM LAMPION PRESS

The writings of C. S. Lewis have touched millions of readers. This new handbook makes clear that it is not just the words and stories of Lewis that capture the attention of the reader; it is also the ideas. The power of words to convey principles and ideas is remarkable, and few contemporary authors do it as well as C. S. Lewis. Matching one idea or aspect of Lewis's writings with each letter of the alphabet, Louis Markos employs a memorable method to demonstrate both the simplicity and the complexity of Lewis. Markos also gives those who want to know more about Lewis an overview of his life and brief guides to his books and three film productions of his works.